Book Three of the Second American War

By

James Rosone & Miranda Watson

Disclaimer

This is a fictional story. All characters in this book are imagined, and any opinions that they express are simply that, fictional thoughts of literary characters. Although policies mentioned in the book may be similar to reality, they are by no means a factual representation of the news. Please enjoy this work as it is, a story to escape the part of life that can sometimes weigh us down in mundaneness or busyness.

Copyright Information

Table of Contents

Chapter 1

A Glimmer of Hope

January 17, 2021

Pennsylvania

Raven Rock Facility

President Sachs noted how painfully quiet it was in the pitch-black tunnel under the Raven Rock facility. The temperature hovered in the low sixty degrees Fahrenheit— not quite cold enough to cause hypothermia, but not warm enough to keep the four of them from shivering in the dark.

"Do you think they're going to find us?" asked Lieutenant Commander Bullard, breaking the silence. He still had the nuclear football handcuffed to his hand; however, its batteries had run out of juice several days ago.

"They'll find us. We just need to keep the faith," replied Harrison, their lone surviving Secret Service agent. "It's only a matter of time until they locate the tunnel entrance and send someone in here."

"How can you be so sure they'll ever find the tunnel?" asked the President, barely above a whisper. His mouth was so parched. He ached for a long drink of water and some food, maybe a nice fat juicy New York strip steak with a twice-baked potato. It had been almost a week since he'd had a real meal.

"Between you and the football, Mr. President, they know where we are," Harrison explained. "They may not know if we're alive, but they know where we are. They'll do whatever they can to find us—even if they think we're dead, they'll be searching for our remains."

"What I wouldn't give for a glass of water right now," General Austin Peterson remarked, speaking more to himself than anyone else.

With nothing else to do in the damp quietness of the tunnel, the President's mind drifted back again to how they had gotten into this situation in the first place. Sachs remembered the short-lived relief he'd felt when he'd sat on the tram and it had started moving toward the bunker complex at Raven Rock. The tram had nearly reached its destination when a thunderous explosion had rocked the earth around them. The tram had stopped abruptly, and they'd lurched forward from the inertia.

General Peterson swore angrily. The reeling motion had caused pain to shoot through every fiber of his already injured body.

Agent Harrison called out, "Hang on, everyone! This tram can operate on battery power." There were a few moments of muffled noises as he searched for the switch, and then two beams pierced the pitch blackness around them. The air was thick with dust and smoke, which seemed to be streaming in from around the edges of the blast door ahead of them.

The President coughed reflexively.

Harrison walked back to the door and touched it cautiously. "Ow! Damn it!" He yanked his hand away and shook it feverishly. "There's a fire behind this door," he announced.

"Well, that's just lovely," General Peterson remarked sarcastically.

"Now what are we going to do?" asked Lieutenant Commander Bullard, concern and fear in his voice. "We barely made it out of Camp David alive."

"Well, obviously, we can't go forward," said Agent Harrison, still nursing his left hand. "Our only real option is to go back."

He sat back down in the tram, and they began their trek toward the violent death trap they'd just escaped. On the battery power, the tram traveled much slower, as if it knew they were marching solemnly to their demise.

They'd only traveled about five hundred meters down the tunnel before they discovered a cave-in. They were trapped.

"The tunnel goes several hundred meters under the actual mountain," General Peterson explained. "If I had to guess, I'd say whoever attacked Raven Rock must have hit all four of the mountain's tunnel entrances to cause this kind of cave-in. They would have had to use tactical nukes or bunker-busting weapons—this shouldn't have happened."

There was a moment of awkward silence as the reality of their situation hit them.

"Well…I guess rescuers would be more likely to find us near the bunker blast door than in the middle of this tunnel," Agent Harrison postulated. "We could go wait closer to that end."

They pulled the tram forward again, and then Harrison announced, "We need to do an inventory of what we have down here. Everyone, empty your pockets." Unfortunately, no one had so much as a granola bar or a pocketknife with them. The only supplies they had were in a small bag in the back of the tram: one flashlight with a fresh battery, an emergency first aid kit, two one-liter bottles of water and two IV bags of normal saline.

They did their best to patch up General Peterson's leg and gave him some Tylenol to help with the pain.

"Go easy on the water, General," Sachs told Peterson. "We don't have that much for the four of us, and we have no idea how long it will take to be rescued."

"I'm going to propose that we only keep the tram headlights on for about ten minutes every five or six hours," Agent Harrison suggested. "That way, we'll be able to explore our surroundings and at least have some periods of light to keep us sane."

Time crept by so slowly in the perpetual midnight. President Sachs found that he had to stop checking his watch—every time he hit the button to light up the display, he was remarkably disappointed by how few hours had elapsed.

About two days in, Bullard made an announcement during one of their explorations. "Hey, guys, I think we have a problem."

"What is it?" asked Agent Harrison.

"There's a crack in the wall that's leaking water."

They all walked over briskly to examine the issue.

"Bullard, that's not a problem—it's a freaking miracle," said General Peterson.

"How do you figure?" asked Sachs.

"It's leaking really slowly. There's not enough water coming in to threaten us, but it might just help us survive," explained Peterson. "Harrison, can you bring me the first aid kit?"

With the deft hand of a survivalist, the general took several of the unused bandages and packed the cloth into the crack. Then he broke off the top of the plastic container that housed the first aid supplies and placed it under the end of the fabric.

"This is going to take a while to fill up. My best guess is we might half fill this container top in a couple of hours. We should all take turns—Mr. President, you'll go first, then Lieutenant Commander Bullard, then Agent Harrison, and I'll go last. Make sure you place this lid back underneath to catch whatever water we can."

"I don't know how clean this will be, but it has to taste better than the pee we've been drinking," Sachs said sarcastically. Agent Harrison had suggested at the outset that they collect their urine. No one had liked the idea, but they all acknowledged that they were going to have to get creative to find ways to stay hydrated long enough to get rescued and see their loved ones again.

The crack on the wall had been discovered three days ago. Not much had happened since then. It left an awful lot of time for the men to think...and for their minds to play tricks on them.

Sachs started hearing noises, but he wasn't sure if they were real or just another figment of his imagination. He waited several minutes before he finally asked, "You guys hear that?"

"I hear something," Peterson confirmed. "Although I have no idea what it is."

They listened intently. "Is that a jackhammer?" asked Bullard.

"It's hard to tell...it's so far away," said Peterson.

The volume grew slowly over time. There seemed to be some other type of machinery running on the other side of the blast door as well. Then, to their dismay, the noises stopped abruptly.

"Hey—we're in here!" shouted Agent Harrison. He tapped on the blast door with the flashlight, hoping the clanging would echo and alert the people on the other end of their presence. The noises on the other end did not return.

Periodically, one of them would use the flashlight to tap on the wall, but it was to no avail. A full twenty-four hours went by without even a hint of activity.

They sat in the tram, trying their best to catch some rest while they waited, but the silence was excruciating.

"Did you hear that?" asked Lieutenant Commander Bullard suddenly.

Sachs sat up in the darkness, holding his breath as he listened to the quiet of the tunnel. His senses slowly returned to him from that groggy place of disoriented sleep, and then he heard the most beautiful clamor of his life.

"Sounds like the jackhammer is back," he said.

"I think it's getting louder," Bullard confirmed.

Agent Harrison turned the flashlight back on and walked to the blast door. He put his ear against the cold steel before shutting off the light to conserve the battery.

"I can feel the vibrations through the door," he announced. "They're definitely chipping away at whatever is on the other side."

The pounding stopped for a minute, and Harrison used the back of the flashlight and tapped against the steel door, hoping that whoever was on the other side might hear him. The machinery kicked back up, and there was nothing to do but wait.

Slowly, the noise grew louder. The President was almost certain that whatever digging machine was on the other side was now nearly at the door. After some time, the racket stopped. Agent Harrison immediately tapped on the metal with his flashlight.

Tap, tap, tap.

"Oh my gosh—did they actually hear us?" asked Sachs.

Harrison quickly tapped on the blast door again.

Tap, tap, tap.

At this point, Harrison turned on the light and whacked the door forcefully.

Bang, bang, bang.

This time, something much more substantial pounded on the steel door.

"Holy crap! They *can* hear us!" shouted Harrison excitedly.

"Try using Morse code!" shouted Bullard, their lone Navy guy.

"I don't know Morse code…hell, who cares. They know we're here. That's all that matters." Agent Harrison pounded on the door several more times, which was answered with a few more bangs from the other side. Then the jackhammer started back up again.

The excavation on the other side went on for several more hours. Then, there was silence once again. Just when Sachs was starting to wonder if their rescuers had abandoned them, he heard a new noise. This time it sounded like a high-pitched dental drill. That brain-piercing hum went on for probably ten or fifteen minutes until a small hole in the blast door appeared, and a tiny light flooded into their dark world.

"Hello? Can anyone hear us?" came a voice from the other side.

"Oh my God. Yes. We can hear you! Please get us out of here," shouted Agent Harrison excitedly.

"Is the President still alive? Is he with you?"

"Yes. Sachs is still alive. He's here."

"Can you please identify who all is with you?" asked the voice from the other side.

Agent Harrison seemed to shift mindsets in that moment. "How about you tell me who *you* are first, and then I'll tell you who all is in here with me."

Sachs heard some voices talking on the other end before a new voice spoke through the hole. "My name is Liam Pritcher. I'm with the Army Corps of Engineers. We've been trying to dig our way to this tunnel for six days. I know you don't have any way to verify who I am, so you're just going to have to trust us. Believe me; if we didn't want to rescue the President, we wouldn't have spent six days trying to dig through this rubble to get to you guys."

After a couple of seconds of calculating, Harrison responded. "I'm Special Agent Darnell Harrison with the Secret Service." He let out a deep breath. "I have the

President, along with Lieutenant Commander Ashton Bullard, who has the nuclear football, and General Austin Peterson, the Chairman of the Joint Chiefs. The general is injured and desperately needs medical attention. The rest of us are fine, other than being dehydrated and hungry. Is it possible for you to pass some water through to us?"

There was some murmuring on the other end. "Hold on, Agent Harrison. We're going to try and get a hose down there and see if we can run it through the hole. Once we get you guys hydrated, we'll bring in a plasma torch. You'll need to move further away from the blast door back into the tunnel. The locking mechanism on the door is in place, so there's no way for us to open the door easily. We'll have to burn a hole that's large enough for you guys to crawl out. It could take the better part of a day, but we'll make it happen."

The President and the other men that had been trapped all reacted differently. Agent Harrison did his best to conceal the tears of joy in his eyes. Bullard let out a "Yes!" and pumped his fist in the air. General Peterson showed little external reaction other than to let out a deep sigh. The President didn't know how to respond at all—he felt like crying and laughing at the same time.

"Oh, by the way, it's damn good to know that you guys are alive," said Liam from the other side of the door. "We'd nearly given up hope on finding you guys."

Sachs made his way over to the hole. "This is President Sachs. Who's in charge of the government right now…and how's the war going?"

"Vice President Powers has taken over as the acting President until we could confirm you were either alive or dead. He's been running the country in your absence," Liam explained. "As to the war, well, let's work on getting you guys out of here first. What I can tell you is we're not losing."

The President grunted at the response. "Fair enough, Liam. I'm glad Luke's taken over. Please send a message to him and let him know we're alive and doing well. We're looking forward to getting out of here."

"Will do, sir. Now, if you'll excuse me, we're going to go find a hose so we can get you guys something to drink before we start using the torch to cut a hole in this door."

President Sachs turned to the three men he'd been stuck in the tunnel with for the last six days. "Gentlemen, when we get out of here, I want you all to know that you guys are coming to the White House for a well-earned private meal with me and the First Lady. I can't thank you enough for not losing faith, even when I felt like I had. You guys kept me alive, and you kept the spirit of America alive in each of us." He paused for a moment. Then, with renewed vigor, he added, "We're going to win this war, gentlemen. God have mercy on those bastards for what they've done to us because I sure as hell won't."

****

Washington, D.C.
White House

An aide walked into the Oval Office just as acting President Luke Powers was signing off on a few documents. The aide stopped in front of his desk, waiting for Powers to acknowledge her presence.

Pausing what he was doing, Luke looked up at the aide. "Oh, hi, Linda. I finished signing those documents for Homeland. Can you please have them processed?" he said as he pointed to the outbox on the right corner of his desk.

Smiling, Linda replied, "Yes, Mr. Vice President. Not a problem...um, sir...we just got a message from the rescue crew at the Raven Rock facility. They believe they may have found the President *alive*. Rich Novella asked for you to come down to the Situation Room. They're working on getting some more information from the crew there."

Vice President Powers lifted his left eyebrow, and then a broad smile spread across his face.

"Then, by all means, let's head down to the Situation Room, Linda."

Linda scooped up the paperwork and then led the way down the hall. As soon as Powers walked into the Situation Room, he saw a secured video teleconference had been set up. He quickly ascertained that the image on the other end was the engineering crew at Raven Rock. A small hole had been drilled into an imposing steel door. Suddenly, he heard the voice of the President.

Turning to the rest of the folks in the room, the Vice President asked, "Can they hear us?"

Rich nodded. "They can. You want to say something to them?"

Powers nodded.

Rich unmuted their connection. "Excuse me, gentlemen. This is Rich Novella, the President's Chief of Staff. I have acting President Powers here with me. We'd like to know if we could say something to President Sachs."

A minute later, they'd fed a microphone through the small hole, and the Vice President heard the voice of his

Commander-in-Chief. "Hey there, Luke. Thanks for running the country for me for a little while," he said lightheartedly.

The Vice President fought back tears. "It's so good to hear your voice, sir," he managed to say. "I've been praying for you to be found safely since the attack."

The two talked for a bit about the situation at large, and the President passed on a few messages for his wife and family. The Vice President cleared his throat.

"Mr. President, God only knows if there's another enemy direct-action unit nearby that could potentially try to finish the job they started. I feel strongly that we need to get you to a secure environment before we announce the story of your incredible survival to the world at large."

"Makes sense, Luke," Sachs responded, clearly a bit unnerved by the implications of what had just been said. "So…I guess that means I could use a few more of those prayers of yours."

Chapter 2

A War of Choice

January 17, 2021

New Delhi, India

Secretariat Building

Prime Minister Bhamre put his tea down when he heard Ambassador Singh mention the phrase *tactical nuclear weapons*. The more his most trusted ambassador explained from his secured video teleconference connection in Washington, D.C., the more alarmed he became.

Could the situation in America really be this bad?

The others present for this emergency meeting of the National Security Council also appeared to be as concerned as he was. Several of them exchanged nervous glances with the Defense Minister, trying to gauge her reaction to the news.

When Singh had finished delivering the summary of his most recent conversation with the American Secretary of State, PM Bhamre felt dumbfounded. "Surely they can't be serious," he remarked.

Deputy National Security Advisor Khandare shook his head, and his lower lip pushed out in a pout.

"You disagree, Khandare?" Bhamre asked curiously.

Lifting his chin, Khandare asserted, "The Americans would never use a nuclear weapon like this—even a tactical nuclear weapon. They just wouldn't. This is an intimidation tactic that they're hoping they won't have to back up with deeds."

Prime Minister Bhamre crossed his arms. "Still, it's pretty concerning that they would even *make* a threat like this, idle or not. Can you imagine if they followed through on it?"

Several of the meeting's attendees nodded.

"I think we should take this proposition seriously," said Dr. Harsh Gandhi, the Head of the Research and Analysis Wing, India's external intelligence agency. "As far as I'm concerned, I think we should agree to the Americans' proposal."

Several people in the room gasped in shock. The Minister of Defense just raised an eyebrow and smiled as she waited for her friend to explain his reasoning.

"You can't be serious, Dr. Gandhi," Prime Minister Khandare remarked. "This could lead us to war, a war of choice, not necessity." Then he reached over and poured himself another cup of tea, dismissing the comment as impractical.

Dr. Gandhi sighed as if he were preparing himself to speak to a hysterical toddler. "Mr. Prime Minister, Deputy NSA—Secretary Kagel is right about one thing. The Chinese military is extremely overleveraged right now. If we made a credible threat against our disputed territorial areas or threatened to liberate Tibet, it would probably cause the Chinese government to halt invasion plans at the southern American border."

"It could also lead us to a war we don't need to fight," the Prime Minister retorted hotly.

Defense Minister Sitharaman shook her head. "That's not entirely true, Prime Minister. Just because we move forces to the line of control and appear to threaten China does *not* mean we have to follow through on that warning and invade. We just have to appear, albeit convincingly, as if we're willing to do so."

Khandare shot her a nasty look, surprised that she'd side with the secretive Dr. Gandhi on this preposterous idea.

"Let's not forget there is an economic component to this offer, Mr. Prime Minister," Ambassador Singh insisted. "If making it appear as if we're willing to attack China prevents them from invading the southern American border, it'll have been worth it."

"Ambassador Singh, Minister Sitharaman—is it true the Chinese H-20 stealth bomber is operational?" the Prime Minister asked.

Dr. Gandhi interjected, "Yes. It has to be true."

"I agree. I don't see any other alternative. The Americans have no reason to lie to us about this," Ambassador Singh concurred. "Plus, I don't think any other aircraft could have gotten close enough to deliver its bombs to hit the Raven Rock bunker. Two of the three pairs of Russian Blackjack bombers were hunted down and destroyed before they even made it to their targets. The H-20 is the only bomber that could have penetrated so deep into their airspace to carry out a raid like this."

"We know the Americans shot down at least one of the H-20s over the state of Maryland, and the other may have been destroyed when they raided the Canadian air base at Cold Lake a few days ago," added Dr. Gandhi. "However, even with the high-powered radar that the Americans have, the Chinese still managed to use these aircraft for maximum impact—just imagine what they would do with our less sophisticated radar networks. Plus, I can all but guarantee you that they didn't use their only H-20s in this single attack. There have to be more of them out there, ready to strike."

Prime Minister Bhamre grimaced at the implications of this new stealth weapon the Chinese appeared to have unveiled. "If the H-20 is operational, then that changes the calculus for everything," he uttered in exasperation. "Do we even have *any* idea of how many of them they have operational or where they even are?"

Dr. Gandhi leaned forward and lit up another cigarette. "My agency believes they have at least twelve of them up and running, but we have no idea how many more they may have in production," he explained. "We believe they have them based at the Foluo Northeast Air Base on Hainan Island." He puffed away nonchalantly—the man was a veritable chimney.

Deputy NSA Khandare wrinkled his eyebrows. "Why Hainan Island? I would think they would have positioned these bombers to be closer to Beijing."

Shaking his head as if he was talking to a student who'd just asked a rudimentary question, Dr. Gandhi replied, "The advantage to Hainan Island is its location. Remember, this aircraft was designed to give the Chinese Air Force the opportunity to strike at the American air and naval facilities in the Pacific. Hainan places them in range of Guam and their budding facilities in the Philippines and Singapore. They could have some of them stationed near

Beijing, but they know more eyes and satellites watch those bases. The Foluo base also has the advantage of multiple aircraft storage facilities built right into the mountain the base is adjacent to. They can hide those bombers under the mountain, out of sight of satellites and prying eyes."

The Prime Minister shook his head. "Regardless of where these bombers are stationed, if they have them in any serious numbers, they're a game changer to our national defense strategy. They could carry out a decapitation strike of our government, and we'd never know it was happening until it was too late." He let out his breath in a huff. "Honestly, I'm not comfortable with making even a perceived threat to China if they have a first-strike capability like this."

"If I could, Mr. Prime Minister, we've made it abundantly clear to China that any first-strike weapon used on our government would be met with a nuclear response by us," Defense Minister Sitharaman insisted. "That has been our declared stance to both the Chinese and the Pakistanis. I don't believe the Chinese would test our resolve to use nuclear weapons if they launched a first strike against us— not when they have a large portion of their air force and army preparing to invade America.

"It's my opinion that the Chinese will tread lightly with us and take any aggression or perceived threat from us seriously. They know they are in no position to fight or win a protracted war against the Americans and us simultaneously. I have to agree with Ambassador Singh and Dr. Gandhi. China is at its weakest point right now. We should not abandon our American friends in their time of need like this. Their economic offer could also help us for decades to come, and that's not something we should just dismiss without careful consideration."

Deputy NSA Khandare folded his arms indignantly. "You can't be taking this proposal into earnest consideration, Prime Minister. This could lead us to a war we neither need to be involved in nor benefit from. This is not a wise decision."

Rubbing the stubble growing on his chin, the PM leaned back in his chair as he thought about all the implications and what to do. He knew if he turned his back on the Americans now and the current administration happened to survive the war, India's relations with the Americans would be severely damaged—especially if Sachs was still in charge. The man could hold a grudge. Then again, if India went to war with China, that could be just as disastrous.

There has to be a middle position somewhere in all of this, he thought.

Sitting forward in his chair, he stared at Sitharaman, his Minister of Defense. "OK. We'll move forward with the American proposal. But before you get excited, I want you to know that I have *no* intention of following through on our warning to invade China. We aren't going to go to war with China. If they see through our threat, then so be it."

Minister Sitharaman smiled as she shared a mischievous look with Dr. Gandhi. He just nodded but didn't say anything. Instead, he lit a third cigarette.

"Very well, Mr. Prime Minister. I'll do my best to make this look as real as possible," she said to his satisfaction.

The others in the room didn't seem as sure, but they didn't say anything to contradict the Prime Minister's decision.

****

When Minister Sitharaman left the National Security Council meeting, Dr. Gandhi joined her as she walked down the hallway back to her office.

"How real do you want this charade to look?" he asked with a devilish expression.

She snickered. "Charade? You think we'll back down, do you?"

Gandhi raised an eyebrow before a smirk spread across his face. "I'll get my people ready then," he responded, and then he broke off from their walk to head back to his own office.

****

Beijing, China

After the dastardly attack across Beijing at the outset of the war, President Chen had moved the entire government and military leadership to the Joint Battle Center. The JBC was a deep underground command bunker just outside Beijing; it was essentially China's version of Raven Rock. The only difference was that their hardened shelter sat nearly two thousand feet below the earth and couldn't be penetrated by American bunker-busters or even tactical nuclear weapons.

The day the American stealth bombers had paid Beijing a visit was a horrific day for the people of China. More than half of the 166 members of the Standing Committee had been killed during the raid on the exclusive

Jade Spring Hill housing development and the Zhongnanhai government compound.

The attack had nearly killed President Chen. The decapitation strike would have found its target had Chen not unexpectedly stayed the night at a military base when his meeting about operations in the American Southwest had gone late into the evening. As it was, his wife and two children had been killed in the raid, leaving Chen emotionally devastated. It had infuriated him to no end that the Americans had not only tried to kill him, but they'd gone after his family.

Fear and panic had gripped the city. More than two thousand people had died during the daylight raid on the capital. Once the immediate anxiety and alarm had subsided, the people became enraged—first at their own government for having failed to protect them, and then at the Americans who had attacked them.

The Ministry of Information quickly went to work crafting and shaping the government's message of what happened and carefully choreographed its dissemination to the rest of the country. By the second day of the conflict, the orchestrated messages began to have their desired effect. The people were clamoring for revenge and American blood. They were also completely oblivious to the fact that China had attacked America first as a part of the UN peacekeeping force, or that China had presumably killed the American president.

****

20 Kilometers Northwest of Beijing
Western Hills National Park
Central Military Commission Joint Battle Center

Turning to look at Foreign Minister Jiang, Chen asked, "What do you make of this threat from India?"

Foreign Minister Jiang squirmed uncomfortably in his chair. "I think it has the fingerprints of America written all over it. I'm not sure we should pay it much attention."

"I'm personally more concerned with the Americans' threat to use tactical nuclear weapons," asserted General Wu. "Do you really think they would attack the Three Gorges Dam?"

Admiral Hu shook his head. "The Americans can't be serious about nuking the dam. It's not a military target," he explained dismissively. "*If* the Americans were ever to use nuclear weapons, either as a first strike or in retaliation, they would hit military targets. That's been a part of their doctrine since the Cold War. I simply can't believe they would attack a civilian dam, especially the Three Gorges Dam. The entire world would turn on them if they did that."

General Ma smiled. "You say the world would turn on the Americans if they used a nuclear weapon on the dam, and they might. But let's not forget our battle plan to defeat the Americans relies exclusively on using EMPs and nuclear weapons on several civilian targets. There's a high likelihood that the Americans will respond by hitting the dam. I think we need to be prepared for that in case it were to happen." Ma Xingrui was the head of the PLA Rocket Force. He was one of the new crops of generals Chen had been moving into the senior ranks of the PLA as part of his plan to modernize the military and replace the old guard with younger men who were loyal and more pliable.

Turning to look at Ma, Admiral Hu retorted, "You may be right, General. However, the loss of life from the destruction of the dam, while tragic, wouldn't collapse our country or government. When we detonate an EMP over parts of America, their technology-dependent society will simply implode. Furthermore, the difference between the Americans and us is that we don't care what the rest of the world says or thinks of us. When our plan is complete, we will be the dominant military and economic power, not just in Asia, but across the globe. When we tell the world to jump, they will ask how high."

President Chen shook his head at the banter between the military men. "Gentlemen, we have war-gamed this out many times the last several years. If we are to defeat the Americans, then we need to continue to fan the flames of their internal civil war and also remove them as a naval power in the Pacific."

He paused for a second before continuing. "Unless we neutralize the American Pacific bases and their remaining carrier strike groups, our convoys to Mexico will be continually interdicted and harassed. We're going to take a serious reputational hit with the international community when we carry out this attack, but it will be worth it. Time has a way of healing old wounds. Let's not forget that it's the victors that write history. We will craft the message the world will read about for generations to come."

Chen turned to his Foreign Minister. "I want our ultimatum issued to the Japanese. They are to either kick the remaining Americans out of their territory or feel our wrath when we attack. Make sure to tell them that we have no intention of invading Japan or occupying their country, but if they are going to remain in a military alliance with the US, then we will be forced to deal with them as a threat. Tell them they have until February first to kick the Americans out of their country."

The Foreign Minister wrote a few notes down, then nodded his head in agreement.

Pausing for a moment, Chen looked at his military leaders and leaned forward. "Back to this Indian intimidation. Here's what we are going to do. We can assume the Americans put the Indians up to making this threat against us. Well, I'm not buying it. I don't believe the Indians would sacrifice their trade relations with us to help the Americans. Let's send a message back to India telling them we know this is a bluff and we're calling them on it. Tell them we have an excellent trade relationship with each other, and they shouldn't risk it over some naïve attempt at helping an illegitimate American government stay in power.

"Furthermore, send a message back to the American Secretary of State. Tell her we see through their idle threat and attempt to coerce the Indians into doing their bidding. Remind her that the world stands united against the administration she represents, and the sooner acting President Powers relinquishes control and Senator Tate is sworn into office, the sooner this conflict can end. Until it does, China is going to work with the UN to liberate the American people from the dictator in the White House.

"In the meantime, I want our military forces made ready to attack the American naval and air bases in the Pacific. We also need to prepare for the eventual nuclear response we are sure to receive. Begin covertly moving as much of our nuclear assets to new bunkers as possible. Make sure we are feeding the Americans enough information to target the bases we want them to hit and not the ones that would hurt us the most. In a few weeks, gentlemen, America will either have a new leader that is amenable to our way of thinking and this war will end, or their nation will simply cease to exist." He sat back in his chair and smiled.

Some of the older men at the table murmured. Not all of them were entirely on board with this all-in approach to dealing with America. However, the younger leaders all smiled and nodded.

Chapter 3
Suwannee Rifles

January 18, 2021
Lincoln Tunnel, New Jersey

Master Sergeant Nick Waters nervously watched as two soldiers inserted the blasting caps into the blocks of C-4 they had fastened to the top of the tunnel. "Are you sure we should do this, Captain?" he asked. Even though there was no traffic due to their roadblock, he spoke in hushed tones as if they were about to be discovered. "Our orders are to bug out of the city and fall back to Morristown with the rest of the battalion."

Captain Fielding shrugged dismissively. "We've gotta find ways to slow this UN force down, Master Sergeant," he retorted. "We don't have enough C-4 to drop any of the bridges, but at least we have enough to flood this tunnel. Besides, have you seen how dilapidated this thing is? We'd be doing the city a service. When this war's over with, they'll get a new tunnel out of it." Fielding smirked.

Master Sergeant Waters shook his head. He trudged back to the JLTV and got in. The guys were nearly done, and they'd be heading out of there shortly. Moments later, the two soldiers and the captain piled into the vehicle. Waters shot them a look of disapproval.

"So, you guys got everything ready? Can I get us out of here now?" he asked.

Captain Fielding snickered at his less-than-enthusiastic response. "We sure are," he said with a warm smile. "Nothing like leaving a little Suwannee Rifle surprise for those UN bastards."

The others in the vehicle laughed as they drove out of the tunnel. They all understood the reference to the Army National Guard unit that had a track record in World War II for blowing things up behind enemy lines. The soldiers of Florida's 868th Engineer Company in the Army National Guard were about to make a devastating impact on the cities of New York and Union City, New Jersey.

******

When the French 7th Armoured Brigade had liberated Albany several days earlier, Governor Tim Shank had returned to his office to begin work on getting things ready for President-elect Marshall Tate to be sworn into office as the forty-sixth president. If they couldn't swear him in in D.C., then they were determined to get him sworn in on the steps of city hall in New York City for the world to see.

Lieutenant General Ryan Jackman and the French contingent he was leading were a part of the lead element to secure New York City for this swearing-in ceremony. His column of Panhard VBLs was making steady progress down I-95 toward what would become the new de facto capital of the United States. Jackman was riding in the lead VBL. He smiled with satisfaction when he spotted signs for New Rochelle. They were now less than an hour away from New York City Hall.

General Jackman had already made contact with the New York City mayor, Mark Townsend, two nights ago. He seemed to be a remarkably compliant leader. Townsend had alerted Jackman to a Florida Army National Guard unit that had taken up residence in the city, but according to him, they were in the process of pulling out as Jackman's French unit traveled their way.

The mayor actually seemed happy to speak with Jackman, but he did have one request. "Please try not to shoot up my city," he'd pleaded. "There's a lot of people living here."

"We'll do our best," Jackman had promised, "but it will largely depend on whether we meet any resistance on our way into the city."

Looking out the windows of his light armored vehicle, Jackman saw a few tanks and armored personnel carriers turn off to head toward the Van Cortlandt Park. The French were going to set up a small firebase at the park and make it their base of operations while the rest of their force continued to filter down into the city.

Two battalions of New York Civil Defense Force units were slated to join a battalion of French armor down the Palisade Interstate Parkway on the New Jersey side of the border. Their orders were to secure the New Jersey sides of the bridges that connected New York and New Jersey so the UN peacekeeping force could advance unencumbered deeper into the state once they were ready.

As Jackman's caravan snaked through the city, one thing was very evident—a lot of people had left the metropolis. The city would typically be thriving with activity right now. However, at nearly 11 a.m., the sidewalks were all but vacant. It was eerie how empty the city was.

Jackman's comrade, Major Gérard Lecointre, turned to him. "This place looks like a ghost town," he remarked.

"Yeah, it's usually hopping. Maybe people are just scared or unsure of what's going on, so they're all indoors," Jackman countered.

Major Lecointre just shrugged. He continued to follow the GPS course without further comment. From Jackman's point of view, Lecointre had a pretty easy duty assignment—his main job was to act as the liaison between Général de Brigade Joffre and the American Civil Defense Force commander.

Ring, ring.

Jackman was startled at the sound of his cell phone. He reached down and pulled it out of the pouch on his body armor.

The mayor's office, he thought with a smile when he saw the number.

"This is Lieutenant General Jackman," he said. He loved the sound of his own introduction. Never in a million years had he thought he'd make general. When he graduated ROTC in 1994, he'd done his obligatory four-year commitment on active duty. Then he'd gotten out of the military and taken a job on Wall Street for his dad's firm and decided to continue his military service by joining the New York Army National Guard. He hadn't realized how much his father's connections with political heavyweights in New York would help him to advance his way through the ranks of the National Guard. In no time at all he'd gone from being a battalion commander in the National Guard to one of the senior leaders of the military resistance.

"General Jackman, I have some bad news for you," said Mayor Townsend.

"Oh?"

"The Lincoln Tunnel was just hit with explosives. It's completely flooded out and unusable."

Jackman grimaced. Losing the tunnel would honestly do more to hurt the city than hurt his force or slow him down.

"Thanks for the heads-up," Jackman replied. "Are there any federal forces that you know of in the city?"

Major Lecointre shot him a sideways glance.

"My intel is that they've all cleared out."

Jackman smiled and shook his head sideways, letting Lecointre know there shouldn't be any problems.

"Excellent. We're probably fifteen minutes from your location. I'll see you shortly," Jackman said. Then he disconnected the call. In a way, it felt good to be able to tell a mayor what to do and when to do it instead of the other way around.

I suppose that's the benefit of having an army at your back, he thought. Jackman held back a snicker.

In what seemed like no time at all, they turned off FDR Drive and found themselves right in front of city hall among a throng of people waving UN, French, and American flags.

"Now *this* is what I'm talking about," said Lecointre, excitement in his voice. He steered them toward a couple of police officers, who guided them to their parking space.

Steadily, the rest of their column of twenty or so vehicles arrived. Crowds of people moved in on the soldiers, waving flags and cheering.

Getting out of the vehicle, General Jackman saw the mayor standing not too far away with the police commissioner by his side. Both men were smiling and genuinely appeared to be happy to see him. As he walked up to them, Jackman extended his hand.

"It's good to see you, Mayor Townsend, Commissioner."

Townsend clasped Jackman's hand with both of his. "It's good to see you as well, Ryan—sorry, I mean Lieutenant General Jackman."

The mayor and Jackman's father were good friends. Jackman had met the man a handful of times, but he didn't have the same relationship with him that his father had.

Seems like he might be trying to suck up now that I'm in with the new administration, Jackman thought. He smiled but also kept his wits about him to evaluate the mayor's true motives.

He waved his hand around. "This is really great, Mr. Mayor. I hope it wasn't too much trouble for you to organize. I know the French and our other militiamen are loving it."

Townsend shook his head. "No, it was no trouble at all for the men who liberated us," said the mayor jovially. "Many people here are very glad to see you guys."

Jackman leaned in. "Can we go to your office and talk?" he asked in a quieter tone. "We have a lot to discuss. We need to get things ready for the President's swearing-in."

Townsend nodded. Steadily, they made their way through the cheering crowds of well-wishers and into the main building. They took the elevator up to the mayor's office and then made their way into his conference room. A handful of police captains were there, along with some of the political staffers that worked for the mayor.

Once the obligatory greetings were complete, Jackman got down to business.

"A man by the name of John Barry is going to be coming down from the governor's office in a couple of hours. He's traveling with two people from Tate's security team. They'll want to speak with you guys about the security situation for the swearing-in, along with other logistics.

However, what I'd like to talk about right now is something a bit more pressing."

The others in the room nodded. Several of them had their pens ready.

"General Guy McKenzie, the Head of the UN force, and Admiral Hill, our soon-to-be Secretary of Defense, have specifically asked me to speak with you about growing the size of the New York militia force. The situation is critical, and they want your help with raising twenty thousand volunteers. If we aren't able to get the numbers we need in the next week, then we're going to need to work out a system to draft them."

The police commissioner scrunched up his face. "So, let me get this straight—you just rode into town on a French armored vehicle, and now you're asking us to help you recruit twenty thousand people to join the governor's militia force in a week? How do you expect us to do that?"

"Commissioner, I know this is a big ask, but it needs to be done. We're in the fight of our lives right now. We have a president who's refused to leave office. The world has come together to help us remove him so our duly elected leader can take charge of the country. We as New Yorkers must do our part too." Jackman leaned forward. "What I'd like you to do is use the emergency alert system and send a message to everyone's phone. Ask those who are physically able to please come down to Yankee Stadium tomorrow and the following day to volunteer to join the CDF."

Mayor Townsend cleared his throat. "We'll send the message out, General," he responded. There was a short awkward silence before he said, "If you don't mind me asking, how is the war going? We're receiving mixed reports as you can imagine."

Jackman sighed. "I won't lie. It's been a tough fight. Some sectors are going better than others."

"We've heard a report that federal forces out west are cutting Canada in half. Is that true?" asked one of the mayor's staffers.

Jackman cocked his head to the side as he calculated his answer. "As I said, some sectors are going better than others. What I can tell you is that the UN just liberated Chicago. Even now, they're working their way to liberate Milwaukee before they expand out to Madison, Wisconsin. We've also liberated the entire upper East Coast and now New York. But we do need more volunteers. Our UN partners have been taking a terrible beating, and they need us to step up and do our part in this. It is, after all, *our* country."

"We'll make sure you get your volunteers," the mayor said.

Everyone nodded their heads, and the police commissioner had at least uncrossed his arms at that point.

******

Bellingham, Washington State

Marcy finished packing a box of some items she felt had some real sentimental value to them. She'd had these family photo albums converted to digital a few years back, but she still liked looking at the old pictures. They reminded her of happier times, canoeing and hiking with her family at Mt. Baker-Snoqualmie National Forest. Those yearly trips with her grandparents and extended family had been a big part of her childhood. In the winter, they'd go snowmobiling through some of the trails, ice fishing and skiing, and then in the summer, they'd fish, canoe, hike, and climb. It was a lot of fun.

She then found an album of her and Jake. She briefly opened it, staring at some of the photos. This particular book started when they were in college, carried through their wedding, and then covered Jake's time in the Army and the years they'd lived in Germany.

Marcy and Jake had met their first year at college. They were both on the cross-country team. She was a nursing student, and he was a civil engineering major. Over the next four years, the two of them spent a lot of time outdoors, running various trails and hiking to keep in shape. Jake had gone to her church and had taken a real liking to her family. He'd join them on their yearly pilgrimage to Mt. Baker and the surrounding area. It was no surprise when he'd proposed to her at the end of their junior year. They'd agreed they would get married the summer after they graduated.

After graduation, Marcy had found a job working as a nurse, and Jake had found a job working for an engineering firm. What Marcy hadn't counted on was that a month after the wedding, Jake's family would be tragically killed in a car accident. The deaths of his parents, brother, and sister had absolutely devastated Jake. He'd withdrawn from friends, and to an extent, from her. He'd said he felt like he didn't have a purpose anymore. She knew that was extreme, but she also knew Jake had been very family-oriented, so the loss of his entire nuclear family had really thrown him for a loop.

When the US had invaded Iraq, several of Jake's friends from college had joined the Army. They told him about how the Army was going to pay off their student loans and was handing out signing bonuses like candy. Then, one day, when Marcy came home from work, he told her he'd talked with an Army recruiter. She thought it was a phase, but when she saw some material on the kitchen table, she asked him more about it.

"I feel like I need to do my part," he'd said. "I want to serve my country in this war."

Marcy had been heartbroken. She'd understood the desire to be a part of something greater, but they had just gotten married. She couldn't bear the thought of him leaving, or worse, possibly getting killed over there.

He told her about the student loan repayment and the sign-on bonus. The payment was large enough to pay off her student loans as well. He reasoned with her that a six-year stint would allow them both to walk away debt-free with a clean slate. The only catch was he had to go enlisted if he wanted both the bonus and student loan repayment, and he'd have to go into EOD. Not knowing what that was, she had agreed, and the next day, he'd started the process of joining the Army.

At first, she didn't mind the Army. After his initial training, they were sent to Fort Lee, Virginia, just south of Richmond. Marcy appreciated Virginia; it was so different than Washington State. When Jake finished his advanced training, he was sent to a unit in Germany. This began their first great adventure as a married couple.

Marcy loved Germany. She just wished Jake had been able to see more of it with her. They had arrived in Germany at the height of the Iraq War, in January of 2005. Over the next four years, Jake had deployed twice, and one of the deployments had ended up being eighteen months. He extended to stay in Germany another four years, this time with a different unit. During the following four years, he only deployed once, to Afghanistan. The only reason he'd been able to come home early from Afghanistan was that he'd caught a piece of shrapnel in his right arm and leg. When his time in Germany ended, so did his Army career.

Truthfully, Marcy had been grateful that he'd left active duty. She was growing tired of being married to a guy who was hardly ever home. Plus, they'd been unsuccessful in starting a family. In between all of those deployments, she'd had a total of three miscarriages. After the third one, they'd decided to stop trying. She couldn't bear the thought of losing another baby. Maybe they could adopt later. Returning to Washington State after the roller coaster they'd been on had been good for her.

"Hey, Marcy. Do you have any more boxes for me to carry?" asked Jake, breaking into her trip down memory lane.

Placing the album back in the box, Marcy called out, "Yeah. I have a few boxes with our albums. I'd really like to take them if we can."

Jake walked into the room, a bit sweaty from all the manual labor, and made his way over to her. He grabbed the first box and lifted it. "I'll come back for the other one in a minute," he said. "Why don't you take a second to do a final walkthrough? We can always come back for one more trip, but I'd like to get this place locked up by nightfall."

"Will do."

She made a quick trip through each of the rooms, looking for anything she thought they would definitely need versus what they could leave behind. She hoped it would all still be there once the dust settled from this new war.

New war, she thought. She realized how strange the words sounded in her mind.

Not seeing anything of importance that she absolutely must have, she grabbed the last box of albums and headed outside. Jake was making some room inside the cab for her. The bed of the truck was already full.

"Anything else, or do you think we're good?" Jake asked.

"Yeah, we're good. You want me to help you with the windows?" Marcy offered.

"Sure. I'll just need your help in holding up one side of the board while I drill the other side in place."

The next three hours went by quickly. Jake covered all the windows with half-inch-thick pieces of plywood and drilled them into the windowsill. He made sure they were snug, so you'd need more than a crowbar to rip them open. When he moved to the front and back door, he did the same thing. Next, he placed several boards across the garage door, sealing it up as well.

"I don't think the neighbors are going to like this one bit if you ask me," Marcy commented when they were done. The place looked like the city had condemned it.

Jake shrugged his shoulders and started to head towards the truck. He turned to look over his shoulder as he replied, "Screw 'em. Half of the people in our neighborhood are welcoming the UN like liberators."

Marcy sighed. It was no secret he'd been angered by the cheering and support for the Canadian and Chinese soldiers passing through their city, and she didn't disagree with him. However, his job at the city still seemed safe, and she hoped he wouldn't spout off to the wrong person and put them in harm's way.

Just as Jake was about to hop into his truck, one of their neighbors, Garret, walked over.

"Hey, Jake. I saw you boarding the place up. What gives? Something I should know about?"

Garret fit all the stereotypes of a granola liberal yogi, even down to the man bun. He and his wife owned five or six yoga studios throughout the county. He was a nice enough guy as long as the conversation stayed away from religion, politics, and guns. Marcy held her breath.

"Hi, Garret. I'm actually glad you stopped by," said Jake in a friendly tone. He motioned for him to come closer.

When Garret reached his open door, Jake replied in a hushed tone. "Garret, you know I work for the county, right?" he asked.

Garret nodded. He had a look of concern on his face, but he didn't say anything.

"Yesterday, we had some soldiers from the UN come to our office. They told us employees that we should take some precautions to keep ourselves safe. They said they had heard reports that some local militia members might try to harm, or worse, kill people they viewed as collaborators with the UN."

Garret looked shocked, then angry. "I can't believe those right-wingers would harm folks like you. I mean, you're just doing your job for the county."

Grimacing as he nodded, Jake put his hand on Garret's shoulder as he added, "I know. It's terrible. I'm just a city engineer, but I have Marcy to think about. One of the Canadian soldiers told me they're setting up a safe place for some of us to stay with our families if we believe we might be in danger, so I'm taking them up on their offer."

Garret looked surprised, then pleased. "Wow. That's great that they're going to help you guys out and keep you safe from those crazy Sachs supporters. I swear those people are going to cause problems, Jake. So how long do you think you'll be gone?"

"Um. I honestly don't know, Garret. They just told us to pack up some valuables and head to their location. I hope you don't mind me not telling you where we're going. They said it needs to stay a secret for security purposes. But, if you could do me a huge favor...," Jake said as his voice trailed off.

"Sure. Anything, Jake," Garret replied warmly. He appeared to have a new sense of respect for his neighbor now that he was being "protected by the UN."

"If you can help look out for the place, I'd greatly appreciate it. I know I'll be able to focus on my duties with the UN a lot easier if I know some of our supporters are looking after our house. I mean, it's boarded up and all, but if you see anything odd, you can call me at work. My number hasn't changed, and it still works. At least until those Sachs supporters find a way to disable our lines."

Marcy struggled to keep herself from laughing at the overt embellishment Jake had added to his story. She watched as her husband handed Garret one of his business cards with his direct line on it.

"Yeah, man. You can count on me, Jake. Thanks for telling me. And thanks for working with the UN. I'm sure things will get sorted soon enough. Tate will be our president soon, and this will just be a hiccup. You wait and see."

Jake shook Garret's hand. "Well, I need to get going to the location. I'll talk with you later, man, when this is all sorted. We'll have you guys over for some wine and cheese. Now that I'm officially working for the UN, I'm going to try and use those privileges to see if I can't get some wine and specialty cheeses from across the border."

Garret shook his head in amusement, "Well, if they're looking for more people, tell them I'd be interested in a job. Talk to you later, neighbor."

A minute later, Jake was back in his truck and headed out of the neighborhood. Marcy turned to look at him and busted a gut laughing. They both did. They laughed so hard they were crying. It felt good to let go of some of the tension they'd both been feeling.

Marcy knew that Jake was doing something to help his old National Guard unit in their efforts to disrupt the UN, but she'd figured that the less she knew, the better. She'd rather help support him in other ways and maintain her plausible deniability.

****

From the *Bellingham Herald*:

City officials have warned that the United Nations still has not found the source of the IED attacks that have been cropping up across the county. In total, six bombs have now exploded, killing more than thirty UN soldiers and wounding close to twice that many. Although the attacks seem to be directed at the peacekeeping force, citizens should reduce travel to only that which is absolutely necessary. If you see any suspicious activities, especially along roadways, please contact your local law enforcement immediately.

****

Bethesda, Maryland
Walter Reed National Military Medical Center

A few dozen armed Marines fanned out around the hospital helipad as a small fleet of flying contraptions made their way toward them. There was a V-22 Osprey in the center, with four attack helicopters flanking it. Behind the first wave of helicopters were four additional V-22s and another group of attack helicopters. Whatever was heading toward the hospital was bringing a lot of firepower.

The first group of helicopters flew over the hospital grounds and loitered in a high orbit while the group of four V-22s landed. They offloaded another company of Marines to add to the group that had already shown up at the hospital.

Then a lone Osprey landed while the attack helicopters hovered nearby, their chin guns at the ready. A swarm of doctors and nurses, ready to treat the four survivors of the Raven Rock facility, rushed forward. After being trapped in the tunnel for nearly seven days, all four of the men were dehydrated and malnourished.

The first person off the helicopter was General Austin Peterson. The injury to his right leg seemed to have developed an infection, and in the daylight, it was a bit more evident that he was now pale and running a fever. He was rushed off to surgery on a gurney. The remaining three men walked out of the helicopter themselves, sporting only minor lacerations and injuries.

When President Jonathan Sachs exited the Osprey, several of the nurses and doctors nearby gasped. It was a shock to see him alive at all, but he was nearly unrecognizable in his dirty, disheveled, and exhausted state. The medical personnel on the helipad obviously realized at that point why there were so many Marines and Secret Service present at the hospital, and they were visibly moved by the knowledge that the President hadn't been killed during the first day of the war.

The doctors and nurses insisted that their three new patients sit down in wheelchairs, despite complaints from each of them that they could walk on their own. With Lieutenant Commander Bullard, Agent Harrison, and President Sachs seated, they were quickly whisked off toward an examination room in the secure wing of the hospital.

Once the doors on the rooftop opened, a dozen heavily armed Marines led the way, making sure the patients were led down the path that they had already cleared. A phalanx of Secret Service agents moved in sync with the doctor and nurses attending the President. Behind them, another platoon of Marines followed, determined to make sure no one was able to breach their protective perimeter of the President ever again.

With the massive increase in security and the whirling thumping of helicopter blades churning above, everyone in the building assumed that the acting President must be paying a visit to some of the wounded. However, as people spotted Jonathan Sachs, the man they all believed had been assassinated, the rumor mill spread like wildfire.

****

From *Reuters Online*:

Unconfirmed reports are coming from Walter Reed Medical Center that a group of four survivors was found in the tunnel system under the DoD's Raven Rock facility. The survivors were purportedly flown to the military hospital so they could be treated for their injuries. A nurse working at the hospital has revealed to us that she saw a disheveled-looking President Jonathan Sachs brought into an examination room along with two other men. As of the time of this publication, we have not been able to confirm this information with the Pentagon, Walter Reed, the Secret Service, or the White House. If it is indeed true that President Sachs survived the attempt on his life, this would be an incredible turn of events.

****

Camp Blanding, Florida

"No. That's not acceptable. You're going to do it again," Seth said in a firm yet commanding voice. He looked sternly at the young female recruit standing next to him.

She grunted in frustration. "I'm trying my best, sir," she complained. "I just seem to be a terrible shot. I don't know why. I'm pretty decent with the M4."

Recruit Amber Ryder had been about to fail her pistol qualification for the second time when Seth had taken a moment to talk with her on the side to see what the problem was.

Smiling, Seth took the pistol from her and motioned for her to follow him down to the end of the firing line, away from the other recruits. He signaled for one of the range sergeants to follow him as well. When they reached the last firing position, he placed the Sig Sauer on the table along with three fresh magazines.

He looked at her with a raised eyebrow. "You do know the difference between a clip and a magazine, right?" he asked.

"Is that a trick question, sir?" she responded with a coy smile.

"No. Just testing you," he replied. Seth did his best to maintain a serious expression.

"A magazine is what we place in a rifle or handgun. A clip is a strip of ammo we use to load our magazines."

Seth smiled. "See? If we can teach you civilians the difference, then we can certainly teach you how to shoot. Now, I've watched you fire the M4, and you do just fine. So, what's the problem with the pistol? What are you uncomfortable with?"

"I guess it just kicks too much. I think I'm flinching right before it fires in anticipation of it kicking, and it causes me to miss."

"That's right. That's *exactly* what you're doing, Ryder. You're afraid it's going to kick in your hand, and it causes you to flinch in anticipation. So, here's what we're going to do. We're going to get you over your fear of it kicking. Once you become used to it, it won't faze you. You'll be able to pick it up and just shoot."

Seth motioned for one of the sergeants nearby to bring them a dozen more magazines for the Sig, along with more ammo. Then Seth had her run through several mags. He had her alternate between firing each bullet one at a time with practiced aim and rapidly firing the pistol to empty the magazine as fast as she could. He showed her some tips for how to grip the weapon differently so that she could control how it felt in her hand.

By the end of the hour, she had run through nearly two hundred rounds of 9mm ammo and had improved her shooting form to where he believed she could now qualify. Seth had her go back to the qualifying lane for her last and final try to qualify with the Sig. It was a requirement for her to graduate training, and Seth was determined not to let any of their recruits fail. In his mind, if a recruit didn't pass, it was because either he'd failed them as an instructor or he'd failed to properly motivate them—in either case, failure was simply not an option in the Special Forces world.

Seth stood behind and to the side of Recruit Ryder. He watched with satisfaction as she shot one of the best scores of the day. When she passed him, she smiled and thanked him before she headed off to rejoin the other recruits, who were busy disassembling their pistols to start the tedious process of cleaning them.

Sergeant Major Wilcock walked up to Seth. "You did good, sir. I thought she was going to be our first failure of this training program."

Turning to look at his sergeant major, Seth leaned in so no one else could hear. "No failures, Wilcock. We've got to get these folks ready for whatever is going to be thrown at them."

The gruff-looking sergeant major nodded, then spat a stream of tobacco juice to his left. "You're right, sir. I'll make sure we give the ones struggling on the range more practice if that's what it'll take." His expression soured. "My concern is we're pushing them through training faster than they're ready for it. We normally spend ten weeks training a raw recruit to be a soldier, and another two to six months for their advanced training before they're even sent to a line unit. Right now, we're pushing these recruits through in four weeks—it's just silly."

"I agree, Sergeant Major, but look at it this way— these recruits are gearing up to be security augmenters, not combat soldiers. This isn't Afghanistan. We're not training a bunch of illiterate farmers and shepherds to go fight the

Taliban. Just keep riding them hard, and let's make sure we're turning out the best possible recruits we can, all right? If you need to draw more ammo from supply—or hell, the local economy—then do it. But no weapon failures."

The sergeant major nodded and then proceeded to berate a recruit for not properly handling their weapon as the next group prepared to qualify with their Sigs.

Smiling at the interlude between the senior NCO and the raw recruit, Seth moved on to the next batch of recruits in training. He walked over to a group being schooled by a couple of their Special Forces trainers on the art of hand-to-hand fighting. The difference between what they were teaching the trainees and what they would normally learn in the civilian world was that their instructors weren't teaching them how to score points or subdue an attacker; they were teaching them how to disarm an aggressor and kill them. There was no pussyfooting around in this training.

"Remember, recruits, your job is to not let the enemy get close enough that you have to rely on this training," bellowed one of the Special Forces sergeants. "If you have to rely on this training, then you've already screwed up. Your best weapon is distance. You keep the enemy at bay, and you take 'em out with carefully aimed shots from your rifle or your pistol. You don't let the bastards get right up on you. You hear me, recruits?"

"Yes, Sergeant!" the group collectively yelled in response.

Hearing someone run up behind him, Seth turned to see his XO, a senior captain. "What's up, XO?" he asked.

"Sir, you're not going to believe it. They're reporting in the news that President Sachs wasn't killed. They found him alive, buried in the tunnel underneath Raven Rock. He's at Walter Reed, being checked on now."

"Holy crap…I can't believe he survived. I'll tell you what, XO—that is one tough man to kill."

"Yeah, no joke. Oh, by the way, I heard some scuttlebutt from a friend of mine still back at SOCOM. Rumor has it we may not be turning our recruits over to DHS after all."

That news came as a bit of a shock. Seth looked around, wanting to make sure no one else could hear them talking. "What do you mean? Isn't that the whole reason why we're out here?" he asked, waving his arm toward the trainees.

"My friend says the new SecDef, Howell, is pushing the acting President to reverse the original DHS plan and have the recruits formed up into DoD militia units to help augment the National Guard and active-duty units." The XO held up his hands in mock surrender. "I don't know how that's any different than just throwing draftees at the units and calling it a day, but apparently the new guy at the Pentagon wants to ramp up a militia force to use for this crisis and then quickly demobilize them when it's done."

Seth snorted. "Sounds like another politician who hasn't served in the military coming up with some harebrained idea," he retorted. Seth looked off in the distance for a second before he returned his gaze to his XO. "All right. For the time being, keep this to yourself. We'll continue to do what we're doing and get these recruits ready for the original mission until we're told otherwise. I'd think if this idea had any merits, our FBI instructors would've heard about it as well, but they haven't said anything to us."

His XO nodded. "Makes sense to me, sir. Just wanted to pass along what I was hearing."

The two of them walked back to their main office. When Seth was alone, he made a quick call back to SOCOM to try and get the skinny on what was really going on.

****

Ottawa, Canada
Lord Elgin Hotel

Marshall Tate heard his Chief of Staff, Jerome Powell, let out a raucous stream of profanity in the next room. His stomach sank. Whatever it was, it couldn't be good. He took a deep breath and walked over.

"What is it, Jerome?" he asked. But in that exact moment, he glanced at the TV and saw the scrolling headline at the bottom. There was his answer.

"Sachs is alive?" he asked incredulously. "Didn't they hit Raven Rock with four bunker-busting bombs?"

Jerome swore a few more times and then slapped his fist down on the conference table. He didn't seem to be able to speak using coherent sentences.

Tate didn't want to wait for him to calm down. He grabbed the phone. It rang twice.

"Admiral David Hill," said his Secretary of Defense.

"Are you watching the news?" Tate asked.

"No, sir," he replied. "But I can turn it on now."

"Don't bother. Sachs is alive."

"What?" Admiral Hill asked, clearly as shocked at the news as Tate was himself.

"You heard me. He survived the attack."

A torrent of obscenities attacked Tate's ears. He moved the phone a bit further from his ear. When Admiral Hill paused to catch his breath, Tate said, "Jerome felt the same way. Now, you and General McKenzie are the ones who got us into this mess—how do you plan on getting us out?"

An awkward pause ensued. "Well?" Tate practically barked.

"I'm going to have to get back to you, sir."

"You struck at the King and you missed, Hill. Now Sachs is going to be angrier than ever. You went against me, and there's going to be hell to pay. Not only is Sachs alive, but the people no longer see us as liberators." He swore. "The next time I talk to you, there'd better be a plan in place, or you're going to regret the day you were born." Then he hung up the phone—wishing the old receiver phones were still in style so he could slam it down in his frustration.

Tate put his head in his hands. Jerome stammered, "Sir—"

"If I were you, I'd go take a walk right now," said Tate. He was angry enough to punch someone.

Jerome followed his advice and exited the room silently. Marshall Tate was left alone with his feelings. He turned off the TV; he didn't want to hear another second of it.

What are we going to do now? he wondered. As he sat there, his rage slowly subsided. He found himself feeling somewhat relieved that this plan hadn't worked. Tate had never wanted to assassinate Sachs. He'd wanted to beat him the old-fashioned way, at the ballot box.

But I didn't do that, did I? he asked himself. He wondered why he was even doing this anymore. He hadn't won. He knew that now. The country was being torn apart over a lie. His country—the one he'd hoped to lead into a new era of freedom and prosperity.

Tate tried to run all the angles, but the more he tried to calculate, the more he realized there was no way out for him. If he tried to back down now, the powers that had propped him up would destroy him and his family in a way that would make him wish he was dead.

He looked over at the bottle of Ambien he'd been using to help him sleep at night. *Maybe I should just take care of it myself*, he thought. But Tate knew he didn't have the courage to end it all. For better or worse, he was stuck now. He was a pawn in someone else's scheme. A scheme that was not going very well…

Chapter 4
Two Presidents

From the Associated Press:

A day after he was rescued, the White House and the Pentagon have finally confirmed that President Jonathan Sachs survived the UN attack on Raven Rock and was found alive. He had been trapped for nearly a week in the tunnel connecting the presidential retreat of Camp David and the Raven Rock facility. The Pentagon reports that the President was one of only four survivors. Rescuers also found one Secret Service agent, the naval officer carrying the nuclear football, and the Chairman of the Joint Chiefs. More than 900 people died in those two attacks.

It's been reported that President Sachs will resume his duties as president the day after Senator Marshall Tate takes a separate presidential oath of office in New York City. Tate still maintains that he is the only duly elected president of the United States.

****

January 20, 2021

New York, New York

Steps of City Hall

For January, it was a beautiful morning in New York City. The temperature hovered somewhere around thirty degrees Fahrenheit, and there wasn't a cloud in sight. There was virtually no wind either. Encouraged by this relatively welcoming weather, a crowd of ten to fifteen thousand people packed every inch of the park and the promenade in front of the city hall building.

Standing on a freshly built stage that had been constructed specially for this event was President-elect Marshall Tate. Next to him stood his wife and two grown children, along with the Chief Justice for the New York Supreme Court. Further down the stage, and at considerable personal risk to himself, was UN Secretary-General Johann Behr, who was flanked by the leaders of Canada, Germany, and France.

Absent, of course, were the military leaders of the UN and CDF forces, along with Tate's soon-to-be-sworn-in Secretary of Defense, Admiral David Hill. Tate and his new administration had decided that they were all taking enough of a risk gathering in a public place for this swearing-in, and they didn't need to tempt the federalists by presenting all the military and political commanders together on one stage. With the cameras of the world pointed at them, they doubted Sachs would order an airstrike on them, but no one was taking chances.

The Chief Justice of the New York Supreme Court walked up to Tate and his wife. He took a deep breath and let it out. The time had finally come. In just a moment, he would finally be sworn in as the President of the United States.

The Chief Justice held a Bible in front of Tate, and a hush fell over the crowd. "Good morning, Mr. President-Elect. Please recite after me."

Tate placed his left hand on the Bible that the justice presented and raised his right hand. He listened intently to each word.

I can't screw up now, he thought. He was very conscious of all of the eyes and cameras that were aimed at him in that moment.

"I, Marshall Tate, do solemnly swear that I will faithfully execute the Office of President of the United States, and will, to the best of my ability, preserve, protect and defend the Constitution of the United States."

When he'd finished uttering the words, it was as if a huge weight had been taken off his shoulders. He felt a surge of optimism and pride in being an American.

The two men shook hands. Then the Chief Justice made way for him to walk up to the microphone at the podium so the newly elected President could give his inauguration speech. Before he spoke, Marshall Tate took a moment to look out onto the crowd, who were bundled up in winter jackets, scarves, gloves and hats, waiting with palpable anticipation for him to speak.

Tate cleared his throat softly, then looked at the teleprompter. "My fellow Americans, these are troubling times we find ourselves in. Here I stand before you, being sworn in as the forty-sixth president of these United States on the steps of city hall in New York City, instead of at the Capitol Building in Washington, D.C., like the US presidents before me."

"Yeah, because your UN army bombed the Capitol Building!" shouted someone from the crowd. Instantly, Tate's supporters and nearby security guards grabbed the man and removed him before he could cause any further disturbance.

Without missing a beat, Tate moved on as if the incident hadn't happened. Methodically, he laid out his vision for America: to provide healthcare to all, free college for those who wanted to attend, and a universal basic income. The crowd ate up every word he said. Then his focus turned to what he called "Occupied America," which is what his administration had begun calling the parts of the country that were still under control of the former president, who simply wouldn't leave office.

"To those citizens in Occupied America—know that we are doing everything in our power to liberate you. With the help of our friends and allies from the United Nations and the rest of the world, we will free you from the shackles of the Sachs administration. I ask that each and every one of you find the resolve within yourselves to either take up arms against the occupiers or to find a way to cross over into Free America and join the ranks of our new Civilian Defense Force as we move to release our country from the yoke of tyranny and oppression."

The crowd went wild as he did his best to rile and stir them up. Page Larson and Admiral Hill had gone over his speech extensively in preparation for this event. They'd sold him on the idea of using his inauguration speech as a rallying cry to try and regain the public support for his administration. They also hoped that his message would help to inspire tens of thousands, or even hundreds of thousands of people, to join their ranks in defeating the federal government.

A lot rode on this speech. If they couldn't grow the ranks of the CDF and do it quickly, the UN force would collapse, and the Second American Civil War would end before it could really get going.

****

From *Der Spiegel*:

Many across the globe are celebrating the official swearing-in of Marshall Tate as the 46th president of the United States. In his public address following the ceremony, Chancellor Kraus stated, "The people of Germany and Europe stand with President Tate and the people of Free America. It is in times of great struggles like these that we must unite as a global village to protect the world from those who are drunk on power."

The Chancellor attended the event to reiterate his support for the UN peacekeeping mission there. The prime ministers of Canada and France were also present to congratulate President Tate. Several other European members of the UN military effort have also made public speeches confirming their support of the new American president.

****

Yankee Stadium
Following Day

Lieutenant General Ryan Jackman looked at the long line of young people volunteering to join the CDF and smiled. He'd hoped President Tate's speech would gin up support, but he had no idea so many people would answer the call. If he had to guess, there were close to twenty or thirty thousand people there, waiting to sign up to volunteer to serve in the CDF.

Jackman's administrative folks were working with the Canadians to get them signed up and processed through the enlistment procedure as quickly as they could. Every half hour, a new batch of enlistees would be sworn in and then moved over into one of two different groups. The first category was the fresh, raw recruits—people who had no prior military experience. Those recruits were going to be moved to a holding area from which they would be shipped off to the recently captured Fort Drum and a few other bases for a very shortened version of basic combat training.

The second batch of recruits were those who had prior military service. These people were immediately given new uniforms and an automatic promotion to either corporal or sergeant, depending on the last rank they'd held. Then they'd be sent over to Fort Totten, where they would be issued weapons and integrated into one of the existing or newly created CDF battalions.

While the federal forces were giving them a short reprieve around Trenton, New Jersey, General Jackman was determined to grow his militia ranks swiftly and get them ready for the next major battle.

****

From *MSNBC Online*:

> Despite nine days of heavy fighting across the American-Canadian border, there appears to be no end in sight to the bloodshed and fighting that is consuming both nations.
>
> After Marshall Tate was officially sworn into office, the governors of California, Oregon, Washington State, Wisconsin, Illinois, New York, New Jersey, Connecticut, Rhode Island, New Hampshire, and Vermont have joined Free America

and have officially declared their support and recognition of Marshall Tate as the duly elected 46th president of the United States.

The other 39 states continue to remain a part of Occupied America, including the following states that are run by Democratic governors: Colorado, New Mexico, Hawaii, North Carolina, Virginia, and Pennsylvania. According to our recent polling, the majority of the country's population still does not recognize Marshall Tate as the legitimate president.

The Sachs administration, for its part, refuses to recognize the results of the recent election and is calling the UN peacekeeping force a "hostile takeover of the American government."

****

From *BBC Online*:

The government of Japan continues to stand by their demand that all US military forces withdraw from their country by 1 February. Sources within the American Department of Defense report that it is a severe logistical challenge to evacuate all of the military members and their families and the equipment on the bases by the deadline. Anonymous informants from the Pentagon have stated that a large amount of military equipment will have to be destroyed in place in order to meet the demands.

The United Nations peacekeeping force, which includes China, continues to put pressure on America to recognize Marshall Tate as the duly elected leader of the United States. Thus far, the Sachs administration shows no signs of deescalating this conflict.

****

From the *Daily Mail*:

As Europe rallies around the fledgling Tate administration in New York, the United Kingdom continues to sit on the sidelines. An official statement from Hughes' office read, "It is not the place of Great Britain to insert herself in the domestic affairs of America, particularly when we have more than one hundred years of friendly relations. As Prime Minister, I intend to keep our nation out of this American civil war and this foolish military adventurism by the United Nations. This folly on behalf of the UN has already cost the lives of more than 20,000 Europeans. I won't sacrifice the lives of our youth to advance the cause of the UN or its German, Russian, and Chinese puppet masters."

The Labour Party decried the Prime Minister's fence-sitting stance, calling it a "swipe at the UN." The Leader of the Opposition described the conflict taking place in America as a "war between the forces of good and evil."

As Canada continues to be torn apart by the federalists loyal to President Jonathan Sachs, many people in the Commonwealth plead for British intervention to help the UN end the bloodshed.

****

Guantanamo Bay, Cuba

Staff Sergeant Lane Haverty and the men of India Company, 3rd Battalion, 6th Marines bobbed up and down a bit as their amphibious assault vehicle hit a few waves. Prior to leaving the USS *Bataan*, their battalion commander had told the NCOs a large contingent of both Cuban and Venezuelan soldiers were preparing to attack the facility within the next twelve to twenty-four hours. As such, the commander of the 24th MEU was going to deploy them now in anticipation of the attack. He'd also said if the Cubans hadn't launched their attack by nightfall, then chances were, they'd go on the offensive and hit them first.

"Staff Sergeant, we're approaching the beach. Get your men ready. When we get off the beach, start scanning your sectors," the vehicle commander announced before he went back to scanning the horizon through the thermal scope.

Haverty grunted. He turned and looked at the two rows of Marines staring back at him, waiting for some nugget of information.

He lifted his chin a bit. "Once we get off the beach, I want those hatches opened and y'all scanning your sectors. Heads on a swivel and stay frosty. We have no idea if the Cubans are going to challenge our landing or attack the base perimeter."

Haverty saw nothing but a sea of faces that were plastered in camouflage paint and looks of determination. They all nodded grimly at the orders. He could tell that many of them had already consumed a few Rip It energy drinks, and some of the Marines had pinches of Skoal chewing tobacco stuffed in their lower lips. These men were ready for a fight.

Minutes later, the engine sounds of the amphibious assault vehicle changed as its tracks found purchase on the gravelly surf just in front of Kittery Beach. The Amtrack lurched forward and then steadily moved up the pebbled coast. A man with a flashlight wand guided them to the patrol road that would lead them to the on-base firing range a kilometer away. The battalion was going to bivouac near the range until they got the rest of their support equipment and units ready to initiate combat operations later that evening.

Haverty checked his watch. It was 2213 hours. When the vehicle finally leveled out, Staff Sergeant Haverty yelled out to be heard above the din of the engine. "Get those hatches opened and start watching your sectors!"

For Haverty, this was his second time at Gitmo. After completing his initial training, his first assignment had been here, as a part of the security detachment on the base, so he was obviously very familiar with the layout of the facility. He also knew if there was a fight, their unit would need to expand out of the base perimeter quickly. It was a small piece of real estate, and they didn't have a lot of maneuver room.

A few minutes into their drive, as Haverty was scanning with his own NVGs, he spotted a growing cluster of vehicles and people as they approached the large open space that represented the on-base firing range. Given the ground guides were doing their best to space the vehicles out as best they could, it had still turned into a chaotic cluster of people and equipment as they tried to cram the entire battalion into the area.

When the vehicle came to a halt, the commander dropped the back hatch, and Haverty's squad piled out of the Amtrack. As the Marines exited, they quickly threw their rucks on and fell into a hastily called platoon formation. As the squads formed up, Haverty moved down his row of men to make sure his guys were ready for whatever assignment they were about to be given. Once the platoon was formed up, the lieutenant walked up to Gunnery Sergeant Mann and relayed some information to him just outside of earshot.

Gunny Mann was a tough Marine, mean as the Devil himself. He'd just finished his twentieth year in the Corps and planned on staying in for as long as they'd let him. Aside from his uniquely brash nature, Mann was a damn good platoon sergeant. He'd served two tours in Iraq and another three tours in Afghanistan. In that time, he'd earned two Purple Hearts, two Bronze Stars with V device, and a Silver Star for his efforts.

When the lieutenant finished relaying to Mann what was up, the gunnery sergeant pulled out a map and quickly pointed to a spot on it. The lieutenant nodded in approval.

Gunny Mann turned to look at his platoon. Using no less than four F-bombs, he yelled at them all to shut up, even though no one was speaking. "Here's the skinny," he continued. "The lieutenant says we've been ordered to go set up a defensive line on the northeast side of the perimeter while we wait for this operation to kick off. I want the squads to dig fighting positions as soon as we get there. The area we're headed to is roughly a mile-and-a-half hike from here. I want us there in twenty minutes, and your fighting holes dug and ready twenty minutes later. Is that clear?" he bellowed.

Without waiting for a reply, he spun around with his gear already on and headed off to their objective. The lieutenant did his best to catch up to Gunny Mann, and the rest of the squads took off at a quick trot, falling into two single-file lines on either side of the patrol road that ran along the perimeter. All around them, other platoons were moving out as well as the newly arrived Marines prepared for the coming offensive.

Eighteen minutes after they'd left the firing range, Haverty's squad arrived at their part of the perimeter. They dropped their rucks and quickly pulled their entrenching tools.

Without a word of complaint or even so much as a murmur, the leathernecks went to work. They swiftly dug two-man positions for the rifle teams and three-man holes for the machine-gun crews, staggered every three to five meters, depending on the terrain. They all knew that the sooner their holes were dug, the sooner they could sack out and catch some sleep before the sun came up. They also knew an attack could happen at nearly any time, so the last thing they wanted was to be caught out in the open during an attack without a fighting hole to crawl into for protection.

Twenty minutes into their digging, one of the Marines called out in a voice barely above a whisper, "Staff Sergeant Haverty, can you inspect our fighting position?"

Turning to see who'd asked the question, Haverty sighed softly and rolled his eyes. Before leaving for this deployment, his squad had been assigned two newbies— young Marines fresh from boot camp. They were both eager and utterly green. This was literally their first time doing anything with their new unit, and like most people on their first day or week on the job, they were enthusiastic but completely ignorant of what they were supposed to do.

Climbing out of his fighting position, Haverty looked down at the other rifleman he was sharing a hole with. "Finish squaring the walls while I'm checking on these cherries. Also, make sure you move more of the dirt to form a bit of a lip facing this direction here," he directed, pointing to the most likely direction where an enemy attack would come from.

His partner in crime just grunted in response and went back to work.

Looking down at his watch, Haverty saw it was now 0122 hours. He really wanted to try and get some shut-eye, but he knew he had to make sure his squad was done with their work before he could even think about catching a few z's.

Walking over to his two greenest recruits, Haverty stood next to their fighting position and nodded in satisfaction. He knelt down so he could be heard as he whispered softly. "Not bad, grunts. Now, shift the dirt from this spot here and place it in an arch around this part of your position. If the enemy's going to attack us, they're going to come from that direction." He pointed to illustrate.

The two of them nodded at the suggestion and immediately went to work on making the adjustment. One of them looked up at him before he had a chance to move on and asked, "Staff Sergeant, do you know what our sleep rotation will be?"

"Yeah. When everyone's done, we're going to stay at fifty-percent manning until half an hour before sunup. Then we'll stand to and wait and to see what happens." Haverty glanced at his watch again. "It looks like we're going to get roughly four or so hours of sleep. You guys figure out how you want to break that up, but one of you has to be awake at all times. Is that understood?"

He saw them both nod, acknowledging his instruction. Satisfied, Haverty moved down the line to check on the rest of his guys. It took him another ten minutes to verify everyone in the squad had completed their fighting holes. Before he went to find their platoon sergeant, he told his guys to start sacking out. If there were a change to their orders, he'd let them know.

An hour later, Haverty found himself finally settling into his own fighting position, ready to sack out for the next two hours. He slipped into a deep sleep, dreaming about the new Chevy El Camino he was planning on buying in April. Haverty ran his hand across the hood of the vehicle, admiring his new chick magnet. He couldn't wait to open that 6.2-liter 550-horsepower engine at the racetrack. Suddenly, the canary-yellow car of his dreams blew up into a million pieces in front of him. The next thing he knew, his body was being thrown across the parking lot of the Chevrolet dealership. Haverty's eyes popped open wide as saucers as his brain registered that his body was actually being flung through the air. His arms flailed about to try and break his fall.

Holy crap! he thought.

He had only just realized that he was no longer dreaming when his body hit the ground a dozen feet away from his fighting position. The wind was violently knocked out of him, and he struggled to fill his lungs with air.

Haverty lay on the ground in shock and confusion, trying to piece together what had just happened. With a fair amount of pain, he was finally able to force a gasp and take a deep breath, sending much-needed oxygen to his brain. Haverty coughed. Then he felt his body being pelted with dirt, rocks, and other debris that was raining down. Finally, his sense of hearing returned, and he was overwhelmed by the sounds of gunfire, explosions, and the screams of the Marines around him.

What the hell is going on? he wondered.

"Here they come!" shouted someone not far from him.

Haverty rolled over to his side and frantically searched for his rifle. He looked to where his fighting position had been and saw his partner was lying half in the hole, and half out of it. He wasn't moving or returning fire.

Lifting himself up to his hands and knees, Haverty coughed a couple more times as he scrambled back to the fighting hole. Bullets kicked up dirt and rocks near him as people all around him were yelling. Someone was shouting commands; others were yelling out in pain, screaming for a corpsman.

As Haverty approached the fighting hole, he saw his battle buddy, Lance Corporal Mendoza, still hadn't stirred. He rolled his comrade over to see why he was still asleep. Haverty nearly threw up. Mendoza's entire face was missing. There was just a pulverized mess of flesh, bone, and tendons where his face should've been.

Brushing off what he'd just seen, Haverty found his M27 still leaning against the side of the fighting hole, right where he had left it when he'd fallen asleep. He crawled in and grabbed it. Positioning himself to face the attackers, Haverty brought his rifle to his shoulder and looked for something to shoot.

"They're breaching the right flank!" shouted Gunnery Sergeant Mann over their internal platoon coms.

"Haverty! Get your damn squad over here now!" he screamed.

Haverty snapped himself out of the fog his mind was still in from the concussion of his fall. He turned to his left and yelled out, "Second squad! On me!" Then he jumped out of his fighting hole and ran down the right side of their platoon's position to where Gunny Mann was calling for him.

As he came around the slight rise in the hill, he saw Gunnery Sergeant Mann with maybe six other Marines doing their best to try and hold their position against what had to be more than thirty enemy soldiers trying to bum rush them through a hole in the perimeter fence.

Raising his rifle to his shoulder as he ran toward them, Haverty squeezed off rounds at a rapid clip as he flicked the selector switch from semiauto to full auto. Enemy soldiers started dropping left and right. Once Haverty reached Mann's position, he jumped into a fighting hole that was currently occupied by two dead Marines. He dropped his spent magazine, reached into his MOLLE gear on the front of his IBA, slapped a fresh magazine in place, and hit the bolt release.

One of the Marines in his squad who had been running just behind him and to his left dropped down to a knee as he raised his M240 Golf to his shoulder and fired off a string of rounds. He cut down a dozen or more attackers who were nearly on top of Gunnery Sergeant Mann's position.

Several of their LAV-25 A3s roared up behind them, opening fire on the attackers with their 25mm chain guns and ripping the remaining enemy soldiers apart. As the LAVs advanced closer to their position, they continued to light up the enemy soldiers with their 25mm chain guns and started using their crew-served M240 machine guns. Marines began piling out of the rear hatches of the LAVs, adding their own firepower to the melee being unleashed on the enemy. Then, as abruptly as the attack had started, it ended.

Lying before the Marines was a carpet of dead bodies. Before anyone could figure out what had happened, artillery guns from further back inside the base fired at some unseen target. Then the Marines' mortar teams pounded the enemy positions a few kilometers away from the perimeter fence.

Gunnery Sergeant Mann stood up in his fighting hole and barked obscenity-laden orders to the remaining survivors of their platoon. The LAVs and a newly arrived platoon of M1 Abrams battle tanks lurched forward, pushing past the perimeter of the base as they sought to hunt down any further enemy units still lurking nearby.

The armored vehicles pushed past their positions, driving over the dead bodies of the attackers. Although they could all hear the morbid sound of bones being crushed, Gunny Mann was completely unfazed. "Form up and follow me!" he ordered.

The enemy might have gotten the first punch in, but the Marines were about to deliver a series of body blows that would knock the Cubans, Russians, and Venezuelans out of the war.

****

Boquerón, Puerto Rico

Colonel Popov of Russia's 61st Naval Infantry Brigade stood on the rear deck of the *Petr Morgunov* landing assault ship. He watched as the last of his landing force of naval infantry disembarked from the ship to head for shore. Sighing, he pulled another cigarette out of his breast pocket and proceeded to light it. Taking a long pull, he watched as the red embers lit up the tobacco.

"You aren't going ashore with your men?" inquired a naval officer who'd walked up behind him.

Turning to see who had asked the question, Popov just shrugged when he saw it was the ship's captain. "They will secure the beachhead. Then I'll transfer my headquarters to shore. For right now, I can communicate better with my brigade from here than I can in a BTR."

The captain nodded. The two stood there in silence for a few minutes as they watched the amphibious assault ships begin to turn toward the shore. It was still dark, and the sea was calm. Some lights were emanating from the buildings on land, but largely it was dark and quiet.

"You know, in a couple of hours, it's going to be very busy on land," the captain commented.

"*Da*. The sun will be up, and the islanders will wake up to find a brigade of Russian naval infantry have occupied their little island."

"Once your equipment and stores have been fully offloaded, I've been instructed to head back to Port of La Guaira."

"*Da*. I know," Colonel Popov said. "Just make sure those Venezuelans don't cheat you out of our supplies and your sailors don't get cold feet and want to stay in port. My men are going to need those provisions." He fixed his naval counterpart with an icy stare.

The captain nodded. "My little flotilla will return in a week," he assured. The plan was to drop the two brigades of Russian naval infantry off in Puerto Rico and the Dominican Republic and let them create yet another thorn in the side for the Americans to deal with.

Taking another pull on his cigarette, Colonel Popov looked at the steely-eyed naval captain. "The Americans can't be everywhere at once. Don't worry, comrade—your ships will be fine."

The captain grunted at the assurance. "You know most of the Northern Fleet is at the bottom of the ocean, don't you?"

Popov snickered. "And so is a third of the US Navy, comrade. Let's not forget that. Just do your job, and we'll do ours. Don't abandon me and my men, OK? I need the rest of that equipment, or I won't be able to hold the island for very long."

The captain grunted. The Navy knew they had a critical job to perform. Once the soldiers made their landing, it was incumbent upon the Navy to then ferry over the thousands of Venezuelan soldiers who would help occupy the two islands while the Russians went to work on building up the island's surface-to-air and antiship missile platforms. If all went according to plan, they'd turn these two islands into a hornet's nest for the American Air Force and Navy to have to contend with.

Chapter 5

Northwest Passage

January 22, 2021
Joint Base Lewis-McChord
I "Eye" Corps HQ

Looking at the map, Major General Scott Stevens saw one major problem with this new offensive his boss was advocating for.

We don't have enough soldiers to make it happen, he realized.

Seeing the perplexed look on his division commander's face, Lieutenant General Andrew Biggs asked, "You're thinking we don't have enough manpower to make this work, aren't you?"

"Yeah. Pretty much, sir. My division is spread fairly thin right now, trying to protect the various naval facilities around the state and making sure the CDF forces down in Oregon don't cause us any problems."

General Biggs nodded. "I can see why you'd think that, but here's why you're wrong." Standing up, Biggs walked over to the map on the wall they were looking at with the disposition of their forces along with the remnants of the

Canadian, Chinese, and Russian forces, as well as a smattering of militia units. Pointing to Joint Base Elmendorf–Richardson in Alaska, Biggs explained, "I spoke with General Markus the other day. He agreed with my assessment that the Russians, Chinese, and Canadians aren't going to be a credible threat to our facilities in Alaska. As such, they've authorized the release of the 25th Infantry Division's 4th Brigade Combat Team to us. They're still going to hold the Stryker brigade in reserve, but they've released the airborne brigade to I Corps."

Smiling and nodding, Stevens replied, "Well, that does change things. How do you want to deploy them?"

Pointing at the map again, Biggs instructed, "Your division is going to press the enemy positions around Kent, just south of Seattle. Because we've finally achieved air supremacy over the battlespace, I'm going to have our paratroopers conduct two airborne assaults. The first one will be at North Marysville. I'm going to have one battalion land there, placing a blocking force north of Seattle. The second battalion will land just north of Monroe, to the east of Seattle. The rest of the brigade will fly in to Ault Field, where they'll offload the rest of their equipment and then link up with their two sister battalions. This will place an entire brigade in the enemy's rear area, cutting off their supply lines—but more importantly—trapping them as your division advances."

"You're trying to ensnare the entire enemy force, aren't you?" Stevens asked.

General Biggs nodded. "That's right. If we pull this off, we'll either capture or defeat the entire UN ground army in the Pacific Northwest. Once we've done that, we'll be able to finish securing the rest of the state before we move down into Oregon and assist our Marine brothers down in California."

"I like it, sir. It's bold and audacious," Stevens remarked with satisfaction. Then it looked as if he suddenly remembered something. "Here's my other concern, though. How are we going to handle the civilian population? Once the fighting finally ends, we need the city governments to go back to work. Right now, most of the city employees are supporting Senator Tate. How are we going to get them to recognize the current administration and do their duties and not fight us? How are we going to keep the cities from collapsing into chaos?"

General Biggs sighed. It was well known that he did not care for politics. "I've brought this very problem up to General Markus. He told me Secretary Hogan's new Federal Protective Service Force is going to start graduating six thousand new federal officers every week starting the first week of February. He's made the argument that two thousand of these newly trained federal law enforcement personnel should be sent to Washington to support our operations. Once they arrive, it'll give us two thousand extra bodies to help us administer the city and state governments."

"That's all fine and dandy, but how is that going to help us with enforcing their cooperation?" Stevens asked. "We need the citizens there to keep basic city functions up, like collecting garbage, paying their police and fire departments, hospitals, etcetera. There are a lot of things that need to get ironed out, sir."

Biggs grimaced at the laundry list his division commander had just brought up.

Stevens wondered if the general was picturing managing the crowd through the use of detention camps. There weren't too many simple scenarios to ensure public compliance.

General Biggs walked over to a nearby table and took a seat. He ran his fingers across his shaved scalp. "Stevens, I don't have an answer for how we handle the political side of things. Right now, I think you and I need to focus on defeating these foreign invaders first. We can figure out how to keep the state and local governments running once we've accomplished that first task. Do you have any further questions for me before we move forward with this plan?"

Stevens contemplated. "When do you want to launch this offensive?" he asked.

"I was thinking we'd kick things off in seventy-two hours. It gives us enough time to get things moved around without tipping our hand that we're about to do something major."

Stevens nodded. "OK. That can work. Let me get with my brigade and battalion commanders and get them ready." He tapped his foot nervously.

"Was there something else?" asked Biggs.

"I've been hearing there's a militia force up in the Burlington area that's been causing the UN all sorts of problems. Do you know any specifics on who they are?"

General Biggs smiled mischievously. "I don't know all the names of the people involved, but I've been told a handful of the local Army National Guard units that didn't side with the governor went rogue. They've been carrying out hit-and-run attacks on the UN."

Stevens grunted. "OK. Good to know we might have some local support up there. My G2 said they appear to have a couple of effective IED builders in their group. They've hit the UN force with close to thirty IEDs since the start of the occupation. That's a lot of IEDs in a short amount of time."

"It is. Let's just be glad whoever is doing that is on *our* side."

****

Monroe, Washington

"Six minutes," announced the jumpmaster. Then, using the appropriate hand signal, he ordered, "Stand up."

Sergeant Schneider, 3rd Battalion, 509th Airborne, did as he'd been instructed.

"Hook up!" shouted the jumpmaster. His arms were raised above his head, and his index fingers were hooked. Schneider reached for the cable, attached his static line hook, and inserted the safety pin.

"Check equipment," the jumpmaster instructed, slapping his chest with both hands.

Mechanically, Sergeant Schneider went through the process of running through his equipment check, and then checked the equipment of the man in front of him. The soldier behind him completed the final examinations of his own parachute as they prepared to make their first-ever combat jump.

Who would have guessed I'd be making a combat jump in my own country? he thought. It seemed very surreal. Soon, they'd be parachuting behind enemy lines in hopes of establishing a blocking force for the 2nd ID, which would be starting a major offensive around the same time they'd be landing.

"Sound off with equipment check," shouted the jumpmaster, cupping both hands behind his ears.

From the front of the plane, the soldiers called out as ordered, then tapped the thigh of the man in front. Then the soldiers nearest the jumpmaster announced, "All OK," and pointed at the jumpmaster with an extended arm. This signaled the loadmaster and the assistant loadmasters to begin the process of opening the side doors and the C-130.

As the doors opened, cold air rushed into the cabin, replacing any warm air that had been comforting the jumpers. The noise of the aircraft intensified to a dominating roar. All four propellers were running at full speed.

When the side doors to the C-130 opened up, the internal lights of the cargo plane turned to a soft red tone, allowing their eyes to adjust to the darkness outside. Sergeant Schneider was glad that it was still dark. In another hour, the sun would start to illuminate the sky. For the time being, the night still belonged to the paratroopers, who'd trained extensively at night using their night vision goggles.

Thus far, their pathfinder unit hadn't reported any enemy units in the area, but that didn't mean the UN coalition wouldn't dispatch some forces to deal with them once they were made aware of an incoming threat in their rear area.

Steadily, the aircraft droned on for a few more minutes until the jumpmaster signaled that they were about to jump. Schneider surveyed the soldiers near him. They all looked pumped—eager to go fight these foreign invaders and get into the war.

The last couple of weeks had been tough for them. Their brigade had been largely sitting on the sidelines as they watched the war unfold in the lower forty-eight. It had pained them to know their brothers in arms were fighting and dying while they'd sat on their duffs in nowhere Alaska, waiting for orders.

The jumpmaster moved to the door and commenced his checks, ensuring no sharp edges that could cut a static line were on the trailing door edge. He grasped the side of the door frame with both hands and stomped on the jump platform, which fell into place with the door open. Then he stomped on the platform with the other foot.

Schneider always breathed a sigh of relief at this point. The doorway was secure and holding on to the door frame.

The jumpmaster leaned out as far as he could to see if anything around the door could impede the jumpers. He also double-checked to make sure the drop zone was in front of the aircraft. Then he stepped back into the C-130.

The jumpmaster got the attention of the first jumpers for each door. "One minute! Stand. In the door!"

Returning his attention to the task at hand, Schneider saw that his fireteam was prepared. His five troopers were ready to get this show on the road. The wind swirled around him.

The first jumpers eagerly moved into position, and each subsequent jumper moved right up behind the next. There would be no hesitation once the command was given—it'd be imperative to empty the plane as fast as possible. They all watched the red light next to the door expectantly.

Finally, the light turned green. "Go, go, go, go, go!" shouted the jumpmaster. The sixty jumpers were out of the C-130 in less than twenty seconds.

Schneider's body freefell through the air for the briefest of moments before his static line caught and deployed his chute. Following his training, he immediately checked to make sure he had a full canopy. He let out a sigh of relief—at this altitude, no one wore a reserve since there wouldn't be time for it to deploy if the main line malfunctioned.

His rucksack, which had been held between his legs as he shuffled out the door, finally dropped below him when he judged he was roughly seventy-five feet above the ground. Looking around him, Schneider saw the chutes of the other paratroopers filling the sky as their battalion slowly drifted down to the ground below them. Drop altitude was only five hundred feet, so their ride would be brief.

It was Tuesday morning. The people of Monroe and the surrounding area would either be starting their morning commutes, or they would be in the process of waking up. In either case, those residents that were awake would be treated to a scene out of the old movie *Red Dawn* with nearly eight hundred paratroopers descending on their sleepy little town.

Schneider looked down and saw that he was quickly approaching the ground. He prepared his mind and body for the landing. Seconds later, his feet touched down. His knees bent as he tucked and rolled, allowing his body's momentum to shift and transfer the energy of the fall.

Coming out of his roll, Schneider quickly disconnected himself from his parachute and then began the process of collecting it so it wouldn't clog the drop zone. With his chute wrapped up in his arms, he dropped it on the ground next to him and unpacked his rifle from its protective case. Next, Schneider disconnected himself from his drop bag and walked over to where his rucksack was. He grabbed his ruck and pulled it over his shoulders.

While no one was shooting at them yet, the paratroopers rushed about, rounding up their equipment, weapons, and everything else they would need. Steadily, the men formed up in their platoons and squads. As the units continued to coalesce, the ones that were ready to roll moved out to secure their objectives.

"Sergeant Schneider, get your fireteam ready to move. We're heading out in three mikes," called out his squad leader, Staff Sergeant Harris.

Looking for the guys in his fireteam, Schneider saw they all had their rucks on and rifles out of their jump cases, ready for action. He walked up to them.

"You all good to go?" he asked, visually inspecting his team.

They each confirmed they were ready, and Schneider turned around, giving Harris a quick thumbs-up. A few minutes later, their platoon moved out, walking toward the Old Snohomish Monroe Road. Their orders were to set up a blocking position on the banks of Snohomish River and State Road 9, which crossed the river and headed north.

The brigade's first battalion would be landing near Everett, cutting off I-5, which connected all the way up to Vancouver. Another battalion would also be jumping into Monroe, but they'd be staying there to cut off State Highway 522. Finally, a recon element would go south to Duvall and watch the bridge there, destroying it if necessary. Together, the battalions were going to set up a thirteen-mile-long line, effectively cutting the UN forces off from retreating north or back to Canada.

Schneider reflected that it felt strange to be walking in two single-file lines on either side of this rural road in America. Five minutes into the road march, the platoon finally got its spacing right with each soldier about three to five meters apart from each other. Two squads walked down each side of the road while the lieutenant, platoon sergeant, and RTO stayed somewhat close to the center of the platoon.

A couple of soldiers had run further ahead of them to act as their scouts. So far, it looked like most of the local citizens were playing it smart and choosing to stay indoors. Schneider imagined that the people in this part of the state had probably felt reasonably safe up to this point; the UN peacekeepers had bypassed them entirely. The closest UN presence was battling with US forces near Kent, some forty-six miles south of them.

Thirty minutes into the march, the hairs stood up on the back of Sergeant Schneider's neck as he spotted some adults and children near the road.

Are they here to greet us or attack us? he asked himself.

When several of the kids smiled and waved, Schneider breathed a sigh of relief. A few of the adults looked much less thrilled to see them, but they refrained from making any negative comments or threatening gestures.

They probably figure we'd rather shoot them than argue politics, Schneider thought, suppressing the urge to chuckle.

The lieutenant broke his reflections. "Sergeant Schneider!" he called, holding the hand receiver for the radio to his shoulder.

"Moving, sir!" Schneider shouted as he ran to find out what the LT wanted.

When he got closer, the lieutenant gruffly said, "Sergeant, take your fireteam and go catch up to the scouts.

Apparently, they've encountered some sort of police roadblock up there. Find out what the issue is with these officers and let me know whether or not we're going to have a problem. I don't want to bring the entire platoon up there if it's a possible ambush."

Schneider nodded. "Roger that, sir. We'll get it sorted."

He then turned around and took off to grab his fireteam. Schneider's squad leader decided to come with them. The rest of the platoon took a knee and fanned out on the side of the road while they waited to see what would happen next.

Schneider and Staff Sergeant Harris took off at a quick trot with the five other soldiers of Alpha Team. After a few minutes, they spotted the four scouts crouching on the side of the road in the underbrush and joined them as quietly as possible.

One of the scouts motioned to Schneider. He followed the soldier's line of sight and saw the police cars that were blocking the road, lights flashing. Schneider noticed four officers standing behind the vehicles. Two were armed with shotguns, and the other two had AR-15-type assault rifles.

Schneider turned to his squad leader, Harris. "How do you want to handle this, Staff Sergeant?" he asked quietly.

"Schneider, you come with me and Jones," Harris responded. "We'll go try and talk with them and find out what the deal is. I want our M240G set up over there, ready to provide covering fire should we need it. You two," he said as pointed to two of the scouts, "I want you guys to set up a position across the road and crawl up to that tree area there. You'll be able to cover our flank should we need it."

With the plan put in motion, the nine paratroopers set to work. Staff Sergeant Harris stepped out of the tree cover with his rifle hanging from his single-point sling, waving a white rag in his right hand. Soon, the police officers noticed him and nervously took up positions behind their cars.

"We just want to talk. Please don't shoot!" shouted Staff Sergeant Harris as he slowly and calmly continued to make his way toward the roadblock. Schneider and Jones also held their hands up and to their sides to let the police officers know they weren't a threat. However, they also remained ready to grab their rifles and start shooting if needed.

When they got to within twenty or so feet of the police cars, one of the officers called out, "That's far enough. Who are you? And what do you want?"

"My name is Staff Sergeant Harris. We're with the 3rd Battalion, 509th Infantry Regiment. We're American paratroopers."

The officers exchanged nervous glances with each other before the leader of the group asked, "Whose side are you guys on?"

Schneider furrowed his brow. *What kind of question is that?*

"Um…we're Americans. We're on the side of America," Harris responded, stumbling over his words.

"Are you guys with the UN peacekeeping force?" yelled out one of the police officers.

Harris exclaimed, "No. We're here to kick those bastards out of our country. Is that going to be a problem?"

Broad smiles spread across the faces of the police officers, who must've liked his response. They immediately lowered their rifles and made their way around their cruisers. The officer in the lead extended his hand.

"I'm Sergeant James, the shift supervisor for the Snohomish County Sheriff Department. It's good to finally see some American soldiers. I served in the 2nd ID twenty years ago. We were starting to think you all had abandoned us when the UN crossed the border."

Shaking the man's hand, Harris replied, "Nah. We've just been busy trying to beat these bastards back in other areas. Let me radio back to the rest of the platoon that you guys are on our side. We're on our way to Snohomish."

Turning to Schneider, Harris said, "Radio back to the LT and tell him the platoon can move up. These guys are with us."

Looking back at the police officers, Harris asked, "Can you tell me if there are any UN or CDF forces in Snohomish or the surrounding area that we should be aware of?"

Sergeant James nodded. "Yeah, there are. The CDF has a small base they set up at the Harvey Airfield, just across the river. They've turned all the hangars into sleeping quarters and makeshift offices. They've even set up a firing range to help teach their new recruits. We see helicopters landing there all the time. Not sure what they're doing, but the helicopters look to be European or Russian types."

"Do you have an idea of how many of them are there? Are we talking a few dozen or a few hundred?"

Sergeant James shrugged his shoulders. "I'm honestly not sure. We aren't really encouraged to patrol around the area. What I do know is they've been holding all sorts of recruitment drives all over the county to grow their ranks. I'm not sure how long their training is, but most of the people appear to be getting sent either south to help out in the fighting or north to be trained by the Canadians."

Harris shook his head. "OK, Sergeant James. This has been helpful." He pulled out a map of the area. "Do you think you could help point out where you've seen any guard towers or machine-gun bunkers? It sounds like we're going to have to deal with this CDF problem before we do anything else."

For the next ten minutes, the police officers took turns showing them on their map where the perimeter was that the CDF had set up. They pointed out any guard towers and bunkers, and then explained some other details they knew about the base. By the time they'd finished giving them a detailed picture of what lay ahead for them, the rest of the platoon had shown up.

When the LT spoke with the sheriff deputies and saw the map, he ordered their scout drones to be launched so they could start to get some eyes on what they were headed into. He also called back to their captain to let him know they'd need the rest of the company to move forward and help them if they were going to take this airfield back. It was too big of a task for a single platoon to reasonably handle.

****

Sergeant Schneider approached the railroad bridge cautiously, looking for any possible signs of trouble. The surveillance drone hadn't picked up any roving patrols or guards watching for foot traffic, but that didn't mean that there wasn't a well-hidden surprise lying in wait.

Looking over his shoulder, Schneider motioned for the rest of his fireteam to follow him. Standing up into a low crouch, he raised his rifle to his shoulder, ready to fire at any possible threat. As he started moving forward toward the entrance of the rail bridge, his troopers slowly followed behind him with their rifles also at the ready.

Schneider kept searching his surroundings. He still hadn't spotted anyone. With no visible signs of trouble, he continued along, making sure to step on the railroad ties so as not to fall or get tripped up. Once on the actual bridge, Schneider moved as quickly as he could without falling to cross to the other side.

On the other end, he took a knee and had the others do the same. They waited at the edge of the bridge and watched and listened for a moment. When he was sure he didn't hear anything, he led his fireteam off the bridge. Three of his troopers broke to the right—they'd search that side of the bridge and riverbank while he moved to the left with two of his other soldiers, doing the same. Once they'd all confirmed that they hadn't found anything of interest, Schneider radioed that it was safe for the rest of the platoon to cross.

While the others traversed the bridge, Schneider and his fireteam moved further along the tracks. There was a pallet factory not too far down, adjacent to the small airfield and CDF base. It was a good staging point for them to gather as much of the company as possible before they could bum rush the airfield and hopefully overrun it before the defenders could react.

On the other side of the river, their heavy weapons platoon had already set up their 60mm mortar tubes, and they were ready to give them some cover when the time came. Now it was just a race to get everyone across without being seen.

Schneider and his team were probably a hundred yards ahead of the rest of their squad and platoon when they heard a single shot ring out. Then a machine gun opened fire.

Turning to see where the gunfire was coming from, Schneider saw a string of tracer rounds fly into the railroad bridge that the rest of their platoon was trying to cross. A couple of soldiers appeared to have been hit. One of them fell into the water.

"Alpha Team, drop your rucks! Patrol packs only, and let's move!" shouted Schneider. They needed to get into a better position to help cover the rest of their platoon.

Running at a near sprint despite having his patrol pack and body armor on, Schneider made it to the edge of the tree line that ran along the railroad and butted up against a heavy engine repair shop and the pallet factory. He pointed to a couple of positions along the edge of the tree line.

"Get your M240 set up now," he exclaimed. Schneider found his M203 gunner next. "I want you to start firing smoke grenades here and here," he ordered, pointing to the intended targets.

Schneider did a brief, broad survey of their surroundings. They were now less than one hundred meters from the newly erected perimeter fence of the CDF base. He grabbed his radio. "Hornet Five, this is Alpha One. I need four rounds HE at target one. Then I need four rounds smoke at target two and target five. How copy?"

It took a moment for their heavy weapons platoon to respond, but they repeated back his fire support order and had the rounds on the way. While they waited, two of the

CDF guard towers continued to fire away at the paratroopers racing across the railroad bridge with their machine guns.

Sergeant Schneider held his breath for a moment until he heard the expected thunderous explosions at the nearby base. He could see that several rounds did score direct hits on the hangars, and then the smoke rounds began to land, shrouding the base in thick white smoke.

At the same time, Schneider's M203 gunner had fired off three of his own smoke grenades along their portion of the fence line. His goal with the smaller localized smoke grenades was to keep the enemy from knowing what was happening along this side of the perimeter until the rest of their platoon was able to join them.

Suddenly, five people carrying a mix of different civilian assault rifles rounded the corner of the engine repair shop, headed right for their position. Before Schneider could even inhale, his M240 gunner had opened fire on them, hitting them with a barrage of bullets. The CDF soldiers had a look of sheer surprise and terror on their faces, right before their bodies were riddled with bullets.

Zip, zap.

Bullets flew in their direction, hitting some of the trees and underbrush around them. One of the guard towers not far from them had let loose on their positions.

"Take that tower out!" shouted Schneider with urgency.

His heavy machine gunner shifted fire, and the M203 gunner aimed his grenade gun at the tower as well.

Pop...bam.

The grenade missed hitting the machine-gun position in the tower directly, but it did hit part of its support structure. Within seconds, the tower toppled over on its side, silencing the machine-gun crew inside it.

The victory was short-lived. By that time, more than a dozen CDF soldiers had started filtering into the grounds around the engine shop and the nearby area, and they were lighting up Schneider's position. One of his soldiers grunted and then moaned in pain from a hit he took.

Just as Sergeant Schneider thought he was going to have to have his guys pull back, the rest of their squad filtered into the positions they had taken up. In the span of ten seconds, there were now more than forty paratroopers laying down fire on the CDF soldiers.

The platoon sergeant shouted, "Advance on these two buildings, one squad at a time! We need to get closer to the base perimeter."

Across the railroad tracks, Schneider and his men could see that additional mortars were making contact. They weren't as large, but they seemed to be doing an excellent job of continuing to cause chaos and confusion at the CDF base, which was the real goal.

As Schneider and his men took up positions at the engine repair shop and the pallet factory, their numbers were suddenly augmented. The remaining two platoons of the company had finally made it across the river.

Five more minutes went by, and then Captain Ira Tabankin fired off a blue flare into the sky. That was the signal for all of the platoons to do their best to start breaching the CDF base. Adrenaline coursed through Schneider's veins as he charged forward—it was finally time to get inside and begin clearing the hangars and surrounding buildings.

Bullets whipped all around Sergeant Schneider and his fireteam as they ran through the hole in the fence that Bravo Team had created. Behind them, the other squads in their platoon followed through the breach, and they all fanned out through the parking lot to the main flight building and the hangars nearby.

As they continued their mad dash forward, Sergeant Schneider saw several CDF soldiers spill out of the hangars and buildings in front of them, weapons drawn. Their presence was very short-lived, however. Very rapidly, each of them dropped to the ground in a growing heap as they were gunned down by the advancing paratroopers.

The slaughter went on for another five minutes as the US soldiers overwhelmed the defenders. After almost a hundred CDF soldiers had been added to the body count, several of the enemy soldiers began coming out with their hands up in surrender, dropping their weapons and clearly hoping they would be spared the same fate as their comrades.

After a few minutes of this, Schneider's squad cautiously approached one of the hangars. A white sheet appeared from a crack in the door.

"We want to surrender!" Schneider heard a man shout urgently.

Sergeant Schneider and his men spread out in front of the entrance to the building. "Come out with your hands held high!" he barked.

His pulse pounded ferociously. *If they try any funny business, we're going to light 'em up*, he thought.

The sounds of gunfire quieted down as more and more CDF soldiers threw down their rifles. One by one, the soldiers exited the entrance of the hangar with their hands up.

"Check them and make sure none of them are still armed!" Schneider ordered. A few of his men moved forward and started patting down the new prisoners.

When they'd all been checked and lined up, his men zip-tied their hands and marched them over to the parking lot and had them sit down. Schneider noted that out of the twenty-six soldiers he now detained, nearly half of them were women. He hadn't expected that.

What exactly am I supposed to do with you? Sergeant Schneider asked himself. Their orders on how to handle these prisoners weren't precisely clear. He knew that if they captured any UN soldiers, he and his men were supposed to treat them in accordance with the Geneva Conventions, but no one had really outlined what to do with CDF militia forces. All he knew for certain was that they had been declared unlawful enemy combatants at the outset of the war.

A few minutes went by as the rest of the company continued to secure the area. Schneider overheard their commander talking on the radio with battalion headquarters about what to do with the prisoners—he apparently had the same questions. When he got off the horn, he called over the platoon leaders. Shortly, they spread out to disseminate the information.

"Listen up," called out Schneider's platoon sergeant. "For right now, we're going to transport these prisoners to the local sheriff's holding cells. Then they'll wait there to be collected by either DHS or FBI for prosecution.

"Now that we've completed our initial objective, it's time to get your positions ready to deal with whatever UN forces may try to retreat past our positions. You should anticipate some action soon—the fight down south of us is in full swing."

Schneider set to work with his men. Although he learned that the front lines were nearly forty miles away, he could still hear a lot of loud explosions in the distance. At times they would get louder, and Schneider questioned if they were already retreating toward him.

Will the enemy try and fight it out in the streets of Seattle or attempt to retreat to Canada? he wondered.

****

Two days went by somewhat uneventfully in terms of combat. Sergeant Schneider and his squad got their positions ready to stop the retreating UN force. They'd been probed a few times, but not by a large force.

It's only a matter of time until the main body of their army shows up, he thought nervously.

Schneider continued his work and walked up and down the line checking on his men. His blood pressure rose when he saw a couple of soldiers jaw-jacking instead of filling sandbags like they were supposed to be doing, and he made a beeline over to them.

"Hey, stop messing around!" he yelled. "Get back to work so we can build those bunkers!"

The men bristled but said nothing.

"We don't know when the UN force is going to show up, but you can bet when they do, they'll hit our positions hard. You're going to want those sandbags to protect yourselves," he snapped.

The group of five soldiers grumbled a bit, like good privates usually do, but they eventually nodded their heads and went back to work.

Schneider shook his head. *Slackers*, he thought. Then he walked away to check on the next group of soldiers.

Sergeant Schneider had to remind himself that his fate was not entirely dependent on the efforts of a few lazy privates. Things were actually going quite well.

After their victory at the CDF base, several townspeople had come out of the shadows. "Thank you for liberating our town," said a man who'd apparently elected himself as a spokesperson.

"Just doing our jobs," Captain Tabankin had responded.

"What can we do to help you?" the man probed.

Not passing up an opportunity, Tabankin had replied, "Actually…do you have any bobcats, backhoes, or dump trucks?"

"I know where we can get some," another man answered. "We'll bring them over to you."

When the construction vehicles had arrived later that day, Captain Tabankin had the company begin building a series of trenches and fortified bunkers all along the Snohomish riverbank. They used the backhoes to break through the tough cold dirt and dug a number of trench lines so they wouldn't be so exposed to the onslaught that was sure to hit them.

They dug the fighting positions to be five feet deep and two feet wide. Every twenty yards, they excavated a section of the trench that was eight feet deep, twenty feet in length, and eight feet wide. These larger sections were slated to be turned into fortified bunkers, in case they needed to ride out any artillery bombardments.

For the next twenty-four hours, close to three hundred civilians from the town and the rest of the company had worked feverishly getting the defensive positions built.

They'd leveraged the nearby pallet factory for many of their wood products and other material needs. A trip to the local Home Depot helped them acquire any of the other last-minute tools required and the four-by-four timbers for the roofs and walls.

After a full day's work, Captain Tabankin spoke to their foreman. "Thank you so much for all of your help. At this point, though, I think you all should leave town and head for Three Lakes or Lake Roesiger. Although that's not that far from your homes, it should keep you out of the way of what is sure to turn into a bloody fight."

****

After the townspeople had promised to do their best to stay out of harm's way, Tabankin had set to work contacting his various counterparts from his new command bunker. Not only was Captain Tabankin the company commander, he was also the senior captain in the battalion—and if casualties across the Army continued, he was most likely going to make major.

First, he spoke to the battalion commander on the radio. After explaining their current situation and capabilities, the commander had told him he'd call the higher-ups to see what he could do.

Twenty minutes later, the commander was back on the horn. "Captain, I spoke with Brigade. They informed me the 2nd ID commander shifted the 4th Battalion, 2nd Aviation Regiment over to Naval Air Station Whidbey Island, further north of you. 4th Battalion's call sign is Death Dealers. They've got sixteen Apaches itching for some trigger time."

Captain Tabankin smiled. When the UN decided to show its face, he could get the Apaches airborne and have them snipe at the enemy armor with their Hellfire missions.

"Do we have any fire support, sir?" Tabankin asked next.

"We have some artillery guns set up several kilometers behind your lines, around ten kilometers to your rear in Machias."

"Good copy, sir," Tabankin replied. He knew that was a good location for the artillery—from there, they'd be able to provide them excellent fire support, but they wouldn't be near any major cities to put civilians at risk when the enemy decided to run counterbattery fire missions.

Next, Tabankin spoke to the tactical air control party on loan from the 22nd Special Tactics Squadron. The TACP liaison officer made contact with his superiors and then informed the captain, "Sir, we've shifted a squadron of A-

10s and F-16s to provide direct air support. We've also moved the drones of the 20th Attack Squadron over to Fairchild Air Force Base on the eastern side of the state. They have sixteen MQ-9 Reaper drones. Not only will they be able to provide you with a lot of persistent ISR capabilities, but they're also armed with four Hellfire missiles and two five-hundred-pound JDAMs."

"Excellent," the captain replied. He felt reasonably confident that with this level of support, they'd be able to crush the UN's armor and maybe take out their command structure.

With support in place, all they could do was continue to reinforce their positions until the UN finally decided to show up.

****

On the eerily quiet morning of January 28, it was almost dawn when Captain Tabankin's radio crackled.

"Captain, this is Private Connor from OP-Two. We've sighted the enemy advance party."

"What're you seeing, Private?"

"Most of the armored vehicles seem to be a mixture of Chinese, Russian, and Canadian infantry fighting vehicles. They have some armored personnel carriers and a few light tanks."

"That's great, but what strength level? Give me some numbers, Private," demanded Tabankin.

"Um, sorry about that. It looks to be about a company-sized element of light tanks and probably two battalion-sized elements of infantry fighting vehicles and other armored vehicles. They look to be five or six kilometers away but steadily moving toward us."

"OK. Continue to monitor their progress. We'll pull you guys back soon," Tabankin ordered. He had the TACP LNO call up the Death Dealers to get the Apaches in the air on standby.

Ten minutes went by as the enemy continued to move closer to their positions. When they got within two kilometers, the edges of the American lines started to get bombarded by enemy artillery. Tabankin could hear the concussions from his vantage point, but they still seemed far away.

Right on cue, the brigade's lone battery of 155mm Howitzers and their two batteries of 105mm guns opened fire. The rounds flew over their heads with a whooshing noise high above. Their sudden impact amongst the enemy formations initiated the battle, letting the attackers know the paratroopers were nearby.

A few minutes later, one of the drone operators who'd been keeping an eye on the enemy formations a few kilometers in front of them shouted, "Here they come!"

"Are you sure? I can't see anything," replied Captain Tabankin, looking off into the horizon with his binoculars.

The specialist didn't even look at the captain. He was wearing a VR headset while his right hand controlled the small drone he was using to spot for them. "Well, I see at least a battalion's worth of armored vehicles heading toward our position. Um…they are probably about two kilometers away but picking up in speed."

"Crap!" replied one of the platoon sergeants. "They're probably going to try and see if they can overrun our positions with their tanks."

Turning to find his weapons platoon leader, Tabankin called out, "Make sure our Javelin operators are ready for what's coming."

Next, he turned to find their TACP LNO. "See if those F-16s can go after some of the larger formations to the rear of the enemy positions," he ordered.

The Air Force NCO nodded and reached for his radio that would connect him to the various aircraft operating in the region. The sergeant had a map of the area laid out on a small table they'd gotten during the Home Depot run they'd made the day earlier. Another airman was working on getting the approximate location of the enemy armor with the soldier wearing the VR headset controlling their surveillance drone.

"Here they come. They're about to pass through Phase Line Alpha," announced the soldier manning the drone.

The Air Force LNO announced, "I've got two Reapers that are about to engage the enemy armor right now. Then the Apaches are going to engage them next. Once they've expended their ammunition, the A-10s will swoop in and plaster what's left."

"What about those F-16s—do you have an ETA on them?" demanded Captain Tabankin.

The TACP LNO nodded. "They're being scrambled out of Fairchild. They'll be on station in about twenty minutes."

This is going to work, thought Tabankin.

Captain Tabankin walked outside of the command bunker to watch the carnage. He winced briefly when an explosion erupted less than a hundred feet away. One of the enemy tanks had fired a round right into another one of the bunkers, blowing it apart.

Then he saw what he'd come to see—a wave of probably more than twenty Hellfire missiles raced over their heads as they flew toward their intended targets. As they sailed toward the enemy, Tabankin's optimism shrunk a bit when he saw several of the missiles fall prey to enemy flares and dazzlers. A couple more were blown up by some sort of antimissile system. Still, he counted twelve explosions. More than half of the missiles had impacted against their targets.

"I see 'em!" Tabankin shouted back into the bunker. "Tell our Javelin crews to start lighting them up."

Pop...swoosh...boom.

Eight of their Javelins raced across the two thousand meters that separated the two opposing forces. Next came the second wave of Hellfires from the Apaches, intermixed with a slew of antimateriel rockets. This volley was quickly followed up with a string of red tracer rounds from their chin-mounted guns.

More infantry fighting vehicles, tanks, and armored personnel carriers exploded as they crossed into Phase Line Bravo. Tabankin could tell they were now approaching fifteen hundred meters because they were in range of their heavy weapons. Unfortunately, they only had two of the venerable Browning M2 fifty-caliber machine guns with them. The gunners started shooting at the lighter-skinned armored personnel carriers, avoiding the tanks they knew they couldn't penetrate with their AP rounds.

Several missiles from the charging enemy vehicles fired at them, headed right for their remaining machine-gun bunkers. Those dugouts also housed their fifty-cals, which meant they were going to be down their last two major weapon systems. Seconds later, both bunkers exploded in spectacular fashion.

More enemy tank rounds, 20mm and 30mm cannon fire raked their positions as the enemy force raced toward the two-vehicle bridges that crossed the Snohomish River. They were closing in on one thousand meters distance. Once they got a bit closer, they'd disgorge their infantry to help them secure the bridges and their escape to Canada.

Captain Tabankin heard the familiar whine of the A-10's engines and turned to look behind him. Two of the Warthogs were coming in for an attack run. They must've swooped down from a much higher altitude because, like a German Stuka bomber, they were coming in at a forty-five-degree angle. Several Maverick laser-guided missiles fired from beneath their wings as the tank killers swooped in to get within range of their seven-barrel 30mm tank-busting nose guns.

As the aircraft got closer to the ground, they leveled out a bit and opened fire on the remaining enemy vehicles. Those 30mm guns made their distinctive ripping sounds as hundreds of depleted uranium rounds strafed across the swarm of enemy vehicles. Dozens of explosions ripped across the UN lines as the Maverick missiles found their marks and the 30mm guns did their thing.

A couple of MANPADs flew up from the UN lines as they tried their best to swat the Warthogs from the sky. The A-10s began spitting out flares at a prodigious rate while the pilots banked hard to the left and applied more power to the engines. Once they'd fired off the series of flares, the planes then swooped lower to the ground as the pilots sought to confuse the enemy missiles.

Both A-10s managed to escape and appeared to get themselves in position for another attack run on the UN forces.

That's the way, Tabankin thought. There was no reason to go back home when they still had some ordnance left and the enemy was gearing up for another attack.

Looking back at the UN forces, Captain Tabankin saw that the field before them was quickly becoming filled with burning wrecks and charred enemy vehicles from the Apache and A-10 attacks.

Grabbing his pocket binoculars, Tabankin looked further back behind the enemy force. He could see that the next group to hurl themselves at his position was a wave of infantry soldiers intermixed with a few infantry fighting vehicles and six light tanks. The tanks appeared to be the new Chinese-made ZTQ-15 light tanks. The smaller, lighter armored tanks still sported a 105mm cannon, which made them deadly to the defense network he and his men had built.

Tabankin turned to his radio operator. "Start relaying what we're encountering back to the battalion headquarters. I want them to know what we're running up against," he ordered.

When the A-10s lined up for their next attack run, they swooped in like hawks, ready to snatch an unsuspecting rabbit. They fired their 30mm guns at the light tanks, specifically looking to take them out first. As they moved over the enemy lines, they also released a stack of six five-hundred-pound dumb bombs across the charging infantry.

Before the explosives hit the ground or the A-10s could get away from the scene, two Type 09 self-propelled anti-aircraft artillery trucks opened fire with their two 35mm autocannons. The sky around the Warthogs suddenly filled with bright red tracers. Those vehicles used a radar-guided system to help lead the guns to where the targeting computer believed the aircraft were traveling next.

The first string of rounds slammed into the lead A-10, shredding its right wing and summarily blowing out its right engine. The second string of bullets tore into the rear half of the same plane, nearly ripping the entire tail section off. Chunks of the aircraft fell to the ground.

The pilot did his best to bank his aircraft hard toward the American lines as he applied power to his remaining engine. As Captain Tabankin watched the scene unfold in horror, he thought about how the pilot was like a racer at the end of a triathlon with a sprained ankle, just hoping he could push just a few more feet to get across that finish line. Another string of tracer rounds found the last engine of the aircraft and blew it up. Tabankin saw the pilot eject and said a prayer that his brother-in-arms would somehow be able to land somewhat close to their lines.

The second A-10 was also met with a barrage of 35mm tracers, but somehow, it didn't seem to sustain any critical damage—at least not until several SAMs flew after it. One of the SAMs homed right in on the left engine and blew it apart. Then several new strings of tracer fire slammed into the plane. It exploded before the aviator had a chance to eject. Tabankin put his hand over his heart.

Captain Tabankin looked to his left down the trench line and saw Staff Sergeant Harris, one of the squad leaders in First Platoon. "Staff Sergeant!" he yelled, waving his arms to gain Harris's attention. "Grab your squad and go fetch our pilot before the Chinese can grab him."

Harris turned and nodded. "Form up on me!" he yelled. Tabankin saw Harris direct his squad before they moved out.

Tabankin had a sinking feeling in the pit of his stomach. The pilot who'd ejected had nearly drifted to the ground at this point. He was probably about three hundred yards in front of their position—right in the middle of no-man's-land.

****

"Sergeant Schneider, I want your fireteam to move forward as quickly as you can to secure the pilot. Bravo Team, we're going to move with them, but if they come under any fire, I want you guys to stop where you are and engage the enemy. We need to make sure Schneider's team can get to the pilot before the Chinese do. OK?"

"Yes, sir!"

With his orders given, Sergeant Schneider yelled out to his fireteam. "Follow me!" Then he climbed up and over their trench wall. Right away, he saw that the pilot had somehow gotten himself hung up on a tree not too far from their position. This made him an easy target for the Chinese soldiers who were now running toward him.

We have to get there first, Schneider thought.

One of the American machine-gun positions opened fire on the charging Chinese soldiers as they tried to keep them from getting too close to the downed pilot while one of their squads tried to recover him.

Schneider ran at a near full sprint, despite his full eighty-four-pound kit. Between his body armor, helmet, magazines, grenades, camelback, sidearm, and his M4, it really was a lot of weight to run with, but he knew speed was life at the moment. They had to get to the pilot before the Chinese did, or he was a goner. The American aviator in that tree had probably saved his entire company from being overrun by this armored horde that had appeared from out of nowhere, and Schneider was going to do everything he could to make sure that he survived. However, as he sprinted like an Olympic athlete competing for a gold medal, bullets started kicking up dirt and splinters of wood from the nearby trees and underbrush all around him.

"I'm hit. I'm hit!" yelled out one of his soldiers somewhere behind him. "Medic!" he shouted.

"On my way!" Schneider heard the medic yell. He must've been farther back with Bravo Team because his voice sounded farther away, but Schneider didn't stop, trusting the medic to take care of his fireteam member.

Behind him, Sergeant Schneider could tell that Bravo Team's M249 SAW had just opened fire on something. His own team's M240 gunner had just passed him in sprinting to the pilot.

That nineteen-year-old kid is a beast, thought Schneider. The guy could run two miles in under ten minutes, and he'd pretty much maxed out every other aspect of the PT test. Running at full speed with that pig of a machine gun and all that ammo and body armor barely made the kid sweat.

As they got closer, Sergeant Schneider could hear the pilot scream, "Help me!" Wood splinters flew as bullets hit the branches near him. The pilot fired two random shots with his pistol in between struggling with the ropes. He'd already thrown his helmet to the ground, and he kept fighting to untangle his left leg. Apparently, his survival knife was attached to that leg, and he couldn't cut himself free from his parachute until he reached it.

Schneider's gunner made it to the pilot first. He stood right under the pilot and yelled, "I'm going to throw you my knife so you can cut yourself free. Catch it, OK?"

The nineteen-year-old made sure the dangling prisoner was ready, then tossed the knife. Sergeant Schneider breathed a little easier when the pilot caught it. He immediately cut away at his chute and fell into some of the lower branches. The pilot had been just high enough that Schneider and his men would have had a tough time cutting him down themselves—especially under heavy enemy fire.

Dozens of Chinese soldiers were closing in on Schneider and his four remaining men. Bravo Team did their best to lay down suppressive fire. Schneider's M240 gunner quickly set up his weapon and began hammering away at the enemy soldiers.

"Incoming!" shouted one of the soldiers just as an RPG sailed over his head and impacted on the tree, blowing apart the lower portion of the pine, knocking it over. The pilot fell to the ground along with the top part of the tree.

Sergeant Schneider dashed forward and found his aviator, pinned to the ground by one of the larger branches. Schneider screamed a torrent of obscenities, then scrambled to figure out how to free the pilot's trapped leg.

One of his soldiers yelled, "Hurry up, Sergeant! They've got a couple of armored personnel carriers heading toward us."

"He's trapped under part of the damn tree!" Schneider barked. "I'm going to need a few minutes to get him out. Johnson—use your AT4 on that APC and take it out before it lights us up."

At that precise moment, Bravo Team bounded up to them and set to work setting up some sort of perimeter.

"You should make a break for it, Sergeant," the pilot said defeatedly. "Save your guys. You did your best."

"Screw that!" Schneider yelled. "We're going to get you out. I'm going to raise this branch just enough for you to slip out. When I lift it, you need to crawl out as fast as you can."

The pilot just nodded. Sergeant Schneider reached behind his body armor and grabbed his breaching prybar and sledgehammer. He unscrewed the breaching tool at the center and extended its telescopic arm with the sledgehammer. That added another six inches to the tool, which he hoped would give him just enough leverage. Schneider looked for a rock or something hard he could place on the ground near the tree branch he needed to lift.

"Hurry up, Schneider!" yelled Staff Sergeant Harris. "We're going to be overrun in a few minutes." The rest of the squad had made it to their position.

Schneider didn't say anything and focused on the task at hand. He finally located a stone he thought could work, then slid the prybar under the branch, keeping the head of the tool on the rock. He looked at the pilot.

"Get ready to move!" he yelled.

He shoved down on the tool with all that he had, putting all his weight and muscle strength into it. The pilot wiggled as hard as he could. For two very tense seconds, it almost looked like he wasn't going to get away, but then he slid an inch. Then he pushed a couple more inches, and he was finally out.

Just as the pilot got out from underneath that large branch, Schneider looked up and saw a wild-eyed Chinese soldier, screaming and charging him with a bayonet. In a Herculean move perpetuated by adrenaline, Sergeant Schneider raised his arm back with the prybar on one end, and the sledgehammer on the other. Then he swung the tool with all the force he could muster toward the charging soldier.

The sledgehammer side of the breaching tool connected with the man's face, driving itself several inches into the mush that used to be his skull. The soldier fell to the ground less than two feet from Schneider. His body twitched a bit, like a chicken that's been separated from its head.

The now-freed pilot grabbed his own pistol and shot at the charging horde, hitting several enemy soldiers.

"Duck, Sergeant Schneider!" yelled his M240 gunner from somewhere to his right.

Schneider jumped on top of the pilot as his machine gunner opened fire, throwing dozens of rounds right over their bodies and cutting down several PLA soldiers.

"Frag out!" yelled another soldier.

Crump.

"We have to get out of here!" yelled Staff Sergeant Harris. "Start falling back!"

Getting up, Schneider grabbed the pilot by his harness and yanked him to his feet. He pointed toward the bunker he'd left and shouted, "Run to our lines! We'll cover your back."

The pilot looked utterly terrified. Sergeant Schneider realized that the man before him was used to flying in the sky, delivering his weapons from a distance, not having to be up close and personal with the enemy like the ground pounders.

After a brief hesitation, the pilot took off, sprinting to safety as the rest of the squad did their best to cover him and keep the enemy off them. First, Alpha Team fell back ten or twenty yards. Then they turned around and provided covering fire for Bravo Team. The two teams alternated covering each other as they progressed toward their lines.

The one big obstacle they still had to overcome right at the end was crossing the vehicle bridge on State Road 9. It was wide open, but it was also close to several of their machine-gun positions.

The Chinese must have seen what was going on because they were doing their level best to gun them all down. Two more of Schneider's guys got hit and tumbled to the ground. Sergeant Schneider saw that one of the guys who'd been hit was being helped by another soldier to cross the bridge.

He stopped to see how bad his trooper's injury was. He'd been hit a couple of times in the leg. Once he discerned that despite the volume of blood, his comrade in arms hadn't been hit in an artery, Schneider made the call that they had to get the heck out of Dodge. He couldn't stop to give him medical aid, not with bullets whipping all around them in front of the bridge. He had to get them to safety first.

Reaching down, Schneider grabbed the private and threw him over his shoulder. The sergeant grunted involuntarily as he felt every pound of the man's weight, but he did his best to race across the bridge. In his peripheral vision, he could see many of the other soldiers doing their best to cover his run. Then Schneider saw one of his men get hit in the face—half of his head disappeared, and his body dropped to the ground.

Twenty more feet. Come on. You can do this, the sergeant told himself.

Suddenly, it felt like a sledgehammer had hit him in the back. Unable to control the momentum from the sudden kick, Schneider tripped and fell forward. The wounded soldier he was carrying let out a scream of agony.

Sergeant Schneider tried to get up, but it felt like a hot poker had been rammed through his left leg around the calf. He realized he couldn't stand up to run the rest of the distance back to their lines, and instinctively yelped in pain.

One of the soldiers jumped out of the trench and ran toward them. Schneider yelled, "Grab him first! He's hurt the most. I'll cover you." He turned onto his back and sat up just enough to see the enemy and proceeded to open fire. He hit several of the PLA soldiers before his bolt locked to the rear, letting him know his magazine was empty.

Of all the times to run out of ammo, Schneider thought.

He cursed Murphy's Law, then dropped his rifle to the ground and grabbed for his Sig Sauer. He pointed it at several of the enemy soldiers closest to him and fired. In less than ten seconds, he had emptied all seventeen rounds from his magazine. Then Schneider dropped the empty magazine and proceeded to grab a fresh one from his pouch. As soon as he'd slapped the fresh magazine in, he slapped the slide release and aimed at the closest enemy soldier to him. He fired a couple of times before he felt someone grab the handle at the top of the back of his body armor. Whoever had grabbed it yanked him hard and pulled him back across the bridge with him, still shooting at the enemy soldiers.

When Schneider had finally been pulled back over the bridge and into one of their fighting positions, a medic ran up to him and examined his leg. He poured some Quick-Clot on his wound and then applied a pressure bandage, which hurt like hell as he pulled it tight.

"I'm going to try and get you back to our aid station," the medic announced. A second later, the man pulled Schneider upright, swung his arm over his shoulder, and helped him back to the rear of their position.

While he hobbled along, Schneider's ears were suddenly overwhelmed by the booming of half a dozen massive explosions nearby. The ground beneath them shook like an earthquake.

"What the hell was that?" Schneider exclaimed.

"I think more air support arrived," replied the medic. "We're nearly to the aid station. I'm going to hand you off to the other medics while I go back for more wounded."

A second later, they were back behind a small cluster of houses near an open field. They had picked this location as their medevac spot two days ago because it had a large enough field but was still just far enough away from their main trench line so the helicopter hopefully wouldn't get all shot up trying to pick up the wounded.

Surveying the other wounded soldiers, Sergeant Schneider spotted three of the five soldiers from his fireteam. He also saw two other soldiers from Bravo Team, along with the Air Force pilot. There were a few more wounded soldiers from some of the other platoons there as well. Less than five minutes later, Schneider heard the thumping sound of incoming helicopter blades.

Soon, a Blackhawk helicopter with a bright red cross painted on several sides of it set down. A couple of soldiers got out of the chopper and ran toward the cluster of wounded soldiers. The ones that could walk on their own started hobbling toward the Blackhawk while the few of them that had leg wounds like Schneider waited for someone to help them or load them on with a stretcher.

Two medics ran up to him and pulled him to his feet. They each grabbed an arm and threw it over their shoulders and then ushered him as swiftly as possible to the helicopter. Schneider flinched as two enemy artillery rounds landed nearby, seeking to take out their angel of mercy before it could leave with its cargo of wounded warriors. As soon as he was inside the Blackhawk, the two medics ran back to their position, waiting for more wounded to show up.

With no more people getting on, the pilot immediately applied power to the engines and got them airborne. Once they broke above the trees, Sergeant Schneider saw the true carnage of the battlefield before the helicopter turned away to race back to the naval air station to their north. There were dozens upon dozens of burning wrecks strewn across the area for nearly two kilometers.

Bodies were lying everywhere, practically covering the ground for more than a kilometer from the edge of the river all the way back to the wooded area. It was horrifying to think their battalion had inflicted that level of destruction and death on the enemy.

One of the soldiers stuck his head out a little further from the bay of the helicopter and threw up. Thankfully, the soldier had had enough reasoning to understand that throwing up inside the helicopter would result in his vomit being thrown around on everyone.

Sergeant Schneider shook his head at everything he'd just gone through in the last sixty minutes. He slumped back against another wounded soldier and did his best to hold on to the helicopter and close his eyes. Tears streamed down his face as the emotional dam gave way. He wanted to put everything he had just seen behind him, but somehow, Schneider knew he'd never forget what had happened that day for the rest of his life.

Chapter 6

Decisions

January 25, 2021

Washington, D.C.

White House

President Jonathan Sachs lay on his back, staring at the ceiling. This was only his third night back in the White House. It felt good to be back in his own bed, but he had to admit, he missed being cooped up with General Peterson and his other two compatriots from the tunnel. Having never served in the military, he had previously not comprehended what soldiers meant when they talked about the "bond of combat." Now he really understood why those connections were so tight.

Sachs looked at his alarm clock. *Damn. Only eighteen minutes since the last time I checked.*

Shaking his head in frustration, the President flipped the covers off his body and swung his feet over the side of the bed. He figured at this point, he might as well get dressed. In a moment, he'd already put on a polo shirt and pair of khaki pants.

Sachs looked back at the bed. His wife was still asleep, her breathing quiet. She'd told him that her sleep had been much more peaceful since he'd returned home.

He glanced at the alarm clock one last time—it was 4:26 a.m. He let out a sigh and headed down to the Oval to get a jump on the day.

As he exited the residence, his Secret Service detail quickly fell in line as he moved down the hallway. The Department of Homeland Security wasn't messing around with the President's safety—not that they had before, but now that he'd been rescued, they'd really beefed up the protective measures. The Marine guards who usually wore their dress uniforms were now tricked out in full body armor and carried their combat rifles. There was no more pretending all was normal and well at the White House.

When the President left for a public event, his head of security made damn sure he was guarded by a phalanx of heavily armed Marines in addition to ordering his Secret Service agents to openly carry assault rifles and wear body armor. He'd nearly been killed once; the Secret Service wasn't about to allow it to happen again.

Once he walked into the Oval Office, the President made his way around the desk and took a seat at his chair. He reached for the inbox on the left side of his desk and immediately read through the materials and reports that required his signature. Sachs pored over some of them in detail, while he'd skim through others. He signed off on several documents, then put a bunch of other papers in a pile—those he either marked with red strikes through specific sections or left comments for the author to amend or clarify before he'd sign off.

In a way, it felt good just to bury his head in work. It kept his mind busy, and it kept him from flashing back to being trapped in the tunnel. For a while, he'd really believed he was going to die down there. It had scared him to think that his life was going to end, that he wouldn't be able to see his kids or his wife again. That feeling made the entire situation he now found himself in feel all the worse. The country was being invaded and in the process of completely unraveling itself—thousands upon thousands of people were being killed across the country, and he felt powerless to stop it.

He ached for the families who were losing loved ones, especially those who were losing family members from the seemingly senseless political violence and retribution that were starting to spread. Yesterday, he'd read a report from the FBI that had said more than eight hundred people had been killed in politically motivated attacks. The

President went down a rabbit trail of thought, trying to figure out how to stop America from becoming like the Balkans.

An hour into the President's work, his Chief of Staff, Rich Novella, walked in.

"Morning, sir. Couldn't sleep?" Rich inquired with a bit of concern in his voice.

Sachs looked up. "No. I figured I might as well do some work," he answered nonchalantly. "But hey, since you're here—what the hell is going on with Japan? How can they possibly expect us to be able to evacuate all our equipment and personnel from the country in two weeks? Hell, the West Coast is causing us all kinds of problems right now, so it's not like we can just relocate most of those forces and equipment there."

Rich sighed frustratedly. "They don't want to be invaded, Mr. President. The Japanese don't exactly have a large combat-ready military. They can't stand up to the Chinese, and with us spread so thin, they know they won't get any reinforcements from us. So rather than try and fight it out in a war they know they'd lose, they're going to try and sit this one out."

"Yeah, but can we reasonably get our stuff out of there in time?"

Rich shrugged his shoulders. "I don't know. That'd be a better question to ask during the military briefing later this morning."

The President shook his head. "What's the situation like down in Cuba and Puerto Rico?"

Rich plopped down in the chair next to the President's desk and shot Sachs an enigmatic look. "The Marines really kicked ass, sir. The Cuban Army landed one hell of a sneak attack on Gitmo, but that lasted for maybe twenty minutes. Once the Marines got themselves organized and retaliated, they managed to capture or liberate the entire eastern half of the country, all the way up to Las Tunas. Hell, if you gave them the order to march on Havana, I think we could probably capture it within a week."

Sachs's jaw dropped slightly in disbelief. "How is it the Cuban military has so thoroughly fallen apart like this? I mean, we don't have a ton of Marines down there. How was that small force able to tear them apart so quickly?"

Rich shrugged his shoulders. "I don't think the Cuban Army is as strong or determined to die for their country as our Marines are. If you want more specifics, I think you'll have to ask the Joint Chiefs. I've told you about as much as I know."

Standing up, Rich walked over to the pot of fresh coffee that one of the stewards had brought in and proceeded to pour himself a cup. When he'd finished adding a dash of milk and a teaspoon of sugar, he carried his mug back to the chair next to the President's desk and resumed his conversation. Sighing, he said, "Puerto Rico and the Dominican Republic are a different story, sir."

"How so? My understanding is that the Navy intercepted the Russians' little convoy of ships on their way back from Venezuela."

Rich took a sip of his coffee and nodded. "They did. But we've still got a brigade of Russian naval infantry on both islands to deal with. They've effectively taken control of Puerto Rico and the DR for the time being. They haven't crossed over into Haiti yet, but I don't think that was their mission."

The President took a sip of his own coffee, then changed the subject. "So, how are things across the rest of the country? I mean, what's the mood like?" He was still trying to get up to speed after being out of the loop for several days.

Rich shifted in his chair. "It's tough right now, Mr. President. The West Coast is in open insurrection, and a good chunk of the Northeast is still under UN control.

Fighting's been pretty tough in the Midwest too. On top of that, people are concerned that we're about to be invaded by the Chinese in the Southwest."

Sachs snorted. "I think the VP's little plan to nuke the Three Gorges Dam seems to have given them some pause."

"It has, but I don't think it's going to stop them," Rich replied glumly. "They haven't slowed down their deployment of troops into Mexico. If anything, it's given them time to beef up the protection of the dam."

The President sighed. "One problem at a time, Rich." He ran his fingers through his hair. "Back to California and the rest of the West Coast—what are *your* thoughts on how to put down this rebellion and bring them back into the fold?"

His long-time Chief of Staff shook his head. "You aren't going to like my suggestions."

Sachs grunted at the honesty. "Why don't you try me? Being trapped in a tunnel for six days has given me a new perspective on life."

Rich smirked at the President's answer. "We dissolve the state governments," he proposed. "If they won't comply with federal law and want to continue to pursue this path of recognizing that traitor Tate as President, then we dissolve their government and arrest them. Anyone that we catch in the act of taking up arms against the federal government, we execute, and we detain anyone who openly supports Tate."

Rich paused for a moment, apparently trying to gauge the President's facial reactions before he continued. "Look, we have to stamp this insurrection out quickly, Mr. President. If we don't get the parts of the country we still control back under our authority, then the situation is only going to get worse and spread."

The President swiveled his chair away to look out the window of his office. He kicked his feet out a bit as his body stretched out in the chair. Lincoln had arrested and detained folks during the first Civil War.

Do the ends justify the means? he asked himself.

****

Four Hours Later
Washington, D.C.
White House
Situation Room

The President looked at Patty Hogan. "What are our options in California and the other states that aren't responding to our inquiries?" he asked.

Leaning forward in her chair, she said, "I think we should use the newly expanded Federal Protective Service we've been training up. They aren't military, and it'll still keep things within the law enforcement community."

General Vance Pruitt grunted at the idea. "I don't think that force is going to be up to the task. Plus, I don't think their first batch of recruits has finished training yet, if I'm not mistaken."

Lifting her chin up in indignation, Patty responded, "It's true that the first batch hasn't finished their training yet, but when they do, this would be a good test for them. Besides, we're going to stir up a negative publicity storm when you dissolve the state governments and move to arrest the legislators who are leading the rebellion. It'd be best to have these arrests made by federal law enforcement officials and *not* soldiers."

"She's right," asserted FBI Director Polanski. "You don't want the military to be the ones making the arrests. I'd recommend my agents go in, and we should use Patty's folks for security and backup if needed."

Sachs stroked his chin. In his opinion, the FBI was one of the few government agencies that were still somewhat respected and trusted by the public on both sides of the aisle. If he was going to follow through on arresting a few hundred legislators in these rebellious states, it'd be best to let the FBI be the public face of it.

Turning to face Patty, the President asked, "When will your first batch of trainees be ready?"

She glanced down at her notepad. "February first," she responded. "Between the six training camps we've established with FLETC and US Special Forces, we're going to start graduating six thousand trainees a week at that point. My goal is to get a thousand of them relocated into the capitals of the eighteen states that are in open insurrection to assist the FBI in restoring order.

"We'll start with the states that are geographically closest to the ones still adhering to our authority and look to expand outwards as we get more folks trained up. It's going to take some time, Mr. President, but it is a better approach for us to use the Federal Protective Service to handle the civil unrest than to place troops in the streets. Coupled with the FBI, I think this will give us much more public support and appear less like a hostile military takeover."

Sachs nodded. "I agree, Patty. That was a good call you made when all of this started falling apart—keeping this in law enforcement lanes as opposed to using soldiers."

The President then turned to his FBI Director. "Polanski, your agents will make the arrests. Coordinate with Patty on when and how you guys will execute the warrants. Start drawing up the papers right now, and let's get things ready. I want this to happen rapidly when it gets moving. Make sure to make as many of those arrests as possible on the same day. Once word gets out about what's happening, you can bet a lot of the conspirators are going to go to ground."

Director Polanski smiled and shot Patty a mischievous look. He seemed like he was going to enjoy this mission.

Sachs stood up. "All right, that concludes the domestic affairs portion of this meeting. It's time to clear the room for the rest of the National Security team," he announced.

A couple of the military folks who were in the room remained while other staffers and military personnel filed in.

General Adrian Markus, who'd taken over for General Austin Peterson as the newly appointed Chairman of the Joint Chiefs, took a seat next to the President. Sachs couldn't help but feel a twinge of sorrow. Unfortunately, General Peterson's leg had become severely infected during their six-day ordeal in the tunnel. The doctors had ended up having to amputate his leg, and now he was still struggling to fight off a series of infections that had spread to other parts of his body.

Sachs had assured Peterson that there would always be a place for him as a senior advisor in the White House when he got better, but for the time being, he'd been forced to appoint a replacement. Ideally, Sachs would have selected General Tibbets from NORTHCOM, but he had proven to be an incredibly effective overall military commander for US forces, and it was determined that he could better serve the country by staying in command of the defense of North America than being cooped up with the President.

After a few moments, General Markus surveyed the room and then cleared his throat. "Mr. President, I'm going to go over the bottom line up front for each sector of the war. We'll stop and address any specific questions you may have as we go along. Otherwise, we'll move through the information at a pretty rapid clip."

The President nodded, and the general continued. "In the North Atlantic, we sank two Russian submarines and two additional UN warships as they attempted to break through the blockade. We lost another destroyer, and one of our guided-missile cruisers took a couple of hits. It looks like they'll be able to limp back to port for repairs, which is a good thing. That said, the blockade continues to stay in effect."

When Sachs didn't have any direct questions, General Markus continued to the next theater. "In the Pacific, we sank five Chinese warships, and eight submarines in the South China Sea and along the Chinese coast just south of Taiwan. We lost two destroyers and two submarines—one *Virginia*-class and one *Los Angeles*-class attack sub. Of particular concern were two submarines we sank off the coast of Alaska. Apparently, a Russian *Oscar* had tried to get in close to Anchorage, probably to try and put their land-attack cruise missiles within range of Elmendorf Air Force Base and our antiballistic missile interceptor base at Fort Greely. The other Russian sub, an older *Kilo*-class, tried to ambush one of our boomers as it made its way under the polar caps. Both Russian subs were sunk with no losses to our own forces."

Pausing for a moment, General Markus traded a nervous glance with Admiral Chester Smith, the Chief of Naval Operations, before he proceeded. "We have some concerns about Hawaii, Mr. President."

Sachs surveyed Smith and Markus's faces. "What specifically are you concerned with?" he asked.

Admiral Smith interjected, "We've received some signals intelligence that indicates that the Chinese are planning some sort of major attack in the near future. We're not sure what specific kind of attack, but suffice it to say, they're planning on hitting our forward bases in the Pacific in advance of any ground combat along the southern border."

The President furrowed his brow. "So based on your most educated guess, what kind of attack are you thinking? What bases are most at risk?"

"They've already made good use of merchant raiders," Admiral Smith asserted. "My money says they're going to try and hit us with some sort of missile swarm attack. As to what bases are most at risk, I'd have to say Guam and Hawaii.

"While our bases in Japan would've been a threat, the Chinese were able to strong-arm the government into kicking us out of the country. The withdrawal has been kind of a mess. We've dispatched as many ships and planes as we can, but there's a lot of equipment that's going to end up being left behind."

"What about getting some help from the Japanese?"

Admiral Smith nodded. "We're working on that. As a matter of fact, the Japanese have offered to let us use several dozen of their large roll-on, roll-off ships to help get our vehicles, tanks, and other armored equipment out. For the moment, they're going to move the equipment to Hawaii, unload it and then make one more trip before the two-week deadline ends. Once everything makes it to Hawaii, we'll work on getting it moved over to California. On the plus side, sir, we'll have the entire Third Marine Expeditionary Force relocating back to California. That will beef up our southern border defense and give us the additional resources we'll need to put down these uprisings in California once DHS is ready to make a move."

Sachs paused for a moment, contemplating the situation. "OK, then here is what I want to have happen," he finally announced. "When those additional Marines get to San Diego, I want you to start having them put down this rebellion in Los Angeles. We need to get that city under control again, and we need those ports."

"Yes, Mr. President," Admiral Smith responded.

The President still had one burning question. "If we know Guam and Hawaii are the most likely targets the Chinese are going to attack, then how do we want to defend them?" he asked.

General Markus jumped back into the conversation. "With your permission, we'd like to deploy additional THAADs to both Guam and Hawaii. I'd also recommend that we position our two carrier strike groups on opposite sides of Hawaii—one to guard the North Pacific and the other on standby to support Guam should the Chinese make a concerted move on it."

The President nodded, giving them the go-ahead to redeploy the necessary forces.

Before they could continue, Sachs asked, "What's going on with Taiwan? If the Chinese really are gearing up to attack us head-on, then Taiwan has to know they're in the crosshairs."

"The Taiwanese are gearing up to repel any invasion attempts by the Mainland," explained Admiral Smith. "I'm not confident they'll be successful, but they will definitely bloody the Chinese up pretty good. Unfortunately, there isn't much more we can do to help them."

The President shook his head in disgust. All the Navy had been able to do so far was sink a few Chinese warships in the area. "I hate to say it, but for the time being, they are on their own. Until we can defeat this UN force in the north and figure out what's going on with the Chinese in the south, we're tapped out. In the meantime, let's continue with the brief. I want to know what's going on along our northern border."

General Markus nodded and continued.

"The 4th Infantry Division has officially secured Regina and Winnipeg, effectively cutting Canada in half. We've isolated the eastern half of Canada from their oil and natural gas pipelines in their western provinces. That's going to have a huge impact on their ability to function as a country and a military."

"What about the Pacific Northwest? How is the offensive going there?"

General Markus replied, "It's actually going better than we thought. At least from a military perspective. We dropped an airborne brigade behind the UN lines, effectively cutting them off from any possible retreat out of the state. Lieutenant General Biggs, the commander for I Corps, was able to effectively drive the remaining Canadian, Russian, and Chinese forces back to the banks of the Snohomish River, where they ran into our airborne brigade. The clash lasted more or less for three days. They saw some really heavy fighting on the first day, but on the last day of the battle, the local UN commander surrendered his force.

"There's also a bit of a partisan fight that's brewing up there. On the positive side, a pro-American militia unit has grown pretty strong around the city of Burlington, not too far from the Canadian border. We don't know a lot about them yet, but what little we do know is they appear to have some of the National Guard deserters who wouldn't side with the governor. The group also appears to have linked up with some other militia groups to create a much larger force."

General Pruitt, the Army Chief of Staff, broke into the conversation. "What's making this group so deadly against both the CDF and the UN force is they appear to have a gifted bomb maker in their midst. My best guess is one or more of the National Guardsmen that deserted or someone in the militia unit is a former explosive ordnance disposal guy with combat experience in Iraq. Whoever is making those IEDs knows what the hell he's doing. He's been wreaking havoc on them since the war started."

General Markus nodded. "The bigger issue we're going to have to deal with now that the UN force has largely been defeated is the remnant of the CDF militia force. We estimate the number of those who haven't surrendered to be between two and four thousand. They're primarily clustered in a handful of densely populated enclaves, which means our soldiers are going to have to root them out in some of the cities.

"We're holding off on starting that part of the operation until we've fully dealt with the UN forces that surrendered. When I spoke with General Biggs earlier this morning, he told me that as of right now, they had collected eighteen thousand UN prisoners. He's having a hard time trying to figure out where to put them and how to logistically feed and guard them all while still carrying out his combat operations."

The President let out a soft whistle. "What were the UN casualties? I mean, if we took eighteen thousand prisoners, how many of them did we end up killing or wounding?"

General Markus paused for a moment as he looked through his notes. "The last report I got from the I Corps staff was roughly somewhere around sixteen thousand killed or wounded during the last two weeks of fighting. We're not sure what the CDF casualties are just yet, but they told me they estimated them to be somewhere around ten or eleven thousand."

Shaking his head in disgust, Sachs commented, "So much killing. I wish it hadn't come down to this." He paused for a moment to collect his thoughts before he asked, "What were our casualties?"

Grimacing at the question, Markus replied, "Three thousand eight hundred. Most of that occurred during the three-day battle. The airborne brigade we dropped in from Alaska bore a lot of those casualties. The UN force made a concerted effort to try and breach their lines to attempt a retreat to Canada. The paratroopers held the line, but took a beating doing so."

Leaning forward, Sachs replied, "Send my regards and congratulations to the brigade commander. Make sure he knows the President said thank you for holding the line and winning this battle for us. While you're at it, award their brigade a presidential unit citation and give those paratroopers some valor medals. I can only imagine what kind of hell it must have been like for them to try and hold off a force of probably more than twenty thousand soldiers with less than two thousand men."

General Markus nodded. He turned to one of his aides. "Make sure you write that down to action it after the meeting," he ordered.

Returning to his briefing, General Markus pulled up a map of the Midwest and pointed to several units. "III Corps has established a line of defense spanning from Cedar Rapids, Iowa, down to Springfield, Illinois, then across to Bloomington, Indiana, through Cincinnati, Ohio, and on up to Cleveland. It's a massive bulge, but Lieutenant General Hightower believes he can hold the line while the rest of his corps continues to take up positions for his coming offensive."

Sachs held up a hand. "When is his offensive supposed to start?" he asked.

"In six days."

"Why the delay?" the President asked, pushing back. "If he's formed up a defensive line and stopped the enemy, then why is he not pushing back on them?" His voice betrayed how irritated he felt with the slow response of the military to recapture lands lost while he had been trapped in the tunnel.

General Tibbets from NORTHCOM interjected, "That's my call, Mr. President. I ordered him to hold his position until we're ready to launch our counteroffensive. I'm still getting more of his units moved into place. Right now, we've been fighting it out with a joint Russian, Canadian, and French unit around Cleveland, Ohio, and Erie, Pennsylvania.

"As a matter of fact, the 82nd Airborne has been fighting hard in the Allegheny Forest in Pennsylvania for the last three days. We lost New York State, and the UN forces are threatening to push down into New Jersey and potentially threaten Washington. Our focus right now has been on stopping them from doing that. Once that has been achieved, I'll allow General Hightower to launch his offensive. Until then, we can't split our forces that sparsely."

The President nodded and uncrossed his arms. He motioned for General Markus to continue with the brief. This was his first time getting a *full* update since he'd fully resumed his duties as President, so he was still drinking from the firehose of information.

"I'm going to bring us up to speed on the Caribbean before we move to the southwest," General Markus said, bringing up a new map.

"The Russians landed a brigade of naval infantry on Puerto Rico and the Dominican Republic. Our Navy interdicted their troop transport ships while they were attempting to ferry over more soldiers from Venezuela and sank them. For the time being, the Russians are going to be stuck on the island. They have the equipment they landed with, but not much else—and fortunately, it doesn't appear that the Russians landed with all the equipment that they'd hoped to bring. The NSA intercepted a communique between them and their headquarters. The second landing was supposed to drop off several S-300 and S-400 surface-to-air missile platforms. We're lucky the Navy was able to intercept them before they got those systems operational on the islands. It would've complicated things for us in the area considerably."

The slides on the PowerPoint now shifted to show Cuba. "The Marines have pushed the Cuban Army back to Las Tunas. We effectively control the entire eastern half of the country. The 24th and 26th MEUs have fully offloaded their brigades at Gitmo. We've now got a combat force of forty-six hundred Marines in Cuba. Do you want us to continue to expand out further and try to drive on Havana, or what would you like us to do, Mr. President?"

Leaning forward in his chair, the President fixed a steely gaze on General Markus. "Can we support them moving on Havana?" he asked.

General Tibbets responded. "Mr. President, the Cubans aren't in good shape right now. The bigger challenge we have if we expand out further on the island is the Russians. They have several fortified positions in and around Havana. That's what we need to take out. They've set up several SAM sites that are causing us some problems. The Navy's done a decent job of going after them, but we need ground pounders to go in there and make sure they're destroyed. My recommendation is we have the Marines hold their current position until we can send the 22nd Marine

Expeditionary Unit from Camp Lejeune to reinforce them. Then I'll feel confident about pushing on Havana."

"OK, then have them hold their positions for the time being until you can get that other brigade moved over to support them. In the meantime, what are we doing with this growing force on our southern border?" the President asked.

The generals shared a nervous glance before they returned the President's eye contact. General Tibbets dared to speak first. "Mr. President, we have a couple of ideas we'd like to get your permission to proceed with…"

****

January 30, 2021
Northwestern Pennsylvania
Allegheny National Forest

Private First Class Johnson of the 2nd Battalion, 501st Infantry Regiment, shifted cautiously from one covered position to another. Each time he moved, he hoped that he wasn't about to be drilled by an unseen bullet.

As his body thudded against a fallen log, he looked over the top of it into the distance, where his sergeant had said he'd spotted movement. Johnson squinted his eyes to try and see better, but he couldn't see it. As his eyes darted to the right and left, what he did spot was fresh snow starting to fall. There were already at least four inches on the ground, and it appeared like Mother Nature was going to give them a few more.

Slumping against the fallen log, Johnson couldn't help but admire the beauty of the forest as the snow started to fall. If the area wasn't crawling with enemy soldiers trying to kill him and his comrades, it might have been a lovely day for a walk in the woods.

"Contact, right!" shouted one of the soldiers in his squad. Then his fellow soldier fired his rifle several times at whatever he'd just seen.

A second later, the entire forested area in front of them erupted in gunfire.

Johnson ducked down below the fallen log, just in time to hear a string of rounds slap into the wood, chipping away at his newfound protective barrier.

"Covering fire!" shouted another private.

Johnson jumped up from behind the log and proceeded to fire off four three-round bursts at a cluster of trees and underbrush where he saw a handful of enemy soldiers.

"Grenade!" someone yelled.

BOOM.

"Take that machine-gun position out!" shouted his sergeant.

"Ah, hell. I'm hit!" screamed one of Johnson's friends, Tippins. "Medic...oh God, medic!"

"Covering fire!"

"Hang in there, Tippins! I'm on my way," their medic bellowed. Johnson couldn't see what was wrong with his friend, but he could hear him continue to scream and thrash about.

Pop...swoosh...BOOM.

"203!"

Johnson watched as the entire tree line maybe two hundred meters in front of him erupted in explosions and fire. One of his squadmates had fired off a couple of M203 grenades at the enemy position while another soldier hit the enemy gun position with one of their AT-4 rockets.

Dropping his now-empty magazine, Johnson slapped a fresh one in its place. He hit the bolt release, ramming a fresh round into the chamber. Johnson rolled over onto his belly and proceeded to crawl over to another firing position, maybe five meters away. He then rescanned his sector, looking for a target to shoot. Meanwhile, the guys in his squad continued to scream out orders and information to each other as they engaged the enemy soldiers.

Just as Johnson got to his new firing position, he heard the unmistakable sound of incoming artillery.

Oh crap, that's not friendly, he realized.

Boom, boom, boom!

Three artillery rounds hit roughly three or four hundred meters behind their position.

"Everyone, move forward!" yelled their lieutenant frantically. "We need to get closer to the enemy so they don't start dropping arty rounds on us!"

Private Johnson shook his head in frustration. The LT had just gotten the rest of the platoon moved over to assist them, and they were finally starting to tear into the enemy positions with the added firepower—but he knew the man was right.

Johnson searched for the next best position to run to and spotted another fallen log maybe twenty meters in front of him. Looking to his right, he saw two of his squadmates. He waved his hand and pointed to the position. They both nodded.

"Cover me!" he shouted. Then he jumped up from his position and charged forward. As he sprinted full out, bullets zipped past him like angry bees. Dirt and snow kicked up all around his feet. He dove for the fallen log, landing hard on the ground just as a grenade exploded maybe ten meters in front of him. Johnson found himself being showered by a cascade of debris mixed with slush.

When the cloud had dissipated enough so that he could see again, he rose up on his right knee and brought his rifle to bear. Ahead of him were a handful of enemy soldiers who were shifting their fire in his direction. Johnson quickly unleashed several three-round bursts from his M4 to provide covering fire for his other squadmates who were now racing forward to join him. In seconds, one of the enemy soldiers' heads had burst into a cloud of red spray, and another clutched at his chest and fell backward.

Sensing he should duck, Johnson dropped to his belly and rolled on his back and to his left. A string of bullets hit right where he had just been. Then an explosion rocked the log he had been hiding behind, and the portion of the fallen tree exploded.

Johnson winced as he felt a couple of sharp objects bite into his left leg. Looking down past his feet, he saw two of his fellow soldiers charging toward him. His sergeant was running with his rifle against his shoulder, firing away at the enemy while he advanced. The other man, his friend Private Miller, had a look of sheer terror on his face as he ran like hell for his position.

Suddenly, Miller's facial expression changed from terror to one of intense pain as an explosion went off near him and his right leg was ripped off. The man tumbled several times as he fell to the ground. The sergeant continued to run toward Johnson, finally landing right next to him.

"Chuck a couple of grenades at those bastards and then go back and grab Miller!" barked the sergeant. He coughed briefly and did his best to get his breathing under control.

Johnson pulled two of the grenades from his IBA and placed them on the ground in front of him. He pulled the pin on one and threw it for all its worth in the direction of the enemy. He then repeated the process with the second grenade.

"I'm hit, Johnson! God, it hurts, man. Someone, help me! Don't leave me here!" his wounded friend continued to cry out.

"I'll cover you, go grab him," his sergeant barked. Then he laid into the enemy position with his new M27 infantry automatic rifle. That beast could lay down some serious suppressive fire.

Crawling back to his feet, Johnson took off the ten meters to his friend, whose leg was still bleeding profusely. Reaching down, he grabbed the handle on the top of the back of Miller's IBA and dragged him as fast as he could to their position.

When Johnson reached the fallen log, he knelt down next to Miller, grabbed his tourniquet from the field dressing pouch, and got it set up on his right leg. Once he had it in place, he cranked it tight, causing his friend to scream wildly from the excruciating pain.

Their sergeant barked, "Hold that scream in! Take the pain, Miller. Your screaming is going to attract more attention to us and get us all killed."

Wrinkling his face in anger, Miller did his best to stifle another scream as Johnson finished tightening the tourniquet.

Looking down at his wounded friend, Johnson said, "I've got it tied off. The bleeding looks to have stopped, but you have to try and not move too much, OK? We'll get you some more help once we finish killing these guys."

With that, Johnson returned his attention to the attackers in front of them, hurling another grenade toward the enemy. Then several loud shrieks that sounded like runaway freight trains headed right for them.

"Everyone down!" screamed their sergeant.

Johnson dropped below the lip of the fallen log again. The world around them disintegrated into utter chaos as artillery round after artillery round landed among the trees where they were hunkering down. Chunks of hot shrapnel and splintered wood flew in every direction. Some of the rounds exploded as air bursts, delivering a rain shower of scorching red metal from the sky.

The barrage lasted maybe ten seconds. When the noise of the explosions died down, the overwhelming sound was screams of agony.

Private Johnson turned to check on Miller—a huge chunk of wood had buried itself in his friend's neck, nearly severing it from the rest of his body. Miller was dead. His eyes were already glazed over.

"Forget him," said his sergeant callously. "Focus on killing the enemy in front of us. We need to take 'em out or we're dead." Then, following his own advice, he let loose a full magazine's worth of bullets at the UN soldiers.

The urge for survival forced Johnson to do his best to shake off the scene of his dead friend. He scanned the forest in front of him. One of the sergeant's rounds caused an enemy soldier to grab at his neck. Another dropped like a sack of potatoes. However, a third soldier brought some sort of light machine gun to bear and cut loose a long string of bullets in their direction.

Johnson ducked. He heard a grunt and a wet, fleshy sound. As he glanced over at his sergeant, Johnson watched him fall backward, hit by multiple bullets. His sergeant was dead before he hit the ground.

Damn! I'm all alone now, Johnson thought.

He turned and looked around behind him. All he saw was either dead bodies of his squad and platoonmates or men crying out for help. There didn't seem to be anyone left unhurt to help him or continue the fight. Johnson turned back to his sergeant, reached over for the M27, and readied himself to use it.

Abruptly, the battlefield became quiet. No one was shooting anymore. All Johnson could hear was the cries for the medics. As he lay on his back, trying to decide if he should jump back up and resume shooting or not, he heard voices.

"Check your sectors and advance," called out a voice in English.

"We got a lot of wounded over here. What do you want us to do with them?" asked another.

Could those be Americans? Johnson wondered.

"If they're wounded, help 'em out. If they give you any trouble, kill 'em," replied another.

Just as Johnson was about to crawl over and engage whoever was moving toward him, he heard a couple of branches snap. "Don't even try it or I'll light you up!" shouted a loud commanding voice near him.

Moving his hands away from his rifle, Johnson held them out and turned to see two soldiers pointing their weapons at him.

"Who the hell are you guys?" Johnson asked. They were clearly speaking English, which confused him.

Smiling, the soldier replied, "48th Highlanders. We're Canadian." He paused for a second as he lowered his rifle.

His comrade did the same before he added, "You damn Yanks cost us a lot of good men."

Sitting up slowly so as not to get shot, Johnson replied, "Yeah, you Canucks cost us a few as well."

With nothing more to say, they gestured for him to get up. Then they trudged him back toward their lines into an uncertain future.

Chapter 7
Detention Camps

January 31, 2021
Fort Stewart, Georgia

Rows and rows of white tents had been set up for as far as the eye could see. Every couple hundred meters, there was a cluster of ten portable toilets positioned between them. Near each group of portable toilets were two prefabricated shower trailers. The site had turned into a truly massive camp, only a couple of miles outside the town of Hinesville, Georgia, and not too far from the coastal city of Savannah.

"What do you suppose they're going to do with these camps?" Tommy asked. He'd just finished inspecting the tent to make sure it had the proper number of bunk beds and footlockers to house twenty-four people. Each tent also had three tables with eighteen folding chairs, where the occupants could play cards, read a book, or otherwise entertain themselves.

Tommy climbed back into the golf cart. His partner, Bill, answered, "I suspect they'll fill 'em up with prisoners from the war. You heard they captured over ten thousand prisoners up there in Washington, right?"

"They captured ten thousand prisoners in D.C.?" Tommy asked skeptically. He stuffed some more chew in his lower lip.

Bill just shook his head. "No. Not D.C. Washington State. You know, up near Canada. It's on the West Coast. Geez, boy, didn't they teach you anything in school?"

"Don't call me 'boy,' old man. And yes, I know there is a state called Washington. I just got confused," Tommy replied. Most days, Bill and Tommy got along pretty well, despite the fact that Bill was in his midfifties and Tommy had just turned nineteen. They were both African American, and Bill pretty much called anyone younger than him "boy," which agitated the hell out of Tommy, who took it as some sort of racial slur.

"Let's go sign off on the next group of showers, Tommy," said Bill, trying to reframe the conversation.

Tommy let out a deep breath, then asked, "You really think I should learn to become a plumber?"

"I do," Bill responded. "Look, I don't mean to insult you when I say this, Tommy, but let's face it: you aren't the sharpest tool in the shed. I know you had to drop out of school to get a job and help support your momma and all, but being a plumber is good work. You don't need a college degree for it, and you can make really good money. You're good with your hands. Heck, a month ago, you wouldn't have had a clue how to set up one of these shower trailers. Now, you can practically do it yourself."

Tommy nodded at the compliment. "I guess I am getting pretty good at this," he said, suddenly sitting up taller. "But still, going to trade school costs money—something I obviously don't have."

Bill was silent for a moment as they pulled forward to the next set of trailers they had to inspect. When they hopped out of the golf cart, he put a hand on Tommy's shoulder. "If you agree to work for my company for three years after you complete trade school, I'll pay for it, Tommy. As you can see, I have more work than I can handle. Besides, I told your mother I'd do my best to help you 'cuz your father was a good friend of mine. But I'd need you to commit to working for me while you're in school, and for three years afterwards. Deal?"

Tommy thought about that for all of two seconds before he stuck his hand out. "Deal. Now, let me do the final inspection on this unit, and you check to make sure I did it right."

Bill smiled at his new apprentice and nodded. For the next couple of hours, they finished signing off on the shower units and the rest of the tents they'd been assigned to inspect.

Once they finished their final checks of each tent and building, they'd let the camp manager know it was ready for whatever was coming next.

As they drove down the rows of tents, they saw another work crew was finishing up a guard tower. The tall structures were being placed along the outer perimeter fence, every two hundred meters apart. The outer barriers themselves were twelve feet tall with a coiled string of razor-sharp concertina wire on the top. Another crew set up light poles every twenty meters facing inward, illuminating the camp.

By the time the sun set on the last day of January, Bill and Tommy certified the camp as complete and ready for operations. In the coming weeks, the camp population would swell to more than eight thousand people as the government filled it up with prisoners of war.

****

Metcalfe, Mississippi
DHS Detention Camp 14

George Thomas wiped the sweat from his forehead as he walked into what would become the camp's administrative office building. He saw the commander of the 34th Military Police Company and walked over to him.

"Afternoon, Captain Quinn," he said jovially. He poured himself a glass of sweet tea and took a seat in the chair next to the man's desk.

Smiling at George, Quinn replied, "Afternoon, sir. I assume you've completed your inspection?"

George nodded as he finished draining the contents of his glass. "I sure did. I must say, Captain, I'm impressed. Your soldiers are quick and professional. This place looks great."

"Well, our unit helped to run a detention camp in Afghanistan, so we have a lot of vets with experience in getting these things going. That said, it didn't hurt having a few hundred KBR contractors and a few hundred FEMA tents as well."

George tilted his head to the side. "So, how many contractors do you think you'll need to help manage the camp?" he asked.

"Do you mean guards or just workers to keep the camp functional?" asked Quinn, leaning forward.

"Both, I suppose. We've got three more of these camps going up right now, so I'm trying to get a handle on the numbers."

Captain Quinn nodded. "Well, I think you'll need roughly eighty contractors to maintain the facilities, and we'll probably need a guard force of roughly six hundred. I plan on having the guards working either eight- or twelve-hour shifts, six days a week, depending upon how many people we have to keep an eye on." He paused for a moment. "Roughly how many people are these camps going to hold, and for how long?"

George shrugged his shoulders. "That's the million-dollar question, Captain. I know our capacity for each camp is roughly five thousand people. As for how long—I can't be sure. I'd guess until this stupid conflict is done with. Could be a few weeks, could be a few months. All I know is when the next big offensive starts, they expect to capture a lot of prisoners."

Leaning in closer, Quinn spoke in a hushed tone. "You have any insight into how the war is going at all? Are we winning, or is the country really going to split apart?"

George looked around the room to make sure no one else was listening. "From what I've been told, the war in the north is going well, or at least as good as can be expected. The big concern right now is what's happening in Mexico and out west. I heard a rumor California and Oregon have been building up a large militia force. They've also started rounding up conservatives and anyone that's giving them problems and putting them in reeducation camps."

Captain Quinn snickered. "Isn't that what we're doing here?"

George shook his head. "Not at all, Captain. This is going to be a POW camp. They're setting up a few other camps just like this for Americans who've chosen to take up arms against the government. If people are caught doing that, then they're getting sent to one of these camps until they can be tried in a court of law. There's a big difference between holding people until they can be prosecuted for a crime and outright rounding people up because you disagree with their politics."

The two of them talked for a bit more as they worked out the details of how many guards and other workers they'd need to make the camps in the area run. George Thomas and Captain Quinn might not have been happy about it, but for better or worse, they found themselves managing some six detention camps in Mississippi. They'd do their best to make them run as safely and efficiently as possible.

******

Camp Pendleton

Brigadier General Shell of Regimental Combat Team One looked at his commanders briefly before he turned to point at a spot the map of Southern California.

"Marines, as most of you know, California and a handful of other states are currently operating in a state of open revolt against our federal government. Thus far, we've been told to stay clear of the political crap going on there. However, with our forces having to withdraw from Japan, the Navy needs us to secure the ports of Long Beach and LA. There's a sizable Japanese-American convoy of some sixty-odd freighters, cargo ships, and roll-on, roll-off ships heading to the ports as we speak.

"Right now, the city government and the local port authorities have denied the federal government and us the use of the facilities. Therefore, we're going to go seize them. Now, I know many of you have some concerns about this, but it has to happen. We need to offload that equipment from Japan and get ready to deal with this Chinese force to our south. RCT One has been tasked with this mission, and we're going to achieve it." He motioned to a man near him. "I'm now going to hand things over to the G2 for the latest intelligence summary of what we're facing."

A major walked up to the front of the room and changed the PowerPoint slide to his portion of the brief.

Once he was ready, he returned his gaze to the battalion and company commanders in front of him.

"Near the hills of San Clemente, the California National Guard's 1st Battalion, 160th Infantry Regiment has set up a series of fortified positions along Interstate 5. Their goal is to keep us bottled up down here in San Diego County. To the north, in Temecula along Interstate 15, 1st Squadron, 18th Cavalry Regiment has set up a blocking force to keep us from gaining entry into the valley. The California Civil Defense Force has also moved a substantial number of militia units to the area. We are uncertain of their level of training, equipment, or numbers, but we're estimating their numbers to be somewhere around two or three thousand. They make up the bulk of the force opposing us.

"Under normal circumstances, we'd land our force behind them and bypass them altogether. However, we need to also secure a route for our equipment that'll be arriving in the ports back to San Diego County. That means we're going to have to clear them out."

General Shell heard a few of the Marines grumble and saw some of them shaking their heads. He stood back up to interject. "Listen. I know none of you guys like the idea of having to shoot fellow Americans, especially our Army brothers—but let's not forget something here. These guys made their choice. They opted to join the renegade government and fight against our country. We can't allow that to happen. We're going to give these guys one chance. They will either surrender peacefully or get crushed by the United States Marine Corps."

The general paused for a second before he added, "I want you to start preparing yourselves and your men for this. We push off to start this show in twelve hours. So we have time to get everything ready and also get a bit of rest. God only knows how long this operation will take, so let's be as prepared as we can for whatever may come next."

****

Interstate 5, Near San Clemente

It was still dark, 0500 hours, as Staff Sergeant Mack's LAV-25 followed behind four M1A1 Abrams main battle tanks down Interstate 5 toward San Clemente. There was a lot of consternation among the men of Regimental Combat Team One as they inched closer and closer to a possible conflict with their Army brothers.

Sergeant Mack had his own reservations. Given, these were Army National Guard units—still, many of them had served with plenty of regular Army and National Guard soldiers in the Iraq and Afghan wars. While they weren't Marines, they were still blood brothers from a war they'd collectively fought together. The thought of having to kill them wasn't sitting well. Mack could tell that the younger Marines who hadn't seen combat in Iraq and Afghanistan didn't seem to be questioning the orders, but the more seasoned Marines were coming to grips with a horrible situation.

Captain Turpin picked up on the foul mood. "You look like your chewing on a lemon, Staff Sergeant," he commented.

Mack shrugged. "A big part of me hopes we don't have to actually fight these guys. I'm hoping they'll just surrender or go away."

"I know how you feel, Sergeant. When I was enlisted, this National Guard unit that's standing in our way in San Clemente was operating in our AO in Iraq during my first deployment. We didn't have a lot of interaction with them, but what I do remember was that despite them being a National Guard unit, they sure knew how to take the fight to the enemy."

Captain Turpin paused for a moment. "I hope the veterans of those deployments don't view us in the same manner. We're not the enemy, and neither are they. We're all just caught up in this three-dimensional chess game some higher-ups are playing. We're just pawns being moved around on a board none of us understand or can see. I pray none of our guys have to get killed because people can't come to their senses."

Before either of them could say anything further, the SINCGARS radio crackled to life with the voice of the tank commander leading the force ahead of them. "Loki Six, Hammer Six. How copy?"

Captain Turpin grabbed the radio and depressed the talk button, waiting for a second for the receiver to beep, signaling that the device had synced. "Hammer Six, Loki Six. Send it."

"I got a roadblock roughly two thousand meters to my front. Thermals are showing multiple enemy positions dug in along the spur leading up to the ridge. How do you want us to proceed?"

Turpin swore under his breath. Then speaking back into the receiver, he asked, "What is the roadblock made of? Do you see any other armored vehicles?"

"The roadblock consists of at least two eighteen-wheel semitrucks and trailers blocking both directions of traffic. As to enemy armor—yeah. There's an Abrams battle tank that just poked his head around a position. He's aimed right at us but hasn't fired yet. Do we try and talk to them?"

Before Turpin could reply, Mack asked, "What if we approach them under a white flag? Let's try and talk to them before we start shooting. If they've got Abrams battle tanks just like ours, chances are they have artillery and other nasty surprises waiting for us. This could get really bloody really quickly."

Nodding at the suggestion, Captain Turpin responded, "Go find me a white flag then, Mack."

Talking into the receiver, Turpin ordered, "Hammer Six, stand by. Don't do anything that may make them want to attack you. As a matter of fact, back up a few hundred meters. I'm coming forward under a white flag to try and talk some sense into these guys."

"Loki Six, this is War Machine Actual. Stand down your approach to the enemy lines. I'm en route to your position. We'll approach them together." Sergeant Mack lifted an eyebrow, as did Captain Turpin. The general had overheard their conversation.

Ten tense minutes went by as more National Guard soldiers filtered into some fighting positions along the hillcrests that dotted this area of Interstate 5. They could hear the sound of tracks moving along—more tanks were nearby.

Brigadier General Shell walked up to Turpin. "This your idea, Captain?" he asked with a wry smile.

Captain Turpin shook his head. "It was my staff sergeant here."

Turpin turned to face Mack. "Good idea, Sergeant. So, since this was your bright idea, I want you to come with us. Stay frosty and be ready to drop these guys if we have to. You got me?"

Smiling, Mack nodded his head. "Yes, sir. Locked and ready to rock."

The four of them headed out down the road past the four Marine battle tanks and a couple of LAVs that had also taken up defensive positions. When they got to the front of the vehicles, Lance Corporal Pyro, who'd been designated as the man to carry the flag, waved it a couple of times high above their heads. He did that for maybe sixty seconds before he led the way, walking toward the enemy roadblock.

It took them a few minutes to walk the two thousand meters to the barricade. When they got a few hundred meters away, a voice called out, "That's far enough!"

"We're under a flag of truce. I'd like to talk to whoever is in charge," General Shell bellowed.

"Stand by. We'll get the colonel."

As the four Marines stood there, they observed that a lot of people had weapons trained on them. Most were wearing the Army's ACU uniform, but there were also a lot of folks who appeared to be wearing a hodgepodge of different camouflage uniforms.

Those must be civilian militia units joining their ranks, thought Staff Sergeant Mack.

Five minutes went by, and then an Army colonel walked forward with several additional soldiers. Two of the people joining him appeared to be wearing civilian camouflage. The two groups of warriors sized each other up.

Eventually, one of the men across from them stepped forward, extending his hand. "I'm Colonel Griffin, the commander of the California Army National Guard 79th Infantry Brigade Combat Team."

One of the men in civilian camouflage stepped forward. He didn't extend his hand, but he puffed out his chest a bit as if to signal his own importance. "And I'm Brigadier General Ryan of the California Civil Defense Force," he said.

"I'm Brigadier General Shell, Commander of Marine Regimental Combat Team One. This is Captain Turpin, one of my company COs. I was hoping us commanders could talk for a few minutes and see if we could defuse this situation before a lot of people end up getting killed."

Colonel Griffin nodded at the comment and smiled. He motioned for them to take a walk over to the center divider of the highway. General Ryan was about to join them when Griffin held a hand up. "Sir, I think it might be best if us military types talked first." Undeterred, Ryan insisted on being a part of the conversation.

****

When the three of them stood next to the center divider, the two military men sat on the dividers while Ryan opted to stand.

Looking at General Shell, Griffin said, "I suppose you're here because you want to pass through our lines on your way to the ports," he commented casually.

Shell nodded. "That's right. I was hoping we could work something out, so none of us have to kill each other over it."

"You guys should have thought about that before you sided with that illegitimate dictator in Washington," Ryan shot back, flashing him a look of scorn.

Undeterred by the man's outburst, Shell continued his conversation with the Army colonel. "We have a large convoy coming in from Japan. It's going to dock at the Ports of LA and Long Beach to begin offloading our equipment being brought back home from Asia. I'd like my boys to be able to pass through without a problem, secure the port and escort their contents back to San Diego County."

"Those ports are off-limits to the federal government. You'll have to find another port to use, General," the CDF officer said gruffly.

Turning to look at the wannabe general, Shell crossed his arms. He'd had enough. "Listen up, you civilian puke—just because they pinned a star on your shoulder doesn't mean you know crap about the military or our capabilities. I have an entire RCT ready to punch its way into LA. We have thirty-two thousand Marines arriving from Japan in forty-eight hours. I have enough firepower to destroy your little world here and kill every last one of you!"

General Shell took a deep breath. In a calmer voice, he said, "I'm trying to talk to the man who's in charge to see if we can prevent our two groups from coming to blows. If fighting starts, I have to afford his men the same rights they'd have to afford my men under the Geneva Conventions. However, if we capture *you* or your men, our orders are to either hang you on sight or execute you by firing squad. You all have been declared unlawful enemy combatants and have no rights. So why don't you shut the hell up and let the professionals talk?"

Ryan was aghast. He huffed and puffed a bit and then walked away, cursing under his breath.

"That guy's been a freaking pain in my ass since the first day he arrived," Colonel Griffin said with a grin on his face. "Hey, maybe you could help me out with something, General. What the hell is going on down in Mexico? We keep hearing there's some grand Chinese army that's going to help us liberate the state of California."

General Shell snorted at the question. "You heard right. There are two large Army groups. One's down near Texas, and the other is south of San Diego County. Right now, I'm stuck having to deal with you guys to my north, and the Chinese to my south. I'd really like it if your force could help us keep these Chinese bastards out of our country instead of viewing them as liberators. You know what'll happen if they get a foothold here. We'll never get rid of them."

Colonel Griffin nodded. "I don't doubt you, General. Hell, I wish I could deploy my brigade down to the border to help you guys right now. But I've got my orders from the governor. I'm supposed to keep your Marines bottled up in San Diego County and away from the rest of the state."

"Colonel, you know if I want to punch through your force, I can do it. I may lose some Marines in the process, but I've got gunships, F/A-18s, and other support I can call on to take you guys out. I'd rather not because, at the end of the day, I need your tanks, Stryker vehicles, and soldiers to help me defeat this Chinese army to my south. But if you're going to be a problem, Colonel, then I'm going to have to deal with you guys as quickly as I can. Is there any way we can avoid having to fight each other? Do you need me to take these militia guys out for you?"

Now it was Griffin's turn to sigh and think about the problem. Shell imagined that he was weighing his oath to the Constitution and his allegiance to California. Suddenly, he seemed to have an idea.

"What if we did this, General? What if you were to pull your force back and then appear like you were going to circumvent us here and make a run for Interstate 15 instead? I could convince Ryan that he needs to hold his boys in place here while I shift my force around to meet you guys. This will leave you facing only the CDF. You can solve my problem of having to deal with Ryan and his men, and then our two forces will completely avoid each other altogether. If I'm going to make a case to my troopers that we should switch sides *again*, and this time work with you to defeat the

Chinese, I'm going to need more than five minutes, and I'm certainly going to need those CDF bastards dealt with. I'm pretty sure when my guys see your Marines slaughter them, they'll have second thoughts about wanting to fight you."

Smiling, General Shell held his hand out for him to shake it. "Deal. I'll pull my guys back. But come hell or high water, tomorrow around this same time, my guys are going to come through this area like a freight train. We won't stop, and we won't be taking prisoners. Understood? Just make sure it's those CDF guys left here, and I'll take care of them for you.

"Once the rest of Three MEF arrives in port, you'll have an easier time of making the case to switch sides. We're going to have two full Marine divisions down here. You guys wouldn't stand a chance if you chose to fight. That said, we sure could use your help dealing with these Chinese soldiers that are gearing up to invade us."

Almost breathing a sigh of relief, Colonel Griffin took his hand. "Deal. Just don't leave any of these CDF guys alive. You might even want to drop some heliborne troops behind them to make sure they don't fade away. These militia guys aren't real soldiers. They're radical leftists that view this conflict as a way to settle scores and fashion

California into the socialist, leftist model they want. I'll be glad when you're done with them."

The two military leaders parted ways, and within thirty minutes, General Shell had his entire RCT turned around to head back to Pendleton. He made sure to send a force over to Interstate 15 to be a part of the ruse they'd agreed on.

When his scout units launched a few drones over the area, they confirmed that the Army colonel was, in fact, moving his units to I-15, just as they'd agreed. Come tomorrow morning, they'd find out if they had just been suckered into a bigger trap, or if they might have found a new ally.

****

"Stand by for contact. We're five minutes out from the roadblock," the vehicle commander said to Captain Turpin.

Unlike yesterday, their convoy of vehicles was racing down Interstate 5 on their way to deal with the California Civil Defense Force.

Now that their scout drones had confirmed there were no tanks, Strykers, or Bradley fighting vehicles at the roadblock or anywhere nearby, the four tanks in the lead opted to barrel down the highway and punch a hole right through the barricade and clear a path for the infantry.

Depressing the talk button on his radio, Captain Turpin called out, "All Loki elements, when the tanks clear us a path through the barricade, I want you guys to push through the newly created hole and head for Objective Foxtrot. Platoon leaders, you need to secure the housing development overlooking the interstate before you expand further up the ridgeline. If you run into any serious challenges, we have MAG-39 on standby, ready to bring the pain. Let's do this, Marines. Loki Six out."

With his little pep talk done, Turpin turned to Staff Sergeant Mack. "Remember, Sergeant, no prisoners, unless they are wearing an Army ACU. Copy?"

Mack just nodded, and so did the three other Marines of his squad in the vehicle. The rest of his team was in the following two LAVs.

Boom! Boom!

The lead tanks fired two rounds, blowing the semitrucks apart. They then charged forward toward the tractor-trailers. While this was happening, the militia soldiers all along the spur, ridge, and other fixed positions around the choke point along the interstate opened fire on the armored column.

Seconds after the fireworks started, the gunner in the LAV Mack and Turpin were riding in fired his 25mm at some unseen target. As they got closer to the barricade, they heard bullets pinging and bouncing off their armored shell. They were taking fire from the militia.

"We're through the barricade, Captain. We're headed to your objective now," the vehicle commander announced as they turned off the interstate.

Once they were through the barricade, they found that the volume of enemy fire being directed at their vehicle dwindled immensely. The sounds of war, however, only increased. They heard more tank rounds, along with a new sound. Mortars.

"We're here!" shouted out the vehicle commander. The roar of gunfire continued to build outside their armored shell.

"OK. Everyone out!" Mack ordered. "Let's get formed up and do this thing."

Crump, crump, crump.

Mortar rounds landed where the barricade had just been. Most of the rounds missed the Marine vehicles, but every now and then, a lucky one would score a direct hit on one of the LAVs, AAVs, or troop trucks, killing a lot of good Marines.

Ping, zip, zap.

Bullets smacked against the LAV that Mack and his guys had just exited. Turning to see where the enemy fire was coming from, Sergeant Mack spotted a cluster of houses at the top of the spur. It looked like they had set up some fighting positions at the top. The place gave the militiamen an excellent position to rain fire down on them. It had to be taken out.

"First squad! Form up on me!" shouted Staff Sergeant Mack. He ran past the LAV to a small embankment at the base of the spur. He needed to get his squad under some sort of cover so they could formulate a plan on how to take out that enemy position.

Looking to his right and left, Mack saw the thirteen Marines of his squad were ready for his next set of orders. Several of his men were returning fire at the attackers. The enemy was probably about five hundred meters above them, so it was almost pointless for them to fire back with their rifles, although it did make them feel like they were doing something.

"What do you want us to do, Sarge?" asked one of his fireteam leaders.

"Where's my RTO?" Mack asked.

"Here, Staff Sergeant." The Marine who was carrying their SINCGARS radio stepped forward and took a knee next to him. The young man looked at him with the expression of a nervous puppy in a thunderstorm. Bullets randomly hit all around them. At this distance, the enemy fire wasn't particularly accurate, but it did keep them on their toes.

"Get MAG-38 on the horn," Mack ordered. "I want to see if we can get one of those gunships to take those guys out or at least provide us some covering fire while we bound up this spur."

The young Marine pulled out his notepad, which had the frequencies and call signs on it for the units in their company, battalion, and support elements. Once he found what he was looking for, he contacted one of the gunships and handed the radio hand receiver over to Sergeant Mack.

Mack glanced at the young man's notepad and saw the call sign before he depressed the talk button. "Thunderbolt Two, this is Loki One Six. I've got an enemy position that needs some love. How copy?"

"Loki One Six, that's a good copy. Send the grid."

"Enemy bunker and multiple fighting positions on top of the spur. Grid SC 7854 8543. How copy?"

There was a short pause, and then the gunship replied, "Good copy. Enemy bunker and fighting positions on top of the spur. We'll make a quick pass of the area to confirm the targets, and then we'll engage. Can you pop some smoke at your position so we can know where you are in relationship to the target?" asked the pilot.

Mack was more than happy to oblige the request. He wanted to make sure they didn't accidentally hit the Marines they were supposed to support. He turned to one of his squad leaders. "Pop a smoke grenade for the gunships," Mack ordered.

A second later, a purple smoke grenade started puffing away a handful of feet in front of their positions. The wind caused the trail to drift upwards into the early-morning light.

"Thunderbolt Two. What color smoke do you see?"

"Loki One Six. I see purple smoke."

"That's us."

"Good copy. Stand by. We're making our run now."

Sergeant Mack looked off toward the ocean. He heard the rhythmic thumping sound of helicopter blades. Eventually, he spotted a pair of Super Cobra attack helicopters swoop in. They made a quick pass over the targeted area, attracting a ton of enemy gunfire.

Then both of the Cobras spat out flares and banked hard to one side, attempting to gain altitude at the same time. Mack saw two small objects fly up from the ground and chase after them. The helicopters split up. One dove for the deck while the other tried to lose the missile in a nearby canyon. Unfortunately, the Cobra that flew toward the canyon soared into another small pocket of militiamen, who summarily fired off a second Stinger at them. A second later, the missile hit the helicopter, blowing it apart.

The second Cobra managed to escape. It circled back around to where it had been attacked and fired off two missiles before it headed back out to sea.

"Loki One Six. We're going to see if we can't get some fast movers to plaster that enemy position for you," the Cobra pilot announced. "It looks like these guys have some Stingers. Helicopters don't like Stingers."

"That's a good copy. We'll stand by for the fast movers."

While Mack's squad continued to hold their position, the rest of the platoon fanned out nearby as they waited for the Hornets to plaster the top of the spur. Then they'd bound up the hill and secure their first objective.

Looking again out toward the sea, Mack saw two objects flying fast toward them. The F/A-18s flew right over the enemy positions, releasing several small objects from beneath their wings. With their special delivery made, the Super Hornets released a series of flares as they went almost vertical, lighting up their afterburners in the process. In the blink of an eye, they were gone, nothing more than noisy specks in the sky.

Sergeant Mack returned his gaze to the top of the spur just in time to see the entire area explode in a series of massive fireballs.

"That's it. All Loki elements charge!" came the call over the radio from their captain.

"You heard the captain. Charge!" Mack yelled. He lifted his body up and over the embankment where they'd been hiding, and raced up the hill, willing his muscles and mind to overcome the pain and burning he felt as his body, laden down with over one hundred pounds of body armor and gear, tried to run for all its worth up the steep incline.

As he rushed forward, Mack saw the fireballs starting to dissipate.

Crap! he thought. Whatever defenders had survived the attack would resume shooting at him and his men soon. He needed to get to the top of this position swiftly.

As he continued to struggle up the hill, his quad muscles burned intensely. His chest started to hurt as his lungs fought to keep his muscles oxygenated. Several Marines charged right past him, which only spurred him to push harder.

Zip, zap, zip, zap.

As they got closer to the top of the hill, bullets flew back down at them. They were now less than a hundred yards from the top. Kneeling beside some rocks, Mack looked up and saw a handful of defenders had somehow survived the barbeque the Hornets had delivered—they were geared up for revenge.

Lifting his rifle to his shoulder, Mack aimed at one determined militiaman who kept firing at his Marines. He heard some of his guys calling out for a corpsman, so he knew some of them were getting hit. It infuriated him that his Marines were dying because of these militia groups. Sighting in on the guy, who was firing what appeared to be an AR-15, Mack fired a single shot. His round hit the guy and knocked him down.

Sergeant Mack smiled. *At least I took one of them out.*

Then to his dismay, the militia soldier got back up and started shooting back at them again. Shaking his head in disbelief, Mack realized the man must have been wearing some sort of body armor. He took aim at the man again but moved his selector from semi to burst. Once Mack got a good sight picture on the man, he squeezed the trigger. He felt the three-round burst leave the barrel. This time, the militiaman didn't get back up.

Seeing the immediate threat gone, Sergeant Mack continued to charge up the hill with the rest of his squad and platoon. When he got within twenty meters of the top, he saw half a dozen of his Marines charge right over it. They were firing away at something just outside of his vision.

"Grenade!"

Crump.

"Take that machine gun out!"

"Covering fire!"

Crump, crump.

"Corpsman! Oh, God! I'm hit. Corpsman."

When he reached the top of the hill, Mack was greeted by a dystopian wasteland. More than a dozen houses were burning, and several dozen cars, pickup trucks, and SUVs were nothing more than charred wrecks. Bodies were strewn everywhere.

Pushing past the initial shocked reaction, Sergeant Mack spotted some militiamen shooting at his Marines from deeper into the housing development. Small clusters of

Marines were advancing cautiously from one covered position to another, returning fire.

Mack was horrified as he realized that this was a civilian community that was being destroyed. *This isn't what I signed up for.* He had no desire to devastate an American neighborhood at all—but he also didn't see any way around it.

Just then, Mack heard the familiar engine sounds of an LAV and looked down toward the incoming noise. He watched as several of the vehicles crashed through the front gate of the housing community, then made their way up to the top of the hill, where the rest of his platoon was.

A new sound that didn't fit in with all the clamor of war reached Mack's ears. "Please help!" a woman screamed. "Someone, please help us. Don't shoot! My daughter's been shot."

Mack saw a woman carrying a small child in her arms, running toward him, tears in her eyes. He rushed forward and shouted, "Corpsman!"

A couple of other Marines joined him as they raced to the woman and her daughter. Her little girl was probably only four or five years old, and she cried uncontrollably, barely able to catch her breath. Blood streamed down from her left leg. Mack found an apparent gunshot wound. Her face looked pale and clammy, probably from loss of blood and shock.

"We need to apply pressure to the wound," Mack instructed.

Just then, their squad's corpsman arrived and took charge of the little girl's care. Mack and the other Marines who'd come to assist took a knee, creating a small circle to protect them.

"Ma'am, I need you to put the girl down so I can start working on her." The Navy corpsman pulled his aid bag off his back and pulled out a pair of scissors. "I just need to cut the pants a bit so I can see your leg better, OK?" he explained to the little girl.

She sobbed but nodded.

As the corpsman continued working on her, several bullets ricocheted off the asphalt near them. The little girl screamed, and the mother started crying hysterically.

"Take those bastards out!" yelled Mack to a couple of the Marines nearby.

One of the Marines leveled his M240 Golf at the house where the shots had just come from and opened fire. The mother and daughter screamed some more as they heard the roar of the machine gun open up next to them. Hot spent shell casings landed on the ground around the mother's feet.

Mack and another Marine ran toward the house while the machine gunner provided them with some covering fire. When the two of them got to the wall of the house, the machine gunner stopped shooting but stayed ready to provide covering fire for their medic.

Now that Mack had made it to the wall of the house, he motioned for his comrade to get one of his grenades ready. The two of them moved toward two of the windows facing the street where their medic was working on the little girl.

Holding a hand up with his fingers out, Mack silently counted down as he pulled one finger down after another. He then pulled the pin on his grenade just as his comrade did. Then the two of them held the grenades for two seconds, cooking down the fuse just a bit before they lobbed them inside.

Boom! Boom!

They heard a couple of curse words and at least two people moaning in pain. A third voice said something they couldn't understand. Knowing the defenders were stunned and hurt, Mack motioned for his squadmate to breach the door with him.

In one swift movement, Mack kicked the door hard right at the handle, breaking it open. The door swung inward, and he rushed in with his rifle at the ready. He swept the room to the left while his partner swept to the right. Mack saw one defender lying on the ground, attempting to stop the bleeding from a wound in his leg. Without thinking, Mack fired several rounds into the man's chest, killing him.

"Moving right!" shouted the Marine as he moved to clear the next room. Sergeant Mack heard a couple of shots before the man called, "Room cleared!"

As he advanced down the hallway, Mack heard some voices coming from one of the other rooms, so he paused. He grabbed another one of his grenades from his IBA and pulled the pin. He let it cook down for two seconds before he tossed it in the room where he'd heard the voices.

"Grenade! Get down!" Mack heard.

Boom!

Several pieces of shrapnel blew through the wall, and Mack winced as he felt something bite at his left arm. Brushing the pain off, Mack whirled around the corner and saw the two defenders. Both of them were dead, ripped apart by the grenade.

"You all right, Staff Sergeant?" his partner asked.

"Yeah. I think I got clipped by a piece of my own grenade."

"I'm going to clear the next room."

It took them a couple of minutes to finish clearing the house. With no more defenders hiding inside, they moved back outside and headed back to where the medic had been working on the little girl. They didn't find them there.

"Where's Doc?" Sergeant Mack asked.

Lance Corporal Pyro explained, "He took the girl and her mother over to the casualty collection point over there." Pyro pointed to a section further down the road where it looked like two of their corpsmen were treating several wounded Marines along with a few wounded civilians.

Looking around, Mack saw most of his squad was engaging another house further up the block. Seeing that the little girl had been taken care of and this house had been cleared of threats, he had the two other Marines follow him and catch back up with their squad.

Bang, bang, bang!

Sergeant Mack breathed a sigh of relief. One of the LAVs had finally made it to their location and began using its 25mm cannon to tear into another house that had been turned into a bunker.

Soon, a second, third, and fourth LAV had arrived in the neighborhood. Behind them was a JLTV that had a bright red cross painted on the sides. As he continued forward, Mack glanced back to see the tactical ambulance make its way over to the casualty collection point where they'd be able to load up the wounded.

The fight in this area went on for another hour as the last holdouts were found and killed. By midmorning, the battle for San Clemente was over. A battalion of Marines continued to stay in the area to keep the highway open and clear it of any remnants still wanting to fight, while the rest of the RCT continued to the ports.

****

The following day, Colonel Griffin drove up to the Auld Dubliner in Long Beach. It was a nice little Irish pub near the port facility that the Marines had taken over. Attached to the antenna of his JLTV was a white pillowcase they were using for a flag. He wanted to make sure his vehicle didn't get lit up by some trigger-happy jarheads on his way to meet with their general.

Pulling up to the Irish pub, Griffin spotted a couple of LAVs and Amtracks, along with probably thirty or so Marines that he assumed were either pulling guard duty or eating at the pub. It was odd seeing so many military vehicles inside such a large city—it reminded him of Iraq or Afghanistan, not America.

There wasn't any official polling out to gauge the mood of the people of Long Beach, but Colonel Griffin's impression was that many of the residents were glad to be rid of their CDF overlords. Still, others were definitely concerned that fighting could break out at any moment, especially if the California Army National Guard opted to fight.

Last night, a few gangbangers had thought they could take advantage of the situation and tried to ambush a squad of Marines a few blocks away. Needless to say, that didn't go very well for them. Since that incident occurred, the Marines had pretty much been shooting anyone on sight that looked like a gang member or who made an overt threat toward them. It might have been overkill, but they were tired of being shot at, and with much of the police force giving the Marines a wide berth, there weren't a lot of options left to dealing with threats like that.

As Colonel Griffin's vehicle pulled up to the restaurant, a young Marine guided them to a spot where they wanted them to park. For the most part, they kept their rifles at the low ready, which made him feel a bit better about the meeting.

When he exited his JLTV, a couple of Marines walked toward him and saluted. Griffin returned the salute.

"I'm supposed to meet with General Shell," he announced.

The Marines nodded and gestured for him to follow them inside. When Griffin entered the pub, he spotted the general sitting at a long table with a handful of other officers and NCOs. He also saw a number of maps spread out on the table.

General Shell stood when he saw him, and the two shook hands. Shell took a moment to introduce some of the officers at the table, and then they sat down. They placed an order for some fish 'n chips before the two military commanders got down to business.

"Well, Colonel, you held up your end of the bargain. My men stayed clear of your guys, and we took out that militia force for you. I can't be certain that we killed that wannabe general, but we certainly took his force out. Are your men ready to cross back over to our side and come back into the fold?"

Griffin had talked with his officers and senior NCOs the night before. The consensus was that they should take the Marines up on their offer. His men told him they felt caught between a rock and a hard place. While they owed their loyalty to the state and their community, they also knew in their hearts and heads that breaking away from the federal government and joining this UN peacekeeping force was tearing the country and the state apart. Everything about it just felt wrong. His officers and NCOs felt like they'd just been given a golden opportunity to receive mercy for a crime they didn't want to commit, and they were determined to take the pardon.

"General Shell, my men and I have come to the conclusion that while we have a responsibility to our governor, we also have a responsibility to the Constitution. I can't guarantee that *all* my men will switch back over, but what I can tell you is that all my battalion and company-grade officers and commanders, along with my senior NCOs, will. We'll do our best to make sure our men comply with our orders as well."

The Marines at the table were visibly relieved by the news. Colonel Griffin related to those sentiments. This whole business of fighting your countrymen was sickening.

Chapter 8

Tactical Surprise

February 5, 2021
940 Miles West of Hawaii
Johnston Atoll

Colonel Peng couldn't believe their luck when he heard the heliborne troops had landed on the island and found it deserted. He had thought the Americans would have reinforced the atoll, or at least placed a contingent of Marines there to prevent them from seizing it. Then again, the Americans had wholly underestimated them up to this point, so why should this be any different?

Looking back at the *Longhu Shan*, Peng observed a couple of sailors acting as ground guides as the drivers got the Wanshan special vehicles off the *Longhu*. Each W2400 was a specially equipped launcher platform vehicle that could carry three CJ-10 long-range cruise missiles, very similar to the American HIMARS system. The *Longhu* had transported twenty of these vehicles, along with their crews, to the abandoned American base. The other transport ship, the *Dabie Shan*, was carrying three additional missile pods per truck. All told, they had 120 CJ-10s for their upcoming mission.

It took the soldiers and sailors close to an hour to get the vehicles and the additional missile pods offloaded from the two transport ships. Once that task had been completed, the launchers were driven over to the east side of the abandoned runway, where they'd be set up and made ready to fire.

Peng and his crew were on a strict timeline. They had to have all twenty vehicles ready to fire their missiles at precisely 2100 hours, which only gave them about nine hours before the final attack on the remaining American forces in the Pacific would start.

****

Clear Air Force Station, Alaska

Despite the cold-weather gear and tight-fitting body armor he was wearing, Senior Airman Dutt was freezing. After spending ten minutes letting the two JLTVs' engines run, he couldn't wait to get back inside the building. Every few hours, one of the guys from the QRF had to go outside and turn the trucks on to let the engines run. Otherwise, they couldn't be sure they'd crank in the cold when they needed them. Dutt had drawn the short stick.

While Airman Dutt loved being in the Air Force, it was moments like this he hated being stationed in Alaska. When he'd initially received his orders for Eielson AFB, he had been excited. Growing up in Montana, Dutt was an avid hunter and fisherman, so an assignment to Alaska had sounded like a dream. Then he'd arrived at the 354th Security Forces Squadron and had summarily been assigned to Clear Air Force Station, nearly two hours away.

Fortunately, they had a rotation system in place, so he only had to serve a week at the remote radar station once every three weeks. Still, he hated being at the secluded base. With the war going on, Dutt wanted to be down where the action was. A number of his friends in other squadrons had already regaled him with their combat experiences.

Senior Airman Dutt had also learned that several of his classmates from technical school had been killed at Beale Air Force Base in California at the outset of the war. It angered him that here he was, itching to get into the fight, and he was stuck pulling guard duty on a remote radar base in the middle of nowhere Alaska, far from the fighting.

As Dutt reached the door that would lead him back into the warmth of their security detachment's QRF office, he entered his six-digit code. The green light came on, letting him know the magnetic lock had turned off. Once he heard the click, he pulled the handle and walked in. The heat from inside slapped him in the face, and he immediately felt better.

"Hey, close the door, man. You're letting the cold in."

Grumbling to himself, Dutt closed the door and stomped his feet a couple of times to get the snow off of them. He placed his rifle on the gun rack and then began the process of unwrapping himself from all the cold-weather gear and body armor.

He looked over at his counterparts. Two of them were taking a catnap in a chair, two more were playing something on the Xbox, and the other three were watching the computer monitors that displayed several different camera images from around the base.

Just as Dutt finished stripping off his cold-weather gear, one of the perimeter sensors detected something. The red flashing light hanging from the ceiling in the center of the room turned on and spun rapidly in a circle.

"What the hell is that?" Dutt asked.

"Crap! Those look like snowmobiles," his technical sergeant remarked. "Hit the alarm and alert the QRF at Eielson that we have a perimeter breach!"

"Everyone, suit up and grab your weapons," ordered one of the staff sergeants, who quickly threw on his winter jacket. "Someone call Bravo Team and tell them to head over to Alpha's position. Tell them they are cleared to engage those hostiles." The sergeant moved faster than Dutt had ever seen the portly man move.

"Miller, you stay here and monitor what's going on," called out the section chief. "You're our eyes right now, so stay on the radio and let us know what you see. The rest of you follow me out to the JLTVs and let's get going. I want those M240s manned, so don't forget your goggles and gloves. Let's go!" As soon as he finished issuing orders, he hit the green lock release button on the side of the wall.

The sergeant pushed the door open. Before any of them knew what had happened, an object slammed into his chest plate, throwing him backward into several of the airmen. He knocked several of them over, like a bowling ball hitting a stack of pins.

Dutt had been standing to the side of the door, so he hadn't fallen, but as he looked down at his section chief, his eyes went wide. It was an RPG rocket that had hit him. For whatever reason, the rocket hadn't gone off. Whoever was out there was real trouble.

Flicking his selector switch from safe to semi, Dutt dropped down and took a knee. He arched his body over to peer outside the door. Several dark-clad figures were practically on top of them, their rifles at the ready.

One of the attackers fired several rounds that flew over Dutt's head and thudded into the chest of one of his friends. Dutt immediately fired several shots into the men charging toward him. His first shot hit the lead soldier right in the face, killing the man instantly. His second and third shots hit the man just to his right, clipping his neck just above his body armor.

Dutt swept his rifle slightly to the left. He was just about to squeeze the trigger when his world went black.

****

Tan Zheng fired several rounds from his QBZ-95 into the face of the American soldier who had just killed his two comrades. When the man dropped, Tan kept charging forward, shooting his rifle at the remaining Americans in his line of sight.

As he crossed over the threshold, he could see the looks of surprise and terror on the faces of the two soldiers as they reached for their sidearms. Tan fired several bullets into each of them—two shots to the chest and one to the head, just like he had done a thousand times in training.

Tan could smell the cordite and sulfur from the rifle fire, followed by the feces and urine from the dead bodies he now found himself surrounded by. Seeing no one else left alive in the room, Tan walked over to the computer terminal. He pushed the dead American out of the chair, letting his body fall in a heap on the floor amongst the shell casings and blood. Then he grabbed a couple of tissues from his pocket and wiped the blood and brain matter off the computer monitor so he could see it.

One team of snowmobiles was headed toward the phased radar array they'd come to blow up. The other group was moving in on the building their intelligence briefer had said was the operations room, directly behind the radar building. After a couple of seconds, he realized that two armored vehicles were heading toward the team that was speeding toward the radar—Tan grabbed his radio and sent that team a quick warning.

With his work here done, Tan pulled the pin on two thermite grenades and tossed them to either side of the building as he exited. Once they'd exploded, he grabbed the corpses of his two dead comrades and placed them in one of the American JLTV vehicles. He took the knife from one of his friend's pockets, pulled out one of their Siberian Tiger playing cards, and stabbed it to the outer wall of the building he'd just torched, leaving their unit's calling card behind.

As Tan drove the American vehicle toward the radar building, the sounds of battle intensified. When he made it over the top of the slight hill he'd been climbing, he saw the 105-foot-tall building that enclosed the world's largest phased array radar system. This tall but unassuming structure fed information to NORAD and US Space Command about ground- and submarine-launched missiles across much of Asia, as well as all space-based objects that passed through its massive arc of coverage.

As he approached the building, Tan saw that one of the American JLTVs had several of his comrades pinned down. He floored it a bit more, until he was within a hundred meters of the Americans. They didn't respond to his approach, most likely assuming that he was there to reinforce them.

Tan climbed out of the driver's side of the vehicle and climbed back into the rear of the truck. He was just about to move up to the turret when he spotted something. He smiled and reached for the AT4 rocket he'd found. Tan flipped the turret hatch open and climbed up. Pulling the

227

safety pin off the AT4, he aimed it at the JLTV that was firing on his comrades and depressed the trigger.

Pop...swoosh...BAM!

The truck exploded. The Americans in the other gun truck turned around with a look of shock and confusion on their faces at what had just happened. Tan grabbed the machine gun mounted on the turret and let loose a string of bullets at them. Several of them scattered for cover while a couple more were mowed down.

Tan's comrades, who moments earlier had been completely pinned down, now joined the fray. Together they finished off the remaining airmen still shooting at them.

With the immediate threats neutralized, the two teams went to work completing their mission. One of the teams blew open the door to the building that housed the phased array while the other group proceeded to breach the main building where the radar operators were located.

A flurry of shots rang out as the Chinese soldiers moved through the building, killing the operators inside. Tan knew that in the meantime, the other group would apply explosives to the radar equipment inside the massive structure.

When they were ready to leave, the remaining team members climbed into Tan's vehicle and the other JLTV that hadn't been blown up. The group quickly made their way off the little base to head for their next target. As they left the air station, one of the soldiers depressed the red button on the remote detonator.

Behind them, a massive explosion blossomed in the darkness.

Mission accomplished, Tan thought with satisfaction.

Despite the loss of half of their Special Forces group, they had effectively blinded the Americans' ability to monitor sea and ground-launched ballistic missiles, as well as any space-based weapons and satellites over much of the Asian continent.

****

Cavalier Air Force Station, North Dakota

One of Rip's fellow Special Forces soldiers broke the early-morning quiet. "I've got movement," he announced. "Three SUVs moving down County Road 89. They just passed mile marker twelve."

Rip looked through his own night vision goggles, scanning until he spotted what looked like three Chevy Tahoes moving at a rapid clip toward the base.

He grabbed his radio receiver and pushed depressed the talk button. "Hellboy to Reaper Five. We've got confirmation of the target. You're cleared to engage."

Ten thousand feet above them, an MQ-9 Reaper drone was loitering, steered by a UAV pilot at Creech Air Force Base nearly a thousand miles away.

"Reaper Five to Hellboy. That's a good copy. I have three Chevy Tahoes passing mile marker eleven. Is that the right target?" The drone pilot had to confirm before he fired off his Hellfire missiles.

"Yes, that's the target. Take 'em out!"

Rip watched and waited as the group of SUVs continued to get closer and closer to the radar installation.

BOOM, BOOM, BOOM.

Three deafening explosions ripped through the darkness. The flaming blasts briefly turned the scene into a spectacular display of precision firepower.

"Reaper Five, Hellboy. Good hit. Continue to stay on station. There may be additional hostiles in the area."

"That's a good copy. Returning to station. From our vantage point, we don't show any additional vehicle traffic within a twenty-mile radius of your position."

Smiling, Rip felt a certain level of satisfaction at having just prevented a major attack that could have debilitated his nation's early-warning radar system.

****

February 6, 2021, 12:41 a.m.
NORAD Facility

General Tibbets had just lain down on the couch in his office to take a much-needed nap. As of today, they were officially three weeks into this civil war and UN-led invasion of his country, and the unrelenting tempo was exhausting.

How could this have happened to our country? he wondered as he tried to calm his mind for some rest.

Tibbets would have paid good money for twenty-four hours of uninterrupted sleep. He needed a chance to rest his mind and allow his body to unwind from the constant stress of his position. He hadn't left the mountain or seen his wife in nearly four days.

I can't go on like this indefinitely, Tibbets realized. He made plans to try and escape back to his home in the near future.

Tibbets knew he'd been pushing himself too hard. The twenty-plus-hour days and lack of sleep, exercise, and proper diet were all taking their toll on him physically and mentally. The truth was he had a hard time allowing himself a chance to relax when so many men and women were fighting and dying on the front lines. A big part of him felt that if they couldn't have a break, then neither should he.

His mind had just slipped into a dreamless sleep when his office door suddenly burst open. He practically jumped off his couch, ready to attack whoever had stormed his office.

Seeing the startled look on the general's sleepy face, the intruding Air Force major immediately declared, "Sir, I apologize for not knocking. I'm so sorry to disturb you."

General Tibbets half-growled. "This had better be good," he said grumpily. "I told everyone I didn't want to be interrupted for at least four hours."

"Sir, the Special Forces team we placed near Cavalier Air Force Station just took out those Chinese Special Forces the NSA said was going to attack the facility."

Crap. The attack is really going to happen today, he thought. Tibbets stood up and immediately started walking to the watch center. "What about Clear Station?" he asked. "Please tell me it's still operational."

The major shook his head as they walked together down the hallway. "We received a message from them a few minutes ago, saying they were under some sort of attack. Their QRF was moving to engage, but then the base went silent, and the radar feed cut out. Eielson launched *their* QRF, but they are still twenty minutes out."

As he entered the cavernous room that constituted the watch center, General Tibbets immediately confirmed that their radar coverage over much of Asia was gone. With Thulu Station, Beale, and Cape Cod having gone down at the outset of the war, they were now essentially operating in the dark. This left them utterly open to a sneak attack by either Russia or China. Tibbets said a prayer that their few remaining satellites continued to stay functional.

General Tibbets heard the watch officer on duty, Colonel Jessup, issuing orders. "Someone send a message over to STRATCOM to scramble their birds. I want additional global hawks launched. See if we can reposition some of our satellites to plug the holes in our coverage until we can figure out what the heck is going on."

Tibbets strode over. "Jessup, talk to me. What's happening?"

Jessup, a rising star in the space operations side of the Army, turned to face the general. "Sir, approximately forty-two minutes ago, one of our SOSUS sensors detected a Type-94 *Jin*-class ballistic missile submarine pass near our Wake Island monitoring facility. We immediately ordered a *Poseidon* to go hunt it down and sink it. Then our PAVE PAW radar system at Clear Air Station went down, and we got a report that Cavalier Air Station was in the process of being attacked by what appeared to be a Chinese Special Forces team. While I had a runner go wake you up, I authorized the Special Forces on the ground to engage the enemy before they could reach the base. A Reaper drone just blew up the three SUVs carrying the assault team."

Tibbets nodded. "Good job ordering that assault team to be taken out with the Reaper, Colonel." He ran his fingers through his hair. "So, do you think everything that's happening is a precursor to them hitting us with some sort of ballistic missile attack?"

"It's what I would do if I were them," Jessup responded, a look of concern on his face.

Just then, a flashing red light turned on, and a voice came on over the PA system. "Ballistic missile launch detected."

Tibbets cursed to himself. "This is it, the big attack," he muttered. He'd barely been able to get brought up to speed and now this. It was all happening too fast.

"Someone find out what kind of missile that is and where it's going!" demanded Jessup.

A few seconds went by before one of the satellite operators responded. "We have another bird coming online now. Should have data on the missile location momentarily."

For roughly twenty seconds, they saw several missile tracks appear to come from the ocean near Wake Island, where they had detected that Chinese boomer sub. Then the satellite went offline before they could confirm the type and number of missiles.

"What the hell happened to our satellite?" barked Tibbets.

"It looks like it was just taken out—probably by a ground-based laser," one of the specialists replied.

Tibbets popped his knuckles angrily. He knew he needed to get more information about what was going on before he called the President. Whether or not those missiles were nuclear and where they were headed would make a huge difference in determining how they responded.

"Sir, that P-8 that was heading over to engage that enemy submarine is giving us a visual report of six subsurface missile launches," called out another officer who was also monitoring the situation. "They've just released their torpedoes and should have the enemy sub taken care of shortly."

For the moment, Tibbets waved off the naval success. "Where are those missiles heading now?" he barked.

"We'll know in three more minutes," called out one of the communication officers. "We have another satellite coming over the horizon. Some of our *Arleigh Burkes* on picket duty around Hawaii will also be able to start transmitting some telemetry shortly. We're in the process of repositioning one of our E4 aircraft to fill the communications gap from the loss of the satellites."

While they waited for more data to stream in, Tibbets worked on getting the National Military Command Center at the Pentagon spun up on what was going on. He also ordered the Secret Service to work on getting the President woken up.

"Telemetry's starting to come up!" shouted one of the officers at a computer terminal.

Data finally streamed in to them as the coms gap started to get filled in. Jessup and Tibbets both turned to look at the big board, which was now tracking the missiles. Two of them appeared to be turning to head on a westward track, while the other two were now headed on an eastward trajectory. The last two missiles appeared to have split off from their formation, with one heading south while the other headed north, still gaining altitude as they raced toward their intended targets.

An Air Force captain sitting at one of the computer terminals turned to look at the general. "We'll have definitive targeting data on these missiles in a couple of minutes from the Pine Gap facility. Right now, it appears four of the missiles are headed for Guam and Hawaii. I'm not sure about the other two—there isn't an obvious land target further north or south of where those missiles are headed."

One of the naval officers suddenly stood up. "Sir, the *Roosevelt* strike group is north of Hawaii. That missile heading north could be meant for them."

"The *Reagan* strike group is to the south. They could be trying to take out our carriers in one swoop," another officer said.

A stream of obscenities flew out of Tibbets's mouth. "Get me the President!" he barked. "And close the blast doors. Move us from DEFCON 3 to DEFCON 2."

Warning. Missile Launch Detected.

The automated alarm blared out a new warning for them to worry about. This missile launched appeared to originate from Manzanillo, Mexico. Seconds later, the alarm blared a third time.

Warning. Missile Launch Detected.

To their collective horror, they saw a single missile track emanate from Base 22 in Taibai, Central China—the primary nuclear weapons storage facility for the PLA Rocket Force and where their main ICBM base was located.

"What the hell? Where are those missiles headed, and what type are they?" demanded General Tibbets. He watched in horror as the new missile tracks were being plotted on the big screen for them to watch. He felt a bead of sweat dripping down his forehead as he realized this was likely a major nuclear attack underway.

"Pine Gap's starting to get some telemetry readings on those submarine-launched missiles. They're CSS-N-14s, sir. It's definitive—those are nukes, not conventional warheads."

Pointing at the two tracks rising in altitude and beginning to take a separate arc over the American Southwest, Tibbets demanded, "What type of missiles are *those* and what are they targeting?"

"This is STRATCOM," said one of the technicians from the Omaha base, speaking through a telecom. "Those missile launches from Mexico are confirmed Dongfeng 26s. Sensors confirmed they are carrying nuclear warheads."

"What about that new launch from the Mainland?" demanded Tibbets.

An Air Force major was on the phone with his counterpart at the Pine Gap facility in central Australia. For the briefest of moments, everyone waited for his response to the general's question. He pulled the receiver down to his shoulder and looked up at the general. "The single launch from Taibai is a Dongfeng 31A. It's one of their long-range ICBMs. This one is headed for Pine Gap, and it appears to be nuclear as well."

Colonel Jessup smacked his fist into his hand angrily. "The Chinese are looking to take us out in the Pacific," he remarked to Tibbets, just above a whisper.

Tibbets cursed under his breath.

Just as they were starting to collect all the information they needed to brief the President, more of the satellites that had been providing them with real-time intelligence over Asia blinked out of existence. Then several of their satellites providing communications and surveillance over the continental US went offline, leaving them entirely in the dark.

"What the hell just happened, people?" General Tibbets roared.

Colonel Jessup started barking at some folks for answers. Then he made a beeline over to a station being manned by an Army NCO who was responsible for maintaining their UHF, VHF, and FM ground radios.

"Sergeant, patch us through to STRATCOM, the Pentagon, and the White House through our backup system *now*," Jessup ordered. The sergeant speedily began the process of making contact with those parties via their alternate communication protocols.

Tibbets turned to the officer who, moments ago, had had the President on the line. "Is he still there?"

The young man nodded. "Yes. This line is a dedicated hardline."

"I've got STRATCOM on the radio," called out the Army sergeant as he made his first successful connection.

Tibbets walked over and was handed the radio receiver before the sergeant went back to work, trying to raise the Pentagon.

"Talk to me, Norman," Tibbets said gruffly.

"They just took our satellites out. That's why we've lost communications," General Norman responded. "We think they hit them with a DDoS attack, because Cavalier

Air Force Station is still showing them in orbit. I've directed CyberCom to figure out what the hell is going on, and the NSA is working on a counterattack right now.

"In the meantime, I'm switching the national command authority over to our alternate systems while we scramble some RC-135 Rivet Joints out of Offutt Air Force Base. I've also ordered the E-4 NEACPs to get airborne and help fill in the gaps. Give me fifteen minutes, General, and I'll have most of our capabilities back up and running."

"Norman, get the Looking Glass airborne and scramble our TACAMO planes," Tibbets ordered. "This appears to be a first strike, and I have no idea if we're going to have more missiles raining down on us soon or not. We're not going to get caught flatfooted like we did on the first day of the war."

I can't believe this is happening, General Tibbets thought. The whole thing seemed like a nightmare unfolding. Two nuclear powers on a collision course could see the world destroyed multiple times over if things couldn't be brought back under control.

The Army sergeant nearby announced, "I have the President. They've moved him down to the PEOC, so we're communicating with him from there."

Before Tibbets started briefing the President, he turned to Colonel Jessup. "Move us from DEFCON 2 to DEFCON 1. Begin dispersing our strategic assets and scramble all of our bombers and boomers *now*," he ordered.

He grabbed the phone from the sergeant. "Mr. President, this is General Tibbets."

"General, what the hell is going on?" Sachs demanded. "Did I just hear you say you're moving us to DEFCON 1 and scrambling our bombers?"

"Yes, Mr. President. We're tracking a total of nine ballistic missiles launched by the Chinese at the continental US and our military forces overseas. Six missiles were launched from one of China's ballistic missile subs around Wake Island. We have a high degree of certainty that these missiles are nukes. Four of them are heading toward our bases at Guam and Hawaii. We also have single missiles headed toward the *Roosevelt* and *Reagan* carrier strike groups in the North and South Pacific."

He paused for a second. "Sir, we're also tracking a single missile launched from Mainland China and two originating from Mexico." When Tibbets didn't hear an immediate response from Sachs, he continued. "The missile launch from Mainland China appears to be going after the Pine Gap facility in central Australia. It's a key base in our global signals intelligence apparatus. Judging by the targets they are going after, it would appear they are trying to take out our naval and air presence in the Pacific and completely blind us as to what's going on along the West Coast and the Southwest border. To further compound the problem, they've just taken down more than a dozen of our satellites covering Asia and the continental US."

President Sachs groaned. "You said there were two missiles fired at us from Mexico—where are they headed, and when are they expected to hit?" he asked.

"The two missile launches from Mexico are still gaining in altitude, but one appears to be targeting Southern California while the other appears to be heading towards Texas."

Tibbets heard a short pause followed by a few curse words from those in the room with the President. The phone went silent for a moment—Tibbets confirmed that the line hadn't gone dead. Sachs must have placed the call on mute temporarily.

When he came back, the President said, "General, my advisors here tell me we should have some of our digital communications back up again, once more of the E-4s get airborne. I'm also being told by the Secret Service that they'd like to get me in the air in case Washington is a possible target. Let's reconvene in ten minutes. I'd like you to have some recommendations for how we should respond to this attack once I'm airborne."

General Tibbets let out his breath in a huff. He knew it would take them longer than ten minutes to get the President to Air Force One. They needed a decision *now*. Hoping to get Sachs's attention before he ended the call, he practically shouted, "We don't have ten minutes, Mr. President! Some of these missiles are going to hit in the next eight minutes."

Sachs dropped a few F-bombs before he responded, "What do you want me to do, General? I'm not staying in another flipping bunker and waiting for the Chinese to nuke me. I'm getting on that helicopter to Andrews." He let out a grunt. "We'll reconvene when I'm on Air Force One, Tibbets. Do your best to shoot these missiles down, and we'll go over our response once I'm in the air."

The President then hung up the phone, leaving Tibbets fuming. He wanted to get an immediate response on the way to China, but he'd need Sachs's permission for that.

He smacked his hand down on the table in frustration. Then he took a deep breath and let it out in a huff. He realized he needed to get back to the task at hand— figuring out how they were going to stop these missiles from wiping out their only forward naval bases and carriers in the Pacific.

"OK, people," he said loudly to whoever was in earshot. "We've temporarily lost our picture over the Pacific and Asia, but that doesn't mean we don't know what's inbound and what's going to happen. Let's get a flash message to the strike groups to begin dispersing their ships and prepare for a nuclear attack. Get a message out to our bases on Guam and Hawaii that they have an inbound ballistic missile attack. Then send an alert to our missile bases out west of a possible inbound nuclear attack."

"Yes, sir," several people replied. A flurry of activity began.

"What are our options for stopping these missiles?" bellowed Tibbets.

An Army captain stood up from behind his computer terminal. "Sir, we have a THAAD system at Andersen and another one on Wheeler Army Airfield. They should be engaging those missiles now."

One of the naval LNOs interjected. "We've got the USS *Hopper* on patrol near Pearl. I'm sure they are working in tandem with the THAADs to knock those missiles out of the sky."

One of the Air Force officers piped up. "General, one of our Rivet joint aircraft is sending us the targeting data from that missile launch from Mexico. It's beginning to arc towards Southern California and Texas. Impact in four and five minutes, respectively."

"The USS *Princeton*'s SM-3s are engaging the missile headed toward Southern California," one of the naval LNOs announced.

One of the Air Force officers stood up. "We've got a problem!" he yelled. He still had a hand receiver held to his ear from whatever group he was talking to. "Our radar just detected a cone shroud being ejected right after that last booster phase completed."

"Holy crap! Those two missiles are MIRVs," called out an Air Force colonel.

"Get more interceptors airborne now!" Colonel Jessup shouted.

They watched the monitors in horror as the reentry vehicles made their final turn and course correction before their final descent. At first, they'd each started off as one warhead, but then a second, third, fourth, fifth, and sixth were released. Now the twelve projectiles angled towards their targets, starting their final descent towards the

American west and southwest border at a rate of twenty-five thousand miles per hour.

As Tibbets looked at the big board displaying the twelve warheads, dozens of missiles began to lift off from several locations along the US southern border. The Army's THAAD systems fired their interceptors to try and interdict the warheads. In another three minutes, the Patriot PAC-3 batteries would join the fray, sending their own interceptors up.

A naval officer frantically shouted, "The *Princeton*'s firing more SM-3s."

A few seconds later, the blue naval icon identifying the *Princeton* showed a new interceptor icon appearing every couple of seconds as the ship fired off additional missiles as quickly as it could. Two more *Arleigh Burke* destroyers joined in, firing their SM-3s at the incoming threats.

Steadily, the interceptors raced towards their assigned targets until the first one appeared to collide with its target. One of the naval officers yelled, "Splash one!" as the two objects impacted.

A few cheers erupted as one of the five warheads was destroyed.

"Splash two!"

"Splash three!"

"Splash four!"

General Tibbets was starting to feel cautiously optimistic, until the interceptor heading for the warhead descending on the Yuma proving grounds suddenly missed. The missile and warhead sailed right past each other.

Tibbets held his breath as the next layer of interceptors from the Patriot PAC-3 went after the remaining warhead. The first interceptor missed, then the second. The third missile didn't connect either.

Ten seconds after the interceptors missed, the warhead reached five thousand feet in altitude and detonated, whiting out the aerial picture over the base and dozens of kilometers around the city of Yuma.

Several people shouted torrents of curse words. Others stopped what they were doing and silently stared at the screens, unable to take their eyes off what had just happened.

Colonel Jessup clapped his hands together loudly to snap everyone out of their state of shock. "We still have other warheads to worry about, people! Let's stay focused," he bellowed.

Just then, Major General Estrada came running into the room. "Where are those warheads over Texas targeting?" he demanded.

Estrada made his way over to General Tibbets as people scrambled to find him an answer. Estrada still had his gym clothes on and sweat streaked down his back. He'd run across the mountain fortress through one checkpoint after another to get to the ops center when the missile launch warning had blared over the PA and the facility had begun to go on lockdown.

The last remaining warhead falling on San Diego managed to dodge the remaining SM-3s and then detonated at an altitude of fifty thousand feet.

"I think it blew it up early," commented an Air Force lieutenant, apparently unaware of what a high-altitude detonation meant.

Colonel Jessup shook his head. "It didn't blow up early. The electromagnetic pulse generated from that blast just blanketed Southern California, northern Mexico, and the entire US military force along the border. That EMP will plunge the region back into the Dark Ages."

Turning to one of the communications officers, Jessup ordered, "Send a flash message out to our strike groups and facilities, letting them know some of these warheads may be EMPs. They need to power down their radios, radars, and any other electronic equipment. Make sure they get our planes and other assets indoors if there's still time."

General Tibbets barely restrained himself from punching a wall. This situation was unfolding into an utter disaster—his forces in Yuma had already been obliterated, an EMP had neutered his California forces, and the attack wasn't even over yet. On top of it all, they still didn't have a clear picture of what was happening in Hawaii and the rest of the Pacific.

One of the Air Force officers announced, "The THAAD missiles are starting their intercepts over Texas."

The warhead descending on El Paso and the US ground forces at Fort Bliss blinked out of existence. Tibbets let out a huge sigh of relief as his eyes now turned to the one heading towards Dyess Air Force Base. An interceptor nailed it too. Then the one heading to Fort Hood disappeared as well.

The remaining warheads were heading towards the McAlester Army ammunition plant in McAlester, Oklahoma, the Red River Army depot near Texarkana, Texas, and the Pine Bluff arsenal in Arkansas. Without a second to spare, the missiles headed toward Red River and

Pine Bluff collided with their targets. Then a white spot generated on the map over the McAlester Army ammunition plant.

A mixture of gasps and profanity filled the room. In less than thirty seconds, they had witnessed two nuclear detonations on American soil, something no one could have imagined.

General Tibbets was frozen for a moment, unable to respond to the horror show he'd been watching. General Estrada leaned over to him and put his hand on his shoulder. "I know this isn't going to bring you a lot of comfort right now, sir, but we did a good job. We just intercepted nine out of twelve warheads. The enemy didn't take out our forces along the Texas border, nor did they nail our strategic air bases. Right now, the Chinese hit us with an EMP over San Diego and two conventional nukes that didn't cripple us. We still have those missiles in the Pacific to worry about, but we'll pull through this."

Just then, one of the computer monitors near General Tibbets's desk came on with the image of the President and several of his advisors aboard Air Force One.

"Thanks, Estrada. I needed that," Tibbets said. He took a deep breath and let it out. Then he moved over to the chair in front of the monitors so he could speak with the President.

When Sachs saw Tibbets, he immediately tore into him. "General, what the hell is going on?! We're looking at a map right now that shows nuclear detonations in Arizona, California, and Oklahoma. We still have multiple missiles heading towards Hawaii, Guam, Australia, and two of our naval strike groups that we aren't even able to see right now. What are we doing to stop them?"

Tibbets steeled his nerves. "The detonation over San Diego was an EMP, Mr. President. It wasn't a direct nuclear detonation over the city. This warhead was designed to fry the electronics of Southern California and northern Mexico, probably in anticipation of a Chinese ground invasion. The other two detonations were air bursts, around five thousand feet above their intended targets. Unfortunately, the hit we took in Yuma effectively wiped out about twelve thousand soldiers and Marines we had positioned there to defend the border. The detonation in Oklahoma hit the McAlester munitions plant and the nearby city. Before you ask me any further questions, Mr. President, we should have data on those missiles heading towards Hawaii, Guam, Australia, and our two carrier strike groups momentarily."

"Damn it! What are we doing to *stop* those missiles, General?" the President shouted. His face looked ashen.

"We've got a THAAD in Guam and Hawaii, along with *Arleigh Burke* destroyers that should be engaging those missiles as we speak. The strike groups are also engaging the missiles with their own interceptors. We're in the process of repositioning some new satellites, along with moving some aircraft around to get our communications with Hawaii and the Pacific back up and running. Unfortunately, though, that EMP over Southern California did put another dent in our communications ability."

There was a lot of commotion going on around behind Tibbets. He knew more information was coming in, and he should probably get back to it. "Mr. President, I'd like to keep this link open, but I need to keep an eye on what's happening," he insisted.

"Yes, General. Please do, but I'd like to start working on getting some sort of response going right now," Sachs responded. "General Markus is telling me that with our satellites and other radar stations down, it's possible the Chinese may have launched more missiles at us, and we won't even know about it right away." His face registered a mix of fear and concern.

Tibbets saw General Markus sitting next to the President, along with the military officer carrying the nuclear football. He had the briefcase opened on the table next to Sachs. While Tibbets couldn't see the new Secretary of Defense with him, he did see the National Security Advisor.

"Where's Secretary Howell?" asked General Tibbets. Secretary Mike Howell had taken over as the new head of the Pentagon a few days ago.

General Markus explained, "He was visiting Fort Benning when everything started. I've directed one of the Looking Glass planes to go pick him up and get him airborne. They should be there in another hour. Secretary Kagel wasn't able to make it to Andrews in time, so we're having her picked up by one of the TACAMO planes before it heads out to run figure eights over the Atlantic."

"What are your orders for us, Mr. President?" Tibbets asked. Solemnly, he pulled his nuclear codebook out. Then he removed the dog tags from under his shirt and used a small key on the chain to unlock the codebook.

Before the President could respond, one of the officers behind Tibbets announced, "Sir, we've re-established our link with the *Roosevelt* strike group."

The general turned to look at the new information and saw that all six of the warheads had been successfully intercepted.

The same officer explained, "Sir, the strike group commander says they succeeded in intercepting the warheads targeting them. They said the THAAD in Hawaii destroyed eleven of the twelve warheads fired at them, but it appears one warhead detonated at a high altitude above the island. They believe this was a targeted EMP blast. Right now, the strike group commander says they are tracking close to a hundred CJ-10 long-range cruise missiles inbound to our facilities on Hawaii emanating from the Johnston Atoll."

Turning to face the naval LNO, Tibbets asked, "What about the *Reagan*? Are they able to intercept those cruise missiles?"

The naval officer's face looked ashen as he replied, "No...the *Reagan* strike group has been destroyed. Two of the warheads got through. We haven't been able to make contact with anyone from the strike group."

General Markus called out to Tibbets. "General, we just spoke with the Brits. They are piping us into their satellite system right now. The NSA should have a new picture for us of the Pacific shortly."

"Did the Ministry of Defence tell you how it's looking? Do we have more missiles inbound?" asked Tibbets. He hoped this was it.

The President jumped in. "They said Guam's gone. At least two of the warheads hit the island. There isn't anything left. They also said Pine Gap was knocked out. The missile aimed at Australia hit most of the country with a series of EMPs detonating at fifty thousand feet and thirty thousand feet. It looks like a huge part of the country is going to be in the dark."

Then, just as the NSA got the British satellite system linked to the DoD, the entire system went down. Not only did they lose their momentary picture, but now the entire Department of Defense NIPR, SIPR, and JWICS communication systems had blacked out.

The President shouted, "Oh my God! Seriously, what is happening? Why are our screens blacked out again?"

General Norman's face suddenly appeared on the screen to answer the question. "Mr. President, one of my folks is telling me we just got hit with some sort of cyberattack. We're not sure how it happened, but it appears it's trying to take our communications system down." The general paused for a moment as someone off-camera handed him a sheet of paper, which he quickly scanned before returning his gaze to Sachs. "Mr. President, I was just informed that AT&T, Verizon, T-Mobile, and Sprint are all experiencing a massive cyberattack against their cellular and internet networks as well."

General Tibbets broke back into the conversation. "Mr. President, the Chinese just hit us with a concerted nuclear first-strike attack against our forces in the Pacific and the continental US. They're now in the process of blinding and muting our military by taking out our satellites, cellular communications and email system. They're shutting down our civilian internet and cellular networks, which will cripple our ability to communicate domestically and inhibit our government's ability to govern and manage the country. I must recommend that you order an immediate counterstrike against the Chinese and their military."

General Norman from STRATCOM announced, "I second that recommendation. We certainly have our justification, sir."

There was a short pause as the President talked briefly with General Markus. Finally, Sachs looked back to General Tibbets. "I agree, General," he confirmed. "It's time to hit back."

Tibbets nodded. "Has General Markus advised you on some possible scenarios? Do you have a particular one you'd like to discuss?"

At this point, Tibbets had flipped open his launch book, which had a multitude of different attack options. He thumbed his way over to the China tab, revealing the target package names that had been preselected.

"Right now, I'm leaning towards Red Diamond Five," Sachs responded. "What are your thoughts?"

Tibbets moved his finger down the page until he found the target package the President had suggested. Red Diamond Five was an attack on PLA Rocket Force silos, storage and launch facilities, command-and-control bunkers, and PLA group headquarters throughout the country.

Yeah, this should neutralize them from launching any further nuclear attacks on us, Tibbets thought.

General Tibbets looked back up at Sachs. "I concur, Mr. President. This is a well-measured response. It'll hit them hard and send the right message." He paused for a second before he added, "Mr. President, I highly recommend that you try to get through to the Russian president and inform him of what we're about to do. I don't want them to think this attack may be directed at them. Tell them we are retaliating against the Chinese attack on our soil, and although we don't want to involve them in this issue, if they attempt to intercede or prevent us from striking back, we will not hesitate to attack them as well."

"That's a good call, General," President Sachs answered. "Yes. I'll place a call to him immediately. If that bastard tries to intervene, we'll unleash our missiles on them. Let's go ahead and get the ball rolling, Tibbets. I want to know when our response is on the way." Then Sachs resumed his conversation with some of the others in the room with him.

Just as Tibbets was about to execute the President's directive, Sachs added, "Oh and General, I want you to hit that dam. We warned them what would happen if they attacked us. They detonated a nuke on US soil and took out Guam. I want the Three Gorges Dam included in our response."

****

Guam
Andersen Air Force Base

Major Jillian Heinkel of the 11th Bomb Squadron grabbed for her flight helmet as she followed her copilot out the door of the building. As she burst through the door and onto the parking ramp of the flight line, she heard the air raid klaxons wailing. Their high-pitched scream swelled before fading out and then repeating the sequence.

Running towards her B-52H bomber, Heinkel saw that the ground crew was already pulling the engine covers off and removing the chocks from the wheels. Another airman rolled out the aircraft generation equipment and hooked it up to the plane, ready to give the engines the jolt of electricity they needed until the aircraft was able to provide its own power.

As Major Heinkel raced to her baby, the sudden roar of a bomber racing down the runway at full power only caused her to run harder. The two bombers that had been strip alert were already getting themselves airborne. She needed to hurry.

When she reached the ladder that would allow her to climb into the bomber, she had to wait a moment for her copilot, who had beat her to the aircraft, to finish getting in. Heinkel looked back. Behind her, the rest of the flight crew was huffing and puffing from the mad dash they had just made from the ready room.

Once she had climbed aboard the bomber, Major Heinkel raced up the second flight of steps to get to the flight deck. She practically jumped into her seat. Her copilot was already going through his reduced checklist to get them ready. Heinkel had just fastened her helmet on and attached it to the aircraft's coms and life support system when she heard the first radio call.

"All Jiggs elements, this is not a drill! I say again, this is not a drill," said the commanding voice of her squadron leader. "The command post is tracking multiple ballistic missiles inbound. All Jiggs elements are to get airborne and head to your rally points and await further orders."

As Heinkel began flipping some power switches and prepared to start the main engines, her copilot asked, "What the hell is going on, Major? Missiles inbound?" His voice cracked and trembled with fear.

Without turning to look at the junior officer, Heinkel pushed the start button to activate her engines. "Hey, snap out of it," she quipped. "Just do your job, and let's get this bird airborne. We can talk about it once we're off the ground. Right now, I need you focused on the task at hand, got it?" She knew she didn't have time to get distracted or hold his hand through this crisis.

Moments later, the engines fired up. She revved them up a bit and then released the parking brakes, allowing them to start rolling down the parking ramp.

Major Heinkel depressed the talk button on her coms system. "This is Big Bella. We're heading down taxiway One Alpha. Permission for immediate takeoff?"

A moment later, her radio crackled. "Tower to Big Bella. Permission granted. Hurry up. You don't have much time until impact," the voice said. Heinkel could hear the fear in the man's voice even over the radio. She knew they were scared because whatever was headed their way, they weren't going to be able to hide from it. At least she stood a chance of getting out of Dodge.

Heinkel turned the lumbering aircraft hard as she moved off the taxiway and onto the runway. She felt as though the plane almost tipped over to one side, and she knew the wing wheel was probably straining severely from the maneuver she had just done.

"Major! I'm showing a missile impact in less than sixty seconds!" called out the radar control officer below the flight deck.

Heinkel pushed the engine throttle all the way forward as she gave the engines as much power as she possibly could. Instantly, the massive bomber lurched forward as it sped down the runway, breaking every procedure in the book on how to take off without damaging the aircraft or its engines. Right now, she was just hoping and praying they had enough time to get off the runway before that missile hit. She also prayed it wasn't a nuclear missile headed their direction, or none of this would matter—they'd be vaporized before they got far enough away.

Big Bella raced down the runway—palm trees and hangars whipping past her window with blinding speed. She felt the wings start to lift as her speed continued to climb. She pulled back on the wheel and felt the bomber's nose start to lift up. It took a second or two more before she felt the plane leave the runway and begin to claw its way into the sky.

The landscape below her began to change as their bomber left the island and made it over the water. Her altimeter read five hundred feet and still climbing.

"Brace for impact!" shouted the radar operator moments later.

As Major Heinkel continued to will her aircraft further away from Andersen Air Force Base, everything suddenly whited out. What had moments before been a bright blue sky with a few clouds interspersed was suddenly bright as the sun. In that instant, Jillian Heinkel knew she was dead. They hadn't made it far enough outside the blast wave.

Fractions of a second later, Big Bella was violently tossed through the air and then ripped apart by the force of the nuclear detonation.

******

Johnston Atoll

Colonel Peng watched the horizon as he listened to 690 AM on the radio, a news talk station broadcasting out of Hawaii. Peng smiled when he heard the emergency alert noise, which reminded him of a fax signal, interrupted the broadcast.

"This is the emergency alert broadcasting system. This is not a test. All residents of the Hawaiian Islands are advised that a ballistic missile has been detected targeting the island chain. Again, this is not a test. Please seek immediate shelter and stay away from any glass windows. This has been a message from the emergency alert broadcasting system."

Peng felt a feeling of glee considering the fear and panic that must be spreading across the islands. The people of Hawaii had nowhere to go and no way of avoiding the nuclear fire that was about to rain down on them.

"The missile to our south should be impacting shortly," announced a young captain to the officers who had gathered around him.

They all looked to the south, waiting with bated breath for the flash that would indicate a successful detonation. They were more than eight hundred miles away, so the flash wouldn't blind them, and the EMP wouldn't reach them. The seconds ticked by anxiously. Then they saw a bright flash off in the horizon, like a prolonged lightning strike.

"I wish we could see the mushroom cloud," commented one of the officers.

Turning to look at the soldier manning the computer terminal, Peng asked, "What about the other missile, the one north of Hawaii?"

The man had a perplexed look on his face. "Sir, it appears that all but one of the warheads were intercepted."

Grunting at the info, Peng asked, "Do we know which one hit?"

The soldier nodded. "It looks like the EMP got through, but the others didn't."

Peng let out a sigh of relief. He knew the EMP would help them in their own attack. However, he had hoped one of the nukes would have nailed the American fleet at Pearl

Harbor. They really needed to take out those remaining carriers that were in port for repairs.

Sensing the other officers staring at him, waiting for his orders, Peng exclaimed, "Prepare our missiles to launch. The Americans may have taken a lot of our warheads out, but I'd wager they expended a lot of their missile interceptors to do it. That means more of our own missiles should have a better chance of getting through. I want our missiles ready to start firing in the next five minutes."

With his orders issued, the Chinese prepared to land their second blow against the American fleet and naval facilities on Hawaii.

****

Ojos Negros, Mexico

The air in the bunker felt warm and stifling as sweat ran down the side of General Han Lei's face. He was nervous—more nervous than at any other time in his military career. His life trajectory rode on what would happen today.

As he rubbed his hands together, General Han could feel the sweat forming on them. He listened to the various news feeds and other data being supplied to them from around the world, but suddenly realized his right leg had started bouncing up and down under the table due to nerves. He surveyed the other faces of the 38th PLA Army Group around him—they all looked just as nervous—unsure if they were about to die in the next thirty minutes or if their ruse was really going to work.

When they had fired off their EMP missiles at California and Texas, they had known the Americans would retaliate. What they didn't know was whether the Americans would try and hit them with their own EMP weapons or if they would attempt to burn them all to ash in a nuclear fireball.

For more than a week, they had been carefully moving most of their vehicles to a series of large abandoned warehouses in the city of Ojos Negros, some 97 miles south of the California border, and the town of Chihuahua, 235 miles south of El Paso, Texas. They were keeping their army close to where they had previously established a military encampment, hoping the Americans wouldn't notice they'd moved their troops and equipment a few days before the EMP attack.

Meanwhile, they had worked with the Mexican government and army to build up massive military encampments around Guadalupe, north of the port city of Ensenada, and Galeana, near the Texas border, to make it appear like they were gearing up to attack from those two points. The Chinese and Mexicans had spent the last three weeks making those encampments appear to be the main staging areas for the 38th and 65th PLA Army Groups. Hundreds of radio transmissions were generated daily from the camps, along with other fake communications. They had even moved mock tanks and artillery by collaborating with news outlets and TV and movie producers to incorporate special effects and launch a coordinated disinformation campaign.

Meanwhile, both army groups had been dispersed into a couple of other cities further away. General Han had chosen to hunker down with the 38th Army Group in a series of caves and bunkers while their vehicles were hidden in specially designed warehouses that would protect them from the effects of the EMP.

"I sure hope the Americans don't find us," one of the officers commented nervously.

Turning to look at his men, General Han puffed his chest out a bit as he spoke, attempting to project more confidence than he currently felt. "We have done all we can. Our fate has already been decided. We will either live and fight, or we will die today. If the Americans do attack and we survive, I'm going to need you to rally your men quickly to retrieve our equipment and get it ready to move. Our orders are to invade America in forty-eight hours."

****

California-Mexico Border
Naval Outlying Landing Field, Imperial Beach

Corporal Isaacs of the 11th Marine Expeditionary Unit looked at the control panel of the V-22 Osprey. He held his breath as he depressed the power button. A second later, he was rewarded by a series of buttons lighting up and the whirring sound of the generator starting the engine.

Looking out the cockpit, he flashed a quick thumbs-up and smiled to the others outside. After swapping out a circuit board that wasn't as hardened as the manufacturer had led the Marines to believe, they were back in business.

Shortly after the Chinese had detonated the EMP, the mechanics that were responsible for the maintenance of the Marine Medium Tiltrotor Squadron 163 swiftly ran through a systems check of the squadron's V-22 Ospreys. They soon discovered that a few control boards responsible for providing the engines and the rest of the aircraft with power had shorted out. Fortunately for them, this was a part that often had problems, so their supply section kept a lot of them on hand. They were doubly lucky in that the supply building had been hardened against EMPs back during the Cold War era.

As the aircraft mechanics went to work getting the squadron's helicopters operational again, the motor pool mechanics likewise did their best to prepare the 3/5 Marines' LAVs, AAVs, and JLTVs for combat. No one knew for sure when the Chinese would attack, but after they had hit the area with an EMP, it was only a matter of when, not if.

****

Staff Sergeant Mack saw Lance Corporal Pyro shifting uncomfortably in his peripheral vision. "Staff Sergeant, you really think the Chinese are going to invade soon?" Pyro asked.

Mack lifted his head to look at his troop more carefully before he spat a stream of tobacco juice on the ground. "Does it matter, Pyro?" he asked dismissively. "I'd rather be shooting and killing Chinese than stuck pulling garrison duty in LA or dealing with those CDF militia types."

"My friend that works over at headquarters told me the Chinese nuked one of our carrier strike groups—took the *Reagan* right out."

Staff Sergeant Mack ignored the comment. He'd spotted movement over to the side and had pulled his field glasses back up to his eyes.

"What do you see?" Pyro asked nervously.

"Three o'clock, about twenty meters past the fence— I think I spotted a soldier."

Looking through the more advanced spotter scope, Pyro scanned the dilapidated buildings, alleyways, and homes that were near the border wall. "Got it," he confirmed. "You're right. It looks like a soldier. He's wearing some kind of body armor. You want me to send up the drone?"

"No. They'll hear it. But I'm calling this in," Mack said. Then he reached down to hit the talk button on his radio.

"Loki Six, this is Loki One Six. We've got movement along the border. Sector Three Delta. How copy?"

A few seconds went by before they got a reply.

"One Six, this is Loki Six. Copy that. Movement in sector Three Delta. What do you have for us?"

"Tell them I now see six soldiers," Pyro called out as he continued to look through his spotter scope. "It looks like two of them are setting up some optics on the roof of that building just to the left of the blue liquor store."

Mack passed on the message before he asked, "Do you want us to attack these guys or continue to observe and report?" Truthfully, Sergeant Mack hoped they'd be given permission to engage them. He didn't like the idea of another sniper team setting up a position a few hundred meters away from him. The slightest movement on their part could result in a bullet.

A minute went by this time before they got a reply.

"One-Six, you're cleared to engage. Report back when you've neutralized the hostiles."

Kicking Pyro's foot slightly, Mack whispered, "We're cleared to attack. Let's figure out where they're all at before we take out that team on the roof. I don't want to start shooting and suddenly find out there's a damn platoon of them nearby, and we just didn't see them."

Lance Corporal Pyro nodded and went back to looking for enemy soldiers in his scope. While Pyro was busy, Mack decided to crawl out of his position and make sure the rest of his squad knew what was going on.

When Sergeant Mack found their resident sharpshooter, Private First Class Tapper, he smiled. "Tapper, just the man I was looking for," Mack remarked. "I want you to set up your long gun next to Pyro. If we can, I'd like to try and take these guys out with our long guns so we can avoid attracting more attention than necessary."

Tapper nodded and dutifully went to work. Soon, they were both sitting next to Lance Corporal Pyro, scanning for additional targets. Unexpectedly, a single shot rang out. None of Mack's soldiers took their eyes off the targets in front of them, but they heard the radio squawk. The friendly sniper team further down the line and to their left was engaging a target.

Sergeant Mack continued to peer through his scope and saw that the enemy soldiers had set up a high-powered optical lens on the top of the building. One of the hostiles was looking through the lens while another soldier nearby wrote something down on a clipboard. If Mack had to guess, these guys were range-finding certain terrain features and possible routes for an attacker to use.

Speaking barely above a whisper to Tapper, Mack ordered, "Hit the guy with the clipboard first. He looks like he may be an officer."

Taking a deep breath, Tapper slowly let it out and then pulled the trigger.

Bang.

Mack saw the soldier with the clipboard flop to the ground like a broken doll. Tapper worked the bolt quickly, ejecting the spent casing and slamming a fresh round into the chamber. In a fraction of a second, he had the rifle aimed at the soldier looking through the spotting scope and pulled the trigger a second time.

Bang.

Sergeant Mack witnessed the second soldier being thrown backward from the force of the bullet as it hit his head. As bloody mist and chunks of brain matter splattered on the other soldiers on the roof, they dove for cover.

Staying calm, Tapper moved his reticle down to the ground floor, where two other soldiers were standing guard. Sergeant Mack had noticed that those men had moved inside the building; however, one of them was looking through a window, trying to see if he could spot what was going on. Mack watched in suspense as his squad's best shooter sent another round across the US-Mexican border, taking the man out.

"Damn good shot, Tapper," Mack praised.

Private First Class Tapper was still somewhat new to his squad. He hailed from Wyoming and was an avid elk hunter. Clearly, shooting long-range game had helped him become an excellent shot.

"The guys on the roof have come out to play again," called out Lance Corporal Pyro, who had continued to watch the building with the spotter scope.

Tapper shifted his aim.

I hope he can take 'em out before they call an artillery strike on us, thought Sergeant Mack.

Bang.

The round flew flat and true, slamming right into the spotting lens and into the face of the enemy soldier who'd been looking through it.

"Hot damn! That was a good shot, Private!" exclaimed one of the Marines in their squad.

Before any of them could say anything else, a machine gun opened fire further down the line. Turning to look at what was going on a few hundred meters to their left, Mack saw one of the fireteams was exchanging gunfire with at least a squad-sized element of enemy soldiers on the opposite side of the border.

A minute later, the small skirmish had already escalated into a much larger clash. A platoon-sized element was closing in on the lone Marine machine-gun position.

At least the fireteam is positioned in a good spot overlooking the border, thought Sergeant Mack. If an enemy unit was going to cross, they'd have to pass under heavy fire from that position.

As the shooting continued to escalate, Mack heard a call for a fire mission come through over the radio. The higher-ups must not have wanted to tip off the enemy that they had a battery of 155mm Howitzers not too far away because they opted to hit the enemy with mortars from their heavy weapons platoon.

Soon the telltale whistling flew overhead toward the enemy. The first mortar slammed into a building the enemy soldiers were using for cover. A column of smoke and debris climbed into the sky. A few more mortar rounds landed in the area, damaging other nearby structures. Shortly after the dust settled, the shooting ended.

****

From the *Daily Mail*:

The world stands aghast at China's use of nuclear bombs and electromagnetic pulse weapons. Yesterday, the Chinese government detonated two separate EMP devices. One, which was released just north of San Diego, California, has disabled the power for much of Southern California and has destroyed most electronic devices and equipment in the vicinity. The second EMP device was detonated over Oahu and is thought to have been targeting the American military bases around Pearl Harbor, Hawaii.

In addition, six additional nuclear weapons were detonated by Chinese forces against the US. One nuclear device targeted the Arizona city of Yuma along the American Southwest border. Another hit a critical munitions factory on the northeast side of the state of Oklahoma. Two nuclear devices destroyed the USS *Reagan* carrier strike group, and two additional nuclear weapons destroyed the island territory and American forward military bases on Guam.

During this unprecedented nuclear and EMP attack by the Chinese, the Australian city of Alice Springs was also hit by a high-altitude EMP device, causing a blackout across much of the Australian Northwest Territory. It is believed the Chinese were targeting the joint Australian-US electronic spy base at Pine Gap.

The US government has confirmed that the Chinese attempted to detonate a total of 36 nuclear weapons against US forces and American cities. Most of these warheads were successfully intercepted by the US Army's THAAD missile defense system.

Thirty-two minutes into the nuclear attack by the Chinese, President Jonathan Sachs ordered a nuclear response on the People's Republic of China. The US hit various Chinese nuclear missile bases, storage facilities, and other military bases associated with China's nuclear weapons program. American nuclear missiles also hit more than a dozen People's Liberation Army military headquarters and other command and control centers. In addition, the Americans also used two tactical nuclear weapons on Chinese military formations in Mexico. It is unclear how many casualties the Chinese or Mexicans have sustained during the nuclear counterattack.

President Sachs further ordered a nuclear attack on the Three Gorges Dam in China as a part of the American retaliation. When the dam collapsed, it released 22 cubic kilometers of water into the Yangtze River and valley below. A wall of water as high as 100 meters raced down the valley toward the Chinese cities of Yichang, Jingzhou, Changsha, and

Wuhan. It is unclear how many people may have died in the ensuing flood, or what the damage has been to these cities. It is expected that destruction is going to be severe, and the loss of life will probably be in the tens of millions, if not more.

United Nations Secretary-General Johann Behr has pleaded with both sides to refrain from further use of nuclear weapons and has decried their use by both nations.

****

Ramona, California

"Do you think the power will come back on soon?" Julie asked her husband, Bill.

Their six-year-old daughter donned her most convincing pouty face and exclaimed, "I want to watch *Masha and the Bear*!"

Bill looked at his daughter, trying his best to be brave for her. "Molly-bear, remember when Daddy said the power may not come back on for a while?" he asked.

His daughter looked up at him and nodded but didn't say anything.

"I don't know when it'll come back on, honey," Bill said, gently hugging her. "But tomorrow we're going to go on a little hike. We're going to go stay with Auntie Jessy. Remember?"

"Yeah. Can I bring my Momma Bear with me?" she asked. Her face showed genuine concern at the possibility of leaving her giant stuffy behind.

"We'll see. I need to go outside and work on the truck, OK? Stay in here and help your mother." She nodded and grabbed her mama's hand.

Bill put his shoes on and headed into the garage. He opened the large door so the natural light could flood in. He still had a few things he needed to fix on the old 1973 Ford F-100 XLT. It had been a hobby of his since he was a teenager, fixing up old cars.

Bill's dad had been a Vietnam vet and an alcoholic. Their relationship had been pretty volatile growing up, but when his dad had quit drinking his freshman year in high school, things had changed for the better. To help make up for lost time, his dad had bought an old Ford pickup truck. Despite being an alcoholic, his father had maintained a job as an ASC master tech mechanic; it was the one thing he had always been good at, aside from drinking. When he had given up alcohol, he'd sought to rebuild his relationship with his son by teaching him how to work on trucks.

During that freshman year of high school, they'd rebuilt that truck and then sold it during the summer. His dad had let him keep the money from the sale, and Bill had bought two more old trucks—one to fix up and use to drive himself to school, and the other to sell and make some money. Fixing up cars and trucks became a bonding experience for them. When Bill had turned eighteen, he had gone to a technical school and learned how to become an even better mechanic.

What Bill liked most was working on the cars built before 1977, before the automakers began to introduce computer chips into them. Vehicles continued to get more complicated and harder to work on with each passing decade. When Bill had found this 1973 F-100 truck on Facebook Marketplace four months ago, he'd swiftly snatched it up. He'd just gotten the last major set of parts he needed to make it run two weeks ago. Judging by what was going on in the world, it couldn't have come at a better time.

Bill glanced up and saw his neighbor from down the road approaching his driveway. "Hey, John. How are things going?" asked Bill.

John smiled as he walked up toward the garage. "They're going all right. I thought I'd come over here and check in on you guys."

Bill wiped some grease off his hands as he walked up to John. The two shook hands. "I was listening to that little AM radio you gave me yesterday," Bill said. "They say all of Southern California is without power."

John nodded. "I was talking with a guy on the HAM radio earlier this morning. He lives over in Utah. He was telling me the Chinese detonated an EMP over Southern California—hit Arizona and Oklahoma with a nuke as well."

Bill let out a low whistle. They'd heard bits and pieces of what had happened a couple of days ago, but nothing definitive. One of their other neighbors a few houses down the road was a retired Marine. He'd said the Chinese were probably going to invade California soon. He also had an older car that still worked. He'd packed up his wife and some of their belongings and they'd left a day ago. He told them they should work on getting out of the area as soon as they could.

"You think you're going to have it running today?" asked John as he leaned up against the workbench.

"I think so. I just need to put a few finishing touches on it."

"What are you doing for fuel?" John asked.

"I siphoned the gas out of our other cars. Got enough for a full tank on this thing and a couple of five-gallon cans to bring along with us. Are you and Jill going to come with us?" Bill inquired. He'd offered to give them a ride out of the area if they wanted.

Smiling, John nodded. "We will. I've got a pistol and a deer rifle I'll bring with us. I don't have a lot of ammo, but hopefully we won't need it."

Bill grabbed a wrench and tightened something before he replied. "That's good, John. I hate to say this, but I don't even own a gun. I'll be glad to have you bring yours. Just make sure you get your stuff over here tonight. We're going to leave at dawn tomorrow. I don't want to be on the road at night if possible."

"Makes sense to me. It's starting to get crazy at night. I heard a few gunshots last night. I think things are starting to fall apart the longer we go without power."

Bill shook his head in disgust and set his wrench down on his tool chest. "This is crazy, John. Everything that's going on right now…I don't understand it. I don't understand how it's all come to this. I mean, I walked down to Main Street yesterday afternoon to see if the pharmacy was possibly open. I wanted to see if I'd somehow be able to get a refill of Julie's thyroid medication, but the entire place had been looted. I mean, who loots a CVS when the power's been out for two days?"

"People are freaking out. What I'd like to know is when these CDF or National Guard soldiers are going to start helping out. The governor keeps telling us help is on the way, but I've yet to see a single National Guard vehicle or anyone else come to Ramona."

"Yeah. I'm not counting on help to arrive anytime soon," Bill replied. "I'm just glad my wife's built up a six-month supply of Julie's medicine. She'd be dead in a couple of weeks without it. I just hope when we get to Las Vegas, things will be better." He used a rachet to tighten down a bolt.

John rubbed the back of his neck. "Hey, Bill, if you don't mind, we're going to spend the night at your place. I think we all might be safer if we stay together. Also, don't start the truck. I know you'll want to make sure she runs, but it's best to wait and do that tomorrow when we're ready to leave. If you start it now, people will hear it. That could attract some attention we don't need or want."

"Wow, I hadn't even thought about that, John. Good call. Why don't you and Jill start getting your stuff brought over here now then? I want to get this thing loaded up as soon as I get this last thing here finished."

John agreed and left to go back to his house. An hour later, he and his wife came over with two rolling suitcases. They went back to their house and came back with a second load of stuff, only this time they had a small garden cart full. It was packed with five flats of water and a lot of freeze-dried food.

The three of them went to work, loading the bed of the truck with the essentials they'd need for the trip to Vegas. It was roughly a 350-mile journey, and God only knew what they'd encounter along the way. If they were able to use the interstate and there wasn't much traffic, the drive would normally take around six hours, but Bill doubted that would be an option.

Once they had the truck loaded up, they looked over an old AAA road atlas John had and started mapping out their path. Their plan was to travel along the backroads as much as possible, trying to avoid any major cities or towns along the way.

The following morning, just before dawn, everyone loaded up in the pickup. John and Bill were going to sit in the front with their wives and Bill's daughter would sit in the back of the bay right behind the cab. They did their best to keep their supplies below the lip of the bed so as to not attract more attention than they wanted.

When John raised the garage door up, Bill placed the key in the ignition. He was pretty confident it would start. He turned the key and hoped for the best. An instant later, the truck roared to life. Bill put the truck into gear and drove out of the garage. John closed the door and locked it—not that they'd be coming back to their house anytime soon, but still, it felt good to leave it locked.

John climbed in and they started driving out of the neighborhood. Fortunately, the sun had just come up and most people were still sleeping. They made it a few miles down the road before they saw the first signs of life. A couple of people were sitting on their front porch. They nodded toward them as they drove on by, as if they hadn't a care in the world.

For the next hour, they managed to avoid nearly every major city and town along the way, although they knew they'd eventually have to drive along the frontage road of I-10 as they headed to Desert Center. There was a small state road, Highway 177, that would lead them to Highway 62. From there, they'd continue on until they reached Vidal Junction. Then they'd turn onto Highway 95 and stay on that road until they reached Las Vegas.

The scariest moment of the trip was when they reached the frontage road along I-10. The highway was littered with dead vehicles. Cars, trucks, semitrucks…all stopped right where their electronics had fried. They saw some people among the abandoned cars. A few of them tried to flag them down for help, but John insisted they not stop.

"I hate to say it, but chances are, they'd try to rob us and steal the truck," he insisted.

The entire drive along I-10 was nerve-racking. When they eventually made it onto the less-traveled state road, they all breathed a sigh of relief. With such slow going, they did ultimately have to stop for the night. When they did, Bill used the two five-gallon jerry cans and topped off their tank. They had burned through most of their gas having to take all the detours.

It was a long, frigid evening. The next morning, they got back on the road just as the sun started to crest into the sky. It took them another hour until they reached a small town called Searchlight, roughly fifty-two miles south of Vegas.

As they approached the town, they spotted a couple of military vehicles blocking the highway. Bill slowed the truck down as they neared the roadblock. Several soldiers walked out from around the vehicles and held their arms up, signaling for them to stop.

One of the soldiers walked up to them with his rifle at the low ready; the other soldiers had their rifles raised slightly as they covered their friend.

"Morning. Where are you folks headed?" asked the soldier as he eyed them and their vehicle suspiciously.

Bill smiled as he replied, "My sister lives over in Henderson. That's where we're trying to go."

The soldier nodded. "Where did you guys come from?" he asked.

"Ramona. It's a small town in East San Diego County. We've been out of power for a few days now. I needed to try and get my wife and daughter to a safer place. I hope you can understand," Bill replied.

God, I hope this isn't going to be a problem, he wished, eyeing the soldiers' weapons with trepidation.

The soldier's demeanor seemed to soften a bit. "I understand. Word has it the Chinese are going to invade California soon. You probably got out at the right time."

The man stretched as he eyed the contents of the back of the truck. Finally, he announced, "So here is what I'm going to do. I'm going to allow you to pass through and head to Henderson—but nowhere else. We'll write up a travel pass. You'll need to present this to any other checkpoints you come across. We're trying to limit the number of people crossing over into the Las Vegas area right now, especially those coming from California. So what I need you to do is pull over to that parking lane over there. We'll do a quick search of your vehicle, give you ten gallons of gas, and have you on your way, all right?"

Bill nodded, relieved that they'd be allowed to pass through. He followed the other soldiers' directions, and they pulled into one of the vehicle lanes and got out. The soldiers spent a few minutes searching through their meager belongings while a couple of other soldiers questioned them about what they had seen on their way up here. They asked a lot of questions about California CDF units and any signs of Chinese soldiers. Fortunately, Bill and his family hadn't come across any of those two groups.

Half an hour later, they were finally sent on their way. They made it to his sister's house an hour later. She and her husband welcomed them with open arms, along with Bill's neighbor and his wife. They had now officially joined the ranks of internally displaced refugees in their own country.

Chapter 9

Operation Snowman

February 7, 2021

The Ritz-Carlton New York, Central Park

Marshall Tate reviewed the intelligence summary put together for him by some of Page Larson's people. The more he read, the sicker he felt. Tate wanted to vomit, but he knew this was not the time or place. He needed to push through and read this information so he'd be ready for his private meeting with his Secretary of Defense, David Hill, and his National Security Advisor, Page Larson. The three of them were trying to come up with a joint statement responding to this latest round of hostility.

I didn't sign up for this, Tate thought. This wasn't the way he'd been told this would play out. He had to find a way to put an end to this before the country was completely ripped apart.

He couldn't concentrate. Tate decided a moment of procrastination was needed and flipped on the flat-screen TV in his room. A CNN report immediately caught his attention, and he turned the volume up. Soon he sat there transfixed.

The television anchor asked, "Jay, can you explain to the viewers what you're seeing?"

The reporter responded, "Yes. Apparently, earlier this morning, nineteen Republican state legislators and their families were apprehended by state militia and brought to a detention facility outside the city of Milwaukee. The details of what happened next are still a bit murky as we've been unable to confirm exactly what transpired, but what we do know for sure is that the buses that were transporting these individuals were attacked."

The reporter paused, letting out a deep breath. "No one survived the assault. Along with the legislators and their families, eight state militia members that had been transporting these individuals were also killed."

This is getting out of control, Tate thought. He clenched his fist angrily before changing the channel to RT Worldwide. A reporter who looked like he'd been up all night was speaking.

"Looting is running rampant in the city of Los Angeles as all civil functions have completely broken down. The entire southern half of the state is without power. Without electricity, there is no running water, no refrigeration for food or medication, no working traffic lights, and for now, no cellular service. It's pure chaos here. The police are completely overwhelmed."

The anchor asked, "What about the California Civil Defense Force? Or any other government support? Is anyone providing them with assistance in this terrible tragedy?"

"It would appear that the southern half of the state is completely on its own," the reporter answered. "After a large percentage of the California Army National Guard defected back to the US government's control, the California CDF in this part of the state was largely slaughtered by the US Marines when they captured the ports of LA and Long Beach. At this time, the US Marines have not ventured into the city and have primarily remained camped out on the ports and along the US-Mexico border.

"The elements of the California Army National Guard that defected to the Marines are also nowhere to be seen. The last we heard, they were also along the US-Mexico border, working with the Marines to prevent the Chinese from liberating the state from federal control. We received a message via our satellite phone from the governor of the state, pleading with the Chinese to expedite their plans to free them and provide immediate support and assistance to the people of Southern California.

"We'll continue to report on what we're seeing. We anticipate that the Chinese ground forces will make a concerted move to help bring humanitarian assistance to this portion of the state that President Sachs has abandoned."

Disgusted, Tate shut the TV off and went to the bathroom. He closed the door and looked at himself in the mirror. The dark circles under his eyes seemed far more apparent than before, and he wondered if he had developed more gray hair and wrinkles overnight.

Suddenly, he bent over the toilet and puked his guts out. After a few minutes, he had emptied his stomach but continued to dry-heave several more times until he felt like he could finally regain control of himself.

Someone knocked on the bathroom door. "Are you OK, Marshall?" asked his wife.

"I'm fine," he responded, trying to sound calmer than he felt. "I must have eaten something that didn't agree with me." He hoped that the answer would keep her off his case for now.

Tate splashed some water on his face. Then he pulled his razor out and proceeded to shave the evening stubble off. Next, he proceeded to take a very long, hot shower as he wrestled in his mind with what to do.

The jig is up, he thought. *We can't keep doing this.* He couldn't help but be horrified by the realization that millions of people were dying unnecessarily. *All of this so Sachs wouldn't be president a second term?* he wondered. Couldn't his "sponsors" have simply waited him out?

Turning the water off, Tate grabbed for a towel and began to dry himself off. Things started to become clearer in his mind. He knew what he needed to do. Now he just had to figure out how to tell the others and make sure they listened to him.

****

Marshall Tate meandered down the hallway of the Ritz-Carlton, making his way to the series of working offices and briefing rooms that had been set up for his exiled government to use. Each door he walked past represented a staffer running a key part of the administration or a cabinet secretary. Too many of the critical positions remained unfilled—until his government controlled Washington, they only had influence in the liberated states and cities. Even that was fluid as the front lines continued to ebb and flow.

Tate shook his head. Every time he walked through one of these fancy corridors, he couldn't help but feel it was pathetic being in a hotel instead of governing from the White House.

He reached his destination: a smaller briefing room situated in the center of the hallway. Several guards held the door open for him. When he entered the room, those in attendance stood out of respect and stayed at attention until he had taken his seat at the center of the table.

Seated before him were Admiral David Hill, his Secretary of Defense, Page Larson, his National Security Advisor, Richard Isaacson, his Secretary of State, General Ryan Jackman, the head of his military/CDF, and Janey Roberts, his Attorney General. These were his most trusted advisors. Tate surveyed their faces—several of them looked as somber as he felt. He hoped that maybe some of them had come to the same conclusion he had and knew that they couldn't continue to keep this charade up.

Before Marshall could say anything, SecDef Admiral Hill chimed in. "Mr. President, what happened last night was appalling. I...," he stammered. "I don't even know what to say or how to respond. This wasn't part of the plan."

Secretary of State Richard Isaacson pounded his fist on the table. "This was never supposed to be part of the plan!" he yelled. "The Chinese were *supposed* to join the Europeans and invade at the same time. By applying pressure on Sachs from all angles, we were going to force him to realize it was futile to resist. Then he should have resigned. By waiting and then losing their ever-loving minds and using nuclear weapons, they've screwed us all over!"

Attorney General Janey Roberts jumped in. "Have you seen what's happening in California?" she asked, exasperated. "More than half of the state is blacked out—none of their electronics work. I got a call from the governor last night right after this happened, and he told me most of the state was going to fall into anarchy, and he has no way of stopping it. What few National Guard forces he has that are still loyal to him are caught up in conflicts with military forces loyal to Sachs—more than half of his CDF force was wiped out by the Marines last week."

"Yes, we know it's bleak," replied Page Larson nonchalantly, flicking her wrist, "but they'll have to make do."

AG Roberts's face turned crimson. "Are you mad?" she growled. "California represents an enormous block of the constituency that supports us. We need to hold on to the state! Writing them off like you just did will alienate a huge chunk of our voters that backed us at a time when we are still struggling to maintain our legitimacy."

Marshall Tate stood and waved his arms downward. "Let's just take this all down a notch, shall we?" he urged. Both women crossed their arms and stared daggers at each other, but they remained silent for the time being.

Tate turned to his Secretary of State. "What about international aid, Rich?" he asked. "Are there any foreign efforts we could mobilize to help the people in California?"

Page Larson shot him a look that implied she thought this was a tremendously stupid question, but she managed not to say anything aloud.

Richard shook his head. "No, Mr. President. There is no foreign aid that can be sent to California. For one, it's an active warzone right now, so no aid organization is going to want to get involved. Second, while we largely control things on the ground out west, we do not control the skies. We don't really have an Air Force to speak of, and unfortunately, our UN allies who had an air force have been soundly defeated."

He sighed. "Sir, I don't like this any more than you, but Ms. Larson is right. The people in California are largely on their own until the Chinese are able to break through the Marines at the border. Once they have captured San Diego and Los Angeles, they can begin to restore order and bring in help."

Lieutenant General Ryan Jackman leaned forward. "Richard, when you spoke with the Chinese, did they give you an estimate of when they will be launching their main offensive?" he pressed.

"Soon was all they told me."

Jackman snorted and shook his head. He and Admiral Hill exchanged nervous glances.

Tate couldn't let the interplay between them go unaddressed. "Secretary Hill, General Jackman—I know we don't have General McKenzie with us, but can you give me an update on how things are progressing on our side of the equation?"

The two looked at each other for a moment before Hill spoke up first. "Mr. President, the CDF continues to grow following your inspirational inauguration speech. We've grown our ranks from approximately thirty-five thousand to over one hundred and sixty thousand members. The biggest challenge we have is equipping and training them, and keeping them supplied so they can fight—not to mention there have been issues keeping them under our control."

"What exactly do you *mean* by that?" Tate retorted.

Admiral Hill tilted his head toward General Jackman as if to tell him, "You take this one."

General Jackman let out his breath in a huff. "Mr. President, we've broken the CDF down into battalion-level commands and largely kept them local. The challenge I'm having right now is being able to mobilize the units. For example, how do I move a unit from Boston down to New Jersey to help the New York and New Jersey CDF battalions fight federal forces around Trenton? The chain of command becomes muffled. Also, in terms of 'control,' we do have some issues keeping this relatively green force disciplined when pressed by the federal Army—at times, they can tend to evaporate. Some have also gone off on their own to carry out unsanctioned attacks."

Tate held up a hand. "Hold up. What do you mean 'unsanctioned' attacks?"

Jackman sighed. "OK. Here's an example, Mr. President. Yesterday, one of my battalion commanders in Ohio called me directly and told me he had to relieve one of his company commanders and place half of the unit in jail. They'd apparently taken it upon themselves to get some political payback, and a group of them went to a neighborhood outside of the Toledo area and raped and killed as many people as they could in a day."

Aghast, AG Janey Roberts blurted out, "They did *what*? How many people were attacked before this battalion commander stopped it?!"

General Jackman shifted uncomfortably in his seat. "I, um…the details are still a bit sketchy, but he told me they probably killed somewhere around three or four hundred people. As to the number of people raped, I honestly couldn't even give you an idea."

Tate leaned forward. "And what have you done to these men?" he asked pointedly.

"Um. Nothing yet," Jackman mumbled. "I mean, I know it's bad what they did, but we need all the fighters and help we can get right now. I don't think you understand how precarious the situation is on the ground, sir."

Admiral Hill quickly added, "Mr. President, we all agree this was a terrible act of barbarism and it shouldn't have happened, but let's be honest—this is a civil war. This isn't the first atrocity, and it won't be the last. We can't come down on units every time we hear of something like this. The fact is, we need units like this to help us win this war."

Tate shook his head in disgust. "We may need units like this to fight and win, but we'll never win the peace if we conduct the war like this. I want it to stop. As a matter of fact, I want an example made of these men. Execute them.

Make it known that this type of behavior is not tolerated. We are liberators, not a raping, marauding army to be feared."

Page Larson stood. "Sir, could I have a moment to speak with you privately?" she asked.

Tate paused for a few seconds, then agreed. "All right, everyone. Clear the room for a minute, please."

There was a bustle of activity as the rest of the advisors stood and walked out. When it was just the two of them, Page moved around the table so that she was sitting in the chair next to Tate. Looking at him, she asked, "What's the problem, Marshall?"

"What do you mean, Page?" Tate asked, crossing his arms.

"You can't have units like this executed," she asserted. "David's right. We need units like them to win this war."

He shook his head. "No. Not that kind of win," he insisted. "I didn't sign up for this, Page. This isn't what we agreed to."

Page sat back in her chair and laughed. "Of course you did, Marshall," she said icily. "You said you'd do anything to become President. You said you'd go along with the plan and you'd do as you're told. In exchange, you'd be made President and serve two terms."

Stiffening at the comment, Marshall quickly shot back, "The plan obviously hasn't worked, or we'd be having this discussion in the White House and not in New York."

"Yes. Things haven't gone exactly according to plan, but that doesn't mean we abandon the strategy," she insisted. "The dominoes have started to fall, and none of us can stop them. We need to see our piece through to the end."

"And what is that end, Page? The Chinese controlling half of America? They clearly had a different agenda than what everyone else agreed to. They let the UN force die on the vine and waited to attack until Sachs's forces had largely defeated the UN. Now they can come in like a knight on a shining white horse to liberate us from the evil Jonathan Sachs, and in exchange, they get what…the West Coast and the American Southwest in compensation?"

Page sat there for a moment, calculating her response. Finally, she sighed. "If this civil war ends and you are President, will it matter if the Chinese control Texas and California? You'll still control the rest of the country. The Chinese will have the resources and people to help us rebuild. You'll be the fearless leader who fought and defeated a horrible tyrant in the White House. You'll go down as one of the greatest American presidents in history, the man who saved the Republic."

"And all it'll have cost me is two of America's most valuable states in exchange?" Tate asked incredulously. "Page, you are striking a bargain too one-sided for anyone to accept. Even if I did win, the American people would never settle for the Chinese controlling the American Southwest. They'd demand they leave, or that we fight until we force them to."

Page leaned forward and fixed Tate with a steely look. "Marshall, if you aren't willing to see this plan through to the end and honor the bargain that's been struck to make you President, then another person will take your place. Is that understood?" Page stared at him for a second before her expression softened to a smile. "Just continue to play your part. You're doing great."

****

February 9, 2021
Monticello, Illinois

First Lieutenant Trey Regan had just been promoted to captain. He had been given command of the newly reconstituted Bravo Company as the 198th Armor Regiment geared up for the much-anticipated Midwest counterattack. They were going to retake the central Midwest and push the

European and Russian forces back across the Canadian border. Regan was excited at the prospect of helping to finally defeat this foreign invasion.

Most of Regan's original company, along with Echo Company, had been slaughtered during the mad dash of the first couple weeks of the war by the German-Dutch Division Schnelle Kräfte. After nearly a ten-day lull in fighting, their brigade had been augmented with a few hundred new recruits from basic and advanced training, along with thirty-six new M1A2 main battle tanks from a cold storage depot. Having been reconstituted and brought up to ninety percent strength, they'd been moved to a position between Decatur and Champaign, Illinois.

The regimental briefing had just finished a few minutes earlier, but Captain Regan wanted to get a better picture of what was going on all around them, so he headed to the part of the tent where a map board was hanging from some five-fifty cord. He stared at it blankly for a moment before the overall strategy began to make more sense to him.

To the left flank of their current location, their sister regiment, the 137th Infantry, was waiting in the city of Decatur. They'd advance behind his regiment's tanks once they broke through the enemy lines. Screening to their right was 1st Squadron, 98th Cavalry Regiment. They were hunkered down in Monticello and would cover their right flank as they advanced to contact. Once Regan's regiment made a hole in the enemy's lines, their two sister regiments would rush through behind them. Following their advance was 1st Battalion, 155th Infantry Regiment. They were going to act as their mobile reserve should they get bogged down in a particular spot.

The 2nd Battalion, 198th Armor Regiment would accompany Regan's unit as they worked to find, fix, and then destroy the German-Dutch army somewhere in front of them.

Colonel Beasley walked up behind him. "It looks more complicated than it really is," he remarked.

Regan shrugged. "I just wanted to get a better picture of what we're headed into," he explained.

"When I was at the division meeting last night, the G2 said the bulk of the German armor was hunkered down around this point here," Colonel Beasley said, pointing to the area of contention.

Regan saw that the spot was a large patch of flat farmland stretching between Bloomington and Onarga. "That's good tank country. Nice, flat, and wide open."

Beasley grunted. "It sure is. That's why you guys are going to have to stay frosty, Regan. I don't have to tell you not to underestimate these German tankers. They're better tankers than the Russians we first fought. They also know if we break through their lines here, we may be able to roll their entire line up all the way back to Kankakee. If we do that, we'll be in spitting distance from Gary, Indiana, and we can cut off their entire force in northern Illinois and Wisconsin."

Regan turned to look at Colonel Beasley. "We'll find the bastards, sir. And then we'll kill 'em all."

****

As he walked back, Regan saw that Sergeant First Class Miller had finished painting four new rings on the barrel of their tank. There was a total of twenty-two of them now, each one representing an armor kill they'd managed since the beginning of the war.

When Regan had been promoted to captain, one of the first things he'd done was get the brigade commander to promote Miller two grades, making him an E-7. That way, Miller could help him manage the company better. Regan wanted and needed an experienced tank commander in the vehicle with him when the shooting started so he could hand off the duties of fighting the tank while he coordinated the rest of the company.

Miller heard Regan approach and turned around. "When do we push off?" he asked. He hopped down from the turret and immediately began to help one of the other guys tie down a couple of five-gallon jerry cans of water to the rear of the turret.

"Two hours," Captain Regan replied. "Two more hours, and we finally get this show on the road."

Corporal Tipman stuck his head out of the gunner's hatch of the turret. "Hey, Miller. Can you see if we can get a couple more sabot rounds? I still have room for three more in the locker."

"That's Sergeant or Sergeant First Class Miller, Tipman—not 'hey, Miller.' Got it?"

Corporal Tipman sighed. "Yes, Sergeant," he answered, annoyed but appropriately respectful. "Sergeant, can you please check on getting us some additional sabot rounds?" he asked.

Sergeant Miller smiled. "Yes, Corporal," he answered. "I will go check on getting us a few extra rounds. Help Jaysic get these water cans loaded in the cage and make sure you guys have that new camouflage netting properly secured."

Miller turned to Captain Regan. "I'll be back shortly, sir. I'm going to go hunt down some more tank rounds. You need me for anything else?"

"No, Sergeant. I'm OK," Regan responded. "Make sure you're back in thirty minutes though, OK? I'm going to go over our objectives with the rest of the company, and I want you there."

Miller nodded, then took off to find some additional tank rounds to top off their stores.

****

Looking at his watch, Regan saw it was now 0934 hours. They were thirty-four minutes late in starting this new offensive, and he was growing more agitated by the minute. Just as he was about to pick up the radio and inquire with headquarters as to what the holdup was, he heard the rumble of artillery further behind them.

Captain Regan poked his head out of the turret. Behind them, their artillery, the 2-114th field artillery regiment, had finally started the show. The 155mm M109 self-propelled Paladins were going to hit the known and suspected enemy tank positions with a short barrage before the regiment kicked off their attack.

Miller popped his head out of the gunner's hatch to see what Regan was looking at. "It's about time they started firing," Miller commented. "Those freaking gun bunnies are always late."

Captain Regan turned back to the front and lifted his field glasses to his eyes. He couldn't see where the artillery rounds were hitting, but he still felt the urge to look anyway. "Agreed," he remarked. "Time to get this show on the road."

Regan slipped back inside the turret and depressed the talk button on his radio. He had enough experience to wait a second for the familiar beep indicating the SINCGARS had synced before he started talking. "Dixie Six to all Dixie elements: let's roll," Regan announced.

Time for the Mississippi Guard to go kick some ass, he thought to himself.

Regan switched to the vehicle intercom. "Driver, head to Waypoint One. Keep us moving at twenty-five miles per hour and watch for obstacles."

With the order given, the tank lurched forward, and they took up the lead position in the arrow formation. Regan knew his tank should probably be further back in the formation, but he didn't care. He firmly believed that you led from the front. Regan had read somewhere that General Patton used to like to ride in the lead tank or have a jeep lead the charge as he held his pearl-handled revolvers. Not that Regan fashioned himself after Patton, but he figured if Old Blood and Guts could do it, so could he.

Standing up in the turret, Regan looked to his right and left. His platoons were emerging from their covered positions as they steadily advanced over the small engineering bridge that spanned Sangamon Creek next to a small bridge on County Road 320 East.

A week earlier, a driver in their scout platoon had mistakenly thought the bridge would hold up as he drove his Bradley over it. Sadly, the bridge had fallen apart on them, and the vehicle had crashed into the creek. It had taken them a few hours to get a wrecker to pull the Bradley out of the water. The next day, the engineers had moved one of their heavy assault bridge spans to the spot so the tanks could get across the creek.

"We're over the bridge," their driver called out over the intercom. The tank started picking up speed again.

Miller was peering through the gunner's sight when he called out, "I don't see anything just yet. Nothing on thermals or infrared, either."

Regan nodded, more to himself than anyone else. He kept looking through his own commander's sight extension, switching between thermals and their regular lens. With it still being winter, it was relatively easy to spot a vehicle or person against the cold air and ground.

Artillery rounds were still flying over their heads, heading toward an unseen enemy. Their rhythmic thudding and explosions could be heard off in the distance, reminding them that a war was still raging, even if no one was shooting at them right this moment.

Either our artillery scouts have found something, or those guys are wasting a lot of ammo firing at something they can't see, Regan thought pensively.

As they drove down the county road, they spotted the small town of Cisco to the left, along with Interstate 72. I-72 was the first waypoint. Once the regiment made it there, they'd line up and prepare to make their mad dash across roughly twenty or so miles of open ground to the town of Farmer City, or Waypoint Two. Once they reached Farmer City, they expected to meet the first line of resistance.

Five more minutes went by as they continued down the road to the embankment of I-72. Standing in the turret, Regan looked to his right and caught sight of a handful of homes nestled on the side of the road up against the trees. He saw a few adults and some kids standing on their front porches or in their yards. The little kids held up tiny American flags, and the parents waved briefly as they caught his eye. They were all smiling and looking like they were delighted to see them instead of the Germans.

Captain Regan suddenly felt a wave of anger wash over him. He couldn't believe that he was driving a tank through southern Illinois in order to liberate parts of his own country. As they rolled past more homes and saw civilians waving, he felt a sinking feeling in the pit of his stomach—these were the true victims of all of this chaos. Regan pushed past these emotions and forced himself to smile and wave. No sense in making things worse.

When they reached the embankment of the interstate, Captain Regan ordered his company to stop. His tank came abreast as they waited for the rest of the regiment to move forward. The next dash they were going to make was across some pretty flat farmland, with little in the way of cover. Since it was ideal tank country, it would probably be where they'd meet their first signs of resistance.

****

Peering out of their IR camouflage netting, Oberfeldwebel Karl Haag observed the sky, checking to see if he could spot any reconnaissance drones or surveillance aircraft leading the advance of the American force.

His German paratrooper unit had known the Americans would eventually attack them. Knowing that this assault was imminent and that they couldn't rely on any air support or substantial armor support of their own, the men of the 310th Airborne Reconnaissance Company had set out a series of ambush points in hopes of bloodying the Americans up and possibly forcing them to halt their new offensive.

Covering their ambush position was a specially designed infrared shielding camouflage net. It was the latest in German technology and should help to conceal their location from any thermal or other types of surveillance devices on the enemy tanks or drones that might be flying overhead.

Turning to look at the three other soldiers in the shallow trench they called home these past five days, Haag saw that his men were tired but ready for action. Thus far, their highly trained unit had been kicking the crap out of the Americans, although Haag knew deep down that was primarily because they had caught them by surprise. Once the Americans got themselves organized, they'd come at them like banshees.

As the four of them were eating their morning Einmannpackung, the German version of an MRE, they were interrupted by the unmistakable sound of artillery rounds flying over their positions. Not far behind them, the ground shook as the high-explosive rounds hit targets to their rear.

Looking at his soldiers, Haag exclaimed, "Toss your breakfast and grab your weapons. The Americans are coming!"

The four of them grabbed one last bite of food and began to get their weapons ready. Aside from their personal rifles, they had one Heckler & Koch MG4 and two Panzerfaust 3s. As they prepared their weapons and extra rockets, Haag made a point of making sure they had their white sheet unfurled and attached to the stick they'd found a while back.

Three days ago, Haag and his men had agreed that after they carried out their attack, if it looked like they were going to get killed, they'd voluntarily give up. There was no point in dying in this hole if they genuinely had no hope of winning the battle or making a difference. But, until that time came, they'd do their best to rough the Americans up.

Ten minutes went by. Eventually, the artillery barrage lifted. As it did, they made a quick check of their field phone to see if it was still working. The artillery hadn't destroyed the telephone cable, which was good. Now they just had to hope their command wire to their explosives hadn't been cut either.

As Oberfeldwebel Haag listened, he realized that the enemy artillery hadn't stopped entirely but had merely drifted further away. He also heard a new noise. It was faint at first, but unmistakable—the clinking mechanical sound of tank treads and the almost high-pitched whine of the Honeywell multifuel turbine engines of Abrams tanks.

Sensing the enemy was getting closer to them, Haag lifted his field glasses to his eyes and scanned the sector to their front. A couple of minutes went by as the tanks drew closer. Then, Haag spotted them. At first, all he could see was the radio antennas of the vehicles swaying and rocking as they made their way through the farm field. Eventually, the shape of the turrets appeared as the lead tanks moved closer to the southern embankment of Interstate 72.

Intermixed with the tanks were several M2A4 Bradley fighting vehicles and a group of Strykers. Those concerned Haag the most. An armored force almost always traveled with a contingent of infantry. The infantry soldiers accompanying the tanks were there to protect them from the very type of ambush Haag and his men had planned. They were also the force that was best suited to hunting his men down and killing them.

The armored force stopped on the southside of the interstate, just as the Germans had anticipated. Haag looked for the reflective tape they'd placed on a couple of trees near those positions. Those were their range points. It would let them know when the enemy tanks had entered the kill box.

A smile spread across his face. The tanks and Bradleys had just entered their trap. Haag lowered his field glasses and handed them off to his second-in-command, Unteroffizier Reichman, who took the glasses and confirmed the enemy was in position.

Haag grabbed the field phone. He cranked the handle a couple of times, which sent an electronic chirp back to the operator on the other end. Haag grabbed the handset and depressed the talk button.

"Artus Six, Artus Two. How copy?" he said in a hushed tone.

Haag's soldiers stared at him as they did their best to listen in on the conversation.

The voice on the other end quickly responded, "Good copy, Artus Two. What do you have?"

"The Americans have reached the interstate, and they've entered our kill box." Haag reflected that it was odd using an old-fashioned field phone for their communications. However, it was a tried and tested means of talking without the risk of being jammed or someone listening in on what they were saying.

A short pause ensued before the soft voice on the other end replied, "Commence your attack. Good hunting, Artus Two." Then the line went dead.

Turning to look at the four other soldiers in the hideout with him, Haag could feel the tension in the air. Excitement, uncertainty, and terror hung in the air around them.

A mischievous smile spread across his lips. "Blow the charges," he ordered.

Unteroffizier Reichman reached over and grabbed the detonator. He removed the safety switch on the device, twisted the plunger a quarter turn, and then depressed it.

In a fraction of a second, an electrical charge was sent across the command wire some one thousand meters away from their position to a series of twelve blasting caps that were inserted into the nose of the daisy-chained 155mm artillery rounds they had buried more than a week ago.

The world in front of them burst into a brilliant and thunderous boom. Rocks, dirt, chunks of trees, cement, and parts of vehicles and bodies were blown hundreds of feet into the air. The entire southern embankment of Interstate 72 erupted in fire and shrapnel.

Seconds after the blast, a handful of Abrams tanks emerged from the smoke and dust as they raced forward, toward their positions.

"Here they come. Get those Panzerfaust ready!" Haag yelled to his motley crew.

A slight breeze blew in from the east, which helped to clear away the smoke and dust from the IEDs. Using his field glasses, Haag saw they had succeeded in blowing up at least one tank and looked to have damaged two more. What really made his day was the three Bradleys he saw on fire. Three JLTVs also appeared to have been destroyed.

The enemy tanks were now six hundred meters and rapidly closing in. A new series of explosions rocked the path in front of their position as four additional IEDs were detonated by the other ambush crew four hundred meters to their left. This second round of IEDs succeeded in disabling one more tank.

"Ready…fire!" Haag yelled.

Two of his soldiers popped up from their concealed positions and fired off their Panzerfaust at the remaining enemy tanks.

****

Captain Regan's tank was rocked hard by the second set of IEDs as they continued to charge forward. The driver was giving the engine as much gas as possible as their sixty-plus-ton beast, barreling ahead into whatever may come next.

"Keep an eye out for possible RPG teams!" Regan shouted. They still hadn't found any enemy tanks or vehicles yet, but clearly, someone was out there watching them.

"Rocket team to our four o'clock! Engaging them now," Miller shouted as he swiveled the remote-controlled gun system.

Bang, bang, bang.

The Browning fifty-caliber machine gun that sat in front of the commander's hatch fired a handful of rounds, cutting the two attackers apart before they could fire off their rockets.

"Good shot, Miller. Rake that position they were hiding in again and let's make sure there aren't any more of them playing possum," Regan ordered. Miller proceeded to pump a dozen or so rounds into the makeshift hideout.

An urgent call came from one of the tankers in Blue Platoon. "Enemy tanks to our front, twenty-eight hundred meters, my nine o'clock!"

Miller immediately shifted the main gun to Blue-Two's location and scanned for a target.

"Enemy tank, 2,300 meters to our three o'clock. He's right behind that barn to the left of that blue farmhouse. See it, sir?" Miller shouted. He was clearly looking for verification that he wasn't just seeing things.

Captain Regan peered through the commander's sight extension. It was hard to see, but he could make out the silhouette of the barrel. Whoever had positioned that tank there had done a damn good job. They'd nearly missed it.

Turning to look at Miller, Regan shouted, "Tank identified. Load sabot."

"Sabot up," echoed their loader.

Knowing they already had a sabot in the tube, the loader lifted the arming handle up, letting the computer know the gun was ready to fire.

Looking through the targeting sight one last time, Miller yelled, "Firing!"

Boom.

The cannon belched flames out the front as it recoiled back inside the turret, and the spent aft cap dropped to the floor, making a metallic clink. The cabin filled with the smells of burnt cordite and powder.

"Load sabot!" Miller shouted as he got them ready to engage another tank.

The loader hit the ammo locker door with his knee, bent over, and grabbed the back of a sabot round with his gloved hand. As he pulled the round out of the ammo locker, his knee knocked the door button, closing it again as he shifted his body around to ram the next round into the empty breach. With the round now seated, he closed the breach, lifting the arming handle up again.

"Sabot up!" he shouted.

The tank continued to bounce a bit as they made their way over a lot of uneven farm fields. Their company was continuing to move toward the known German lines, which were still another fifteen miles to their front. As they jolted around a bit from the terrain, Miller continued to scan to their left for additional targets while Regan looked to their right.

BOOM, BOOM.

Two enormous explosions went off, nearly knocking Miller and Regan out of their seats. The loader fell backward, hitting his head on something sharp. The gash was bleeding profusely as he tried to shake off what had just happened.

"What the hell was that?" yelled their driver over the crew net.

"Driver, halt. I need to go topside. Miller, see if you can help Mouse. That cut looks pretty bad."

The vehicle came to a quick halt, and Regan unlocked the commander's hatch and pushed it open. He reached above the lip with his hands and pulled himself out of the turret. Standing up, Regan looked out to see what had blown up. To his surprise, he saw the remains of a minivan nearby were ablaze and completely torn apart. A few feet away from the van was a Stryker vehicle that had been blown over on its side. Half a dozen soldiers had set up a defensive perimeter while the other soldiers were tending to their wounded.

Looking further behind them, Regan saw a Bradley on fire. It appeared to have hit a mine or an IED. In either case, it wasn't operational.

Shaking his head in frustration, Captain Regan cursed at himself for allowing them to have been ambushed like this. He wondered if they had been too predictable in their attack.

Several more of the tanks from his company pulled up alongside his vehicle, with their commanders looking out of their hatches to get a better view of the area. Regan nodded toward a few of them as he pulled out his map. A few Bradleys rumbled up next to them, and the second echelon of troops that were going to support them joined them as well.

Looking down at the map, Regan saw they were in front of the small town of Weldon. Then an idea hit him. Sensing they needed to make a change in strategy, Regan switched his radio to the battalion net. It was time to call an audible.

"Dixie Six to all Rebel elements, pull your maps out and listen up. Our initial plan was to assault from Waypoint Bravo. Break." He paused for just a second before resuming. "The enemy must have anticipated us moving there because they hit us with one hell of an ambush. Break."

Feeling like the plan was all coming together in his head, Regan continued. "Right now, we're supposed to advance to Waypoint Charlie, but that's the most likely avenue of attack for our tanks with our current battle plan. I think there's also another ambush waiting for us, so I'm calling a FRAGO. Break.

"I'm going to shift my Dixie element around Lake Clinton and jump on the hardball on State Road 54 and advance behind Farmer City. I'm requesting all Rebel elements follow my lead through Clinton. How copy?"

Now came the moment of truth. Captain Regan wondered if the colonel would chew him out for breaking away from the stated plan or if he'd back him. The radio crackled and then beeped, letting him know the SINCGARS had synced. "Dixie Six, Rebel Actual. Good call on the change of plans. Proceed with your FRAGO. All Rebel elements follow Dixie through Clinton. Good hunting, Dixie elements. Rebel out."

Regan breathed a sigh of relief. He lifted his field glasses to his eyes again so he could survey further ahead. Looking toward the city of Clinton, Regan spotted the two JLTVs zipping ahead of their armored column as they scouted the area for them. The vehicles drove fast; they'd already reached the outskirts of the city, and thus far, they hadn't encountered any problems.

Five minutes later, Regan's tank passed by a large trucking company that had a sign on the side of its building for Miller Container Corporation. A handful of people had come outside to gawk at the armored chariots and the men riding in them as they got closer. They also pointed and stared at the dozens of black smoke pyres rising into the sky from the earlier fighting.

Just as Regan was about to return his attention to the nuclear power plant that was down the road, a couple of men in overalls and trucker hats started waving their hands and walking toward his men.

Regan shouted for the driver to halt the vehicle and asked Miller to come up. As the tank stopped, the men approached them cautiously. "Keep an eye on them," Regan ordered. "I'm going to go talk with them and see why they wanted to stop us."

Miller undogged the M240 machine gun in front of his hatch and made sure the safety was off. He kept the weapon trained on the civilians as Regan walked toward them.

As Regan approached, one of the men held up his hands as if surrendering. "We saw you guys coming and wanted to give you a warning," he said. "The Germans came through here a couple of weeks ago. They've been setting up all sorts of booby traps for you guys."

Regan's left eyebrow rose. "If I show you a map, can you tell me where and what kind of trap they've placed?" he asked.

"I'm Eric, by the way," the civilian replied. "And, yes, if you show me a map, Bill and I can show you what they've been doing. We're just glad you all are here and didn't abandon us. We've been hearing all sorts of reports out of Chicago about how they're calling the areas liberated by the UN 'Free America' and the rest of the country 'Occupied America.'"

Regan shook his head in disgust. "Follow me over to my tank," he directed. Meanwhile, the column of vehicles behind them was once again bunching up as they all came to a halt.

After spending a few minutes with a map, the locals were able to tell them where the Germans had laid several IEDs and explained where they had set up a couple of fortified bunkers.

Armed with the new information, Regan got on the radio and passed along what he'd learned. He called his vehicle commanders, and they made a few adjustments to their routes. Five minutes later, the group of tankers was back on the move. This time, instead of driving down County Road 54, the road that would take them near the Clinton Power Station, they headed north, down Walnut Street to Heyworth. It was a twenty-minute detour, but it kept them away from the ambushes the locals had told them about.

When they reached Heyworth, they turned east again. This time, they'd approach Farmer City from further behind the enemy position. Five minutes into the drive down US Highway 136, they found their first sign of enemy activity.

"Infantry fighting vehicle, twenty-one hundred meters to our four o'clock!" shouted an excited Miller.

Regan looked through the commander's sight extension. "Got it. Load HEAT."

Mouse echoed, "Loading HEAT." In one fluid motion, he removed the unspent sabot round, placing it into an empty hole and grabbed one of the HEAT rounds from the second-to-bottom layer of the rack. Slamming the HEAT round in the breech, he yelled, "HEAT up!"

Regan sent a quick message out to the rest of his tankers about what they'd found, and they reported back to him that they'd found some targets of their own. Seconds later, one of the other tanks in his crew fired first.

When he heard the first shot, Regan shouted, "Fire!"

BOOM.

The cannon recoiled inside, spitting out the aft cap.

"Tank! One thousand, four hundred meters to our two o'clock," shouted Miller. "He's inside that barn across I-74. You see it?"

Captain Regan squinted to try and see better. However, even after zooming in on the spot where Miller had said the tank was hiding, he couldn't spot it.

Where is he? he wondered.

Just then, he saw a flash. Some flame spat out of the darkness from within the barn. He couldn't believe they'd actually placed a tank in there.

"I see it," Regan shouted. "Fire!"

BOOM.

Their round flew flat and sailed like a red-hot lawn dart right into the barn. They saw some sparks from within, but no explosion.

"Damn! I think we missed, or maybe it ricocheted. Load another sabot," Regan yelled apprehensively.

Bam.

Debris rained down on their tank. They heard small chunks of metal and rocks bounce off their armored shell.

Ping, ping, ping.

"We got infantry to our right flank shooting at us!" shouted the driver. His voice was barely audible over the noise of everything going on around them.

"Miller, get another round in that barn and take him out!" Regan ordered. "I'm climbing up to deal with the infantry." Then he undogged the hatch above him and climbed out.

Zing, whiz, zap.

Bullets whipped past Captain Regan. A few of them dinged off the armor around him. He scanned their right flank and spotted several enemy soldiers. Regan unlocked the Ma Deuce from the remote firing system and manually moved it to face the infantry. He spotted about a dozen infantrymen shooting away at his tank and the others near him. The soldiers likely knew that their bullets couldn't penetrate their armor, but that didn't stop them from sending a lot of lead his way.

Swoosh…bang.

Out of nowhere, the tank to his right, maybe two hundred meters away, was suddenly hit by a rocket of some sort. The tank clanked to a halt, its track having been blown off its sprocket.

Captain Regan swiveled the Ma Deuce in the direction the rocket had originated from and spotted the attackers. A German soldier had just sighted in on one of the Stryker vehicles; he fired just as the fifty-caliber rounds from Regan's gun ripped the man's body apart.

Captain Regan hit the talk button on his CVC. "All Dixie elements, beware. They have rocket teams in the area. They just took two of our guys out. Either the gunners or tank commanders need to get up on their crew serve weapons and take 'em out."

In that instant, another enemy tank round flew out of the barn and slammed into one of his tanks, hitting its right rear section. The round cut right through the thin armor on that side of the vehicle and tore right into the engine compartment. A fraction of a second later, the entire rear section of the tank blew up as the vehicle's fuel bladder caught fire. That explosion caused the tank's ammo locker to explode, sending flames to vent some thirty feet in the air for a few seconds as the ammo cooked off.

"Damn it, Miller! Take that tank out—he just nailed another one of our guys."

BOOM.

Regan's tank belched flame and fire as their second round flew right into the barn. This time they were rewarded with a blast. A second after the initial burst, the roof of the barn exploded skywards as the tank's ammo cooked off. The resulting fire ravished the structure.

"All Dixie elements, shift your fire southeast toward Farmer City and *charge!*"

Captain Regan's tank practically jumped as his driver gunned the engine. They roared through the farmer's field, closing in on Interstate 74. As they neared the rest stop attached to the side of the road, Regan saw a few explosions up ahead. Some of his tankers had clearly found some targets to engage.

Zip, zip, zip.

Regan saw several strings of 30mm tracer rounds rip right into one of his unit's Bradleys and a Stryker. The Stryker summarily blew apart—some of the bullets must have hit one of their TOW missiles. A couple of infantrymen were thrown into the air from the rear troop hatches, their bodies on fire.

The Bradley spun to one side as the driver sought to get them out of the line of fire. Unfortunately, the driver must have overcorrected, because he summarily rolled the vehicle. Whoever was shooting at them pumped a few dozen more rounds into the stricken Bradley, causing it to explode before the infantrymen and the crew could crawl out.

"Take that IFV out, Miller!" Regan shouted.

"I'm looking for it," Miller replied.

Suddenly, the area around the rear side of the town they were charging into was filled up with IR-inhibiting smoke. The Germans were attempting to blind them.

Regan was overwhelmed by the sounds of gunfire. There was the singular popping of semiautomatic assault rifles, the staccato of light and heavy machine guns, and occasionally, the swooshing of a rocket followed by an explosion. It suddenly hit him how surreal the scene was. The charging tanks, the infantry fighting vehicles shooting their 25mm cannons, the Strykers rushing the infantrymen forward—it all seemed like a scene from a movie. Yet it was very real.

Miller pulled him out of his reflections. "Tank! Eight hundred meters. He's behind that grain silo."

Regan dropped back inside the tank and placed his eyes against his sight extension. He spotted the tank immediately.

"Sabot up!" shouted Mouse.

"Fire," Regan ordered.

BOOM.

"Got him!" shouted Miller excitedly.

Hitting the talk button, Regan called out to his company, "All Dixie elements, halt. Dismount the infantry and prepare to support them. Continue to look for targets of opportunity, but let's not destroy the entire town in the process if we can avoid it."

The next thirty minutes saw some fierce fighting between a handful of enemy infantry fighting vehicles, two more tanks, and about two companies' worth of soldiers. When a couple of Apache gunships were finally able to assist them, the remaining Germans in the town finally gave up. At first, it was just a couple of pockets waving white flags, but soon, the entire lot followed suit.

When the sun had finally set, Regan's regiment had punched through forty miles of enemy territory. That evening, his tanks were refueled and rearmed. At 0300 hours, they'd set out for Kankakee—their next objective and the last major enemy stronghold between them and Gary, Indiana.

****

New Delhi, India

Dr. Harsh Gandhi looked at the printed photo of Yichang, shaking his head as he did. He set the picture down, then examined an aerial shot of Wuhan next. The devastation of the two cities was massive. Virtually no building was left standing in Yichang.

"It's pretty incredible, isn't it?" asked Minister of Defense Sitharaman as she slipped into his office. She closed the door behind her and took a seat in front of his desk.

Dr. Gandhi looked up at her. "It *is* incredible. I honestly didn't think the Americans would do it."

Her left eyebrow rose. "Really? After Sachs had been trapped in that bunker for more than a week, I'm surprised he didn't nuke China much harder."

"Destroying the Three Gorges Dam wasn't exactly a small strike. It probably killed more than ten million people," Dr. Gandhi countered. "I just read a report yesterday that said the country is experiencing a series of blackouts in southern and central China. This is going to wreak havoc on their economy." He paused. "How is the PM reacting to it all?"

She snorted. "Like a dithering fool," Sitharaman replied flatly. "On the one hand, he's appalled by the nuclear attack on America, but then he's equally appalled by the American response to it. If you ask me, he seems paralyzed with what to do next."

She was growing more and more frustrated with the PM's unwillingness to confront China. She had warned him the Americans would hit the Chinese hard if they invaded, and now they had.

Dr. Gandhi nodded. "If we ever want to settle our border dispute with China or liberate Tibet, we aren't going to get a better chance than now. My sources on the ground are reporting that the PLA is moving several of their divisions away from the frontier to assist in the rescue efforts in Hubei province. If we acted soon, we could catch them completely by surprise." He showed her a couple of recent intelligence reports to back up what he was saying.

She'd been reading over the intel reports too. She knew what was going on—she was just not in a position to make the Prime Minister move. "The PM is concerned that if we join this war now, the Chinese in their weakened state might respond by hitting us with tactical nuclear weapons. I'm not yet confident the PLA wouldn't use them on our forces, either. Have your sources been able to confirm the current status is of the PLA's nuclear force structure?" Sitharaman asked.

Reaching for his pack of cigarettes, Dr. Gandhi pulled one out and lit it up. He held the smoke in and waited until he felt the rush from the nicotine hit before exhaling. "I can confirm their ICBM fields are destroyed," he responded. "The Americans wiped those out. They also hit every nuclear storage site that we knew of. What I can't say for certain is how many of their smaller tactical warheads they dispersed before they launched their attack on the Americans."

She shook her head in frustration. "Harsh, I can't push the PM into our corner to attack if I don't know how many tactical nukes they may still have or where they are. If I convince him to give the go order and the PLA hits us with a few nukes, we'll have to respond. If that happens, it'll most certainly drag Pakistan in. I can fight and win a conventional war against the PLA, but I can't fight and win against the PLA *and* Pakistan. The Chinese know that, and so does Pakistan."

"And therein lies the rub," Dr. Gandhi replied, blowing a smoke ring. "Pakistan—the bane of our existence. How many times have we been hampered in what we can do because of Pakistan?" Gandhi asked angrily. For decades, Indian foreign policy had been constrained by China to their east and Pakistan to their west—both nuclear-armed powers.

"I know. I'm flying to Washington to meet with the Americans' new Secretary of Defense and President Sachs," Sitharaman announced. "I'm going to ask them if there is a way they can help us neutralize the Pakistani threat so we can have a freer hand in dealing with China."

"Really? And the PM is OK with this trip?" Gandhi asked, skeptical that he would authorize such a trip.

She shrugged her shoulders. "I told him if I could not work out some sort of arrangement with the Americans to help us deal with Pakistan, then I'd back his position to remain neutral."

Gandhi's eyes went wide as saucers. "That is a big risk. You've already moved several divisions to the border. We've been activating our reserves in preparation for an invasion. If the PM completely walks away from this threat, it'll have long-lasting repercussions."

She sighed loudly. "I know. But you live in the world of spies and espionage. I live in reality, and I have to face the fact that right now we have a divided government. There is little appetite for war with Pakistan or China, especially since it's already turned nuclear. If the Americans want our help, then they need to provide us with some military assurance against Pakistan, or it isn't going to happen."

****

Kankakee, Illinois
Kankakee Country Club

DeShawn had always wanted to go inside the Kankakee Country Club. However, being a poor kid from the wrong part of town meant he'd never be allowed inside. But that wasn't the case today. Today, DeShawn and thirty others from his Section 8 housing development were being fed a stellar meal by the kitchen staff. Of course, about thirty German soldiers and roughly the same number of Russians were enjoying the same feast.

DeShawn and his friends, mostly gangbangers, had been told by the Germans that if they agreed to fight with them until the end of February, they'd each be paid five thousand dollars, and they'd get to keep whatever guns they were given to fight with, no questions asked.

Halfway through this splendid dinner, one of the German officers received a phone call. When he got done with the conversation, he started shouting orders to his men and the Russians. One of the Germans walked over to DeShawn.

"Your crew needs to get to your positions," the man ordered. "The Americans aren't far away from the city."

DeShawn just nodded. He started barking orders to his guys to get them moving. As they left the table, he made sure to grab a couple of rolls and stuffed them in one of his pockets.

A few minutes later, they were trudging through the cold to get down to their positions along the Kankakee River. When the Germans had hired DeShawn's crew, they'd ordered them to dig some trenches and bunkers there. Now that they'd been activated, it was time for them to shoot at any of the American vehicles or soldiers that tried to cross the river on Interstate 57.

The river was the last major natural barrier between southern Illinois and Chicago. If the Americans made it across the Kankakee, they'd have a clear shot at either taking the city or cutting the UN forces off from Indiana and the supply lines that ran all the way back to Canada.

DeShawn plopped himself down in one of the bunkers and pulled out one of the rolls he'd grabbed from the restaurant. As he scarfed it down, the other three guys looked at him with hungry eyes, ticked that they hadn't thought to grab a roll for themselves.

Three long hours went by without hearing or seeing anything. The men in the bunker were getting tired, and they were more than a bit annoyed that they had been dragged away from their dinner only to sit in the cold.

Where are they? thought DeShawn. The Germans had made it seem like they'd barely have enough time to make it to the river.

Then they heard an explosion in the distance. Another blast erupted—this time, much closer. The four of them looked out the slits in the bunker to see if they could spot where the explosions were coming from.

"Over there," one of them said excitedly.

Before he could spot the source of the attacks, DeShawn's ears registered a giant boom. Something had really gone up a few miles in front of them. Then he saw strings of red and green tracer fire start to crisscross the sky. Every now and then, he'd see some red tracer fire pelt the ground. Some kind of rockets or missiles ignited from the black sky to race down to an object in the dark and blow up.

Suddenly, the five thousand dollars the Germans were paying him didn't seem like very much. DeShawn could see his guys starting to get anxious. As each explosion got closer and the reports of the machine guns inched closer to them, they were visibly nervous. One of his friend's hand was shaking so obviously, there was no hiding it.

A German soldier walked into their bunker. He seemed to sense that they might be losing their will to fight. "The Americans are a couple of miles away," he announced. The soldier pointed at a spot in the dark. "They will try to rush their tanks and infantry fighting vehicles across the bridge here. When they do, you need to use that gun," he directed, pointing at the Heckler & Koch MG5. "Shoot their vehicles up."

DeShawn crossed his arms. "How is that *gun* going to stop a tank?" he asked, obviously doubtful.

The German smiled. "It won't. But it will give our rocket teams that are hiding near the bridge covering fire to disable them."

"What about that rocket or missile thing over there?" one of DeShawn's men asked as he pointed to a nearby position that was being manned by a couple of German soldiers.

"*Ja*. We'll be using that too. Just do your jobs, we'll do ours, and we'll stop them here at the river," the German replied nonchalantly. Then he left to go back to his position.

The minutes felt like hours as the battle continued to inch closer and closer to the river. Then DeShawn detected a noise he'd only heard before in movies or video games—the mechanical grinding and crunching of tank tracks. He wondered if it were closer if he would have felt the ground tremble. DeShawn hadn't allowed himself to be easily intimidated in life, but with each boom from a tank's cannon, his heart skipped a couple of beats.

The Germans fired multiple illumination flares across the river. Some came from small flare guns, and some were fired from the mortar teams further inside the country club. As the illumination rounds descended back to the ground on their little parachutes, they provided light to what was happening on the other side of the river. It was terrifying.

Small pockets of Russian or German soldiers were fighting ferociously against an advancing force, but many of their silhouettes were getting ripped to shreds, torn apart by infantry fighting vehicles. DeShawn watched in horror as several of them were run over by a tank as their bullets bounced uselessly off its armored shell.

"How the hell are we supposed to stop those things?" one of the guys in his bunker exclaimed.

No one said anything for a moment. Then they heard a loud popping noise nearby. A small rocket raced across the river toward one of the armored killing machines. It felt like it took forever as they watched it close the distance with the armored beast. When the rocket connected with its target, DeShawn saw a small flash. That was soon followed by a much larger explosion as the vehicle blew up.

"That's how we stop it," one of the other guys remarked. They all nodded in satisfaction.

Just as they were feeling good about the enemy tank getting blown up, their entire world lit up like the Fourth of July. Red tracers that looked like giant balls started flying right at their position from across the river. They instinctively hit the dirt, lying flat on the ground as whatever was being shot at them tore into everything around their bunker. Occasionally, a few rounds would slap the sandbags that made up the barrier in front of them, scaring them half to death.

It was the most terrifying thing any of them had ever encountered in their lives. Sure, they'd been shot at from time to time in their neighborhoods, but this was something they had never envisioned.

Boom, boom, bang.

Now things around them started to blow up. It wasn't just their side that was throwing rockets across the river— the soldiers on the other side fired their own missiles right back at them.

Suddenly, a towering figure appeared in the entrance to their bunker. "Get up! All of you," the German soldier bellowed. "Someone start manning that machine gun and shoot back! They're going to cross the river soon. You need to start shooting." Then he left their bunker to go get the other groups of DeShawn's crew firing.

"Aw, man. Five G ain't worth this. We have to get out of here," one of his guys grumbled.

DeShawn shook his head. "If you try and run now and those Germans see it, they'll shoot you in the back. The best way for us to stay alive right now is to make sure we keep those bastards on the other side of the river."

Before anyone else could argue with him, they heard the thumping sounds of helicopter blades overhead.

"Get on that gun. Start shooting at them already!" DeShawn barked.

They hadn't fired the machine gun more than ten seconds when a rocket from one of those helicopters blew them all to pieces.

****

Two hours later, the 155th Armored Brigade Combat Team crossed the Kankakee River. It was now a race to get their brigade sixty miles north to Gary, Indiana, and in a blocking position. Once they had the UN forces in Illinois and southeastern Wisconsin cut off from their supply lines in Michigan and Canada, Lieutenant General Hightower's III Corps could begin the job of picking them off one at a time as they ran out of fuel, munitions, and other logistical support an army needs to function.

****

Washington, D.C.
White House

Vice President Luke Powers walked past the map room in the White House. The President was scrutinizing one of the large maps on the wall. Powers took a step back and stopped in the doorway for a moment, trying to figure out what Sachs was staring at. Then he realized it was a map of China. He saw the President reach up and touch part of the map briefly before pulling his hand away. His shoulders slumped, and he looked like he might have cried.

Sachs suddenly realized he wasn't alone and turned around. He hurriedly wiped a tear from the side of his face and mumbled something about letting his emotions get the better of him.

The Vice President approached his friend and put his hand on Sachs's shoulder. "It's OK to cry every once in a while, sir. This war is doing terrible things to us and our country."

The President wiped away another tear before it could streak down his face. "Luke, I just can't help but think of the millions of people that died when I ordered the dam destroyed." Unable to control the flood of emotions any longer, he put his arms around his friend and cried on the Vice President's shoulder.

Powers tried his best to fight back the tears himself. He couldn't imagine surviving an assassination attempt like Sachs had—and then being trapped in a bunker, on top of it. He knew the poor man was suffering—yet he still had to lead the nation in spite of it all.

"They forced your hand, Jon," Powers said reassuringly. "It wasn't your fault. When they launched those nukes at us, we didn't have a choice anymore. We had to react."

He paused for a second as the President pulled away and removed a handkerchief from his pocket and wiped away a few more tears. Looking at the President's eyes, Powers saw sorrow and anguish. He saw how tired and exhausted the man was, and he almost wondered how much longer Sachs would be able to go on like this.

The President took a deep breath and let it out. Then he seemed to steel his nerves. "We have to win this war, Luke," he said. "No matter what happens, we have to win. This can't have all been in vain." He then stood up a little taller. The fire in his eyes had returned and so had the energy that always seemed to surround the man. It was like he'd unburdened himself and now he was ready again to be the Commander-in-Chief.

"We'll win this war, sir. No doubt about that. Would you like me to sit in on this next meeting with you?" Powers asked. Lately, the President had him sitting in on almost every military meeting since he'd been rescued from the tunnel. More often than not, Sachs had turned to him for advice on a host of military options, really using him as a sounding board and partner.

"Yeah, this would be a good one for you to join, Luke," the President replied.

Powers could see that the President wanted blood, but he'd been relying on him to rein him in at times. The war was eating the man up—shoot, it was eating the country up—but deep down, the Vice President was confident they would win.

Chapter 10

Allegheny Bloodbath

February 13, 2021

Northwestern Pennsylvania

Allegheny National Forest

"Contact front!" the point man shouted. Then the entire world in front of them erupted in gunfire.

"Get down!"

Crack, crack, zip, zip.

Bullets flew back and forth between the two groups, and a chorus of orders and angry shouts echoed throughout the woods.

Sergeant Silverman took a knee next to the side of a tree. He calmly leveled his M249 squad automatic weapon at a cluster of enemy soldiers, maybe two hundred meters to his front, and fired several controlled bursts. Silverman saw several of the enemy soldiers go down. Then he lifted up his SAW as he pivoted to the opposite side of the tree—a string of bullets hit where he had just been.

Realizing the enemy knew where he was, Sergeant Silverman dropped to the ground and rolled awkwardly to the left a couple of times to put some distance between himself and his last firing position. Then he popped up with his weapon at the ready and cut loose on four enemy soldiers he saw bounding forward toward his platoon.

Bang, bang, bang.

He stitched the four of them up as they tumbled from their forward momentum. Silverman then dropped to the ground and low-crawled forward to a fallen log he'd spotted. He needed to change firing positions again.

Crump, BOOM.

All around him, grenades went off, and mortar rounds hit. His fellow soldiers fired their M203 grenade launchers. It was pure chaos as his platoon attacked this position for the second time in two days.

Earlier in the morning, they had hammered the place with a battalion of 155mm Howitzers. Now it was time for them to make another attempt at dislodging this Canadian unit that was hellbent on maintaining control of Allegheny National Forest.

"Frag out!" called out one of his platoonmates. Seconds later, Silverman heard the explosion and chose to pop up at that moment to find another target.

Silverman saw two Canadian soldiers reloading one of their FN MAGs. Moving his barrel to face them, Sergeant Silverman let loose a four-second controlled burst and saw both of them get hit with multiple rounds and go down. He also heard and felt the bolt lock to the rear, letting him know he was out of ammo.

Silverman ducked back down behind the fallen tree. He removed the empty box magazine and unfastened another one from his vest. He swiftly seated the new one in place, making sure he stayed ready to keep providing fire support to his platoon.

"Shift fire to the right and advance!" yelled someone down the line.

"Covering fire!"

"Damn, I'm hit. Medic. I need a medic!"

"Grenade!"

"Reloading. Cover me!"

Sergeant Silverman popped back up from behind his log and saw four of his guys bounding forward toward the enemy position. Several meters in front of them, enemy soldiers were shifting their fire toward them.

Silverman pulled the trigger, hitting two hostiles and causing the third guy to duck. Then something out of the periphery of his vision caught his attention, and he turned to see what it was, swinging his SAW around with him.

"Crap! I nearly lit you up, Leary," Silverman exclaimed. Then he ducked back down behind the fallen tree.

"Sorry, man. You move too damn quick for me to keep up, Sergeant," replied Private First Class Leary, his assistant gunner. He was carrying the extra barrel and two extra box magazines of ammo for him.

"Cover me, Leary," Silverman ordered. "I'm going to move up to that next cluster of trees." Then he jumped up and bounded over the fallen log he'd been using for cover.

Leary popped up and fired off a handful of rounds at the enemy position with his M4 before he ducked back down.

"Your turn. I'll cover you!" yelled Silverman. He let loose several controlled bursts from the SAW, and Leary raced forward to try and keep up.

Crump.

"Damn, that was close," Leary remarked. "I think I caught a piece from that grenade." He wiped some blood from his cheek.

"Stop shooting! Stop shooting, you bloody Yanks! We surrender!" a loud voice called out from not too far away.

"You hear that? I think they're trying to surrender," Leary echoed.

It took a couple of attempts, but eventually, a lot of the shooting died down, and it suddenly became quiet.

Poking his head around the tree, Silverman saw several soldiers trying to wave something white as they kept calling out that they were trying to give up.

Taking up a better firing position at the now-exposed enemy soldiers, Silverman yelled to them in his southern accent, "Y'all stand up. Throw your weapons down and walk toward us, nice and slow like."

Then he turned to Leary. "Cover my rear. I'm going to move forward."

Leary nodded.

Sergeant Silverman stood up with his SAW at the ready and slowly advanced. Several other soldiers in his platoon did the same. Silverman counted eleven enemy soldiers standing with their hands held high, slowly walking toward them.

"OK. That's close enough," shouted their platoon leader. "You guys stay right there while we check you for weapons. Are there any more of you?" He moved forward with a couple more soldiers in tow.

"We have some wounded, but I think we're all that's left," called out one of the Canadians.

"If you bastards are trying to play possum on us, we're going kill you all right where you stand," shouted the platoon sergeant.

Now that the shooting had largely died down, everyone could hear the groans of the wounded. Others cried out for a medic.

Walking toward the Canadians, Silverman shouted, "Y'all move over to that cluster of trees so we can search you together." He motioned where he wanted them to go with the barrel of his SAW. "If any of you try to toss a grenade at us or do any other funny business, I'll light you up."

A handful of Silverman's platoonmates had taken up covering positions around the Canadians while a couple of their guys patted them down for weapons. They took their knives, sidearms, and any other weapons from them and dropped them on the ground. Once they had been thoroughly searched and disarmed, several of them led the Canadians back to their rear area, where they could hand them off to another unit for processing.

Meanwhile, the rest of the company had advanced forward to help them. The additional medics also moved in to help treat the US and Canadian wounded. Occasionally, a medic would call out for some help to move one of the more egregiously injured soldiers back to the rear. The area was still way too active with enemy soldiers to try and call in a medevac helicopter.

"OK, listen up, guys," their captain called out. "We're going to wait on an ammo resupply, and then we're going to continue clearing this sector out. It's time we send these Canucks packing back to Canada."

He sent a dozen guys back to their rear to go collect more ammo and water. They'd refill their canteens from the nearby creeks and rely on their water purifiers to make sure it was clean. Water was heavy, and if they had to choose which to carry more of—water or ammo—they were always going to side with ammo.

Sitting down on the ground, Sergeant Silverman opened his patrol pack and grabbed one of the fifty-round belts of ammo. He then took his empty box magazine and placed the belt into it and fed it back through the top lip, so it'd be ready when he needed it. Then he undogged the magazine he currently had in the SAW and tossed it to his assistant gunner.

"Pull one of your belts out from your patrol pack and refill this one, Leary," Silverman directed. "I don't want to have a half-empty magazine when we start again."

PFC Leary nodded and went to work. While he was doing that, Silverman grabbed his last unopened pack of strawberry Pop-Tarts. He tore it open and voraciously took a bite, savoring the sugar and carbs.

God, these taste so much better than an MRE, he thought.

Silverman suddenly realized Leary was looking at him longingly. He tossed him the remaining Pop-Tart.

An hour went by before their ammo runners returned. Everyone grabbed a couple of extra grenades to replace the ones they used, along with additional ammo.

They were just about to head out when their captain got a call from battalion. After the call, he walked past Silverman to inform the platoon leader of the situation. "Apparently, this particular pocket of Canadian soldiers was a rearguard action, meant to slow us down while the rest of their unit pulled back to Warren," Silverman overheard him say. "Charlie Company is maneuvering to get ahead of that retreating Canadian unit. We've been ordered to link up with Delta Company and to try to and get in touch with them. We need to move fast when we get going. Don't slow down or stop for anything until we make contact with them, understood?"

"Copy that, sir," the platoon sergeant answered. "You want my platoon in the lead again?"

"No, I'm going to rotate Third Platoon up," said the captain. "I want you guys to pull rear security for the time being. You guys earned it after this engagement. Good job, Lieutenant."

Silverman smiled at the compliment. He loved how the officers got all the attaboys while it was the NCOs who did the actual work, or in this case, fighting.

Whatever. I survived, he told himself. Plus, none of his friends had gotten killed this time, so he had to count that as a win.

The rest of the company moved out ahead of them while they got a few extra minutes to rest their dogs. Many of the guys took the opportunity to change out their sweat-soaked socks with a pair of dry ones. Most guys in the infantry learned pretty quickly that if they didn't take care of their feet, they wouldn't take care of them. Aside from packing as much ammo as they could carry, every infantryman made sure to carry more than a few pairs of socks, packed away in a Ziplock bag to keep them dry.

****

The next twenty-four hours saw some of the fiercest fighting of the war between the 504th Infantry Regiment of the 82nd Airborne and the Canadian 48th Highlanders. By the end of the second day of fighting, the entire Canadian unit had either been killed or captured. The rest of the Allegheny National Forest was finally retaken by American forces after more than a month of back-and-forth fighting. The heavily wooded area made for a defender's paradise, but with it now securely back in American hands, they could focus on pushing the rest of the UN forces in this sector back toward the border. The remaining Blue Helmets fell back to a new defensive line south of Buffalo in the city of Hamburg.

****

Arlington, Virginia
Pentagon

Admiral Chester Smith was going crazy with the constant hammering and banging just down the hall. While his office had not been hit during the cruise missile attack on the first day of the war, a section of the Pentagon just down the hall from him had been damaged. Construction crews were working around the clock, getting the exterior of the building patched up and at least closed off from the environment while other crews began the laborious task of fixing all the plumbing and electrical wiring. The clatter was a constant reminder to Admiral Smith of the loss of friends and the failure of the military to protect the country.

When Flight 77 had crashed into the western façade of the Pentagon on September 11, 2001, it had caused a lot of damage to the first two rings of the building there. This new attack had caused even more devastation. When the French cruise missiles had hit, they punched through the first ring before detonating in the second. The resulting enormous explosions had damaged both the inner and outer rings of the building near the points of entry. A lot of good people had been killed.

Smith tried not to let the noise bother him, but the constant pounding was starting to drive him nuts.

One of his aides walked in and handed him a SIGACTS. "Sir, I have that report on the latest attack on the blockade you asked for."

Admiral Smith nodded and immediately began to read. He felt his expression sour. "So we lost the *San Jac* and the *Nitze*?" he asked, disappointed and angry.

"I'm afraid so," the aide responded. "The *Gonzalez* and the *Stout* each took a hit but managed to stay afloat. They are both headed back to port for repairs."

"Tell me we at least shot down the Backfires that hit us?"

The aide smiled. "We did. Fourteen of the sixteen that attacked our ships were splashed."

Smith sighed loudly. He felt helpless at that moment. In the span of four weeks, he'd lost more than twenty thousand sailors—nearly a third of the total number of sailors who'd died in all of World War II. Two carriers had sunk, one with all hands. Four other carriers had sustained considerable damage and would be in the shipyards for several months before they could be made ready. Then he had two other carriers still in the process of being brought out of their programmed refueling and retrofitting. That left him with three operational carriers: two on the Atlantic side and one in the Pacific.

In addition to the carrier losses, they'd lost twenty-six *Arleigh Burke* destroyers and eight *Ticonderoga*-guided missile cruisers. The subsurface fleet losses were just as bad. Sixteen *Los Angeles* fast-attack subs and seven *Virginia*-class subs had been sunk. There wasn't a facet of the Navy that hadn't felt the loss of the past five weeks.

Couple all of that with an EMP detonation over Hawaii, and the US Navy was in a world of hurt. The two carriers Admiral Smith had in the shipyard at Pearl were now more or less dead in the water until they could get parts flown in from the Mainland to replace many of the electronics being used to operate the equipment that they needed to repair the flattops. It was an utter mess. There was a debate underway as to whether or not the carriers could be towed back to Bremerton for repairs since Washington State had mostly been recaptured.

The more immediate challenge Admiral Smith faced was figuring out how he could maintain a blockade of North America and continue to protect the US coastal areas. Considering that Hawaii was no longer an effective forward operating base, it would be tough to prevent the Chinese from being able to ferry more troops and equipment to Mexico and the rest of Central America.

While the Navy had reactivated its entire Ghost fleet, it was going to take time to get many of these ships operational. To further add to his headaches, the Navy had to expedite its training programs in order to have these new ships crewed and ready for combat. To make things even more complicated, they'd lost access to Naval Station Great Lakes at the outset of the war, which meant they had to find and set up a new training facility. For the time being, they were turning Naval Station Mayport in Jacksonville, Florida, into their new training facility.

Every time Smith thought they were going to make it—that the worst had passed them—he'd get handed a report like this one. More and more, he just wanted to quit, but he knew he couldn't do that either. His country still needed him, and Admiral Smith knew he couldn't look at his wife if he quit—not after their eldest son had died on the *Truman*. No, he was in this fight to the finish.

Just as his mind was about to slip off into a dark place, he heard a knock at the door. Looking up, he saw Admiral Thomas Ingalls. Smith stood up and waved his friend in.

"It's good to see you, Tom. How are the hell are you?"

Admiral Ingalls smiled and shook his friend's hand. "I'm good, Chester. How are you holding up? I heard we lost a few more ships today."

Admiral Smith grimaced. "We did. I won't lie and say it hasn't been tough, Tom. But what can you do? We have to keep fighting."

"I hear you. How's the wife holding up?"

Admiral Smith sighed. He closed the door and guided his friend over to the set of couches. "She's doing the best she can. It was tough losing Jerry, but the rest of the family is helping her get through it."

Admiral Ingalls nodded and took a seat. "Well, I don't want to dwell on the loss of your son, Chester, so I'll get right down to it. I wanted to provide you with an in-person update on that report you'd asked about."

Smith leaned forward, perking up at the mention of their secretive pet project. "Please tell me the ships are still on schedule," he implored.

Ingalls shook his head. "We're falling behind; that's why I wanted to talk in person. I'm having a hard time sourcing some equipment and getting the skilled labor I need to get them finished."

"What's the problem?"

"Armor plating, reactor fuel, and skilled technicians to work on the ship, for starters."

Admiral Smith rubbed the back of his head, anxiously. "How are we short on those items? I thought I had given your program priority. What's going on?"

Ingalls let out a forceful sigh. "Nearly half of my workforce has been pulled off the project to work on the ships coming back to port for repairs so we can get them turned back around and out to sea again. Plus, the reactor fuel that was slated for my program was reallocated to get our two other carriers refueled and operational. The shipyards have most of my workers crawling over those two ships, and then you add the mess of everything out at Pearl, and you can see why I'm strapped for skilled workers. And then there's the challenge of armor plating."

Admiral Smith held hand up to stop his friend for a moment. "What's the matter with the armor plating? I could have sworn we had that problem corrected several months before the war even started. This shouldn't even be an issue."

Ingalls shrugged. "Well, let's just say the mills are having a hard time sourcing the raw materials right now since most of our suppliers are currently at war with us."

Smith blew air through his lips as if he were creating a smoke ring. Then he leaned back on the couch, thinking about the problem.

"What if you move all the personnel and supplies to just get the first ship operational? Could that solve part of your problem?"

Ingalls shook his head. "No, not entirely. Some of the work needs to be done by skilled labor. Each ship has nearly six hundred electricians running wiring and cabling throughout the superstructure and hull. Then we have

363

another four hundred pipefitters and plumbers that follow in behind them. Until those functions are complete, we can't close many of the floors or the walls up. Also, I'm missing most of the nuclear technicians needed to get the reactors put in place and the fuel to get them started. Until those pieces fall into place, I can't even test the ship's power generation or electrical systems. And we haven't even gotten to the point of testing her weapon systems yet. That's going to be an entirely different problem set we'll have to deal with."

Smith realized that Ingalls looked exhausted and frustrated, just like him. There were too many tasks to handle and not enough hours in the day or people to manage them.

"What if we pulled the work crews from the shipyards in the Gulf and Pearl and sent them up here to you?"

Ingalls's left eyebrow rose skeptically. "You thinking of towing the ships in Pearl back to the Mainland?"

Smith sighed. "I think we're going to have to. The island's a mess. The entire power grid on the bases, with the exception of our microgrid, is out. Heck, we can't even operate most of the cranes or heavy equipment needed to keep the repairs going. If I can't use the shipyard, then there is no reason to leave the ships in port if they can't get repaired. However, right now, I'm not sure we could properly protect the ships if we towed them to Washington. If a Chinese or Russian sub found them, we'd have no way to maneuver them if they were fired upon."

Ingalls laughed uncomfortably. "Man, and I thought *I* had problems to deal with. But back to your offer—yes. It would help. What could speed things up more is if you could either waive or expedite the security clearance required for many of the electricians and plumbers I need. We can advertise the job positions and high-paying salaries all we want, but right now, we have a serious bottleneck when it comes to getting these new hires cleared so they can work on the project."

"I'll see what I can do about that," Smith countered. "In the meantime, you have to find a way to get those ships done. I know we hadn't planned on fielding them for several more years, but the situation has obviously changed, and we need those ships…especially in the Pacific."

"Are you sailing them around Argentina, or are we planning to take Panama back?"

Smith smiled. "Let's say we have a few plans in the works. You just make sure those ships are ready by the end of the year."

Chapter 11

Round One, China

February 13, 2021

Santa Teresa, New Mexico

A day earlier, 1st Battalion, 37th Armor had crossed some thirty miles deep into Mexico looking for the Chinese. They had been told the enemy army group had been hit by a tactical nuke, and this would be a cleanup operation. What they'd found instead was two brigades' worth of tanks and mechanized infantry waiting for them.

The subsequent twenty-four hours had been fought as a delaying action as they waited for the rest of their brigade to get formed up and ready to defend the border. They had been doing what tankers do best in wide open spaces—fire and maneuver—something the American tankers excelled at.

****

"Tank, ten o'clock, 3,200 meters," Sergeant Gomez called out as he found the next T-96 charging toward them.

"I see it. Fire!" yelled Staff Sergeant Melton, sweat dripping down his face.

"Firing!"

Boom.

The cannon recoiled inside the turret, and the tank rocked back on its springs.

"Load sabot!" shouted Gomez. He watched the round they'd fired reach out for its intended target. The projectile slammed right into the base of the turret, missing the tank's reactive armor. The sabot punched a hole right through the weak spot where the turret and the chassis connect. The force of the projectile and the internal explosion blew the turret right off the tank, cartwheeling a hundred or more feet into the sky.

"Good hit, Gomez. Driver, back us the hell out of here and find us another firing position."

While their driver was backing them out, Staff Sergeant Melton was hard at work trying to find them another target. In the span of two hours, they'd taken out twelve T-96s as they continued to fall back into New Mexico and Texas.

"Ranger Actual to all Ranger elements. This is our line in the sand. We hold them here. Thunderbolt element is moving to join us in twenty mikes. Let's try and save a few tanks for them. Out."

"You hear that, Staff Sergeant? Line in the sand. This is it for us, isn't it?" Pittaki asked sarcastically.

Private First Class Andy Pittaki was their loader—the most junior guy on the tank and a real pain in the butt. The guy was a total Debbie Downer. If you asked him if the glass was half-full or half-empty, he always said half-empty.

"Just shut up and keep loading," quipped Sergeant Gomez. "Melton will see us through this, OK?"

"I'm going to park us behind that F-150, Staff Sergeant," their driver announced as he pulled the tank up a few feet behind the truck. They still had plenty of room to let the gun traverse without hitting the cab of the truck or anything nearby.

"That's fine," Melton responded. "Just make sure you don't get us too close to it and be ready to move if I tell you." He scanned for targets from their new vantage point.

They heard some rounds blow up, not too far away. "Hey, is that artillery outgoing or incoming?" asked Pittaki nervously.

"That's incoming. If it was outgoing, you wouldn't hear it blowing up," Gomez replied. He kept his eyes fixed on the scope, scanning for targets with Melton.

"Ranger Three, get your trophy system ready," called one of the nearby tanks. "We have inbound Z-19s."

"What the hell is a Z-19?" asked Pittaki, his voice rising an octave higher.

"Oh, Lord. Don't tell him, Melton," replied their driver. Then he set about making sure their IR-inhibiting smoke grenades were ready.

Pulling the zoom out on his commander's sight extension, Melton scanned the horizon for the aerial threats. "Found it. He's off to our three o'clock."

"Hit the dazzler and make sure he can't get a lock on us."

Melton activated their antitank missile defensive suite and hoped for the best.

"Hey, those don't look like T-96s," Gomez said as he resumed his hunt for targets.

Before Melton could respond, they heard the scream of a jet engine as it flew low and fast over their position.

"Those are ours," explained Melton before any of his guys could ask. He watched as the F-15 fired off a pair of missiles at the helicopters that were gearing up to attack them. Melton laughed out loud before he hit the intercom button. "He just smoked those helicopters. Now, what tanks are you talking about? Where should I be looking?" Melton asked.

"They're still pretty far out. I think it's the next attack wave. To our eleven o'clock, five thousand meters."

Turning his commander's sight in the direction his gunner had said, Melton zoomed in as far as their equipment would let him.

Damn, that kid's got eagle eyes. I would have missed those tanks until they got closer, he reflected.

Melton pulled a Chinese vehicle identifier card out of his breast pocket and looked at it, comparing the tiny image to what he saw on his screen. "It's hard to tell from this distance, but I think that might be a Type-99," he announced. "If it is, then those are their top-tier tanks. This is probably going to be a big push by them."

"All Ranger elements, we're going to let Thunderbolt element work over the enemy tanks," their battalion commander announced over the radio. "They've taken up positions to our west. We've been ordered to go after the infantry fighting vehicles and APCs. We have additional fast movers inbound, so if you hear fighters, they're ours."

"You know, I like that about our battalion commander—he goes out of his way to make sure even us lowly sergeants know what's going on," Gomez commented.

"Here they come. Stand by to engage," Melton directed.

Two new pairs of attack helicopters appeared from further behind the Chinese attacking force and fired off multiple ATGMs at their sister battalion. Melton silently cursed at the new threat, angry that he was powerless to do anything about it.

Then, to his surprise, he saw the sky above the attack force light up with strings of anti-aircraft fire. Next, several missiles took off toward some unseen aerial targets. A few seconds later, two of the four attack helicopters exploded, and the other two dove for cover to try and evade whatever had been fired at them.

Brrrrrr.

"Woohoo. Did you see that A-10? He just took three tanks out in a single pass," Gomez called out excitedly to Melton.

As he watched the scene unfold before him, Melton saw the A-10 bank hard to the left as the pilot sought to regain some altitude after his attack run. The aircraft spat out flares the whole time while multiple strings of anti-aircraft fire raced after it.

Two missiles flew up from the ground and chased the A-10. Both projectiles hit one of the flares. Then one of the strings of enemy tracers managed to cut right across the left side of the aircraft. It blew out one of the engines and ripped part of the wing right off. The damaged aircraft now trailed smoke and flames as the pilot struggled to try and escape the incoming fire.

"ZBD identified: 3,500 meters, three o'clock. Load sabot," Gomez called out.

Melton shook the image of the A-10 from his mind and returned to the job of fighting the tank before him. He mirrored his sight to what his gunner had found for him. Sure enough, there was a wave of ZBDs, ZBLs, and ZSDs charging right behind the tanks. They were the primary infantry fighting vehicles of the PLA's mechanized force and packed an arsenal of antitank guided missiles.

"I got 'em," Melton announced. "Loader, switch to HEAT rounds going forward. I want to save our sabot rounds for actual tanks. Fire as soon as he crosses the 3,200-meter mark. Driver, we're going to fire five rounds from this position and then move—so start thinking about where you want to move us." Once the shooting started, everything was going to happen very rapidly, so Melton wanted to make sure the game plan was set.

A minute went by, and then Gomez started the action. "Firing!" he yelled.

Boom.

The glass windows on the Ford F-150 in front of them exploded from the concussion of their cannon firing. They all watched as his round raced across the more than 3,000-meter divide.

Gomez cursed when he saw the round just miss the vehicle. "Load HEAT!" he barked.

"It's OK, Gomez. We all miss sometimes. You'll get him with this next round," Melton said as he sought to reassure his gunner.

Pittaki hit the button on the ammo locker, opening it up. He reached down and grabbed the HEAT round from the second-to-bottom row. Within six seconds of having fired the first round, Pittaki had the HEAT round loaded and ready to fire.

"HEAT up!"

"Firing!"

Boom.

"Load HEAT."

"ZBS identified," called out Gomez.

The Chinese vehicles were doing their best to change their course, sometimes doing short zigzags or slowing down and then speeding up in an attempt to throw off the tank gunners shooting at them at the last minute.

"Good hit, Gomez. You nailed him," Melton announced.

"HEAT up!"

"Firing!"

Boom.

"Load HEAT!"

Before Gomez could fire another round, their driver threw the vehicle in reverse and gunned it. A fraction of a second later, the F-150 truck in front of them exploded. The front half of the tank got showered with shrapnel and debris.

Then the tank lurched forward as they advanced to the next firing position. While they were moving, a series of artillery rounds plastered everything around them. From inside, it sounded like a hailstorm as shrapnel peppered one side and then the other. The near misses bounced the entire tank around despite its heaviness.

Suddenly their vehicle stopped, and the gears made an odd noise.

"What's going on?" called out Melton, fearing one of those misses might have hit something important.

"I think we threw a track," called out the driver.

"Ah, crap! Gomez, start searching for a target. Make sure no one's getting too close to us. I'm going topside to see what kind of damage we're looking at."

Melton undogged the commander's hatch and pushed it open. Pulling himself up and out of the turret, he hopped down onto the chassis and then down to the ground. Looking at the right side of the tank, he saw it was dented in a few spots and had a ton of scratch marks from shrapnel, but the tracks and gears appeared to be in good order.

He then moved around to the left side of the tank and immediately saw the problem. A piece of shrapnel had gotten wedged between one of the tank sprockets and the track. Had their driver tried to power his way through the grinding noise, chances are he would have thrown the track. If that had happened, they would've been stuck until a wrecker could've come to help them. Given they were in the middle of a battle, that would pretty much have been the end of them as a fighting tank.

Melton climbed back up into the vehicle and stuck his head in the turret. "Pittaki, I need your help," he hollered. "Grab the tool kit and come assist me. Gomez, get up here on the gun in case we need you to cover us."

While Melton and Pittaki used a crowbar and some other tools to pry the piece of metal out of where it had gotten stuck, the sounds of battle continued to rage. All around them, tanks, infantry fighting vehicles, mortars, artillery, and helicopters from both sides were in a desperate clash. It was terrifying being stuck outside their armored shell, unable to fight or do anything until they got their track system fixed.

After a couple of minutes, Melton and Pittaki finally got the piece of metal yanked out of where it had gotten wedged, and their driver moved the tank forward a couple of feet with them, observing it to make sure the track and the sprocket were good to keep moving.

Once they were back in the tank, their driver sped forward. At this point, the enemy had closed to within fifteen hundred meters. They were now at the edge of the US-Mexico border.

"Staff Sergeant, I'm going to reposition us over near the Sunland Park Elementary School," the driver announced over the intercom. "There's a couple Bradleys and Strykers taking up a position near the neighborhood. They look like they could use a tank, and we need some infantry support."

"Good call. Get us moving," Melton replied. "Gomez, turn the gun around, and let's try and see what we can find."

Looking through the commander's sight extension, Melton saw most of the enemy armor was moving further west. He also saw additional helicopters on the horizon, which could prove problematic for them.

He grabbed the radio. "Ranger Six, this is Ranger Three. We've relocated to the Sunland Park Elementary School. I see some helicopters on the horizon. Do we have any additional air support that can deal with them?"

It took a minute for Melton to get a reply. Their CO knew about the helicopters and had placed a call in for help, but he was unsure if or when they'd receive it.

An hour went by as their company consolidated on the elementary school and formed up with the two Bradleys and three Strykers. Including Melton's tank, they had seven of them left. Twenty-eight hours of combat and they had been whittled down from sixteen tanks to just seven. They had lost a lot of friends already, and they were far from safe.

****

Sergeant Higgins felt a lot better now that a few tanks had come over to their position. For a while there, the 1st Battalion, 6th Infantry Regiment was down to just their couple of Stryker vehicles and a few Bradleys—not exactly an ideal setup when facing down a brigade of enemy tanks and mechanized infantry. They needed armor to deal with this threat, and that was something the Americans appeared to be short of.

His lieutenant walked up to him in a rush. "Higgins, get your fireteam up on the top floor of that building and set your machine gun up in one of the windows. Your team needs to cover this field of fire. See if you can't get a couple of Javelins positioned in some of the nearby classrooms as well. If you spot any troops or armor heading our way, radio me and let me know. I'm sending Bravo Team to that building over there. They'll cover your flank while you help cover theirs. Got it?" He pointed to the two buildings where he was deploying First Squad.

Looking at the school building, Higgins nodded. "On it, sir."

Higgins turned to find his guys, then barked out some orders for them to each grab a Javelin and some extra ammo for their lone M240G machine gun. If the LT wanted them to set up a position on the top floor, then he wanted to make sure they had enough ammo and supplies for whatever might be coming their way.

After his fireteam entered the school, they eventually found their way to a stairwell that led them to the third floor. It took them a few minutes to find the best room for setting up the machine gun. While Higgins initially wanted to set it up in the corner room, he realized that it'd be the most likely room the enemy would blow up, so he moved one room over.

He then had his guys place a Javelin in the next couple of rooms down the hallway. His thinking was that his team could fire one, then move down the hall to shoot the next one. This way, if the enemy fired at them, they'd be long gone and shooting from a different position.

"Sergeant, I think we have some vehicles headed our way," called out one of the corporals.

A second later, they heard two of the tanks nearby fire their main guns. Clearly, they had found something to shoot.

Walking up to his corporal, Higgins pulled his pocket binos out of a pouch on his vest and put them to his eyes.

Damn. That looks like a dozen of 'em headed our way, he realized.

"Good eye, Corporal."

Higgins pressed the talk button on his radio. "Lieutenant, we've got movement," he explained. "Looks like about a dozen or so IFVs and APCs headed our way. I spotted a couple of tanks with them, but it looks like our tanks are taking them out. Do you want us to start using the Javelins on the IFVs or APCs?"

"Take out the IFVs first. They have more firepower, and we only have a handful of them."

"Good copy. Out."

He turned to Corporal Meyers. "Start hitting those IFVs with our Javelins, Corporal," he ordered. "When you've shot them all off, come back here and get ready to help these guys."

He then moved over to the two privates manning their machine gun. "We've got some APCs and IFVs headed our way. Make sure you guys are watching that neighborhood over there. If I were those Chinese soldiers, I'd do my best to get inside that area and use it for cover to attack us."

"Roger that, Sergeant. We'll be ready for them," the soldiers replied.

This fight was gearing up to be their first actual conflict of this new war. While they had been accompanying the armor battalion for the last day, they hadn't had the opportunity to engage any enemy infantry. Their Stryker had fired a couple of TOWs at some tanks, but they were out of missiles. All their platoon had left was six Javelins spread between the four squads.

The radio came to life. "Sergeant Higgins, I'm ready to engage those vehicles," announced Corporal Meyers from next door. "You want me to start?"

"Yeah. Let's get this show started."

Pop...swoosh...bang.

Higgins watched the Javelin fly out toward the enemy vehicles. They were shooting it like an AT4, straight and level as opposed to a top-down attack—there wasn't room for that kind of shot from inside the school. As the antitank guided missile raced through the air toward the enemy vehicles, some of them popped some IR-inhibiting smoke to try and throw the guidance system off.

The missile was halfway to its target when Higgins heard the second Javelin fire. The beautiful thing about the Javelin over the TOW or the older Dragon ATGMs was that the Javelin was a true fire-and-forget weapon. Once the target was locked in, the onboard targeting computer would guide the missile to the objective without any operator guidance.

BOOM.

Higgins saw the ZBD-04 Meyers had shot at explode. The vehicle came to a halt as flames engulfed it.

Higgins scanned to watch the second missile. Unfortunately, he did so just in time to watch it get blown up by some sort of countermeasure, right before it was about to make impact.

Dang! It was going to hit one of the Type 89s too, he thought. The Type 89 tracked armored fighting vehicles were considered deadly, and they could carry thirteen soldiers—a full squad.

"Get down!" yelled one of the privates. He dove at Higgins, knocking him to the floor.

An instant later, the entire room was suddenly getting ripped to shreds by a heavy-caliber machine gun. Then it sounded like one of the rooms they'd fired the Javelin from blew up. A second later, the room right next to them was hit, showering them with dust, smoke, and pieces of the ceiling.

"Get back on the gun!" shouted Higgins. He pushed himself up and went to check on Meyers.

As he entered the hallway, Sergeant Higgins was shocked by the scene before him. The passageway was strewn with debris, burning papers and school supplies. He kept walking forward anyway. As his eyes focused on an object further down, he realized he was looking at an arm.

What the hell? he thought. And then it occurred to him that this was all that was left of Corporal Meyers. Shaking the image from his mind, he turned to head back to his machine-gun crew.

Ratatat, ratatat.

His machine-gun team was already firing at something, which meant the enemy must be close. Higgins got a couple of feet away from the room when an explosion blew him backward. His body slammed against the wall of lockers behind him. He slumped down on the ground, his head spinning. Trying to shake off the effects of the blast, Higgins looked at the room the rest of his squad was in and saw that the door and most of the wall was missing. Something had blown it up.

No, no, no…I can't lose more of my guys, he thought.

Higgins suddenly felt a surge of adrenaline. He popped up and raced through the hole that used to be a doorway into the room. His heart sank…the two privates were torn apart. They were both dead—their bodies ripped apart by the explosion.

Zip, pop, bang!

The front of the school building was being lit up by small-arms fire now. In addition to the bullets smacking the walls, Higgins heard explosions nearby and felt the reverberations in his chest.

His radio came to life. "Higgins, if you're still alive, I need you to get your machine gun back up and running," said his lieutenant. "We have Chinese soldiers trying to push through the neighborhood nearby." The sound of rifles and machine guns in the background of the transmission came through loud and clear.

Sergeant Higgins depressed the talk button. "I'm on it, LT."

Looking around, Higgins found the M240G and grabbed it. He moved over to the blown-out wall of the building. It was easy to see what the lieutenant was talking about—at least thirty or forty enemy soldiers were bounding toward them. Scanning the area swiftly, he also saw that two of the three Strykers had been blown up, and so had both of the Bradleys. A couple of the tanks were raging infernos, but a few of them were still firing away at the enemy vehicles.

Higgins leveled the machine gun at a group of enemy soldiers, depressed the trigger, and fired several three- and five-second bursts at them. Some of the Chinese infantry went down while many more scrambled to find cover. He shifted his fire to another group of enemy soldiers he spotted charging forward.

The next five minutes went by in a blur as Sergeant Higgins went through three belts of ammo. After several attempts by the Chinese to take the school, they fell back to tried and regroup. Higgins and the other fireteam had done it—they had held the enemy off from taking their position, at least for the time being.

****

Fountain, Colorado

Chip Peterson sat in his Dodge Ram, parked on the side of the frontage road that ran alongside Interstate 25, just south of Colorado Springs. He grabbed a strip of the beef jerky he'd picked up a few hours earlier and took a bite. Then he watched the cars zip past him as he waited.

After a few more bites of jerky, he grabbed the Bing energy drink he'd purchased and guzzled half of it down before he turned on the radio. It was time for his favorite show. Tim "The Professor" Long, who hailed from the University of Colorado-Boulder, held a three-hour block on Saturdays during which he usually gave a political and economic analysis of what had been going on in the world during the last week. The program had started out as a local affair, mostly followed by students who were stuck having to listen to it, but it had taken off during the primaries and election cycle in 2020.

When President-elect Marshall Tate called for the formation of a Civil Defense Force in every state, the Professor had jumped right on board. The man had been a recruiting genius on the college campuses, rallying thousands of people to join the Colorado CDF. When the governor opted to stay on the side of the federal government instead of siding with the man Chip saw as the true president, the Professor's popularity rose even more. He and officials from the CDF often postulated about ways to remove the Colorado governor and replace him with other state legislators that had sided with Marshall Tate's camp.

As Chip sat in the truck listening to the Professor go on about how more people needed to rise up against the federal government, Chip's phone chirped, letting him know he had a new text. One of his scouts had spotted the Army convoy leaving the base.

A smile crept across his face. *It won't be long until they pass through our ambush.*

Chip polished off the rest of his energy drink, and then he finally spotted what he had been waiting for—a convoy of JLTVs, Humvees, Stryker vehicles, and FMTVs was heading right for him.

The 4th Infantry Division's 3rd Armored Brigade Combat Team had redeployed from the Dakotas. Now they were moving down to reinforce the Army in New Mexico and Texas. Chip knew that if they reached their destination, they would blunt or at least slow down the Chinese liberating force.

Chip continued to scan the advancing convoy with his binoculars until he spotted a long line of M1070 heavy equipment transporters moving toward him. The HETs were massive tractor-trailers and flatbeds that the Army used to transport the sixty-two-ton Abrams battle tanks cross-country when not using the railroads.

Chip reached for his smartphone and placed a quick call to Dusty.

"Hey. The trucks are on the way. Tell Jimmy to deliver the package."

"Roger that," came the reply, and then the line went dead.

Chip turned his truck back on and pulled a quick U-turn so he could see down the opposite direction of traffic. He wanted to witness the results of their handiwork. He also pulled out his phone and got it ready to record what was about to happen.

This will make for YouTube gold when I'm done with it, he thought.

Lifting his binoculars to his eyes, he saw Jimmy's fuel tanker head down Sante Fe Avenue. At that point, Chip put his binos down and started recording what was about to unfold.

Once Jimmy's eighteen-wheeler and fuel tank drove over the southbound lanes, he pulled the truck over to the shoulder as best he could and stopped. He hit the hazard lights and went to work. Chip watched as Jimmy got out of the rig and walked around to the passenger side of the trailer. Chip couldn't zoom in to see exactly what he was doing next, but he knew from what they had talked about earlier that he'd take a packet of matches out of his breast pocket and affix a lit cigarette to it. He'd then place it on the ground near the front tire. It would take a few moments to burn down to the matches, but once it did, it would give them the needed flash to make things go boom.

Chip continued to follow Jimmy as he made his way down to the center of the trailer and unscrewed the caps on the fuel outlet valves. He then opened the tanks up, releasing the eleven thousand gallons of diesel and gasoline stored in the four different storage tanks.

At this point, Chip pulled the image back a little bit so the viewer could see the fuel running over the bridge and spilling onto the southbound lanes below.

With this last task completed, Chip watched as Jimmy ran to the old Chevy on the opposite shoulder of the road that was waiting for him. Chip returned the camera to the tanker that was leaking fuel everywhere. Knowing that he was still recording, Chip used his best radio voice to say, "You don't have to be a soldier or own a weapon to help the CDF. Even this truck driver was able to do his part. We need more people like this—people willing to stand up to tyranny and fight for this country. Fight against this fascist dictator that won't leave office."

As he finished his little recruitment speech, Chip watched as the first HETs began to pass underneath the bridge and were thoroughly dowsed with diesel and gasoline.

Meanwhile, traffic on the bridge was starting to back up behind the truck as people realized it was now leaking fuel everywhere. The fuel continued to roll onto the overpass, and a steady stream of it spilled off the bridge to the interstate below, splashing on the vehicles and trucks passing underneath.

Many of the drivers below began to apply their brakes, while others did their best to either pull over and see what had dowsed their vehicle or try to move around to avoid getting hit with the unknown liquid.

A police car approaching the area spotted the mess and immediately turned on his lights as he sought to gain control of the situation and figure out what was going on. Chip felt a moment of panic as he saw the police officer get out of the cruiser and head for the truck, looking for the driver. He kept the smartphone recording though, waiting for the flash that would ignite the entire thing.

The third and fourth HETs passed under the overpass, and then it happened—the cigarette had finally burned down to the packet of matches, igniting them. A fraction of a second later, the entire bridge blew up in a massive fireball of flaming liquid. Burning fuel was thrown in all directions from the force of the blast, including onto the interstate below. The Army's tanks were covered in liquid flame.

Dozens of vehicles and trucks slammed on their brakes, trying to escape the flaming cauldron that had become the overpass. The multivehicle pile-up that ensued would take hours to unravel.

God only knows how long it'd take to put the fires out, Chip thought happily.

He kept his smartphone recording for another five minutes. He wanted to make sure he had plenty of footage for them to cut and use later. If they were lucky, this single act would inspire many more people to carry out similar attacks on the military.

For his part, Chip and his motley crew of five CDF members had just delivered what they hoped would be the first of many blows against the fascist in the White House.

Chapter 12
The Hunt

February 20, 2021
Bakerton, West Virginia

Master Sergeant Bruce "Deuce" Wilder shivered. The night air felt extra cold as it whipped through the open bay of the Blackhawk. Their helicopter raced along, just above the tree line as they sped their human cargo toward the target.

Deuce pulled his earbuds out and turned off his fight song as they got closer to the objective. He liked listening to Rob Bailey's song "Hungry" right before a kill mission— something about the lyrics got his blood pumping.

Looking across the jump seat, Deuce saw his partner and friend, Sergeant First Class "Larry" Flint, going through his own pre-mission ritual. Each man on the team had their own thing they did prior to a mission like this, one that was explicitly designated as a kill mission. They'd been instructed there were to be no prisoners during this op.

It had taken the NSA several weeks to track down the Russian Spetsnaz unit that had devastated their ranks during a brazen attack on the industrial park opposite their headquarters. However, through an extensive electronic collection of traffic cameras, home security cameras, business security cameras, and then some good old-fashioned human intelligence, they'd finally tracked down the Russians to an Airbnb in the small West Virginia town of Bakerton.

Given the intelligence, the President had authorized JSOC to terminate the threat with extreme prejudice. Brigadier General Lancaster, who'd led the missions in Kosovo, tasked Delta with the job.

"Five mikes!" shouted the crew chief to the Spartans in the back.

Looking out the door, Deuce saw the two Little Birds flying in formation with them. Further back were two Apache gunships, which would be responsible for any direct fire support they needed.

The pilot banked the helicopter hard to the right, gaining some altitude as they climbed over a ridge. The Blackhawk twisted slightly in the air as it dove back down and headed for the farmhouse.

"Here we go!" shouted Deuce over their team's internal coms system.

The pilot pulled up hard on the helicopter, bleeding off speed at an incredible rate before he leveled out and landed on the front yard of the property. In seconds, Deuce and the six operators in the helicopter had dashed off, guns aimed at the farmhouse.

A hundred meters to their right, the two Little Birds landed, dropping the four-man team that would clear the barn and the outbuildings on the property.

As the helicopters lifted off, the front window of the farmhouse erupted in shards of glass. Flame spat out from the barrel of a rifle that began firing at them.

"Contact front!" yelled Deuce. He aimed his weapon at the window, then sent a couple of three-round bursts that way.

"Engaging!" yelled Larry as they continued their charge. While still running forward, he fired his Mk 48 into the front room of the farmhouse, shattering the window and splintering the walls with 7.62mm bullets. The covering fire would force the enemy down while they advanced.

Deuce rapidly closed the distance to the house and bounded up the front stairs, taking them two at a time. He slammed against the wall near the door from his momentum. He and another team member waited to the side as Sergeant First Class Pedro "Spider" Santos, their breacher, slapped the stick of explosives on the door. As soon as they were on,

Spider pulled back to the rest of the team, who were stacked along the side of the wall, ready to assault the house.

"Breaching!" Spider yelled as he detonated the small charge, blowing the door inward. Then he tossed in a flashbang, and they all shielded their eyes for just a moment.

Bang.

As soon as they heard it go off, they dashed inside with guns at the ready.

"Clear!" yelled Deuce as he finished sweeping the front room. He'd found two bodies, but no active threat.

"Movement in the kitchen!" shouted Spider from the opposite side of the house.

Deuce swept his SCAR in the direction of the kitchen and fired a dozen rounds into the wall and door frame, hoping to catch whoever was in there. Two other members from his team fired their own rifles into the kitchen and eating area as they charged forward to clear the rest of the first floor.

Deuce was about to head upstairs with his partner Larry when he heard footsteps above them. Pointing his SCAR to the ceiling, Deuce fired a string of shots into the room above them. Plaster rained down on him. Larry ran to the next room and lit up the ceiling there as well, in case another shooter was up there waiting for them.

Deuce made a beeline toward the staircase to try and catch whoever was up there by surprise and take 'em out. He tossed his now empty magazine into his drop bag and slapped a fresh one in place to get ready.

He bounded up the steps but stopped just short of the top when a string of bullets flew right in front of him. Deuce dropped down to a knee, then popped up to fire his SCAR at the attacker, hitting him several times in the chest and face.

Sensing something coming up behind him, Deuce turned right as a burly man pounced on top of him with a large hunting knife in hand. Deuce caught the man's arms just in time to prevent him from driving the blade right through the side of his body armor. The two of them fought on the ground for a moment, grunting and screaming at each other as they struggled for their lives.

The fight lasted less than ten seconds. Larry had run up the stairs to aid his friend, and when he reached the landing, he kicked the attacker across his face with his steel-toed boot.

The man was flung off Deuce from the force of the kick. He appeared stunned by the blow to the head, but his eyes went wide for the briefest of seconds as Larry leveled his Mk 48 at the man's chest and fired a dozen rounds into him.

After rolling onto his knees, Deuce jumped up with his SCAR still attached to his rig and proceeded to finish clearing the rest of the rooms on that level.

"Top floor cleared."

"Ground floor cleared."

"Cellar cleared."

With no more Russians alive in the house, Deuce's team headed outside to make sure their other comrades didn't need any help. They heard some shooting coming from the barn, and they rushed to assist their fellow soldiers. Seconds later, they heard the call.

"Barn cleared."

"Outbuildings cleared."

The two Apaches circled the farm, using their thermal scanners to make sure no one had escaped. They hovered in opposite ends of the property, eventually calling an all-clear over the radio.

With the location now cleared, the operators started dragging all the dead bodies outside to the front of the farmhouse as a sensitive site exploitation team landed. The SSE team would go through the farmhouse and the surrounding buildings on the property, collecting evidence and biometrics on everything they could. All of this information would be fed back to the NSA for further analysis as they sought to determine if the group of ten bodies constituted the entire Russian team or if more of them may still be alive out there somewhere.

Slowly and steadily, the NSA and FBI were tracking down the enemy Special Forces teams operating within the country while the Unit systematically wiped them out as they were found.

****

Starke, Florida
Camp Blanding

Lieutenant Colonel Seth Mitchell sat at his desk, looking at the mountain of paperwork before him. He sighed. Shifting his gaze out the window, Seth saw that the sun was creating a beautiful dawn display. The orangish-red hues were mixing with the white clouds and the blue hues of the new day. Sunrises in Florida were always beautiful; at least, that's how he felt about them.

Over the early morning chirping of birds, Seth could hear the morning cadence calls of the NCOs working the new batch of recruits over on the parade field. One group of recruits was being run hard by their platoon sergeant. Another group was being smoked, doing endless front-back-goes until they vomited their guts out. A third group was doing a CrossFit routine while a fourth group was participating in morning yoga.

Seth snickered at the yogis. He gave his NCOs a lot of latitude in how they wanted to PT their recruits. His only guidance was to get them fit without breaking their bones or excessively injuring them. In a way, this new assignment General Royal had given him was an ideal Special Forces mission. Instead of training up an indigenous force in a foreign country, they were helping Homeland Security train up a federal law enforcement force to put down an internal rebellion growing within their own country.

The training they were putting the recruits through was rough. The first week of training focused a lot on stretching and cardiovascular training. They gradually worked them into more physical exercises. It was challenging because they only had four weeks with the recruits before they shipped them off to wherever they were being assigned.

The recruits' days were long, beginning at 0430 hours with ninety minutes of physical training. They were only given sixty minutes to get a shower, change, and eat before they started class at 0700 hours. One platoon would be handed off to a group of federal law enforcement training instructors from the FLETC academy, who'd spend a few hours going over the law enforcement procedures they'd be responsible for as a member of the Federal Protective Service. Then the platoon would rotate back to their Special Forces instructors for weapons training, patrolling, combat maneuvers, or other military tactics and training they may need to perform their new duties.

It was slow going, but Seth's training brigade was now fully running. They were churning out a thousand new FPS officers every week. His training command had initially started with a couple of FBI, DHS, and FLETC trainers and fifty Special Forces soldiers. By the end of their third week of operations, the FBI had sent another eighty instructors, and the DoD had finally seen fit to provide with him with an additional three hundred soldiers to help run the training and a hundred more to fill in a lot of the support functions. In the span of seven weeks, they had transformed Camp Blanding into a world-class training facility.

Seth realized he'd spaced off looking at the sunrise long enough and refocused himself on the mountain of paperwork before him. The packet he opened first contained the personnel files of four of their new recruits that one of the first sergeants had singled out. The individuals had prior college or showed a level of leadership that would make them prime candidates to become sergeants or officers at the end of the training course. Seth's unit was under a lot of pressure to not only get these recruits trained but also identify potential leaders to lead them.

Once approved, the candidates would stay to receive additional training: sergeants would be given three weeks of training, and officers would receive four. During those courses, they would learn advanced small unit tactics, communications, and some necessary administrative functions they'd need to know as first- and second-line managers in what was essentially a very military-centric force.

Seth knew the job he was performing was essential to the mission and kept him out of harm's way, but he missed being assigned to a team. The short stint in Kosovo reminded him of how much he liked being in the thick of the action, where it was easy to see that he was making an impact. Now his country had been invaded, and instead of carrying out Special Forces missions against the invaders, he was stuck trying to rapidly train up an internal DHS security force.

Knock, knock.

Looking up, Seth saw a face he hadn't expected to see.

"Smith. What are you doing down here?" he asked, bewildered.

"It's good to see you too," Smith responded with a mischievous grin. "Mind if we go for a walk?"

"Um. Yeah...sure," Seth stammered. He grabbed his beret as they headed out the door.

Neither of them said a word as they walked through the hallway of the old building on their way to the exit. They ambled past the parade ground where the recruits were doing their morning routine and continued to stroll toward the dock along the lake.

Finally, Smith turned to look at Seth. "Are you enjoying this training gig your boss set you up with?" he asked.

Seth snickered. "Mine is not to ask why, but to do or die," he replied, giving the standard military nonresponse to such a troublesome question.

"That's what I thought," Smith said with a smile. He pointed to a bench on the dock. "Here, let's take a seat. No one can hear us talk out here, and you don't exactly have a SCIF at this joint."

"You know, we could go for a drive if you'd like," Seth offered.

"No. I'd rather talk out here and watch the sunrise. It's a beautiful day, isn't it?"

Nodding, Seth didn't say anything. He just waited for Smith to get to the point of why he was here.

"Remember when we were in Kosovo, and you interrogated that Chinese national?" Smith asked.

"Wen Zhenyu. Yeah, I remember him. What about it?"

"We've had him at one of our black sites, and we've continued our conversation. Let's just say he's provided a bit more information since you last spoke with him."

Seth's left eyebrow rose.

"As a matter of fact, he's helped us piece together a few aspects of what's been going on with this whole UN-led mission and the Chinese invasion. The whole world, and in particular, our country, has been played from the beginning. It's been very Sun Tzu if you ask me."

Seth shook his head. He'd thought from the beginning that there was a larger grand plan involved in orchestrating this charade—he just hadn't been able to put his finger on who was pulling the strings. While he was managing this training program at Camp Blanding, he'd gotten removed from that world, effectively cut off from the classified side of things.

"So, how do I fit into all of this?" Seth asked. "You're clearly here talking to me for a reason."

Now it was Smith's turn to smile. "You always were sharp, Seth. I like that about you. Well, you're right. I'm not here for a social call, or to inspect your training program—which I will say looks impressive considering how little time you had to throw it together. I'm here because I need you."

Seth slumped his shoulders. "Well, you're talking to the wrong person," he responded. "General Royal specifically assigned me to this program."

Smith waved his hand in the air as if swatting off a fly. "That's already been taken care of, Seth. You've been effectively reassigned back to the Agency."

"What?" asked Seth incredulously. "How'd you manage to pull that off?"

"Once you work for us, Seth, you never really leave. I made the case that we needed you and your specific skill set, and it was signed off on. When we get back to your office, your new orders will be on your desk, and your replacement should be there waiting for us," Smith explained with a mischievous grin.

Seth shook his head in disbelief. "Who are you really, and what is your position within the Agency?" he pressed.

"That's not important," Smith said jovially. "What *is* important is that we uncovered some new information, and I've put together a small team to go hunt down the missing pieces. This is important, Seth. The world has been hoodwinked, and it's up to us to uncover this plot and reveal its true nature to the rest of humanity. Our country's future depends on us getting this right and doing it sooner rather than later."

"OK, Smith," Seth replied with a nod. "Count me in. Not that I really have a choice, but yes, let's go hunt these guys down and expose this plot."

****

Warrenton, Virginia
Camp Perry

Seth entered the dormitory and summarily plopped his hockey bag down on the bed. He walked over to the closet and opened it up. There were about a dozen wooden hangers in there, along with an ironing board and iron. Looking at his watch, he saw he had about forty minutes before he was needed in the briefing room. Unzipping his bag, he went to work on getting his clothes and few personal items he'd brought unpacked. Seth wasn't sure how long he'd be here, but he didn't like living out of a suitcase or duffel bag if he didn't have to.

Midway through, he pulled his picture frame out and sighed as he looked at his most recent family photo, a picture of all of them at Disney. It was hard to comprehend that this memory was from four short months ago—it felt like a lifetime had happened since then.

It angered Seth to know that his country was being torn apart by some outside force. As a husband, father, and soldier, he felt powerless to stop it. When Smith had shown up in Florida the other day, he'd had a twinge of hope that he might just have a shot at going after the people or group that had started this whole thing.

Thirty minutes later, Seth made his way down the hallway to the briefing room where he'd been told to meet his new team. As he reached the entrance, he stopped and took a deep breath. Then he pulled the door open and walked in.

Seth smiled when he saw Brigadier General William Lancaster from JSOC, who was now sporting a second star. Sitting next to him was Lieutenant Colonel Patrick "Paddy" Maine. Seth knew he was a squadron commander at Delta—he'd been with them in Kosovo. Both men returned the smile, obviously glad that Seth was joining them on this new team.

Seth walked up to Lancaster with his hand extended. "Congrats, sir, on the second star. I hadn't heard you were promoted."

Standing, Lancaster shook his hand. "Thanks, Seth. I owe it in large part to your cracking Wen back in Kosovo. It's good to have you on the team with us. I have a feeling we're going to need your area of expertise again soon."

Paddy also stood up and shook Seth's hand. "It's good to have you with us, Mitchell."

Just then, a handful of scruffy-looking men wearing 5.11 clothes walked in and took a seat near Paddy. They nodded at Seth but mostly kept to themselves.

More people started filtering into the room, some wearing military uniforms, others wearing civilian attire. A few minutes went by, and eventually, the room filled. The crowd was nearly split between those in the military and those who weren't. Clearly, whatever was in the works was going to require both skill sets.

A woman in a business suit walked in and made her way to the front of the room. She cleared her throat to get their attention. "Good morning, everyone. I'm going to pass out a sign-in roster that I need everyone to sign. Use your legal name and social security number. Next, I'm going to have each of you sign a document reading you on to the Special Access Program you're now a part of. This is non-optional. You either sign, or you will be reassigned immediately. When everyone has completed this, I'll collect the papers and signatures, and we'll begin."

She walked up and down each of the rows, handing everyone the appropriate paperwork. The legalese on the document was mostly benign, except for the line stating, "I understand that if I talk about this program or my participation in this program, I will be tried for treason." Seth almost laughed at that, but when he thought back to what Smith had told him, he realized the secrecy involved and the importance of the program—they were serious. He swallowed and signed, feeling a bit more somber.

After a moment, the woman in the business suit came around and collected everyone's signed papers. Then she placed them all in a folder and left the room.

Next, FBI Director Nolan Polanski walked in. He was quickly followed by Tony Wildes, the Deputy Director of the NSA, and Marcus Ryerson, the Director of the CIA. Then, to their collective surprise, President Jonathan Sachs came through the door, flanked by a handful of heavily armed men kitted out in combat gear and weapons.

Everyone jumped to their feet when the President entered the room. The military men moved to the position of attention until told otherwise. Whatever they were about to be a part of was extremely important if the leaders of the nation had come here to talk with them personally.

Not missing a beat, the President walked to the front of the room. He surveyed the men and women gathered there before he announced, "I won't take up a lot of your time. Director Polanski and Ryerson will brief you on the details of why you're here and what you'll be doing. I'm here because I first want to thank you for volunteering for this mission. Second, I want to instill upon you the importance of what you're about to embark upon.

"Our nation has been attacked and invaded. A small group of people has put into motion a series of events designed to destroy our nation and supplant America as a world power—we can't allow that to happen. Each of you has been chosen because you have a specific skill set needed to accomplish this mission. I want each of you to know that you have my backing to do whatever is necessary to accomplish this mission. You will be given every available resource you need, and every effort will be made to assist you in completing the tasks ahead of you. I don't want to say you guys have a blank check to do whatever you want, but the leash has been taken off, so to speak. With that, I'm going to leave and let these gentlemen get you guys up to speed on what's transpired these past few weeks."

The President then turned and left the room with his bodyguards in tow. All eyes then turned to the remaining national leaders in front of them.

The FBI man spoke next. "I'm Director Polanski of the FBI, for those of you who don't know who I am. I've tasked Assistant Deputy Director Ashley Bonhauf to be the FBI liaison officer for this task force. She's a career FBI agent with fifteen years of experience working both in our counterintelligence and cybersecurity departments. Ashley brings a wealth of experience and is one of the key individuals who uncovered the postal worker scheme to rig the election.

"As an FBI agent, she will also provide your task force with the legal oversight and authority to operate within the US. This is critically important as we look to build a legal case against those who've orchestrated this grand scheme to take down our government. Ashley has the complete backing of the FBI and a direct line to me personally for any help or assistance your task force may need."

Ashley stood and waved to identify herself to the group.

Polanski continued. "During the operation in Kosovo, JSOC apprehended a Chinese national by the name of Wen Zhenyu. Many of you have no idea who he is, but thanks to some unique interrogation techniques, we learned that he was a deep-cover agent for the Ministry of State Security. Since his initial interrogation in Kosovo, he's disclosed some new information that led us to discover that this entire UN-led peacekeeping mission, the rigging of our election, and the killing of our Supreme Court justices were all planned out many years ago."

Several people in the room shared nervous glances. A few others gasped at the allegation, and a few more cursed quietly.

Deputy Director Wildes from the NSA jumped in. "Once we knew when and where to look based on the intelligence Wen provided, we uncovered some information that painted a bigger picture for us of what's going on and who all is involved.

"If you'll remember back a few years ago, Google announced a major cyber breach. They learned that the account logins and passwords to every Gmail account had somehow been compromised. Once the FBI and FireEye got involved in the forensic analysis of what had happened, we eventually traced it back to ATP10. It was initially believed the Kosova Hacker's Security group or KHS was the group responsible; however, when we peeled away the onion, it became clear they were just the patsy to the real culprits. ATP10 is an elite Chinese cyber-hacking unit. They go by the name Unit 61398, and they're essentially the Delta Force of cyber-hackers.

"This group is probably responsible for the bulk of China's cyber-espionage efforts globally. More importantly, Wen Zhenyu has admitted to not just being a member of this unit, but he was one of its senior commanders and deep undercover assets in Europe. He's the reason why the EU and nearby countries gave us so much grief while we were in Kosovo and why parts of the Serbian government got involved in protecting the Islamic State in Serbia. They were being coerced by the Chinese government to impede our efforts in the region. They wanted to keep us from uncovering the true nature of the terrorist attacks happening in our country prior to the election and put pressure on us to release Wen back to their custody.

"We obviously needed to hang on to Wen and continue to debrief him. However, we couldn't continue to hold him in Kosovo, and we couldn't move him out of the country—not with the Chinese using their economic and political power against Kosovo and the surrounding countries. So, we reluctantly agreed to hand him over."

Seth heard a few grumbles in the room. "General Lancaster here," Wildes said, pointing to the general from JSOC, "came up with a clever way for us to make the Chinese believe Wen had been killed so we wouldn't have to lose him as an intelligence source. Using something called Deepfake technology, we developed a computer program that pieced together some very convincing CCTV footage of Wen that would pass a forensic analysis test. We made it appear like Wen had attacked and killed several of his guards, then acquired their weapons and broken himself out of Camp Bondsteel.

"We knew the Chinese were watching the base like a hawk with their satellites and probably human sources nearby, so we needed to make this look convincing from all vantage points. When Wen would have supposedly found his way out of the building, we used a body double and had him make his way over to a US government-plated SUV, get in and drive off the base. Through some further trickery, when the vehicle had driven about three miles away from Camp Bondsteel, we had it get blown up by an IED.

"The subsequent 'investigation' into the blast, which we made sure was leaked, revealed that the IED had been placed by Luan Rexhepi's group, Islamic State in Kosovo. Supposedly, the ISK blew up the US government vehicle in retaliation for the US's attack on their training camps and the capture of their leader.

"We weren't sure the PLA would buy it, but we made sure the CCTV video and report of what had happened was compromised and able to fall into their hands. Our hope was once they pieced the information together, they'd believe Wen was killed and no longer a loose end or asset they had to recover. Thus far, that cover story has held up, and it appears they have written Wen Zhenyu off as a casualty of this new war."

Director Ryerson from the CIA jumped into the conversation. "Once Wen had been assured his government no longer believed he was alive, he told us what they were really after. While all of you know about the public Gmail attack, what you don't know is that was just the face of it. It was the PLA's cover for what they were really after—the White House secured email system."

Now everyone leaned forward in their chairs, eager to know what all of this was about.

"Unit 61398 had been tasked with obtaining the secret communications between the President, the Secretary of Commerce, Treasury, and the President's key trade advisors, discussing a series of tough sanctions and trade regulations that were going to be aimed at reining in China. Armed with this information, the Chinese leaders had had an inside track on every move our government made economically. They also used that information to help foment a conspiracy between some other powerful individuals and groups to insert their Manchurian candidate into the 2020 race.

"What your task force is now being assigned to find out is who all is part of this conspiracy. Right now, the only person we know is involved for sure is Peng An. He's the CEO of the China Investment Corporation, which essentially runs China's sovereign wealth fund. He's also a close friend of President Chen. We need to find out who his co-conspirators are."

"Now that you guys know what's at stake, and what your overall mission is, I'm going to hand you over to Major General Lancaster, who's going to be your task force commander. He has the full support of our agencies and the President." Ryerson signaled for the general to come forward, then he and Wildes left the room—their part in all of this was done.

All eyes turned to the general from JSOC. It was suddenly apparent to Seth how he'd ended up in this room, since Lancaster was apparently in charge.

"Ryerson and Wildes are right," said Lancaster. "We don't have a lot of time to uncover who all is involved in this conspiracy. The world is steadily uniting against us, and at some point, these powers are going to be more than even our great military can overcome. We have to defuse the situation, and we have to show the world they've been deceived. That means we need to track down everyone involved in this. Right now, we have one name—Peng An. We need to figure out how we can capture him so we can debrief him on what he knows. That, or we need to find another link that can provide us with the other conspirators."

Lancaster took a step back, softening his demeanor. "Prior to us digging into this, I'd like us to take a few minutes to go around the room. Briefly tell us who you are, what agency or group you work for, and what your area of expertise is."

The next hour was spent getting to know everyone. The group quickly learned that the people in the room all brought a unique set of experiences and skills—a broad spectrum of expertise that would be needed to track a global adversary. They had a financial crimes expert from the IRS, a cyber-hacker working for the NSA, and a plethora of military and counterintelligence operators.

Once the introductions had been made, they got down to the business of trying to figure out how they were going to capture and question Peng An.

Chapter 13

United Nations

Geneva, Switzerland

"You said this plan would *not* lead to a conflict, and if it did, it would be over in a matter of days. We're now entering our seventh week of this war! Do you know what this has done to my country?" shouted Prime Minister Martin of Canada through the video teleconference. The man was irate. His country was in the process of being systematically destroyed by the fighting raging across its borders.

Several others in the meeting all nodded their heads in agreement.

Johann could feel their glares, wrought with misgivings. They had blindly followed him down this path, and now it appeared like everything was in the process of falling apart.

"If the Chinese had held up their end of the bargain, we wouldn't be in this predicament," chided the French Foreign Minister.

"China has invaded the southern American border," Foreign Minister Jiang shot back angrily. "I might also add that it was China who neutralized the American Navy in the Pacific and China who has suffered the wrath of American nuclear weapons, not France."

"Your military was supposed to invade America in coordination with our northern force," countered the Frenchman in his usual condescending manner. "Had you done that, the Americans would have crumbled under our combined weight. As it is, our northern force has been nearly defeated."

Slapping the table hard, the Russian Foreign Minister shouted, "This war was supposed to stay conventional, not go nuclear!" He pointed his finger angrily at the Chinese delegation. "You were supposed to have attacked when our forces invaded. Our combined invasion should have toppled the government and destroyed their military. Instead, you got cold feet and waited a month. Then you thought you could get away with nuking Guam, Arizona, Oklahoma, and one of their carrier battle groups on top of using an EMP over Southern California, Hawaii, and Australia.

"At the start of the war, we had the American public divided and moving in our direction…China has somehow succeeded in uniting the vast majority of their country together. Now, not only are they fiercely fighting our forces in the north, but they are demanding vengeance on every nation involved in this war. China has lost this war for us all!"

Foreign Minister Jiang Yi glared at the Russian and the other members of the UN peacekeeping force as they all nodded in agreement to what he'd just said.

"I will remind you, China has suffered more than sixty million civilian and military casualties since the start of this war. *None* of your nations have suffered loss like ours." Jiang paused for a second before chiding them further. "You Europeans and Russians are pathetic. Your nations have ranked among the top economies in the world, and yet your combined military force has been crushed by less than half of the American military in less than four weeks of combat."

He shook his head in disgust. "No. It is you who are the weakest links in this grand coalition. You have lost the war all by yourselves. China will win this fight, and we will defeat America without you. We alone will bask in the spoils of this war, you pathetic weaklings. China shall laugh as the Americans rain bombs on your cities. China is done pandering to you."

As soon as he finished his blistering speech, Jiang stood up and walked out of the room, followed closely by his aides.

"Come back to the table and let us talk things out," Johann called out. A few others joined him in attempting to convince the Chinese Foreign Minister to stay, but those efforts were fruitless.

As Johann watched the door close behind the Chinese delegation, he was seething with anger inside.

How do the Russians and the French manage to ruin everything they touch? he wondered.

He turned to look at the remaining delegations of the UN peacekeeping force. He pulled his shoulders back to project as much confidence as humanly possible. "We need to reinforce our soldiers in Canada," he commanded. "The weather is warming up, which will open up more ways for us to send supplies into Canada."

The German Foreign Minister, who was also known as a war hawk, chimed in. "While I think it was foolish for the Chinese to use EMPs and nuclear weapons against the Americans, the one advantage they just gave us is stealth. The US lost a lot of its early warning radar systems and satellites during the attack, and while the Americans aren't completely blind, there are now significant holes in their satellite and radar coverage. We need to exploit those holes and push as many supplies and reinforcements through them as we can."

The Russian Foreign Minister uncrossed his arms. "Well, now that we control the American air base at Thule in Greenland, we can use that base as a midway point," he offered. "I was told by General McKenzie that they have largely repaired the runways at Bagotville, Gandor, and Goose Bay air bases. We can begin airlifting soldiers to Thule and then land them at one of those three airfields."

The Canadian PM joined the conversation via teleconference. "If you can get them to Gandor, we can use our fishing boats to ferry them across the Gulf of St. Lawrence." He paused for a moment as if having seconds thoughts. Then looked pointedly at Johann. "If we aren't able to secure some sort of victory against the Americans or slow their advance down on our border within the next few weeks, I believe we will need to strongly consider seeking terms to end this war."

Johann nodded. He realized the man was right. This war had started out with a lot of optimism, but victory had slipped away from them. He sighed. Seeing the others look at him expectantly, Johann lifted his chin. "Then let's work to slow the American advance and get our boys the reinforcements and supplies they need," he announced.

****

A couple of hours later, Johann sat in his office, rubbing his temples. He was getting another stress-induced headache.

Knock, knock.

Johann looked up and saw his old friend, Roberto Lamy, the Director-General of the World Trade Organization. The two of them had been friends now for more than three decades. They had originally met when they were graduate students at the London School of Economics many years ago. They'd managed to stay close friends as each of them rose through the corporate and political ranks.

He happily waved his friend in. "Come in, Roberto. It's good to see you."

"Likewise," Roberto responded as he walked into the spacious office. As he got a little closer, he gently said, "You look tired, my friend."

Johann nodded. The exhaustion he felt seemed to be draining the very life out of his body. "This job is more stressful than I thought it would be," he admitted.

Roberto laughed softly. "You're the first UN Secretary-General to try and wage a world war against the Americans. Did you think it would be easy?"

Johann sighed. "No, I thought this war would have been over with by now. The American president was

422

supposed to have left office with his tail tucked between his legs. How did things go so wrong?" he lamented.

Roberto sat down on the couch next to the large window that overlooked Lake Geneva. "I heard there was a bit of a problem with the Chinese yesterday," he remarked.

Johann joined his friend in staring at the view. He was still trying to figure out if Jiang was serious about the Chinese no longer going to be a part of the UN peacekeeping force. He hadn't explicitly said they were withdrawing, but he wasn't returning his calls right now either. "The Russians and the French pushed them a bit too far," Johann offered. "I think they may pull out of our peacekeeping force."

Roberto's expression betrayed his concern. "You need to call Peng, then. He needs to talk with Jiang and Chen to make sure the Chinese continue to stick to the plan. Everything is riding on remaining a united front against the Americans."

Johann shook his head in defeat. "No, you call him," he insisted. "He'll respond better to you than me right now."

Roberto nodded. No further conversation was needed on that topic.

Johann decided it would be good to speak with someone who had a broader perspective on global affairs.

"Economically, how is the world holding up right now?" he asked.

Now it was Roberto's turn to sigh. "Not nearly as good as it should be. Losing access to the American market has been difficult for many nations. OPEC is under a lot of pressure from the Americans to not sell their oil and LNG to the member nations participating in this peacekeeping force. Fortunately, several OPEC members are also part of this force and have thus far kept the syndicate from giving in to the Americans. However, if the war starts to move decidedly in the Americans' favor, that may change. They will remain neutral until they see who's going to win."

"How bad will things get if the war drags on a couple more months?"

Roberto grimaced. "It will be disastrous, Johann," he insisted. "This war was never supposed to last two months. The global economy is on the brink right now. If it wasn't for heavy defense spending in Europe and Russia and the Chinese propping things up, it might well have collapsed already."

"It can't be that bad," Johann countered. "America isn't the be-all, end-all to the world economy."

"My friend, politics is your field, economics and trade is mine. The world has effectively lost half of its trading partners overnight. A twenty trillion-dollar economy just disappeared. That can't be easily replaced. Look at your own home country, Germany. Daimler, BMW, and Volkswagen aren't exactly shipping cars to America. Even their foreign plants in America are being converted to produce military equipment for this war, and if they don't comply, they are being taken over by the government and handed over to Ford or General Motors to manage. If this conflict isn't resolved in the next month, two months tops— Johann, we'll be looking at a full worldwide economic collapse."

****

Fort Meade, Maryland
National Security Agency

"Got it!" announced one of the analysts excitedly.

"Excellent. Get it over to the crypto guys," Deputy Director Tony Wildes ordered. "Once they're done with it, send it directly to me. I'll handle getting it translated and sent to the task force."

Maybe we finally have our first major break, thought Tony.

He walked back to his office, picked up his secured phone, and placed a call down to Camp Perry. The phone rang twice. "Leah Riesling," said the voice on the other end.

He smiled. "Leah, it's Tony. I think we just caught the break we've been looking for."

"Oh. Do tell," she replied, the excitement clear in her voice.

"Peng An just received a call from Roberto Lamy, the Director-General of the WTO. The call lasted for roughly two and a half minutes. Roberto then made another call to Johann Behr at the UN, which lasted four minutes. Peng returned Roberto's call later in the day, and they talked for another five minutes."

"Wow, that is a lead," remarked Leah. "Tell me we're able to decrypt their conversations."

"It's with the crypto guys right now. Should have it decoded shortly. I wanted to give you a heads up of what's coming your way."

The two talked for a few more minutes before they ended the call. An hour later, Tony got the decrypted call and couldn't believe what he read. They had their link—now they needed to figure out how to question one of them and find out who else was involved.

****

Camp Perry

General Lancaster looked at the decoded transcript of the messages between the Director of the WTO, the Head of the Chinese Investment Bank, and the leader of the UN. He shook his head, unable to believe what he was reading. At least things were starting to make sense.

Lancaster turned to the senior NSA, CIA, and FBI liaison reps for Task Force Avenger, hands on his hips. "So, who do we snatch to question further, and how do we go about doing it?" he asked.

The CIA LNO leaned forward. "Well, I'd say we nab Peng, but even if we could grab him in Geneva, we'd never be able to get him out of the country. Plus, the Swiss are pretty damn good at tracking people down inside their borders. I hate to say it, but if we want to grab him, we have to get him outside of Europe and China."

The group talked over some of the options of carrying out a snatch-and-grab operation in Geneva. It wasn't sounding very optimistic. Finally, Ashley said, "Why don't we grab Roberto? He'll be a much easier target than Peng, and we can probably get just as much information from him."

There was a moment of silence as they all mulled that over. Leah countered, "We'd still have the problem of grabbing him in Geneva."

Ashley shook her head. "No. Roberto's family lives in the Leblon neighborhood of Rio de Janeiro. We could engineer a family emergency that requires him to have to fly back home. When he arrives in-country, we snatch him there."

"What would require him to have to fly all the way back to Brazil?" asked Lancaster, left eyebrow raised skeptically.

"Let me have until dinner to come up with something. I know the legal attaché in Brasilia. Let me place a call down to him and get some ideas."

The group agreed to meet again just before dinner. They'd formulate their plan then and start moving people to get in place.

Chapter 14
Battle of Chicago

March 5, 2021
Calumet City, Illinois
River Oaks Center

Lieutenant General Hugh Ridgeway stood next to the JLTV and waited for the action to start. He watched the sunrise; at least the view was beautiful. Plus, a warm front was moving through the area. The temperatures were moving from the fifties to the low sixties.

"Here they come," announced a soldier who'd been sitting up in the turret of the JLTV looking through a pair of field glasses.

General Ridgeway looked at his watch. They were a few minutes late.

Two Dutch Fenneks stopped roughly twenty meters in front of them, a white flag affixed to each of their antennas. A second after the vehicles stopped, a German general walked toward them, accompanied by a Dutch colonel. Behind them were two men wearing American military uniforms, modified by CDF name tapes and a UN patch on their shoulders.

Ridgeway held up his hand, letting the men know they had come close enough. He didn't fully trust them.

"Thank you for agreeing to speak with me under a flag of truce. I'm Lieutenant General Ridgeway, Commander of the XVIII Airborne Corps," he announced.

"I'm Major General Hans Vollmer, Commander of Division Schnelle Kräfte. This is my Dutch counterpart," the German said as he nodded toward his compatriot.

Apparently not wanting to be left out, the two civilians introduced themselves as the Illinois and Wisconsin Civil Defense Force commanders. Once the introductions had been made, the group stood there for a moment, sizing each other up. The German and Dutch soldiers looked over Ridgeway's shoulder into the shopping center parking lot— they clearly caught a glimpse of the armored force being assembled.

"General Vollmer, your division has fought hard and achieved many victories, but this war needs to end," Ridgeway insisted. "You're now cut off from your supply lines and routes of retreat to Canada. When our forces left Michigan at the start of the war, we declared the major cities open cities to spare them destruction and keep the people living in them from being killed. Sadly, your force has not done the same during your retreat—many thousands of civilians have been killed as a consequence. My corps is assembled and ready to finish you off. I am asking you to accept my offer of surrender and to save the lives of your men and the lives of tens of thousands of civilians."

The German quickly replied, "I have not been authorized to surrender. Furthermore, my orders by my government are to turn every town and city into a fortress to slow your advance and bleed your corps dry."

"You don't care that thousands of civilians are going to die in the process?" Ridgeway asked incredulously.

The German sighed. "I don't want to kill civilians any more than you do, but sadly, they are caught in the middle, and there is little I can do. I have my orders, and you have yours."

General Ridgeway was growing angry at the callousness this foreign invader was showing toward his fellow Americans. "General, if your division surrenders now, they will be treated in accordance with the Geneva Convention. However, if you choose to turn these cities into meat grinders and intentionally place civilians in harm's way, I will instruct my men that any German or Dutch soldier that is captured is to be executed. We won't take any prisoners. There won't be a single person left alive from your division when this war is over. Surely you can see you are losing this war. At this point, you should be trying to figure out how you can keep as many of your soldiers alive so they can return home to their families."

"You would execute prisoners?" the German exclaimed, aghast at the very thought.

"I'd kill them myself if you intend on making my soldiers fight you in the city of Chicago. You're placing the lives of civilians in harm's way for no reason. You think I won't have your soldiers executed for that? This is your last chance to surrender, General. If you want to take a few hours to consult with your commanders and think about it, you may, but at 1800 hours tonight, I start my offensive. I'll be issuing orders for all German and Dutch soldiers to be executed if they are captured."

With nothing further to discuss, the Americans got back in their vehicle and left. They'd give the Germans a bit of time to stew on what he had said and hope they'd come to their senses.

****

"General Tibbets, I made the offer to the German commander," Ridgeway explained. "He seems intent on having his remaining force fight it out in the city of Chicago. Sir, if he does that, it's going to result in thousands of civilians getting killed—not to mention the destruction of huge swaths of the city. How do you want me to proceed?"

"I see, General," said Tibbets. "For the time being, I want you to hold in place. Don't launch your attack tonight. I'm going to talk to the President and propose something." Tibbets paused before confirming, "You said his government had ordered him to turn the cities into fortresses?"

General Ridgeway depressed the talk button on the radio. "Yes, sir. That's what he said. If you ask me, he didn't seem pleased with it, but he's a soldier, and my impression is he'll do as he's told."

"So, if we can convince his government to order him to surrender, he'll surrender. Is that what you're saying?"

"I believe so."

"OK. I think I have an idea then. I'm pretty sure I know how to bring an end to this conflict a lot sooner than I had first thought. Continue to stand by, General."

With that, the conversation was ended, leaving Ridgeway wondering what Tibbets meant.

****

Cheyenne Mountain
NORAD

General Tibbets took a seat at his desk and turned on his SECRET Tanberg. He dialed General Markus's line, hoping he'd be at his desk.

A second later, the Chairman of the Joint Chiefs' image appeared on the screen, looking tired and haggard from the pressures of his job.

"Adrian, it's Joe. We need to talk," said Tibbets.

General Markus seemed somewhat deflated, as if he couldn't handle the thought of one more problem. "What's going on, Joe?" he asked tepidly.

"It's Chicago. General Ridgeway made contact with the German division commander in the city. The Kraut told him he was under orders from his government not to surrender. He also said they've been under orders to turn every city and suburb into a meat grinder. When *our* forces had to withdraw, we made it a point to declare the cities open to spare the population from being caught in the crossfire. This division, however, has the opposite approach."

General Markus shook his head in anger and frustration. "What are your suggestions, Joe? I mean, I can see about sending more infantry to your position, but we're being pressed hard in the southwest right now."

"We need to change the minds of the German high command and their Chancellor. They need to order him to surrender," insisted General Tibbets.

"And how do you propose we do that?" asked General Markus skeptically. "We don't exactly have a lot of resources in the European theater we can use."

"See if the President can get them to order their surrender. If they don't, then bomb one of their cities. If they are going turn Chicago into rubble, then let's make sure they know we can turn one of their cities into rubble in exchange."

General Markus coughed. The idea was hard to stomach.

"Our goal here is to save the lives of civilians and both our forces," Tibbets insisted. "There is no reason why the German division shouldn't surrender. They're cut off, surrounded, and their back is against Lake Michigan. There is no hope of them breaking out. I don't want to have to kill everyone in that division, but we aren't being left with a lot of options here."

General Markus sighed and made a sour face. "I'll talk to the President about it. I...um, I'm not comfortable with this option. But I agree with you, we have tens of thousands of civilians at risk right now, and I'm not wanting to sacrifice them when there is an alternative that can save them."

The call ended. General Tibbets hoped the Germans would see reason and not force the Americans to do something more drastic.

****

Dyess Air Force Base

Standing inside the enclosed hangar, Colonel Webb of the 9th Bomb Squadron completed his final preflight checklist of America's newest global strike weapon, the highly secretive B-21 Raider.

As far as the rest of the world was concerned, the B-21 was years away from production, let alone being combat-ready. Specially designed leaks of testing mishaps, budget problems, production delays and other selective details had been dropped in certain circles to help spread the misinformation. It had worked, too.

Webb had just signed off on the checklist when one of the bomb techs walked up to him.

"Sir, all weapons have been loaded and are ready for your final inspection," announced the technical sergeant. He motioned for Webb to follow him over to the bomb bay doors, which were still open.

As they approached, Colonel Webb saw four other airmen standing at ease while they waited for him to review their work. He nodded toward them as he began his inspection. He knew they had really worked hard getting the bomber ready on such short notice.

Webb gently glided his hand over the nose of the two-thousand-pound bomb. He used a small light to check a few things inside the cavernous space that made up the bomb bay. The weapons had been loaded onto specially designed racks to allow the internal bay to hold as many of them as possible. When it came time to release them, they'd fall systematically, ensuring a clean release. He'd then turn his bomber around and head home.

Turning to look at the technical sergeant and his crew, Webb said, "Thank you, airmen, for your hard work. I'm impressed you got this bird ready on such short notice. I know you don't know where I'm headed, and it's probably best you don't. This mission I'm about to embark upon will save the lives of thousands, maybe even tens of thousands of Americans. Your country owes you a debt of gratitude. When I return, the beers at the Dyess Club are on me."

When he finished his little speech, he reached into his pocket and pulled out a B-21 Raider challenge coin. It had an image of the bomber on one side, and his colonel's eagle as the commander on the other. The command had just gotten them last week, and this was the first time he'd ever given them out. He made sure each of them got one, then made sure they understood the importance of not talking about this mission or their aircraft.

"Colonel, sir...we're ready," announced his co-pilot, who'd stuck his head out of the entrance to the bomber.

Colonel Webb nodded, then climbed inside. He made his way over to the cockpit, sat down, and did his best to make his body comfortable for the long flight.

Now that the ordnance inspection had been completed, his co-pilot, Major Hawkey, closed the bomb bay doors. He went through his own checklist, making sure all systems were 'green' before he turned to Webb and announced, "We're ready for engine start."

Webb fastened his helmet in place, making sure it was hooked up to their communications system and internal life support equipment. Then he called the control tower, letting them know they were ready for engine ignition and requesting permission to start the aircraft and leave the hangar.

Once permission was granted, the hangar doors were opened, revealing a pitch-black night sky. There was heavy cloud cover, which blotted out the moon and stars. Most of the base's lights near the parking ramp and the runway were also off, to help further hide the fact that they were gearing up to take flight.

This was Colonel Webb's third combat mission of this war. His first mission had been against the Russian capital of Moscow, and his second mission had been to deliver America's nuclear response to China. Now, they were being used to carry out a terror mission. He wasn't sure how he felt about it, but he knew the lives of a lot of civilians in Chicago depended on him succeeding.

Five minutes later, their plane, dubbed *Black Death*, was at the end of the runway, like a cocked pistol waiting to be fired. Having received their final authorization for takeoff, they powered up the engines and raced down the blackened runway. About three-quarters of the way down, Major Hawkey pulled back on the controls, and the Raider took to the skies.

He turned the aircraft to head toward the Atlantic. They would top off their fuel tanks a few hundred miles off the East Coast before they'd head toward their target. Once they delivered their message to Europe, they'd be met in the middle of the Atlantic by a second refueler to give them enough fuel to make it back to Dyess.

****

Washington, D.C.
White House
Situation Room

President Sachs watched the path of the B-21 on his computer monitor as it left US air space and began its long journey across the ocean. Even at Mach 1.3, it would still take them many hours to reach their target. Those long hours would give him more time to contemplate the situation. The more he thought about the orders he'd issued, the sicker to his stomach he felt.

When he'd spoken to the German Chancellor, he'd given him his warning and asked that calmer heads prevail. The Chancellor had insisted that his military advisors believed their division was still in good shape and could continue to fight on for many more weeks. He'd also insisted that they weren't going to end their involvement in the UN peacekeeping mission or yield to Sachs's demands.

With no other obvious choice, President Sachs had ordered the Air Force to do its best to level the German city of Hamburg. That was twelve hours ago. Now, they had a bomber on its way to do just that, and Sachs felt like he was going to throw up.

The Chairman of the Joint Chiefs, along with several other advisors, had all agreed that while this was a deplorable act, it could save the lives of thousands, maybe even tens of thousands or more Americans in Chicago. If they were successful in getting the Germans to surrender their forces, it might even collapse the entire UN peacekeeping force in the north.

Still, Sachs couldn't help but feel like he'd go down in history as a monster for ordering this strike. He looked down at the casualty projections in Hamburg and shook his head in anger and disgust that it had come down to this.

He was already having nightmares, knowing that he had ordered the death of millions of Chinese citizens when they blew up the Three Gorges Dam. The images he saw on the news and YouTube haunted him. The knowledge that his order had caused all that death and misery was almost more than he could bear.

However, when Sachs saw the images of the nuclear destruction in Arizona and Oklahoma, part of him just wanted to kill every person in China. He loathed these feelings of hate, regret, sorrow, and anger that put him on an emotional roller coaster. Sachs wanted nothing more than for this nightmare to end and get the new election going so he could hand these duties off to the next person, but he knew that couldn't happen until the country was once again united.

I won't be the last American president, he determined. *That distinction will go to someone else.*

As he returned his attention to the aerial image of the surrounding area of Hamburg, an idea popped into Sachs's head. He turned to General Markus.

"General, I have a proposal," he announced.

The Chairman of the Joint Chiefs raised an eyebrow but said nothing as he waited for the President to share more information.

"If we go through with this attack, we may achieve our goal, but we are going to get crucified in the press and with the international community. We're already being taken to task with our response to China. I think if we do this, we're going to damage our standing in the world beyond repair. They'll view us as a threat that must be stopped at all costs."

The others in the room held their comments, but Sachs could see many of them silently agreed with him by the looks on their faces.

"Let's change their target and go after one specific piece of their infrastructure."

Leaning forward, General Markus asked, "What do you have in mind, Mr. President?"

Sachs pulled out the map of Hamburg out that he had been looking at and pointed to a location on it.

"This report says one of the buildings that'll be hit by the current mission is this power plant. That got me to thinking—what if we specifically went after the German power grid?" he asked.

"You mean we intentionally take out their power plants?" Markus queried.

"Exactly. We can hit their five largest generating plants on this mission and then tell the Chancellor if he doesn't order the division in Chicago to surrender, we'll destroy another five power plants, and we'll continue to destroy five plants every day until the surrender," the President offered. He felt like this might be a decent compromise to destroying an entire city and hoped the general would agree.

General Markus let a giant breath out through pursed lips. Then he looked at the other Air Force general in the room with him. "What are your thoughts, Frank? Can the

Raider use their current payload to accomplish the change in mission, or do they need to come home to rearm?"

"Eh. The ordnance they are carrying isn't ideal for this mission, but it'll certainly do the job. That said, we're not going to be able to hit five targets, not with this current loadout configuration."

"Why not?" countered the President.

General Frank Ayers explained, "The Raider is dropping these bombs from some pretty high altitudes, and these are essentially unguided dumb bombs. There's no way for us to make sure each of them hits the right target. Our goal with this mission wasn't precision—it was to cause fear and destruction. Right now, the payload consists of six sticks of five two-thousand-pound bombs. If you'll give us an hour, Mr. President, we can figure out which power plant we could effectively take offline with the least number of civilian casualties given the Raider's current payload."

The President silently nodded, and the group went to work making the requested change to the mission package. Meanwhile, the B-21 continued on its original mission to Germany.

Ninety minutes later, the group reconvened. Several Air Force members walked to the front of the room and presented the President with an alternate target to bomb.

"Sir, we've looked at multiple power plants," General Ayers began. "We've decided that the best one to attack, given the plane's current payload and your direction to minimize casualties, is the Niederaussem Power Station located in Bergheim. It's Germany's second-largest coal plant, situated near the Dutch and Belgian border in northern Germany. It produces 3,864 megawatts of power on a daily basis.

"The second plant we've suggested to attack is the Neurath Power Station, located in Grevenbroich. It isn't far from the first target, so it wouldn't be out of the way for the Raider to hit it. This station produces 4,300 megawatts. Taking the two of them out would remove 7,864 megawatts of power production in northern Germany."

Sachs nodded his approval.

"Mr. President, if you'd like to continue this strategy of taking out coal plants, we will refit the Raider with JDAMs so that we can be a lot more precise on follow-on missions. Chances are, we'll be able to hit between ten and fifteen power plants on a single B-21 mission with the right ordnance."

"Hopefully, the Germans will come to their senses and not make us have to carry out any more of these types of attacks," countered the President.

****

Mid-Atlantic

Colonel Webb looked at the EAM message they'd just received from the National Military Command Center. He had Major Hawkey check twice to make sure it was legit. It was.

To Webb's surprise and relief, their target had changed. Instead of attacking the city of Hamburg—a mission that he knew would have resulted in the death of hundreds and probably thousands of people—they'd now been given a new purpose.

"I like this target a lot better than our original one," Hawkey stated bluntly after they'd sent their reply to the Pentagon to acknowledge the change.

Colonel Webb turned to look at his partner. "I agree, but we would have carried out our original orders." He paused. "But, yes, I think this is a better target given our current payload."

The two of them rode in silence for another thirty minutes. They had topped off their tanks when they received the mission change. They still had another six hours in the air. It was a long flight, even at the increased speed.

Seeing they had some time, Webb finally told Hawkey, "I'm going to do my best to catch a catnap for a couple of hours."

"All right. I guess it'll be my turn on the way home, eh?" joked Hawkey. The round trip on this mission was about twenty-eight hours of continuous flight. They had to make sure they took some time to get a few hours of sleep if they wanted to stay sharp. Given, the plane could mostly fly itself, but someone needed to stay awake in case something happened, or they received another change in their orders.

The hours dragged on as they got closer and closer to their first target. When they turned and flew over the North Sea, Major Hawkey woke Colonel Webb back up.

"We've got a lot of enemy search radar activity," he alerted him. "I also see a handful of enemy aircraft on the radar scope, flying combat patrols along the coast."

Colonel Webb tapped his chair. "OK, Raider, we're trusting you to keep us hidden right now," he said encouragingly, as if speaking to a pet.

When they neared the first target, they descended to a lower altitude, roughly ten thousand feet, and reduced their speed. This way, their bombs would be held in a much tighter group to ensure the facility was destroyed. Had they been carrying JDAMs, they probably could have parked one or two bombs into a critical section of the plant and called it a day.

A few minutes from weapons release, their threat board showed no apparent signs of danger in the immediate area. Colonel Webb went through the weapons release checklist, making sure they hadn't missed anything or skipped any steps. Less than sixty seconds from the target, he opened the bomb bay doors and made sure the bombs were ready for release.

When the targeting computer said they were over the target, they released their three sticks of five bombs each. In less than twenty seconds, thirty thousand pounds of high explosives had been dropped on Germany's largest coal power plant.

After closing the bomb bay doors, Major Hawkey applied more power to the engines and pulled up so they climbed in altitude. Now, they'd head to their second target and repeat the process. If things went according to plan, they'd be able to get out of the area before the Germans or anyone else could scramble any fighters to try and hunt them down.

Webb looked at his watch. It was just after 2300 hours. They had five more minutes of flying until they came to their next objective.

"Target destroyed," Hawkey announced. All the lights below them suddenly blinked out.

Webb snorted. "Let's hope."

A moment went by before Hawkey stated, "Sixty seconds from the next target. Opening bomb bay doors."

"Acknowledged," Webb responded. Then he prepared the last set of bombs. He had just finished releasing control of the bombs when the computer said they were over the target. The automated bombing system began releasing its payload. Webb observed that the bomber suddenly felt a lot lighter, and its handling had improved significantly.

Just as they got the bomb doors closed, the warning alarms blared. Half a dozen radars suddenly turned on, searching the air for them. Two pairs of Eurofighters also entered the area with their search radars on. They were being hunted.

Despite the danger, Major Hawkey remained cool as a cucumber. He applied more power to the engines and moved them into a cloud bank to help hide them.

Looking at their airspeed, Webb saw they had just crept above Mach 1 and were now approaching Mach 1.3. Their max speed in this beast was Mach 2.1. As they continued to speed up, Colonel Webb started thinking about all the fuel they would begin to go through. The plane was incredibly fuel-efficient when it flew at its cruising speed of Mach 0.9. However, it became a pig when they flew above Mach 1.5. If they kept their current pace for more than thirty minutes, they were going to need to tank up a lot sooner than they'd anticipated.

For five tense minutes, they cruised through the dense cloud cover at Mach 1.3. Major Hawkey finally announced, "I think we lost them. I'm not showing any fighters within a hundred-mile radius of us. It appears we slipped past them."

"I agree. Good job, Major. You stayed calm and didn't panic when they lit the place up. You're going to make a good aircraft commander when I finally retire."

"Retire? Hell, I thought you had your eyes on a star," retorted his partner good-naturedly.

Webb laughed, more to release the tension than at the question. "Oh, I don't know. I'd like the bump in retirement pay, sure. Northrop knows I'm getting close to retirement. They made me a hell of an offer to go work for them."

Hawkey turned to look at his partner. "Really? What would you be doing?"

Webb shrugged his shoulders. "I think they want me to stay on the Raider program—either as a pilot or something in the engineering or sales side of things."

"Sales? Congress said they're going to buy more than a hundred of these things. They're finally going to phase out those dinosaurs we have."

Webb snickered. "I think you heard wrong, my friend. They plan on keeping those bad boys around a bit longer. They're going to phase out the B-1s and the B-2s in favor of the B-21 and keep those flying deathtraps going a couple more decades."

"Wow, I thought that was still just speculation," Hawkey countered. "Well, if you want my two cents, sir, I think you should stay in. Get that star and take over as our group commander and head the first fully equipped B-21 bombardment group."

Webb laughed at the prospect. "Yeah, well, we'll have to wait and see what the boss says. I've made her follow me around for thirty years. If she wants to stick around a few more for me to get pinned, then I will. If she wants me to take the Northrop contract, well, then that's what I'll do."

The rest of the flight over the Atlantic went relatively smoothly. They linked up with their tanker a few hours later and continued back to Texas. Word had it they might be relocating in another week if the Army couldn't stop the Chinese.

****

Hamburg, Germany

The air was cool and crisp. The sky was gray, and the clouds continued to roll in. There was a buzz in the city, but not the kind of jovial energy one would come to expect. The mood in Hamburg had changed dramatically over the last few months. This sudden war between the UN and America had caught many of the residents of the city by surprise. Practically without warning, Germany had somehow found itself at war with America for the third time in less than a hundred years—not a good position to be in considering how the last two wars against the Yanks had gone.

"*Hier ist seine Kaffee*," a waitress announced as she delivered the hot cup of joe to Captain Flecker.

The British 22 SAS officer smiled at the young woman. "*Danke*," he replied. Flecker slipped her a five-euro note and motioned with his hand for her to keep the change. She smiled warmly at him as she walked off to help another customer.

Captain Flecker sipped on his coffee and took a bite out of the still-warm cheese-covered pretzel. While he ate, his eyes shifted to the sprawling harbor of Hamburg across the shipping channel. Black oily smoke still rose into the air from more than a dozen different locations.

Firemen were still trying to battle some of the blazes, while other workers took to the task of cleaning up the mess the Yanks had left behind. American stealth bombers had paid the city a visit two days ago. They had wrecked many of the large industrial cranes used to load and unload the massive ships that would tie up.

Reaching his hand up ever so slightly to adjust his glasses, Flecker depressed the tiny button on the frames that would allow him to record what he was seeing. He slowly looked at the different shipping terminals, making sure he paused at each one long enough to capture a few seconds of video. The recording would be chopped down into still images later on and examined before being passed on to the Americans.

A couple of minutes later, another man walked up to his table and pulled out a chair as he took a seat. "They really tore that place up, didn't they?"

Flecker snickered at the overly obvious statement from his sergeant. "The Yanks have a way of doing that, don't they?" he countered.

"I think we have everything. Are you ready to go?" asked the sergeant, who was holding up his copy of *Der Spiegel* as if he were there to read the paper.

"Yes. Let's head back to the safehouse," Flecker responded as he finished off his coffee.

The two of them got up and headed down the road, making sure to stop periodically and check to make sure they weren't being followed.

Before they stopped into a pub for a quick drink, the two of them eyed the door and the window, looking for any telltale signs that they might be under surveillance. Not spotting any, the two of them went in and drank their beers in private while they observed the people around them.

Captain Flecker and his sergeant both spoke German fluently, which was why they had been selected for this mission. Their job was to conduct battle damage assessment of the American bombing missions and to observe German troop movements to the ports. If they spotted a cluster of vehicles or military equipment arriving at the port, they'd send a message back to Hereford, where it'd be passed on to the US intel community. Usually sometime the next day, a stealth bomber or cruise missile would pay the port a visit. It wasn't a direct-action mission as they would have liked, but it was the kind of cloak and dagger stuff they were still good at.

The sergeant lifted his beer to his lips. Speaking softly so as not to be heard, he asked, "How much longer do you think it'll be until we join the Yanks in their little war?"

Flecker put his mug down and thought about his answer for a moment. There was a lot of talk within the Ministry of Defence about this subject. The politicians, of course, wanted to keep Great Britain out of the conflict, but many others inside the MOD wanted to aid their American cousins. The two nations had maintained a special bond since the end of World War II. It was ironic that now it was America who was being invaded and attacked by Europe instead of the other way around.

Looking at his sergeant, Flecker whispered, "Soon, sergeant. Soon."

****

March 10, 2021
Calumet City, Illinois
River Oaks Center

Captain Regan sat on the top of the turret with Sergeant First Class Miller, eating their MREs while one of the POL guys refueled their tank. Now that they'd been stationary for more than a few days, the ammo and fuel train had finally caught up to them. As soon as they were fueled up, they'd drive over to the ammo section and replenish their stores.

Once he finished his MRE, Miller stuffed his spork in the empty pouch and looked at Regan. "I suppose you want us to load up on extra HEAT and canister rounds for this next operation," he posited.

Regan grabbed his canteen and took a couple of gulps to help wash down his lunch. "I think that'd be best."

"I heard from a guy in the 519th MI that the Chinese finally captured Fort Bliss," said Miller. "They pushed the 1st AD all the way back to Odessa."

Regan nodded. "They did. They also pushed the 1st Cav back to Las Lunas, just south of Albuquerque."

"Holy crap. Really? I have a sister that lives in Albuquerque. Do you think the Chinese are going to capture it?"

Regan shrugged. "I have no idea. I know parts of the 4th ID were moving down to help them when some of their units got jumped by the Colorado militia. I think most of the division has now moved into New Mexico and Arizona, but they lost some tanks in that ambush."

"What? How could the militia have taken out tanks?" Miller asked, shaking his head in disbelief.

"They apparently emptied a fuel truck on an overpass as the battalion of tanks was passing underneath on the highway," Regan responded. "They blew the truck up which collapsed the bridge and dowsed a dozen or so tanks in flaming liquid. Someone in ops was telling me about it this morning at the brief."

"Man, that is some crazy Mad Max stuff right there," Miller said, running his fingers through his hair. "I don't know what the hell is happening to our country, sir. It's like a switch was turned on last September and everyone and everything has just gone nuts. I mean, we used to be able to agree to disagree. Now people are shooting at each other and trying to form their own countries or whatever it is these yahoos in Chicago are doing."

Regan sighed. He tried to avoid politics—he hated how it turned people against each other. Realizing that Miller was watching him, waiting for him to say something, Regan just shrugged. "I don't know, Miller. I'm just trying to do my best to stay alive and keep the rest of the guys in our unit from getting killed. I just want to get back home and do my regular job."

Miller grunted. "You know, sometimes I forget we're National Guard and not regular Army. I suppose that's because I've only been out of the regular Army for a year, so I'm not fully adjusted to civilian life yet."

"I had just accepted a job as a public defender in Meridian a month before this craziness started. I hadn't even unpacked my stuff into my new apartment when the call came," Regan said glumly.

When he'd graduated law school, Regan had opted to become a public defender rather than going into private practice or working in the district attorney's office. Mississippi had a program in place where if someone worked in the public defender's office for five years, the state would forgive their student loan debt. When Regan had joined the National Guard, they'd agreed to pay off thirty thousand dollars of his student loans, but that still left him with a balance of fifty thousand dollars. Despite the fact that the pay as a public defender in Mississippi stunk, it was worth it to him to have all that debt paid off in just five years. Then he'd be able to start whatever law practice he wanted at thirty years old, completely debt-free.

Miller shot Regan a quizzical look. "Public defender? That's an interesting choice. As for me, my uncle had gotten me a job at the Nissan plant in Blue Springs. The

458

pay was pretty good, but the employee discount on the cars was the best. I was lucky though—my uncle says the company has to hold my job for me if I'm called up, so I know my job is still waiting for me when we get back from all this crap."

Just then, the first sergeant walked toward them. "Captain Regan," he called. "There's an officer call over at the battalion CP. I was told to come tell you."

Regan nodded. "Thanks, Top. Why don't you come with me? This way, we can put out whatever needs to be put out when they're done."

The two of them walked off to see what the news was. They'd been sitting on their hands outside the city of Chicago now for five days. Neither side was really shooting at each other as an uneasy truce continued to hold. Word had it some sort of terms for surrender were being discussed.

When the headquarters group knew they were going to be in a static position for more than a day, they tended to line a couple of the APCs up together to form a working headquarters section. One track would be responsible for managing the battalion's supply and logistics, another would manage the ops and intel. As he approached the back of the M117 track, Regan saw several of the other company commanders standing around under the tent canopy.

After a couple of minutes, the battalion commander cleared his throat to get everyone's attention. "I know some rumors have been swirling around the camp. It's true—surrender terms have been reached with the German-Dutch division we've been facing. However, the Illinois and Wisconsin Civil Defense Force units have vowed to continue the fight."

Murmurs spread through the small crowd. Colonel Beasley, who had come over from Brigade HQ, held up a hand to get everyone to calm down and stop talking. "In the next few hours, the German and Dutch soldiers will begin to form up into company-sized elements. They'll disarm themselves and then march toward our positions. When that happens, the MPs are going to search them one more time before they begin to process them as prisoners of war. They'll be moved further back behind our lines to whatever POW camps the MPs are setting up.

"The German commander said they are going to place most of their equipment in a couple of locations for us to collect. Some Special Forces units are over there right now and will guard the equipment until we can move forward and secure it. We want to keep as much of their equipment out of the CDF's hands as possible. Chances are, the CDF is going to capture a lot of small arms equipment and ammo, but we want to keep the armored vehicles and other systems out of their hands if possible."

He nodded to one of the lieutenants who had been working as one of his aides. The man turned on one of the large computer monitors they had with them. It displayed a map of the greater Chicago area.

"Our brigade is going to move forward into the city," Colonel Beasley continued. "Our first objective is to reach Grant Park. We'll set up our initial headquarters there while we wait for the 45th Infantry Brigade Combat Team to relieve us in seventy-two hours. Once they've relieved us, we'll head up to liberate the Army reserve base at Fort Sheridan and then Naval Base Great Lakes. We'll continue to move up the coast and into Wisconsin, with our end objective being Milwaukee, and then Madison if we have to. Are there any questions?"

Colonel Beasley looked around. One of the officers had raised his hand.

"Sir, if we're moving up to Wisconsin, who's going to liberate Michigan and the rest of Indiana?"

Beasley nodded. "That task is mostly being handed down to the 38th Infantry Division. The plan right now is for the 116th Infantry Brigade Combat Team to relieve us in Wisconsin in roughly two weeks. Once our brigade has been relieved of our primary combat duties in Wisconsin and Illinois, we'll rejoin the rest of our division down in Texas and face off against the Chinese. So, let's continue to stay frosty, heads on a swivel, and get through these next couple of weeks. Things are either going to go easily for us now that the Germans are surrendering, or we're about to enter a whole new phase to this civil war."

With the overall strategy having been dished out, the company commanders left the meeting, more informed than they'd been in the past several weeks of what their overall objectives were.

Chapter 15

Texas Nightmare

March 12, 2021
El Paso, Texas

Colonel Li did not agree with the orders he had been given. He knew this strategy was not going to play well in the occupied territories. More importantly, he knew that carrying these orders out would turn all of the American people against them—there wouldn't be any left who viewed them as liberators.

Li sighed softly to himself. Like the other PLA officers, he knew he didn't have a choice in the matter. He had been given his orders from on high, and it was his duty to make sure the regular army implemented them.

He looked out the window of his vehicle. They were approaching the University of Texas campus, the site that the PLA had designated as the central processing point for the Chinese Q program.

The occupation of captured America was presenting the PLA with a serious challenge. They had to manage and feed millions of civilians in addition to their ever-growing army. To accomplish this, they had to cull the herd—

separating those who couldn't contribute from those who could. That meant a lot of tough decisions would have to be made rapidly as they captured more land, towns, and cities.

"We're nearly there, sir," his driver announced.

Soon, their vehicle pulled into the parking lot of the Sun Bowl Stadium. Colonel Li could never understand why the Americans would erect such massive edifices just for the game of football. Outside the stadium were rows upon rows of yellow school buses, intermixed with city commuter buses. Disheveled civilians poured out of them and filtered into various lines to the entrances.

The giant facility was also ringed by hundreds of Chinese soldiers and armored personnel carriers, to make sure the civilians couldn't decide they wanted to leave all at the same time. A couple of people had tried to escape, but they'd summarily been shot. Those public deaths had put a damper on the fighting spirit of those who remained.

As he climbed out of his vehicle, Colonel Li was greeted by General Xi, the PLA garrison commander for Texas. Li saluted and Xi returned the greeting, but both men knew who was in charge. While Xi may be a PLA general, Li was a colonel in the Political Work Department of the CMC—Li was the man who made sure the PLA soldiers and officers continued to stay loyal to the party and President

Chen. Colonel Li even had the power to have a general removed from his position and sent to a work gang or one of the newly formed penal battalions that were arriving daily.

"We've gathered the civilians from the city as requested," stated General Xi. "They are currently being moved through the various in-processing centers."

Li smiled. "Excellent, General. I'm impressed. You have gotten things under control and set up quickly. How are you separating the ones that don't fit the program parameters?"

Pointing to the smaller stadium nearby, Xi explained, "The ones who are too old and frail or require continuous medication to live, are being moved over to the smaller stadium. In the larger stadium, we are separating the younger women who fit the Q program requirements from the rest of the population. The ones that are staying here are assigned a work detail and sent home once they are chipped. The women who fit the criteria given to us are being kept underneath the stadium and away from the others. Every four hours, we plan on loading them onto buses and will transport them to the Ciudad Juárez airport."

"Excellent. Are you having any problems with the transport aircraft?"

General Xi shook his head. "No. Four planes arrive each hour: two cargo planes and two passenger planes. Each Air China Airbus A350 brings in 312 soldiers. Soon, they'll be returning to China with the same number of women for the Q program."

Li smiled. He felt good about how well the system appeared to be working. The planes were bringing in 14,900 new soldiers a day and would soon transport the same number of women to the Mainland.

The two of them walked to one of the mobile command centers set up in the back of one of the ZBDs. As they entered the tent, Colonel Li saw many maps of the city, broken down into quadrants. There was also a whiteboard that listed the number of firearms that had been captured and a listing of the units that were assigned to go house-to-house to search and seize the Americans' guns.

"General, the civilians that are too old or require medication to stay alive—what are your plans for dealing with them?" asked Li.

Xi leaned in closer so the others couldn't hear. "We're going to give them a vitamin shot and then load them onto some of our troop transport trucks that will 'take them home,'" he explained, using air quotes. "However, within twenty minutes of receiving the shot, they will fall asleep and not wake up. The trucks will be driven out to a mass grave site we are establishing in the desert. They'll be buried far away from prying eyes so no one will find them."

Colonel Li nodded. "And the healthy ones?"

"They are all being given an RFID chip in their right hand, and they're being marked with a tattoo, letting us know they've been processed. They'll be assigned to work gangs and put to work growing food, managing cattle, and repairing the infrastructure to keep the city running. They'll earn their keep, or they'll be shot."

"Excellent. Why don't you walk me through the rest of the occupation plans, and let's see how things are going," Li said. The two of them discussed the situation for a while longer. Their efforts to transform the state and the country were now well underway.

Chapter 16
First Break

March 22, 2021
Camp Perry

Ashley Bonhauf stood at the front of the briefing room; all eyes fixed on her as she began her brief. Behind Ashley, on a corkboard, was an image of Wen Zhenyu on the lower left side of the board attached to a line at the top left side with a picture of Peng. Next to that photo of Peng were pictures of Johann Behr and Roberto Lamy, connected by different-colored lines.

"A couple of weeks ago, we found a possible break in the case of uncovering this conspiracy to rig our country's election and foment this civil war and UN intervention. From our interrogations of Wen Zhenyu, we learned that Peng An, the Head of the China Investment Corporation, was somehow involved. What we didn't know was who his other co-conspirators were, and how deep this conspiracy ran.

"A week ago, Peng received a series of calls from the Director-General of the World Trade Organization. The NSA was able to intercept the call and decoded their conversation. It's clear now that not only is Peng a pivotal player in this conspiracy, but so is Johann Behr, the leader of the UN. Roberto Lamy, the head of the WTO, is also involved as well. What we *don't* know is who else is involved and if they have an American connection."

Ashley leaned forward on the podium. "Several days ago, we initiated a plan that would lure Mr. Lamy away from Geneva to come back home, and it worked. We've just confirmed that Mr. Lamy booked flights to Rio, departing two days from now." She paused for a second before adding, "Our plan is to snatch him as he leaves the airport. Then our crack interrogation team will then begin the process of questioning him."

She heard a couple of soft whistles from a few of the JSOC operators as they realized this would more or less be their task.

Walking up to the front of the room to join Ashley, General Lancaster added, "It is critically important that we snatch Mr. Lamy and not get caught. While the President has sanctioned this operation, we are doing this on Brazilian soil and without their permission or oversight. Our plane to Brazil is wheels up in three hours. Those of you heading down there should pack whatever you need quickly. The van will be out front in two hours to take us to the airport. The rest of you who aren't traveling to Brazil will stay ready to analyze the data our interrogators obtain and continue to help us connect the dots. It's imperative that you help us find the other pieces to this puzzle. Is that understood?"

A chorus of "yes, sir" rang out. Excitement hung in the air.

****

While moving along in the Gulf Stream, Seth sat in an overstuffed leather chair, reading everything he could about Mr. Roberto Lamy. He looked at the man's social media posts, the types of papers he wrote about in college, books he read, movies and TV shows he watched, and any other pieces of information the CIA and NSA had put together on the man. Seth made it his mission to learn as much about the man as he could before he sat down to talk with him.

A few hours in, Ashley Bonhauf plopped herself down in the chair opposite him. "So, Seth—what's your deal? Why are you on this mission?"

Seth put the dossier down on the table between them. "What do you mean?" he asked.

"Well, a few weeks ago, you were in charge of running one of the DHS protective service training brigades—a job I might add I heard you were very good at.

One of my FBI friends from the FLETC academy was working there. He said you had the training camp up and running like a well-oiled machine in a week. So, if you were kicking butt there, why would they pull you from there to put you on this team?"

"Let's just say I have a special skill set Lancaster thinks he can use on this mission," Seth replied cryptically.

Lifting an eyebrow, she asked, "You mean you'll be the one interrogating him?"

Seth just shrugged.

"You know, I'm pretty good at questioning too. I used to work on the counterterrorism team out of the New York field office before I was moved to headquarters. I spent some time questioning terrorists in Iraq and Afghanistan," she added.

Smith sat down in the seat next to Seth and smiled at Ashley. The left side of her lips curled up mischievously. "I suppose you have something to add?" she commented.

Smith tipped his head toward her. "The type of questioning we'll be doing is a bit outside what you FBI types are trained for or allowed to do."

"You mean torture," she retorted, her eyebrows crinkled.

"I wouldn't know what you're talking about," Smith replied, feigning ignorance.

"How can you trust the information you get from the subject if you torture him?" asked Ashley. "For all you know, he's just telling you what you want to hear to get you to stop hurting him. It's not that I totally disagree with the concept, but it's worthless if you can't trust the intelligence you collect."

Seth leaned forward. "Ashley, torture is a broad concept," he asserted. "What you define as torture may be different than what I or what Smith view it as. Your perception of torture is also probably outdated. It's not about breaking people's bones or sticking needles under someone's nail beds. This is the twenty-first century. We've moved way beyond those methods."

Ashley paused for a moment. "You know, a friend of mine on the counterterrorism task force told me about the CIA testing pharmaceutical interrogations on Al Qaeda prisoners in Yemen. He told me they yielded some good results until one of the prisoners died. If I'm not mistaken, Senator Lambert from California shut the program down when she heard about it. She said during the hearing that one of the prisoners had suffered terribly when he'd had an adverse reaction to the drug."

Seth and Smith didn't say a word and listened with unchanging facial expressions as Ashley told them what she knew about the Yemen operation. Eventually, Smith said, "Your friend seemed to have known a lot about it. Was he there?"

Ashley nodded. "He was. He also ended up getting canned by the FBI because he didn't do anything to stop them. He told me one of the interrogators was an Army officer on loan to the CIA. When he was asked by Senator Lambert what the names were of the interrogators, he suddenly developed a case of amnesia. That's when Director Polanski kicked him to the curb. He knew the names before the hearing, but he wouldn't disclose them when asked. He was a good agent. I just wish he'd been truthful during the hearing—he'd probably still be in the FBI."

Seth sighed. "Sometimes, Ashley, doing the right thing isn't always doing the right thing."

Laughing at what he'd just said, she added, "I suppose you're right. That's what he told me his last day in the office as well. You know, come to think of it, I have no idea where he is or what he's doing these days."

Now it was Smith's turn to smile. "I'm sure he found a good job somewhere."

The rest of their flight went by relatively smoothly. Many of the folks aboard either took advantage of the time to sleep or read up on their target.

******

Eventually, they landed at the Tom Jobim International Airport—a large airport that had several small hangars off to the side that were run and managed by companies involved in some aspect of aviation. Five minutes after touching down, their Gulf Stream had taxied over to one of those open hangars on the far side of the airport.

This particular hangar was operated by a small jet engine repair company that specialized in repairing engines on Lear and Gulf Stream jets. It was also a CIA front company that allowed the Agency to have a private place to park planes when they needed to deliver or pick up people or packages without being spotted.

When the hangar had been sealed up, the outer door to their jet opened, and the team disembarked. Two blacked-out SUVs were parked nearby, waiting to whisk them away to their safe house. A couple of attendants swiftly unpacked the cargo compartment of the plane, unloading their gear and essential equipment and placing it into the back of the SUVs.

Ashley had been getting antsy. She always did fine on a flight until they made her wait to get off. She was excited to stretch her tall frame without a ceiling hanging over her. Once she stepped outside, she was surprised by the sight of a friend she hadn't seen in many years.

A broad smile crept across her face. "Speak of the Devil—Ed? Is that really you?" she asked. She couldn't help but feel the irony—Ed Laughlin was the FBI agent she'd just talked to Seth and Smith about on the ride over.

He laughed and smiled. "Yeah, it's me. What are you doing here, Ashley?"

"Polanski put me on the task force," she responded. "It's good to see you." She immediately realized that it was the CIA that had told her friend not to testify on the Hill—and it looked like he'd landed a job with them.

"Come on, Ashley. You can ride in my vehicle. I can fill you in on the situation down here, and we can catch up."

From behind Ashley, Ed suddenly caught sight of Smith and Seth, who were the last to exit the plane. He shook his head in amusement. "How did I know they'd send you two guys down here?"

Smith tilted his head to the left. "Well, when they need the best, they send the best," he replied with an innocent smile.

Ashley shot Ed a quizzical look before asking, "You know these two?"

Ed chuckled as the group walked toward the SUV. "Know them? Of course I do. These were the two interrogators I worked with in Yemen. Seth here is the best interrogator I've ever seen. He's like honey laced in poison when he's in the booth."

Suddenly, Ashley looked at Seth and Smith in a different light. She wasn't sure if she liked them more or if she should be scared of them. If half the stories of what went on in Yemen were true, then she was certainly glad these guys were on her side.

It took them forty minutes to weave their way through the traffic congestion of Rio. It was a beautiful city in certain parts and an outright ghetto in others. Their little motorcade mostly stayed in the good side of town and drove along the water as much as possible. Eventually, they started moving up one of the mountains along the southwest side of Rio. The higher they drove, the better the views of the ocean and this side of the city became.

"Where are we?" asked Ashley.

"We're heading up to my place. I have a house up here that I stay in and keep running for special missions like this. It used to be an old coffee plantation, so it's got a few hectors of land and a number of buildings we use for our activities. It's also situated in a beautiful, well-to-do neighborhood, which means it's well protected by the police force, so there's less likely of a chance of some random burglar stumbling on to our operations."

"Ah, yes. Casa Luxe. It has to be one of the best safe houses I've ever seen," Smith remarked with a smile. "I forgot you oversaw it now."

"Yes, and the views from the infinity pool down to the city and coastline below are pretty spectacular," Ed said with a wink.

Changing the topic, Seth asked, "Is our room set up for us?"

"Yeah, I've got the place rigged for what you guys needed," Ed responded, still obviously in a jovial mood. "We soundproofed the building and the room a year ago. It's got a biometric lock on the doors to get in and out, so it's pretty secure."

The rest of the drive went by quickly, with the passengers simply enjoying the view. Eventually, they came to the front gate of Casa Luxe, which was secured by a guard shack with two armed security guards. Both guards appeared to be armed with pistols, though Ashley wagered they probably had assault rifles inside the guard shack, just out of sight.

The villa itself was beautiful. It sat high above the city and had exceptional views of the water. It was also secluded and perfect for what they needed to do.

****

Roberto Lamy hit the button that would return his leather seat to its upright position. He was tired from the long flight. He'd flown from Geneva to Paris, and then traveled from Paris to Rio. The last leg was the worst; it was a grueling eleven-hour-and-fifty-minute flight from France to Brazil. Fortunately, his position afforded him the ability to travel in first class, so it wasn't all bad.

Besides being drained by the journey, Roberto was saddened by the reason he was having to fly home. His elderly mother had passed away two days ago. She had lived to be ninety-six, so it wasn't as if she hadn't lived a full life. She had. He was just sad that he hadn't been able to visit her in the last six months. With everything going on in the world, he'd been too busy to leave Geneva.

I should have flown her to Geneva when the family joined me out there for Christmas, he thought. Then again, at her age, such a long journey wouldn't have been easy.

The aircraft jolted as it touched down. Roberto could hear the air and wheel brakes engaging, and then he was pushed forward as the plane rapidly decelerated. Once they had slowed down to a normal ground speed, they taxied over to the terminal where they'd begin the process of deplaning.

Once he was finally walking through the terminal, Roberto breathed in deep and held it for just a second before letting it out.

It feels good to be back home.

Roberto made his way to the luggage carousel and stood in line with the rest of the crowd, waiting for his bags to appear. An elderly gentleman suddenly walked up to him. "Excuse me, are you Mr. Roberto Lamy?" he asked.

Roberto looked the man over. He was wearing a sports jacket, slacks, dress shoes, and had a clean, manicured beard and mustache. He was also holding a white placard card with his name on it.

I hadn't arranged a car, Roberto thought.

"I am," he responded cautiously. "Who, may I ask, are you?"

"I'm Francisco. Your wife hired my agency to pick you up at the airport. She wanted to arrange something special for you. She sent me a picture, so I'd recognize you," the man said. He produced a smartphone and showed

Roberto a photo of him and his family at Christmas a few months ago in Geneva. Roberto also noted the text message had been sent from his wife's cell phone number.

Roberto smiled at his wife's gesture, then nodded to Francisco. "Yes, thank you. That was very nice of her to arrange this. I had planned on taking a cab. I just need to collect my bag, and I'll be ready."

The two of them stood there for a moment while they waited for the bags to start arriving. A few minutes later, the carousel started rotating, and before long, Roberto's bag appeared. Francisco reached down and grabbed it off the conveyor belt, and the two of them walked out to his waiting car. Roberto loved how Brazil still maintained a VIP car park near the front of the airport, unlike America and some airports in Europe.

As they approached the parking area, Roberto noticed a Bentley Mulsanne with blacked-out windows. When Francisco opened the trunk, Roberto let out a soft whistle. He'd prepared himself to ride in whatever town car this driver had brought.

Francisco explained, "Your wife said you have always wanted to own one of these cars. It just so happens that our company purchased one a few weeks ago for VIPs such as you."

Roberto was practically speechless. *I love my wife so much*, he thought as he glided into the back seat of this work of art.

Francisco made his way around to the front of the vehicle and climbed in the driver side. In no time, they were leaving the airport and heading in the direction of his home near the water.

This car is beautiful. My wife has outdone herself this time.

About ten minutes into their drive, Francisco announced, "Mr. Lamy, your wife has one more surprise for you. She has arranged for a special dinner party at one of her friend's homes. The house is located in the Gávea neighborhood. It's a beautiful place. It used to be a coffee plantation. I hope you don't mind me driving you straight there—she was rather insistent."

Roberto saw Francisco look at him in the rearview mirror to gauge his response. He was sure his expression must have soured—he was exhausted. All he wanted to do was take a hot shower and go to sleep in his own bed.

"Let me just verify that with my wife if you don't mind."

Francisco smiled and nodded as he continued to drive them toward their destination.

Pulling his smartphone out, Roberto hit the speed dial to his wife's phone. A second later, he realized the call hadn't gone through. He pulled the phone down from the side of his face to look at the screen and noticed that there was no cell reception.

"I think we must be going through a dead zone," Roberto remarked. Then he looked up at Francisco and noticed that his driver was suddenly wearing a small respirator mask that covered the lower half of his face.

"What the hell?" he asked. That was all he managed to get out before a mist was blown in his face from the air vents in front of him. In a fraction of a second, his vision blurred into hazy red stars, and then he was unconscious.

****

"Is he still out?"

"Yeah. He'll be out for at least another hour unless you want us to wake him up," the medical doctor on staff replied.

Smith shook his head. "No. Let him sleep a bit more. It's best if he wakes up naturally to his new environment."

The doctor nodded and went back to watching the man's heart rhythm on the nearby screen.

Smith turned and saw Seth and Ashley nearby, looking at their prisoner.

"Why is he naked and chained to the floor and chair like that?" asked Ashley, concern and curiosity in her voice.

Smith could tell she was uncomfortable with the scene before her, but he just smiled disarmingly. "It's called conditioning. We need to start the disorientation process before we begin the serious questioning," Seth explained.

Ashley looked at him with uncertainty written all over her face.

"You know, you don't need to be a part of this, Ms. Bonhauf," Smith offered. "If you'd like, you can go back to the house and work with the analysts or observe from the monitoring room."

"That's not a bad idea, Ashley," agreed Ed. "What you're about to see isn't something you can un-see."

"Does the ambassador know we're here, and does the legal attaché know what's about to happen?" Then she put her hand to her forehead as if she suddenly felt stupid for asking that question.

Smith sighed. "Ashley, this is a CIA black site. No, the ambassador has no idea we are here or what we're about to do. It's called plausible deniability. He can't lie about something he doesn't know is happening. As to the legat, that's why we have you here. We need someone from the FBI here in case this guy starts to talk about a US person. *If* that happens, then you'll liaise that with the Attorney General, the FBI Director, and no one else."

She bit her lower lip and nodded slowly. "I'm sorry, Smith. I didn't mean to imply anything. I guess I'm just new to this kind of stuff. I didn't know what to expect."

Ed placed a hand on her shoulder. "It's OK, Ashley. I said the same thing back in Yemen. Don't worry. These guys are a lot better at this stuff now than they were back then. They've worked the kinks out, so to speak."

"He's starting to stir," the doctor announced.

They all turned to look into the interrogation room. Mr. Lamy slowly moved his head and mumbled a few unintelligible sounds.

"I guess that's my cue," Seth said. He walked out of the room with the one-way mirror and entered the hallway. A few seconds later, he was opening the door to the interrogation room.

****

Seth made his way over to the table and the only other chair in the room. He picked up the chair, placed it on the ground next to Roberto and sat down.

Roberto slowly started to come to. As he did, he realized he was naked and moaned. He tried to move his arms and discovered they were chained to the floor. There was just enough slack in the chains for him to bring his hands up to the table, but not enough slack for him to rub his eyes unless he bent his face down to his hands.

Roberto blinked several times as he looked around the room. It was a dirty and dingy little hole, with paint peeling off the walls. Two lightbulbs hung at opposite ends of the room, which cast ominous shadows everywhere. Then, as if his eyes had finally regained the ability to focus, he noticed Seth, who was wearing a sports jacket and denim jeans and sitting only about two feet away from him.

Roberto's voice was hoarse as he whispered, "Where am I? What is this place, and who are you?"

Seth cocked his head to the right as if pondering how he wanted to answer his question. "My name is irrelevant. As to where you are…you're still in Brazil. In Rio, to be more precise. As to what this place is—well, it's a quiet place where you and I can have a conversation."

In the middle of Seth's answer, Roberto startled, as if the fog in his mind had cleared enough for him to realize the mystery man before him was speaking English. "I'm a Brazilian citizen on Brazilian soil. You can't do this to me," he frantically stammered. "I'm also the Director-General of the World Trade Organization. You can't just kidnap me like this. There are people who will know I'm missing."

"Mr. Lamy, we have some questions we'd like to ask you, and the sooner you answer them, the sooner we can get this whole situation resolved. I'm sure it's just some sort of big misunderstanding," Seth explained.

Roberto's eyes darted around the room briefly as he listened to Seth. Then he nodded his head. "Yes, I'm sure this is some sort of misunderstanding," he agreed. "I'm sure we can work out whatever it is. What is it you want to know?"

Seth smiled slightly as he scooted his chair in closer, invading Roberto's personal space. Seth leaned in even further, placing his face within a few inches of Roberto's. "Let's talk about Senator Marshall Tate."

Roberto's eyes shot open a little wider before he regained his composure. "You mean President Marshall Tate? What about him?" he asked.

"That's a nice try," said Seth, "but let's talk about how he became President. A week ago, you placed a call to Peng An, saying that Senator Tate was 'holding up his end of the agreement, but China wasn't.'" He read the quote from a piece of paper he'd almost magically produced. "I'd like to know what you meant by that."

Roberto Lamy suddenly became visibly nervous. Sweat beads formed on his forehead, and his cheeks blushed, despite the room temperature hovering around seventy-four degrees. His fingers started to tremble. His eyes darted around as if calculating a method of escape, but there was no way out. He'd been caught.

Seth watched all of these reactions with a calm smile. After a moment, Roberto's eyes looked up and to the right; Seth recognized this as a tell that he was trying to think of something creative or imaginary as opposed to something factual. Seth even observed that Roberto's pulse had increased substantially, to the point that he could see the carotid artery pulsing beneath the skin in his neck.

Roberto stammered as he tried to answer Seth's question. He finally spat out, "I don't know what you're talking about. The only dealings I have with Peng are trade-related. He's head of the China Investment Corporation. They are a substantial and influential sovereign wealth fund."

Seth nodded at the nonresponse, then pressed from another vantage point. "OK, then let's talk about how

Senator Tate fits into all of this. What deal has he made with the WTO that involves China?"

Roberto's body was having a hard time trying to control his emotions. Finally, he whispered under his breath, "I, um, President Tate was wanting to work out a new trade deal with the Chinese when this war was over."

Seth snickered at the response. He sat back in his chair and crossed his arms. "Mr. Lamy—can I call you Roberto?" The man nodded, and Seth proceeded. "Roberto, you and I both know that's not true. You expect me to believe that you and Peng were talking about a trade deal Senator Tate wants to have between the US and China after the Chinese get done invading America? I mean, seriously. Listen to what you just said and how preposterous that sounds. How about you level with me and answer my questions truthfully so we can let you go."

The two of them went back and forth for probably five more minutes before Seth finally made the first ultimatum. "Listen to me, Roberto. If you're unwilling to talk with me here and now, then I'm going to move you out of Brazil, and it may be a very long time before you return home...*if* you are returned at all. Now, tell me about this plan you and Peng were discussing about Senator Marshall Tate and how he fits into it."

"You can't do this!" Roberto screamed in frustration, stress and his emotions finally getting the better of him. "I'm the Director-General of the World Trade Organization! You can't just kidnap me in my own country like this. I *demand* you let me go!"

Without breaking eye contact with Roberto, Seth snapped his fingers, letting the others know it was time to move to the next phase.

"I tried to be reasonable with you, Roberto. I'm sorry, but we're going to have to take you with us to talk in a more conducive environment," Seth explained. Two other men in black 5.11 tactical clothes walked into the room.

One of the men placed a pair of noise-canceling headphones on Roberto's head while the other man placed a sensory device over his eyes. They turned the two systems on. Seth knew that Roberto's ears were being bombarded with a disorienting noise, and his eyes were being flooded by a myriad of flashing and strobing lights. Together, this input would overwhelm the sensory receptors of the detainee's body. His mind would now lose complete track of time and space.

Next, they placed a hard, rubberized ball with several small air holes over his mouth and then snapped the straps behind his head so he couldn't talk or even scream above a whimper. Roberto's entire world now consisted of whatever Seth wanted.

A minute later, the Agency doctor walked into the room. Craning his head around to make sure the subject couldn't hear them talking, he asked, "When do you want us to give him the shot?" In his hand was a hypodermic needle filled with some sort of medication.

Seth looked at his watch. "Give him exactly three minutes, and then give it to him."

He turned to the guards. "Once he's out, I want him moved to the other room. Make sure he's strapped into the chair and it's hung from the ceiling. I want him to feel as if he's floating in space."

The guards nodded, and Seth got up. He headed out of the interrogation room and back to the observation room Smith and Ashley were sitting in. When he walked in, Smith clapped his hands a couple of times. "Well done, Seth. You have him completely terrified of what's coming next."

Ashley looked a little green. She continued to observe the guards as they carried Roberto's limp body out of the room with the sensory deprivation equipment still attached. Then Ashley looked at Seth. "Where are you guys taking him?" she asked.

"Here. Come take a look," Seth replied as he motioned for her to follow him.

They walked down the hallway as they followed the guards to the next interrogation room—a room that looked like it could have come from a completely different building. The walls, floor, and ceiling were a bright white. It looked like a very sterile twelve by sixteen-foot room. In the center of the room was a small table, where a piece of equipment was being fastened down.

"What's that?" she asked, pointing to the device.

"That, my friend, measures all of the detainee's biological tells: their pupil dilation, perspiration, and pulse," explained Smith. "When Mr. Lamy is hooked up to it, we'll be able to easily validate whether what he's telling us is truthful or deceitful in real-time."

While Smith was telling Ashley how the equipment worked, the guards carried Roberto's limp body into the room and strapped him into a soft, plush chair. Next, they grabbed a chain that was attached to the front of the chair between Roberto's legs. They lifted the chair with him in it about six inches off the ground and attached the chain to a hook that was hanging from the ceiling. In a matter of minutes, Roberto was hanging from the chair, suspended in the air. Seconds later, the chair turned in a slow circle.

Ashley looked at Seth and Smith with a quizzical look. Smith motioned for them to walk over to the observation room and sit down.

"What is all of that?" she said as she waved her hands in the direction of the interrogation room.

"Before we hooked Roberto up to the sensory deprivation equipment, I told him we were going to take him to another country where we could talk more," Seth reminded her. "Then we placed the devices on his eyes and ears. Five minutes attached to that thing feels like an hour or more. It completely messes with your mind and eliminates the ability to tell time.

"All of this will make him believe he'd been moved to a new location. In an hour or so, we'll have the doctor slowly wake him up. He'll still have the devices attached to him, doing their work. We'll come back and question him after dinner. By the time we do, he'll believe he's been in that device for several days, maybe even a week or more." Seth paused for a second before he concluded, "Ashley, it's all about preparing his mind. The more we control and prep his environment and his internal perceptions, the more effective this next interrogation will be."

"Wow. I've heard of a lot of crazy interrogations, but this takes the cake," Ashley remarked. "Why do you have him hanging from a chair that's turning in slow circles like that?"

"It helps with the disorientation process," Smith explained. "The subject essentially feels like they are floating through time and space. It completely and utterly disturbs their mind to such a point that they are practically numb and going crazy when it's taken off."

"All right, enough questions," said Seth. "Before we move him to the next stage of the interrogation, it's time to get some grub."

Chapter 17

Partisans

April 2, 2021

Flint, Michigan

Bishop International Airport

Nearly a thousand men and women stood around inside the hangar, waiting for Luitenant-Kolonel Maarten van Rossum of 105 Commando Company and the local Michigan Civil Defense Force leader to address them. The local commander, a man by the name of Treyvon Robinson, appeared nervous.

"Are you sure the German division in Chicago surrendered?" Robinson asked, wringing his hands.

"I'm afraid so," said van Rossum. "A lot of my own countrymen surrendered as well."

Robinson crossed his arms. "What are we supposed to do now? How are we going to stop the federal forces when they head this way?"

Van Rossum didn't know how to respond. He felt bad for the guy. Robinson wasn't a trained military officer— he was a union foreman at the local General Motors plant in town. He'd been appointed to his position as colonel of the

Michigan CDF because he'd rallied a few thousand people to take up arms against the federal government. The initial goal had been to allow these militia forces several months to get trained up before they were thrown into combat, but with the Germans surrendering, that was not going to happen now.

After several seconds of silence, Robinson sighed loudly. "How're you and your guys going to help? Will you be fighting with us?"

Van Rossum tilted his head to the right. "Before the Germans surrendered, they made sure my unit got access to a lot of their weapons and ammunition," he said. "We're going to hand over five thousand Colt C7s—they're basically Canadian versions of your AR-15 assault rifles. I'm told many of your militia members are familiar with these rifles, so we're going to give them to you. We also have roughly fifty million rounds of ammo to go along with them."

Robinson's eyes went wide when he mentioned how much ammo and rifles they were being given.

Van Rossum held a hand up before the man could pepper him with questions. "We've been hiding the ammo and some of the rifles in different weapon cache locations all over Genesee County and nearby counties. We're also going to hand over around a thousand hand grenades, six hundred Panzerfaust 3 rockets, and about eighty launchers. We placed them in different caches as well. This way, if the federal forces capture one, they don't nab your entire supply."

"What about mortars or Stingers?" asked Robinson.

Since Robinson had formed up his militia force nearly nine weeks ago, they had largely been training with their personally owned AR-15s and hunting rifles. They didn't have a lot of ammo to burn, so they hadn't spent a lot of time at the rifle ranges honing their skills. Roughly five weeks ago, van Rossum's unit had started providing them with a lot more individualized training, so they'd had the opportunity to learn how to use the Panzerfaust 3 antitank rockets and the 60mm and 81mm mortars.

"We've placed one Stinger with each of the weapon caches. I'm sorry we couldn't give you more, but we have other militia units we need to arm and prepare for the coming fight."

"OK. This is good though. I think we can do a lot of damage with what you've given us. Should we go out and talk to them now?" Robinson asked.

Van Rossum could tell the crowd was getting restless in the hangar. He nodded, then signaled for Robinson to lead the way. The two of them walked out of the backroom and headed for the podium.

Luitenant-Kolonel Maarten van Rossum walked up to the podium first. "Members of the Flint CDF, I want to tell you personally how proud of you I am. These past five weeks, you've shown yourselves to be true warriors—men and women willing to stand up to tyranny and defend your city and community. I know it is not easy to stand up to a dictator, but that's what you have done.

"The coming weeks and months are going to be some tough times. There are going to be days when you're going to want to give up, to turn yourself in. But I'm here to tell you that you need to stand and fight."

He paused for a moment as he looked over the crowd. They were hanging on his every word, lapping up whatever he said like hungry animals. Van Rossum was loving it.

"I'm reminded of how your great nation was born. Did you know that your war of independence against the British was fought by no more than three percent of the population? It wasn't fought by ten or even twenty percent of the colonies. It was won by three percent—three percent of the most dedicated, hard-core men and women in their communities. Well, as I stand here today, looking at all of you. I see you as the three percent of this war. You are the ones standing up for your community, for your loved ones and families.

"The next couple of months are going to be the toughest times in your life. Some of you—no, many of you—may be killed in the coming fights. But many more of you will live, and the sacrifice you'll have made will help ensure your children and grandchildren will grow up free— free from that tyrannical dictator Sachs and his corrupt government.

"My men and I have been tasked with staying in the area to help advise your leaders on how best to deploy your militia to defeat the federal forces. I can tell you that in the coming days and weeks, Sachs's soldiers are going to make a concerted effort to retake Michigan. We need to stand united against this force. Starting today, we are going to break this force down into smaller company-sized elements. Each company is going to have four of my commandos as advisors. When I dismiss you, my commandos will call you each over to your new section leaders. Listen to them. Follow their orders, and we will do our best to help lead you to victory."

When van Rossum finished his impromptu speech, the crowd roared and clapped. There was a renewed sense of optimism, purpose, and pride.

****

CIA Safe House, Brazil

What the hell is this? thought Roberto. *Where am I? What's going on?*

Roberto Lamy woke up, still attached to the sensory deprivation equipment. His body felt almost weightless, yet he realized some straps were holding him into a chair.

How long have I been here? he wondered. The lights and noise overwhelmed his brain. *Oh, God, make it stop!*

Roberto struggled to wiggle his arms and legs again, but they were firmly tied to the chair. Suddenly he felt a new sensation; it was almost like he was falling. Then he felt his feet plant themselves on the ground. At that moment, the room stopped spinning. As if a miraculous answer to his prayer, the flashing lights and that godawful noise were all turned off. His eyes were a bit shocked by the steady light; everything felt hazy. The last time he felt like this, he was waking up after surgery.

"Mr. Lamy, can you hear me?" asked a voice. The sound was familiar, but he couldn't quite place it.

Roberto blinked his eyes several times, and things became clear. He moved his hands up to his eyes and rubbed away the dried tears and crusts from the corners of his eyes. His vision returned to normal as his pupils finally adjusted to the bright light of the room.

He immediately noticed the whole room was bright white. The floor almost looked like it was illuminated by panel lighting. The walls were white, but he couldn't tell what kind of material they were made of. The ceiling was a mix of paneling and very bright white lights. It almost felt as if he was in a sterile surgical room or laboratory of some sort.

Fingers snapped in front of him, bringing him back to reality. Sitting on a chair opposite a white metal table was the man who had first questioned him.

"Mr. Lamy, can you hear me?" the man asked again.

Practically whispering because of how raw his throat felt, Roberto said, "Water. Can I please have some water?"

Nodding, the mystery man reached down into a small backpack near his chair and produced a water bottle. He handed it to him.

Like a ravenous man who hadn't had anything to drink in days, Roberto chugged the liquid down. In less than a minute, he had drained the bottle of its contents. Roberto immediately felt a lot better as his brain returned to normal and his body rehydrated itself. He no longer felt like he was floating in some black abyss. Then his stomach growled.

"Food. Can I please have some food?" he managed to ask.

Tilting his head to one side slightly, the mystery man smiled somewhat before replying, "All in due time. Do you know why you're here?"

Roberto's mind flooded with the recent memories of their last conversation. He remembered that he'd been asked about his relationship with Peng An. There was something else too...a deal or bargain that President Tate had made...he had to work hard to reach deep into his thoughts.

Yes. He wanted to know about the deal we had struck with him.

Looking back at the mystery man, Roberto pleaded, "Why have you kidnapped me? When can I go home?"

The man shook his head, ever so slightly. "The time to go home was earlier. We aren't in Brazil anymore."

Roberto's jaw dropped open. Then he shouted, "Where am I?"

"Where you are is irrelevant. What is relevant right now is what you tell me next. The more you cooperate and talk, the sooner you can have something to eat, and the sooner I can move you to a more comfortable room."

"I don't know what you think I know, but you have your facts mixed up," Roberto insisted. "I work in trade. My job is to help ensure there is free trade around the world and resolve trade disputes between nations."

Brushing off his comments, the mystery man insisted, "You are far more than that, Mr. Lamy. I want to know what kind of deal you, Peng, and Behr have struck with Senator Marshall Tate."

Roberto felt a bit panicked. He searched through his shattered mind for a way out of this situation. *Maybe there is something else I can give them instead*, he thought.

"The only deal I know about is the formal request Mr. Tate made to the UN to help remove Jonathan Sachs from office and recognize him as the legitimate leader of America."

Roberto saw his answer did not satisfy the man. The man reached down and picked up the bag he had with him, placing it on his lap. He then proceeded to pull out a ball pin hammer and put it on the table. Next, he pulled out a Black & Dekker wireless drill and attached a long, thin drill bit. Each time he reached into his bag, he pulled something insidious out of it. Then he'd pause and look at Roberto, as if he was trying to size him up to see which one scared him the most.

Trying his best to remain calm and stoic in the face of what he could only conclude were devices that'd be used to torture him, Roberto did what he could to keep his face passive and not let the spectacle unfolding in front of him give away his true feelings of absolute terror.

"Which of these are you the most afraid of?" asked the mystery man.

As Roberto sized up the man sitting before him, he couldn't fathom how he could be so stoic like that while talking about torturing someone. It was beyond Roberto's ability to comprehend.

"You are an evil, sick person!" he stammered. He felt rage building up inside him. Roberto was angry that he was still strapped to this chair, irate that he had been kidnapped and that he was going to miss his mother's funeral. Most of all, he was furious that this bastard was taunting him with these devices.

The man just smiled a sick sadistic smile. He grabbed the drill and depressed the button. The high pitch whining of the motor and the rapid spinning of the drill bit caused Roberto to urinate on himself. The warm liquid running down his legs was a bleak reminder of just how powerless he was at this very moment.

That sick monster just smiled when he realized I peed myself, he realized. His captor was getting off on his fear and terror. *Damn these evil Americans!*

The mystery man leaned forward, placing himself closer to Roberto. "Enough games, Mr. Lamy. You are here for a reason. Now tell me about your relationship with Marshall Tate!"

"I don't have a relationship with Mr. Tate," Roberto insisted. "I don't know what you're talking about."

The two of them argued for a few more minutes. The mystery man produced several phone transcripts, which he read aloud. He even made Roberto listen to a couple of audio intercepts to further drive home the point that he already knew quite a bit.

Roberto felt trapped. He knew he wasn't going to hold out under torture, yet he also knew he couldn't tell them everything. He had to figure out what he could share that wouldn't endanger the entire plan.

Roberto's eyes darted around the room. He still had no idea where he was, and he had no idea how long he'd been gone.

Will anyone be coming for me? he wondered. *Does anyone even know what happened to me?*

****

Seth's patience was running thin. This stubborn prisoner continued to deny even basic facts and the evidence being shown to him. He flashed back to Arab men he'd questioned that constantly repeated "*Wa Allah Ma'arf*," which means "I swear to God I don't know," even when asked the most basic of questions.

After going round-and-round a couple more times, Seth knew it was time to bring out his other bag of tricks. Reaching down into his backpack, he grabbed the small leather case containing his other tools of the trade.

After placing the case on the table, Seth unzipped it and looked at the two syringes and the two bottles. Looking up at Roberto, he saw the color drain from the man's face when his eyes settled on the contents of what was inside.

"It doesn't have to be this way, Mr. Lamy. If you would just answer my questions, this could be a pleasant conversation over a meal. I could even have them cook up a few steaks for us if you'd like."

Roberto just stared blankly at him.

Seth sighed. "Mr. Lamy, if you're unwilling to talk with me, then I'm going to inject you with a substance that is going to make every nerve in your body feel as if you're on fire. Your brain will be tricked into believing that you're being burned alive. I can assure you; this is incredibly painful.

"You won't die from it, but you'll wish with every fiber in your body that you were dead. The pain is going to be so intense; you will beg me just to kill you. But I won't. I will let you sit there and suffer until you have decided that you've had enough. When you're ready to tell me the truth, I will give you another drug that will turn the pain off like a switch...but I'll only do that if you tell me the truth."

Seth searched Roberto's face. He could see a flood of conflicting emotions on his prisoner's face as he tried to determine if he should hold out or talk now. Seth had gone through interrogation resistance training, and he'd even had the drug administered to him—he knew exactly what was going through Roberto's mind.

Leaning forward, Seth added, "Mr. Lamy, everyone breaks. There's no shame in it. It's just a fact of life. I know the question that is going through your mind right now—how long can I hold out? My question to you is, 'why bother?' You're ultimately going to break. *Everyone* does. So why endure unimaginable pain and suffering when, at the end of the day, you're going to tell me everything anyway. Save yourself that pain and suffering and just be straight and honest with me now."

Roberto licked his lips, and his eyes darted to the now empty water bottle. A disappointed look appeared on his face.

Sensing that Roberto's mind was now where he wanted it, Seth grabbed the second bottle of water he had in his bag and placed it in front of him.

"Go ahead, Mr. Lamy. Things are about to get painful, and you might as well hydrate yourself," Seth said as he motioned for him to drink.

Grabbing the bottle, the prisoner unscrewed the cap and started downing it. He was apparently very thirsty. He emptied the bottle rapidly.

Seth watched Roberto closely. Maybe sixty seconds after he finished the bottle, his eyes dilated a bit. Smiling, Seth resumed his line of questioning.

"Do you mind if I call you Rob?"

Flashing a dopey smile, Roberto answered, "Sure. Most of my friends call me Rob," Seth could tell from his rather jovial demeanor that the drugs had begun to have the desired effect.

"Thanks, Rob. I'm hungry. Would you like to join me for some lunch?" Seth asked warmly.

Licking his lips, Roberto responded, "I sure would. I'm famished."

"Excellent." Seth turned and said something to someone on the other side of the mirror. "They'll bring us some Picanha and vegetables shortly."

Rob smiled. Seth knew his prisoner was letting his guard down further as the drugs saturated his brain and lowered his mental ability to resist.

"I must say, Rob—that deal you guys struck with Marshall was brilliant. How did you manage to get him to agree to it?"

Roberto laughed out loud. "Never underestimate what a person is willing to do to achieve power," he replied.

Seth played along and joined in the laughter. "Still. It was brilliant. You're a master deal maker. What sealed the deal?" he asked.

"All that jerk cared about was being President. He didn't care how or what he had to do so long as he became President."

Seth snickered at the comment and tried to stay in character. "Do you think he'll hold up his end of the bargain, though? You know, once that bloviating idiot Sachs is removed from office."

Roberto shrugged his shoulders. "I don't know. What I can say is if he doesn't, Johann won't hesitate in the least to expose him. Neither will Peng. Those are two people you don't want to cross. They are the real masterminds."

"Oh, come on. None of this could have happened without you, Rob. You're the glue that holds everything together."

"Me? No. I'm just the money guy. Erik and I were just responsible for making sure Marshall had the money he needed to run his campaign and win. Erik was responsible for funneling all sorts of money to that other SuperPAC. What was it called? Oh, yeah—One World. I don't know how he pulled it off, but he managed to help them raise more than two hundred million dollars."

Seth shook his head in astonishment and beamed at the man. "That's impressive, Rob. How did Erik manage to do that? He's just a small fish in a big pond. You're the big fish," Seth said as he continued to stroke the man's ego.

Roberto laughed. "Erik, a small fish? No way. Erik Jahn is the investment guru at Norges Bank. You realize the portfolio he manages for Norway is valued at over 1.3 trillion USD, right? He has financial contacts all over the world and in nearly every major corporation. Once Johann and Peng put the plan into motion, Erik was able to funnel more money than you could believe to make it all happen. That idiot Sachs has a lot of enemies, you know. Hell, Erik was funding numerous SuperPACs to help Marshall. I only know of the one because that's where my contacts were told to put their money."

Just then, a couple of men opened the door and wheeled in a cart with their food on it. Prior to entering the room, Smith had worked it out that these men would be dressed in high-end suit jackets, slacks, and shoes, to give the appearance that Seth and Roberto were dining at some high-end restaurant. The servers had a white cloth draped across their left arm while they set the table between Seth and Roberto with real silver forks and steak knives.

One of the guards nodded slightly at Seth as he placed another bottle of water in front of Roberto, who greedily opened it up and started drinking from it. Then they pulled the silver cloches off their plates to reveal a wonderfully prepared meal of Picanha, which is almost like an American skirt steak. They also had asparagus that had been specially cooked in bacon fat to give it an even more robust flavor, along with a twice-baked potato. To complete the meal, the servers placed a small bowl next to their plates, which contained a fresh garden salad. Before leaving, one of the servers had managed to remove Roberto's hand restraints without him even realizing it had been done.

When the servers left, Seth picked up his fork and ate his salad. Roberto did the same. As Rob was eating, Seth reached for the bottle of red wine the servers had left behind.

"Would you like a glass?" he asked.

Roberto nodded like a person who has had one too many drinks. At that point, he was definitely feeling the double whammy of the drugs—he was barely able to keep his head from falling into the plate of food in front of him. Based on his experience, Seth knew that as far his prisoner's mind was concerned, he was at a fine restaurant, eating a traditional Brazilian meal with a friend.

Seth poured them both a glass of Casa Valduga, Terroir Leopoldina Merlot, an award-winning Brazilian wine only served at expensive restaurants or in the homes of the wealthy.

Returning them to the task at hand, Seth asked, "What where the details of the deal you all had made with Marshall? I can't help you make sure he stays accountable to them if I don't know all of the details."

Roberto creased his forehead. "What is your position again?" he asked, slurring his words.

"I'm one of Marshall's senior advisors; I've been with him from the beginning. Peng said I'm supposed to help him put the country back together after that treasonous bastard Sachs is finally removed."

Roberto chuckled. "Oh, that's right. I think Peng mentioned something about you to me...you and I met before at a party, didn't we?"

Seth smiled. "Maybe. I've met so many people for Marshall. He has me doing so much these days. I just don't want him to forget something important, especially as regards men such as yourself that got him elected."

After taking several long sips of wine, Rob looked at Seth glassy-eyed. "First, Marshall is going to reverse the trade deals with the EU. You have no idea how bad those have been for the European countries, especially Germany and France. Next, he was going to stay out of eastern Europe and let the Russians do what they want with it. Third and last, he's going to give China preferential pricing and access to American oil and natural gas. He was also going to give Peng a firm fixed price on a host of other trade goods and agriculture products if everyone agrees to help him remove Sachs from office."

Seth furrowed his brow. "Was that all Peng wanted?"

"Oh, I almost forgot. I think he mentioned something about Taiwan and the South China Sea, but those really aren't that big of a deal to America. I think those are more political issues to help President Chen maintain his popularity in China," Rob said, almost as an afterthought.

Seth marveled at how effective a pharmaceutical interrogation could be. Trying to torture that kind of information out of someone was incredibly difficult. Letting a drug do it was far more effective. Still, he couldn't believe what he was hearing. He was thankful the interrogation was being recorded because no one would believe what this guy was saying otherwise.

Slipping back into his roleplay, Seth replied, "Ah, that's right. I think Marshall had mentioned something like this to me a while back. I just wanted to make sure I knew all the parameters of the deal. I think he may have forgotten that last part about the oil and natural gas to China. He said something about that kind of deal to Germany but not China."

"No, that's not right," Roberto asserted. "That deal is for China—not Germany. Peng isn't a man to be trifled with. Make sure Marshall knows that." Roberto stuffed another forkful of potatoes into his mouth.

Seth finished his bite, then asked, "What happened in that meeting in Geneva with Foreign Minister Jiang? I heard he got angry and left to return to China."

Roberto sighed audibly at the mention of Jiang. "There was a big argument between him, the Russians, the French, and Germans. I wasn't in the meeting myself, but Johann told me it revolved around the other peacekeeping members being angry that the Chinese didn't invade America when the EU force in the north did. They accused the Chinese of sabotaging the grand plan and put everything in jeopardy. After the meeting, Johann had me call Peng and try to find out what was going on with Jiang. Peng is in tight with President Chen and Minister Jiang."

Nodding his head, Seth poured Rob another glass of wine. "What did Peng say?"

Roberto shrugged his shoulders. "Not much. He mentioned something about us needing to have more patience—that all would be revealed soon enough. I tried to get more out of him, but Peng was always a secretive kind of guy. I'm supposed to meet him in Geneva in another week. I'll know more after I see him."

Seth returned to their earlier conversation. "I'm still impressed with this entire plan, Rob. How elaborate. Was it Marshall's idea, or was he just the benefactor?"

Rob let out a deep guttural laugh before he looked at Seth. "No, Marshall is just a patsy. He, like every other American president, is chosen and groomed for the position.

That idiot Sachs is the first time since Kennedy that someone outside of the preordained leader managed to sneak their way into the White House. Kennedy didn't even make it through his first term. Sachs wasn't supposed to either, but the narrative about his past business dealings wasn't strong enough to take him down. An assassin's bullet would have been the better, more certain choice. It worked with Kennedy, and it would have worked with Sachs, but no— they wanted to try and publicly humiliate him instead of just eliminating him. Now look at the mess we're stuck having to clean up."

Roberto looked angry about how everything had been playing out with President Sachs. Seth knew he was hitting the right buttons, so he pressed on. "If Marshall is just the patsy, then who's the real powerbroker? Should I be worried about some other arrangement he needs to keep?"

Roberto shrugged his shoulders again as he stuffed another piece of steak in his mouth. Through bites, he answered, "Lance Solomon. He's part of that secret Yale group—what's it called? Bones & Skull...Skull & Bones...yeah, that's it. Skull & Bones. Lance...Lance is the American money guy and kingmaker. I was told at the time that he was a big shot at Goldman Sachs. This was several years ago when the plan was first formed. He's the head of

Goldman's now. Powerful kingmaker that guy is—at least in American politics."

Seth heard a small voice speak into his ear mic. "I think we've gotten enough for now. We need to digest and go over everything to see what more we may need to follow up on with him later. Let's wrap this up and put this guy to bed."

Very subtly, Seth nodded to no one in particular, letting the others monitoring the interrogation know he heard the instructions. Then he smiled as he slipped back into his roleplay. "Wow, Rob. I must say this has been a very informative lunch and great company. I'm glad we were able to make this meeting happen on such short notice," he said cheerfully.

As they finished their meal, Seth made sure to ask Roberto questions about his wife and his adult children. When the servers came back and cleaned up the table, they brought them each a wonderful creamy chocolate mousse cheesecake for dessert, along with some coffee.

As Roberto drank his coffee, his eyes suddenly became heavy, and the man fell asleep in his chair. The servers then helped him over to a bed they pulled out of the wall and laid him down on it, placing a blanket over the top of him and a pillow under his head. The man would be out for hours if not a day as the drugs coursing through his body slowly wore off.

Standing up, Seth looked at his watch. He realized they'd been talking for nearly six hours. No wonder his back was aching and he felt exhausted. It was mentally taxing doing an interrogation beyond four hours.

When he left the interrogation room, Seth walked into the analyst room just down the hall. Several people clapped their hands as he walked in; a few even whistled and verbally congratulated him.

"Seth, you're way too good at this job to stay in the Army. I'm going to have to find a way to convince you to stick around," Smith said as he patted him on the shoulder.

Ashley Bonhauf walked up to him. "For a minute, I really thought you were going to torture that guy. He actually peed his pants when you turned that drill on."

Seth smiled at the memory. "That was the goal," he replied, "to make him so worked up and nervous over being tortured that as soon as we introduced the first drug, he'd be a Chatty Kathy and tell us everything."

"OK, people," Smith announced, loudly enough for everyone in the room to hear, "Seth got us a ton of new information and leads. We now need to start working on tracking it all down. When Mr. Lamy wakes up in twelve or more hours, I want to have additional follow-up questions ready for Seth to ask. So, let's start figuring out what the gaps are and what else we need to close the loop on."

The room then bustled with a renewed urgency. Smith, Seth, and Ashley walked off to one of the other rooms, where they'd have a private conversation with General Lancaster to figure out what to do with the information they'd just learned.

Chapter 18
Battle of Three Rivers

April 4, 2021

Michigan-Indiana Border

While many of the Dutch soldiers participating in this UN peacekeeping force had to surrender when Division Schnelle Kräfte got surrounded in Chicago, the 104th Commando Company had not been ordered to join them.

A day earlier, Wachtmeester Hans de Jager and a handful of Dutch commandos had scouted out the city and identified where they were going to position their company of Michigan militia. After spending five weeks training the various Civil Defense Force militia groups across the state, they were making sure to put small units along all the major roadways that the federal forces would have to use as they made their way to Detroit and eventually into Canada. The commandos knew they ultimately couldn't stop the American Army from capturing Three Rivers or the state of Michigan, but they *could* make that capture costly.

Two yellow school buses pulled into the parking lot of the Walgreens store on the corner of Millard Road and US Highway 131. Everyone exited the buses and milled around for a moment, waiting for any last-minute instructions before they headed out to their positions.

Wachtmeester Hans de Jager saw the gaggle forming and climbed up on the hood of one of the school buses. He motioned with his arms, beckoning everyone to circle around. De Jager looked at the faces of the men and women standing before him. Some showed excitement, some fear, but what he saw in all of them was a determination to defend their state and home from a tyrannical dictator in Washington.

He couldn't be prouder of this militia team if he tried. He'd spent the last five weeks training them how to shoot, how to use machine guns, antitank rockets, grenades, and small unit ambush tactics. He'd grown to like these Americans. He saw their patriotism to their cause and their love of their friends, family, community, and country. It was hard knowing that after today, many of them were going to die. This was going to be their first real test against a professional army. He hoped with every fiber of his being that they'd do well and many of them would survive the day. This was his team now.

De Jager raised his hands to silence the chatter. "Listen up, people," he shouted. "The federal forces are about two hours away from our position. This is the moment we've been training for—our first time we'll be in combat together as the Michigan militia."

A few members of the crowd cheered. Others gave each other a high five or slapped a friend jovially on the shoulder. They were excited.

"I want the Panzerfaust teams to head to your positions. Remember your training. Let the armored vehicles get close before you pop out and fire. Oh, and Carl—don't forget to make sure the safety is off on the launcher before you leave your covered position." Everyone started laughing at the mention of safety. One of the guys had forgotten to do that during their training, and they had summarily called him "Carl" ever since.

De Jager let them laugh for a minute easing the tension. Then he continued. "Once your rocket is ready, you need to aim and fire that bad boy quick. Do *not* stand there and wait to see your rocket hit the target. You need to get back under cover immediately and reload. Those federal soldiers are going to be looking for you guys in particular, and they will light you up if you give them a chance."

De Jager scanned the audience. "Where's Martin?" he asked.

A slender man near the back raised his hand. "I'm here, Staff Sergeant," he called out.

Wachtmeester de Jager smiled. He still had to get used to being called by his American rank. "When you get settled up in your perch, I need you to do your best to stay out of sight and continue to relay what you see back to my command post. I'm not going to tell you guys where I'll be set up for operational security, but I'll be somewhat close by. When Martin here identifies where the federal forces are amassing, that's where I'll send our QRF teams to help."

He took a deep breath before he went on. "This is going to be a tough fight, people. Expect the enemy to be ruthless. Make no mistake, friends—they are here to kill you. That means you need to kill them first. Now, I want everyone to get to their assigned positions and wait. Stay off the walkie-talkies and don't change channels, or none of us will be able to communicate. As Martin relays the enemy positions, I'll tell you when to attack. Don't attack unless I tell you to, OK? This is important. If we're going to win this fight, then I need you guys to listen to me, OK?"

"Yes, Staff Sergeant," came the chorus from his group.

De Jager nodded at them. "OK, head to your positions and wait."

As the group dispersed, de Jager walked up to Martin. "Hey, before you head up to your perch, I want you to have this," he said. "It's a small identification booklet we put together for you. It has some pictures of the various types of military vehicles you may see. When you relay the enemy positions, I need you to also help identify what type of vehicles you're seeing. That'll help me know how many enemy soldiers are coming toward each position, OK?"

Nodding, Martin took the little book. "Can I shoot at any of them?" he asked.

De Jager shook his head. "No. Your job is to help identify where the enemy is headed and what kind of vehicles they have, OK? If you start shooting at them, they'll figure out where it's coming from and take you out. You're too exposed up there to last long. Oh, before you leave— when we start firing those mortars, I need you to help us identify where they are hitting, OK? It's just like in training; tell us if we need to drop fifty meters or move fifty meters to the right. You're our eyes and ears out there. We're counting on you, Martin."

De Jager placed a hand on the man's shoulders and looked him in the eyes. "You can do this, Martin."

Martin simply nodded, then headed off to his observation post.

De Jager turned around as he heard the whining engine noise of an armored vehicle approaching. A Boxer armored fighting vehicle pulled up near him, and one of the soldiers stuck his head out of one of the hatches and called out to him.

"Wachtmeester, are you ready to head to the next location?" they asked.

De Jager nodded. He walked around to the rear of the vehicle, climbed in and sat down. The Boxer immediately took off and started heading to check on their mortar team that was setting up a couple of kilometers away.

When they pulled up to the Hidden Marsh Sanctuary, the commandos hopped out to inspect the team that would be handling their mortars. A couple of trucks were parked nearby underneath some trees, and two Dutch commandos were going over the sighting of the mortars, making sure the first set of rounds would land roughly where they wanted the first ambush team to strike.

"Is everything ready?" de Jager asked.

"We're as ready as we're going to be," his sergeant replied.

"Very well," de Jager responded. "I'm going to head over to the command post. Make sure you keep these guys moving. Don't stay in one firing position too long. The Americans will take you out if they have a mortar truck with them."

With nothing more to be said, de Jager hopped back in the Boxer, and they drove to the command post. Once they pulled up to the home at the edge of the tree line, de Jager got out of the armored fighting vehicle and headed toward the house. Meanwhile, the driver moved the Boxer into the trees to help keep it out of sight of any surveillance drones that might fly over. Before de Jager walked into the house, he turned and looked down the road and surveyed the sky above. The day had started out nice and clear but was swiftly becoming overcast. Across the street and down the road a bit was a large church with a sign that read New Hope Assembly of God. De Jager said a silent prayer for his team of militia and then headed in.

Majoor Willem Graaf, their company commander, was the first to greet him. "Ah, Wachtmeester de Jager. Is everyone ready?"

"*Ja.* They're as ready as they're going to be. I just checked on the mortar team. Two of my sergeants are with them as well."

Majoor Graaf nodded. "Good. The other platoons are ready as well. Our scouts show the American force is here," he explained, pointing to a spot on the map approximately twenty kilometers away from the town. "I'm going to head to Battle Creek to check on the other platoons. Luitenant-kolonel van Rossum has the rest of the regiment spread out, covering the main roads leading to Detroit."

"Good luck, Majoor. We'll do our best to hold out here," de Jager said. Then he snapped off a crisp salute.

Then the Majoor left with one other soldier to head to their next position.

Normally, there'd be at least a lieutenant or captain to help manage the coming battle. Sadly, both officers assigned to de Jager's company had been killed earlier in the war. Thus far, no new replacements had arrived from Europe, so de Jager found himself in command of the unit.

With nothing more to do than wait, the soldiers in the house brewed up some fresh coffee and scrambled up some eggs for breakfast.

****

God, I hope this is going to work, Martin thought.

He crawled over to get in position. Once in his little perch, Martin placed his Remington model 783 rifle down. It was a decent .308-caliber rifle with a scope, but nothing fancy like what the Dutch commandos had.

Martin had to keep reminding himself that he wasn't a sniper, and he wasn't supposed to shoot. He was just supposed to spot what was happening in the city and report what he saw.

Once he got settled in, he unfolded the IR-resistant blanket the commandos had given him and placed it over top of him and his rifle. He made sure his spotter scope was set up, and the little vehicle identification booklet was lying next to it so he could quickly reference it. He also placed a small notepad and pencil on the ground next to him. Before he forgot, he grabbed several protein bars from his patrol pack and put them near his notepad.

Nearly an hour went by before Martin heard something—a soft droning noise like a small airplane. Staying under the blanket, Martin started looking around for what was making the sound. While he couldn't find it, he knew it was probably some sort of army surveillance drone. Those little devils were exactly why the commandos had given him an IR-resistant blanket to hide under. It would help shield him from a casual glance at his position and make sure his heat signature didn't show up.

Pulling back from the spotter scope, he picked up his walkie-talkie to send in his first report.

"Van Gogh-One. I've got movement on US Highway 131. The vehicles are approaching the Meijer supermarket."

"Good copy, Dragon One. What kind of vehicles do you see?" asked the Dutch commando on the other end of the radio.

Hmm...good question. He looked at the vehicle identification sheet they'd given him and then back at the vehicles. There were two Abrams tanks, three JLTVs, four M1117 Guardians, and eight Stryker vehicles.

Depressing the talk button on his radio, he relayed the type and number of vehicles. He also made sure to tell the commandos that several of the Stryker vehicles had pulled off into the Meijer parking lot, and a lot of soldiers were starting to get out of them. Some soldiers had moved to the store to check it out while other soldiers began to set up a perimeter.

Martin continued to relay what the soldiers were doing. He explained that a small cluster of vehicles was heading toward the Walmart parking lot down the street.

"Dragon One, we're going to start the fireworks," the Dutch soldier on the other end replied. "I need you to help adjust them once they start."

Sixty seconds later, Martin heard a soft whistling overhead. An instant later, a loud explosion broke any sense of morning calm.

Boom, boom, boom.

The three mortar rounds landed on the highway, a hundred or so meters in front of the Walmart parking lot.

The armored vehicles that were driving down the road broke off into two groups as they moved out of the way of any future mortars that might land near the highway.

Martin heard more whistling as the next three rounds flew overhead, slightly off from the last three rounds. These mortars landed practically where the vehicles had just been. It was as if the drivers of those vehicles had anticipated that the next set of rounds was going to impact right on top of them.

"Dragon One. Did we hit them?" asked the Dutch commando. "If not, tell us how to adjust fire."

Martin spent a few tense seconds explaining where the enemy vehicles were and what was going on. A minute later, he heard more whistling overhead right before the next set of mortars landed. One of the rounds managed to hit one of the federal vehicles and blow it up.

Many of the federal soldiers dismounted from their vehicles, searching for targets to shoot at. However, several of the Strykers expanded their search for the mortar teams; they drove in different directions, their turret gunners at the ready.

As he looked through his spotter scope at the soldiers down near the Meijer, Martin saw two of them throw something small into the air, almost like a model plane or something. Doing his best to follow the object, Martin saw the little devices zoom off in a couple of directions.

Oh, crap! Those are the drones the commandos warned us about, he realized.

"Van Gogh One, I just saw one group of soldiers launch some of those small drones. You guys better get a move on before they find you."

A short paused ensued before he heard them reply that they were moving positions.

Martin returned his attentions to his scope. Some of the federal soldiers were working on something in the back of one of the Strykers. Martin zoomed in a bit more and saw an elongated tube pivot and turn in his direction. In that instant, he knew his mortar team was in trouble.

Martin didn't have time to radio in his warning before the soldiers in the back of the vehicle dropped their first mortar round. In the blink of an eye, it flew out of the tube and was on its way to its target. Before Martin could even register what he was seeing, the soldiers fired a second round, then a third.

Snapping himself to attention, Martin grabbed his radio. "Van Gogh One. They're firing mortar rounds at you guys. Get out of there!"

In the distance, Martin heard a couple of explosions. Looking back to where he knew his friends had set the tubes up, he saw a massive blast and a lot of black smoke.

Oh man. I think they just got our mortar team, he thought in horror. He hoped his friend George hadn't gotten hurt.

Martin looked back down the road. He saw several troop trucks pulling into the Meijer parking lot. There had to be more than a hundred soldiers getting out of the vehicles. They were starting to break down into smaller groups as they moved toward the apartments and other buildings near his position.

He began to relay where they were headed over the radio. The commandos had given him a map of the city, broken down into squared sectors. All he had to do was name the sector and estimate how many troops were headed that way, and the commandos would take care of coordinating which ambush teams should engage the enemy and when. Martin had to hand it to them; it was a simple stupid way to keep things easy for a newly trained militia force.

Crack, crack, ratatat, ratatat.

Gunfire erupted near the Walmart. Martin swept his scope over there to see what was going on. One of the vehicle turrets had turned toward the parking lot and had opened fire on a handful of abandoned cars. Many of the soldiers joined in shooting at the vehicles. The first ambush team had struck.

Then, Martin saw two of the rocket teams pop out of the Dairy Queen less than a hundred meters from two of the armored vehicles. They aimed their Panzerfaust at the Strykers and fired.

Swoosh...boom.

Swoosh...boom.

Both vehicles exploded, killing the soldiers inside. Martin saw one of the soldiers in the turret get thrown into the air. The man's legs were missing as his torso flew high into the sky. Then his body thudded on the ground, bouncing once. Martin nearly threw up. He had to turn away from the gruesome image, or he knew he'd vomit.

A couple of federal soldiers turned and killed both of the attackers before they could duck back inside the building for cover, taking one of their rocket teams out before they could carry out a second attack.

Two more projectiles flew toward the last two armored vehicles from one of the other rocket teams further down the street. One of the rockets missed and hit something behind the vehicles while the other one nailed what Martin had identified as an M1117 Guardian.

The federal soldiers reacted quickly to the new attack and started firing at the KFC building. The volume of fire from their heavy machine guns shredded the building until something exploded inside and blew the entire structure apart.

Back down by the Meijer parking lot, Martin saw several Strykers start racing down the road. They drove past the three burning vehicles and continued toward the KFC, which had been reduced to a fiery cauldron. When they got within a hundred or so meters from the Spartan Motel, two more guys appeared with Panzerfausts and fired at them.

Both guys managed to duck back into the hotel to reload as the façade of the building was lit up by the Stryker gunners. One of the rockets impacted against the side armored rocket skirt of the Stryker and blew up. Sadly, it did not penetrate the vehicle's armor. The other rocket missed entirely and exploded when it hit a building on the opposite side of the street.

One of the federal soldiers nearby leveled some sort of rocket launcher at the hotel and fired. A second later, Martin saw an explosion as the room the two militiamen had run into blew up.

Martin cringed. He hoped the rocket team had died swiftly. Twisting on the roof of the building, Martin saw a lot of soldiers fanning out into the neighborhoods nearby. They were running up to houses and apartment buildings, kicking down the doors and searching each building.

More gunfire rang out from some of the apartment buildings as small pockets of Martin's militia unit started their attacks. For the most part, their unit had broken themselves down into two-man rocket teams or three- and four-man ambush teams. They had set themselves up in homes, apartment buildings, and businesses all around the highway and the key bridges in the town.

Many of the civilians living in Three Rivers had either fled the town when the UN invaded or when the federal forces approached the state lines. That left very few of the town's residents around, which was a good thing considering how many gunfights were taking place.

As Martin continued to observe what was going on, he realized the federal soldiers had now passed his position, and he was now inside their perimeter. He kept radioing in what he was seeing and where the enemy soldiers were to the various teams that were still alive. As the day wore on, more and more of his militia unit was taken out. Eventually, he had no one left to report to. He heard small pockets of

gunfire, yelling, screaming, and the occasional explosion—
but no one was responding to his radio calls. The silence
unnerved him. He wondered what he should do next.

Time crept by. Martin saw strings of federal soldiers
helping to carry back some of their wounded to the Meijer
parking lot. He spotted several vehicles with a red cross on
them. A lot of soldiers were being laid down near them. He
watched as a few people in uniform worked on the wounded,
moving between them. Then he heard the familiar sound of
a helicopter.

Soon, Martin saw a chopper with a bright red cross
painted on its sides land in a cleared portion of the parking
lot. When it did, small groups of soldiers ran out with some
stretchers, carrying their wounded comrades. Then the
wounded soldiers who could walk on their own climbed into
the helicopter. Once it lifted off, another chopper landed in
its place, and the soldiers rushed the next set of wounded up
to it.

Then Martin heard a loud, thunderous explosion not
too far away. He twisted his body around on the roof and
looked north. Just across the river on the Main Street bridge,
Martin saw that the Shell gas station had blown up. A lot of
gunfire erupted in that area, but he couldn't tell which side

was winning or where most of it even was. All he could do was listen to it unfold and continue to spread across the town.

Looking over the lip of the roof, Martin saw his .308 rifle with his deer scope on it. He wondered if he should have tried to do more to help his comrades out. He'd been told his job wasn't to play sniper. He was supposed to observe and report—but now he didn't have anyone to communicate his information to. Martin tried desperately to raise several of them on the radio, but no one responded to his calls.

He looked back at the Meijer parking lot. It was probably around a three-hundred-meter shot to where those helicopters had previously landed. Martin figured he could do one of two things: he could try and slip away in the darkness and hope he was able to get away, or he could wait until the next medical or transport helicopter landed, and he could try and shoot the pilot or the engine and disable it.

He heard the thudding of helicopter blades approaching the parking lot. He picked up his hunting rifle and looked through the scope. The Blackhawk hovered briefly before it settled down on the ground.

Martin sighted in on the front part of the helicopter. He saw the pilot looking out his side window as some of the medics rushed the next set of wounded soldiers to the back of his bird. Then, doing his best to control his breathing,

Martin zeroed in on the pilot's body and gently squeezed the trigger.

Bang.

As soon as his rifle fired, Martin immediately worked the bolt, ejecting the spent round and ramming the next round into the chamber. He looked through his sight to the helicopter in time to see the pilot droop forward.

Hot damn. I actually hit him, Martin thought.

Some of the soldiers nearby started looking around to try and see where the shot might have come from. Martin immediately lay flat, doing his best to try and stay small and hidden under his IR blanket.

After a few moments, he peeked above the lip of the roof. The helicopter was fully loaded. It took off with the co-pilot flying. Martin regretted that his attack hadn't had the intended effect.

Thirty-some minutes later, another helicopter approached the parking lot. This time it was a CH-47 Chinook. When it landed, a lot of soldiers got off through the rear ramp. Martin sighted in on the pilot in the front, placing his target over the man's center mass. Once again, he gently squeezed the trigger.

Bang.

Martin saw some red splatter hit the windshield. The pilot grabbed at his throat and face.

Got another one. This is almost too easy.

The soldiers around the parking lot looked for where the shot had come from. They fired at a few different locations. Then a squad's worth of soldiers ran toward one building, believing he must be hiding in there.

Looking through his scope again, Martin saw he had a good view of the co-pilot and figured he'd try and take him out as well. He placed the red dot of his scope on the man's chest area, just as the co-pilot applied power to the engines. The helicopter got about twenty feet off the ground before Martin fired his rifle.

The bullet struck the co-pilot in the chest. A fraction of a second later, the helicopter tilted sideways and fell over on its side. While it didn't explode, it thudded pretty hard on the parking lot and threw a lot of debris everywhere as the blades tore at the asphalt around it.

Someone pointed in Martin's direction, which sent a shiver down his spine. His stomach tightened as the soldier pointed again, and several other soldiers joined him. Aiming his rifle at the soldier who had spotted him, Martin fired his fourth shot. The round hit the man at the base of his neck, knocking him to the ground. The soldiers around him dove for cover, anywhere they could find it.

Time to get the hell out of here! Martin realized.

He grabbed the rifle, his notepad, and the IR blanket, and darted to the stairwell that would lead him off the roof and down to the ground floor. He raced down the stairs as quickly as he could. As soon as he made it down to the landing, he swung the door open, hoping to make a break for it.

Before he knew what had happened, something struck him right in the face. He immediately lost consciousness, and his body slumped to the ground.

****

Martin wasn't sure how long he'd been knocked out, but his face sure hurt. He tasted blood; he was pretty sure that whatever had hit him had broken his nose. Opening his eyes, he looked around and saw a couple of familiar faces.

"You're awake," one of them said.

Martin shook his head. "How long have I been out?"

His friend shrugged. "You were out when they brought you here. That was probably around three hours ago."

"Where *is* here, exactly?"

"The Walmart parking lot. They've been bringing all the prisoners here."

"What are they going to do with us?" Martin asked as he gently rubbed his face and around his nose. He did his best to wipe away some of the blood and clear his nose.

"I don't know, but you can bet it won't be good," one of the other prisoners responded.

Another hour went by, and then a couple of federal soldiers walked over to the prisoner pen, escorting two more militiamen. Both were wounded in one form or another.

"Hey, can we get a doctor or medic to help these guys?" demanded Charley. He was one of the militia team leaders.

One of the soldiers stopped and sneered at them. Then he went back to whatever he was doing earlier.

For better or worse, they were prisoners. The soldiers had set up some concertina wire in a somewhat large circle and placed them inside it. Three federal soldiers stood nearby, watching them, smoking cigarettes, and talking amongst themselves.

Martin got up. "Hey. Where are you guys from?" he asked.

One of the soldiers stopped talking with his friends and looked at him. He took a pull from his cigarette, finishing it off as he flicked it to the ground. He stood up and walked over to them. "We're from Virginia," he said as he surveyed the nine of them in the pen.

"What are you guys going to do with us?" Martin asked.

Shrugging, the soldier replied, "I honestly don't know." The soldier was about to turn and go back to talking with his friends when he paused, as if weighing whether he should speak. He sighed and then asked, "Why are you guys fighting us? We're all Americans."

The question took Martin by surprise. In a way, he hadn't given it too much thought. He didn't vote for Sachs and felt the man was using the courts as a means to stay in office beyond his term. He believed it was wrong, and he needed to stand up and be a part of history in stopping him.

He looked the soldier in the eye. "I think Sachs is a dictator who won't leave office. I suppose that's why all of us are fighting you guys."

One of the other soldiers guarding them got up and walked over to them. "You realize our country is being invaded by more than two hundred thousand Chinese soldiers, right? We should be down there, repelling them, not having to fight you guys. Hell, you guys should be down there with us, sending them back to China."

The Chinese invaded? Martin asked himself. *When the hell did that happen?*

The soldier must have seen his perplexed expression. "You guys didn't even know that, did you?" he asked. "Well, the UN forces also nuked Guam, Arizona, and Oklahoma. They used a nuke on one of our carrier battle groups in the Pacific and hit San Diego with an EMP. More than two hundred thousand Americans were killed in less than ten minutes." He shook his head. "You all have been duped. You're fighting on the wrong side of this conflict."

Martin felt like a deer caught in headlights. He didn't say anything else; he just sat down. Judging by the looks on the other prisoners' faces, they probably felt the same way he did.

If this is true, then what have we been fighting for? he asked himself. He sure didn't want the Chinese running the country. He felt compelled to spread this news to others so they could put an end to the fighting.

****

Washington, D.C.
White House
Situation Room

President Sachs zeroed in on his NSA representative, Deputy Director Tony Wildes. He took his seat at the head of the table, then motioned for everyone else to take their seats.

"Tony, I want to get right down to business on bullet six of the agenda. What are we doing to counter these Deepfakes and the horrendous misinformation taking place on social media and in the news?"

Tony stumbled for a moment with his response, seemingly caught off guard that his item would be the first one discussed. "I...Yes, Mr. President. Our organization has been doing our best to try and identify where this misinformation has been originating, as well as how it's being disseminated. We've tracked down several of the largest producers of these Deepfakes to a company located in Shanghai, China."

"Sorry for interrupting, Tony," said the President, "but it occurred to me that the group may need some context. When you say Deepfakes, you're referencing the videos being created of Marshall Tate pleading for peace and calm and then the videos of me looking like a raving maniac demanding the blood of my political enemies, correct?"

Tony Wildes nodded. "Yes, Mr. President. Exactly. But it's worse than that, sir. They are also generating these same types of videos of various congressional members, celebrities, sports figures, musicians, etcetera—all pushing or promoting a specific agenda. It's gotten so bad, no one knows what's real and what isn't."

"Can't people tell these are fake videos being generated?" asked the President's Chief of Staff, a confused look on his face.

Wildes shook his head. "No, they can't. The technology has gotten so good you can't tell that these are just computer-generated videos."

"How the hell is this even possible?" barked the President. He'd seen a number of these videos of him saying some truly outlandish things, and it incensed him to no end.

Tony sighed. "Deepfake is a technique of human image synthesis based on artificial intelligence. They're using something called a generative adversarial network, which basically has one computer using AI creating a video and audio of whatever it is they created, and then a second computer doing whatever it can to detect the falsehoods in the fake video. The two computers essentially wargame this against each other until the Deepfake is so accurate even the AI computer can't detect it. Once they've generated the message they want, they pump it out into the various social media channels and plaster it all over the internet.

"For example, if they want to target women in a certain age range, they may create a message that'll resonate with them and then propagate that message on Pinterest or Instagram to reach that specific audience. Using Facebook and Google data, these groups essentially know exactly what people in a specific neighborhood or congressional district are talking about, researching on the internet, or watching on YouTube, so they can socially engineer a message that will resonate with them. As that message takes root and gets shared, commented on, liked or hated, they integrate that user feedback into new messages they create."

Tony paused for a second as he shook his head and then looked up at the President. "Sir, these outside actors have completely and utterly weaponized social media and the internet against us. Our own message can't even get out or resonate because it's being completely distorted by what these other groups are able to do. I mean, it's not even just China—the Russians are hammering us with this, the Germans—and anyone else that has a laptop and the internet."

The President pounded his fist on the table. "Damn it, Tony! There has to be something we can do to stop this— something we can do to keep this from spreading further and tearing our country apart!"

Tony winced at the outburst. "Mr. President, there is only so much we can do. We don't own or control Facebook, Google, or any of the other tech companies involved in the spread of this."

Jumping in before the President could say anything, Patty Hogan asked, "Is there some sort of executive order or action the executive branch can take to give you the powers your agency needs to deal with this?"

The President nodded as he looked at Tony, waiting for him to tell them something.

Tony took a deep breath. "You could sign an EO giving the NSA inside access to the tech companies and these social media platforms' infrastructure. We could then put in place a delay to review all videos and images being posted to these sites unless they come from an approved source. This could help us try to regain control of the situation."

The President agreed. "We'll get with the AG and craft this up. However, I'm going to have him put a time limit on this EO, Tony. We're not going to allow the NSA to have this kind of access permanently. This is only until the conflict is over. After that, we'll work with Congress to create some new legislation that'll address this problem, and hopefully, we won't have to deal with this kind of crap happening again in the future."

The meeting then continued on with the other agenda items. Truthfully, it all seemed rather mundane to Sachs after the discussion with the NSA.

Chapter 19
Connecting the Dots

April 6, 2021
Camp Perry, Virginia

Director Nolan Polanski sat in the small briefing room, dumbfounded by what he was hearing. Turning to look at Director Ryerson, then-Secretary Hogan, and the National Security Advisor, Robert Grey, he could tell they were equally surprised and angered. They were nearly done watching the interrogation of Roberto Lamy, the Director-General of the World Trade Organization. What he'd said during his questioning was nothing short of crazy and fantastical.

When the video ended, Major General Lancaster looked at them. "We're still verifying much of what he said; however, we've already been able to corroborate a lot of what he's told us thus far."

"What are the major loose ends?" asked Secretary Hogan.

"We need to tie up the connection between Lance Solomon, Marshall Tate, and Peng An."

"OK. Different angle. What are the major pieces you've been able to corroborate thus far?" asked Polanski.

"Now that we knew where to look and roughly when, we've been able to trace a lot of the dark money that went to the SuperPAC Global First and how it was used. This was definitely the primary vehicle that facilitated the majority of the election shenanigans that took place. More importantly, we were able to cross-reference the donors to that PAC to more than a dozen other SuperPACs that were aligned with Marshall Tate's campaign or election efforts. As a matter of fact, two of the PACs were being used to pay protesters to cause problems at President Sachs's political rallies and nearly every public event he attended. One of the PACs is currently being used to pay for Marshall Tate's personal security detail in Ottawa."

Secretary Hogan leaned forward in her chair. "What about that Russian PMC, the Wagner Group? They've recently started showing up in New York, Washington State, and I heard even down in Mexico in large numbers."

General Lancaster nodded. "We found evidence of them being funded by the SuperPAC as well. Global First, which currently has about two hundred and thirty million dollars, recently wire transferred eighty million to Wagner. They also transferred about sixty million to seven state CDF groups as well. We're not sure what they're doing with the money, but our best guess is they're using it to pay their militia members so they can keep them ready to fight."

Attorney General Malcolm Wright, who was sitting in the back of the room, cleared his throat to gather the group's attention. "I think we all need to sit and watch this again. This time, we should all take some notes and figure out exactly what crimes have been committed, by whom, and what additional evidence we need to make this an airtight prosecution. Then we need to synthesize this information down into manageable chunks that we can release to the public. If we're going to reunite this country and put an end to this civil war before it tears us apart, then we need to get this information disseminated promptly."

Everyone in the room expressed agreement with the AG. The group broke briefly to take a bio break, grab some coffee, and had some sandwiches brought in. Once they were ready, they resumed watching the video a second time. They observed both the initial interrogation of Mr. Lamy, the one where he was heavily drugged, and then the second interrogation, where Mr. Lamy was clearly distraught over his involvement in the greatest scam ever perpetrated on the world.

When they finished watching the video for a second time, AG Wright asked, "Where is Mr. Lamy now?"

"He's currently being held at one of our safe houses in Brazil," replied General Lancaster. "We weren't sure where we should take him just yet. I was hoping you might be able to tell me if you'd like him brought back to the US to stand trial, or if you have some other thoughts on what we should do with him."

"I think we need to bring him back to the US," the AG responded. "He's the star witness in all of this. He places Marshall Tate at that fundraiser in Seattle with all the other players at the table. If he's willing to go on the record and repeat all of this publicly in court, I'm pretty sure I can get the President to agree to an immunity deal. We can place him in the witness protection program and make sure he disappears, but he'll have to testify. The public needs to hear what he has to say, and we need him to testify against the other co-conspirators."

****

Seth looked at Smith with a raised eyebrow, as if to say, *Are you serious?*

"Really?" he asked aloud.

"Yeah."

Seth blew the air out of his mouth swiftly, as if trying to blow a smoke ring. "This is going to be tricky," he said.

"I know."

"So, how do we do it?"

Now it was Smith's turn to sigh. "If they wanted us to get him out of Brazil, they should've told us that a week ago before his wife became hysterical about his disappearance. She's been raving in the media about him being missing. His face is all over the media. The Brazilian president has made it a national priority to find him. Hell—as soon as his co-conspirators learned he was gone, they ponied up a multimillion-dollar reward for information leading to his recovery. Moving him is going to be difficult, to say the least."

"What about smuggling him to the hangar and putting him on our jet?" asked Seth.

Smith shook his head. "I already looked into that. The state police are checking all vehicles coming to and going from the airports. I even looked at the smaller regional airports and the private airports out in the countryside—they have those locked down as well. I think our best bet at this point is to either sit tight with him here or try to smuggle him out on a boat."

The mention of a boat got Seth thinking about an old mission he'd been a part of when he first joined Special Forces. His team had gotten into some trouble in an Asian country, and they had to be extracted by the Navy. A Naval Special Warfare Boat Team picked them up with a rigid inflatable boat and then linked up with a mother ship further out at sea.

Looking up at Smith, Seth proclaimed, "I have an idea."

Smith smiled mischievously. "See, I knew you'd figure this out for us."

From the Authors

Miranda and I hope you've enjoyed this book. The next book in our Falling Empires Series, *Vengeance*, is already available for preorder. Simply visit Amazon to reserve your copy.

While you are waiting for the next book to be released, you may wish to enjoy one of our books in audio format. All six books of the Red Storm Series are now available for your listening pleasure, as well as our entire World War III series. We've also had *Traitors Within* and *Interview with a Terrorist* recorded on audio as well.

If you would like to stay up to date on new releases and receive emails about any special pricing deals we may make available, please sign up for our email distribution list. Simply go to http://www.author-james-rosone.com and scroll to the bottom of the page.

As independent authors, reviews are very important to us and make a huge difference to other prospective readers. If you enjoyed this book, we humbly ask you to write up a positive review on Amazon and Goodreads. We sincerely appreciate each person that takes the time to write one.

We have really valued connecting with our readers via social media, especially on our Facebook page https://www.facebook.com/RosoneandWatson/. Sometimes we ask for help from our readers as we write future books—we love to draw upon all your different areas of expertise. We also have a group of beta readers who get to look at the books before they are officially published and help us fine-tune last-minute adjustments. If you would like to be a part of this team, please go to our author website: http://www.author-james-rosone.com, and send us a message through the "Contact" tab. You can also follow us on Twitter: @jamesrosone and @AuthorMirandaW. We look forward to hearing from you.

You may also enjoy some of our other works. A full list can be found below:

Nonfiction:

Iraq Memoir 2006–2007 Troop Surge

Interview with a Terrorist

Fiction:

World War III Series

Prelude to World War III: The Rise of the Islamic Republic and the Rebirth of America

Operation Red Dragon and the Unthinkable

Operation Red Dawn and the Invasion of America

Cyber Warfare and the New World Order

Michael Stone Series

Traitors Within

The Red Storm Series

Battlefield Ukraine

Battlefield Korea

Battlefield Taiwan

Battlefield Pacific

Battlefield Russia

Battlefield China

Second American Civil War Series

Rigged

Peacekeepers

Invasion

Vengeance, available for preorder

Retribution, release date TBD

Children's Books:

My Daddy has PTSD

My Mommy has PTSD

For the Veterans

I have been pretty open with our fans about the fact that PTSD has had a tremendous direct impact on our lives; it affected my relationship with my wife, job opportunities, finances, parenting—everything. It is also no secret that for me, the help from the VA was not the most ideal form of treatment. Although I am still on this journey, I did find one organization that did assist the healing process for me, and I would like to share that information.

Welcome Home Initiative is a ministry of By His Wounds Ministry, and they run seminars for veterans and their spouses for free. The weekends are a combination of prayer and more traditional counseling and left us with resources to aid in moving forward. The entire cost of the retreat—hotel costs, food, and sessions, are completely free from the moment the veteran and their spouse arrive at the location.

If you feel that you or someone you love might benefit from one of Welcome Home Initiative's sessions, please visit their website to learn more: https://welcomehomeinitiative.org/

We have decided to donate a portion of our profits to this organization because it made such an impact in our lives, and we believe in what they are doing. If you would also like to donate to Welcome Home Initiative and help to keep these weekend retreats going, you can do so by going to this website: https://welcomehomeinitiative.org/donate/

Abbreviation Key

AAV	Amphibious Assault Vehicle
ACU	Army Combat Uniform
AD	Armored Division
AO	Area of Operations
APC	Armored Personnel Carrier
ATGM	Antitank Guided Missile
BND	Bundesnachrichtendienst (German intelligence)
BTR	Bronetransportyor (Russian armored transporter)
CDF	Civilian Defense Force
CMC	Central Military Commission
CO	Commanding Officer
CP	Command Post
D.C.	District of Columbia
DHS	Department of Homeland Security
DR	Dominican Republic
EAM	Emergency Action Message
EMP	Electromagnetic Pulse
EOD	Explosive Ordnance Disposal
FDR	Franklin Delano Roosevelt
FEMA	Federal Emergency Management Agency

FLETC	Federal Law Enforcement Training Centers
FN MAG	Belgian machine gun in 7.62 mm, originally manufactured by FN Herstal
FPS	Federal Protection Service
FRAGO	Fragmentary Order
HEAT	High-Explosive Anti-Tank
HET	Heavy Equipment Transports
HIMARS	High Mobility Artillery Rocket System
IBA	Individual Body Armor
ID	Infantry Division
IED	Improvised Explosive Device
IFV	Infantry Fighting Vehicle
ISR	Intelligence, Surveillance, and Reconnaissance
IR	Infrared
JBC	Joint Battle Center
JDAM	Joint Direct Attack Munition
JLTV	Joint Light Tactical Vehicle
JSOC	Joint Special Operations Command
JWICS	Joint Worldwide Intelligence Communications System
KBR	Company, formerly Kellogg, Brown, and Root (American engineering, construction, and private military contracting entity)

LA	Los Angeles
LAV	Light Armored Vehicle
LNG	Liquid Natural Gas
LNO	Liaison Officer
LT	Lieutenant
MANPADs	Man-Portable Air-Defense Systems
MEU	Marine Expeditionary Unit
MI	Military Intelligence
MIRV	Multiple Independent Reentry Vehicle
MOD	Ministry of Defence
MOLLE	Modular Lightweight Load-Carrying Equipment
MP	Military Police
MRE	Meals Ready to Eat
NCO	Noncommissioned Officer
NIPR	Nonclassified Internet Protocol
NORTHCOM	Northern Command
NSA	National Security Advisor OR National Security Agency
NVG	Night Vision Goggles
OP	Observational Post
OPEC	Organization of the Petroleum Exporting Countries
PAC	Political Action Committee

PLA	People's Liberation Army (Chinese army)
PM	Prime Minister
PMC	Private Military Contractor
POL	Petroleum, Oil, Lubricants
POW	Prisoner of War
QRF	Quick Reaction Force
RCT	Regimental Combat Team
RFID	Radio Frequency Identification
RPG	Rocket-Propelled Grenade
RTO	Radiotelephone Operator
SAMs	Surface-to-Air Missiles
SAW	Squad Automatic Weapon
SCAR	Also called FN SCAR. Rifle commonly used in Special Forces
SCIF	Sensitive Compartmented Information Facility
SIGACTS	Significant Activities Report
SINCGARS	Single Channel Ground and Airborne Radio System
SIPR	Secret Internet Protocol
SSE	Sensitive Site Exploitation
TACAMO	Take Charge and Move Out (system of communications links designed to be used in nuclear warfare)

TACP	Tactical Air Control Party
THAAD	Terminal High Altitude Area Defense
UN	United Nations
VBL	Véhicule Blindé Léger (French light armored vehicle)
VP	Vice President
VR	Virtual Reality
WTO	World Trade Organization
XO	Commanding Officer
ZBD	Type of Chinese Infantry Fighting Vehicle
ZBL	Type of Chinese Infantry Fighting Vehicle
ZSD	Type of Chinese Infantry Fighting Vehicle

Made in the USA
Monee, IL
31 July 2020